Charming . . . Witty . . .
Enthralling . . . Luscious . . .

Meredith Duran's passion-filled novels of nineteenth-century London deliver "romance at its finest" (*New York Times* bestselling author Liz Carlyle)!

THAT SCANDALOUS SUMMER

***RT Book Reviews* Top Pick**

"A sophisticated, witty, smart novel that, like a Mary Balogh romance, compels the reader to look deeper and uncover great depth as well as grand passion. Duran's characters . . . give readers a better understanding of humanity and the power of love."

—*RT Book Reviews*

"So adorable and witty. . . . I am fascinated and enthralled by Duran's voice."

—*Smexy Books*

"A powerful story with emotional punch. . . . Her prose is a joy to read."

—*The Romance Dish*

AT YOUR PLEASURE

***RT Book Reviews* Top Pick**

A *Romantic Times* nominee for Most Innovative Romance of 2012

An American Library Association Shortlist selection

"Unforgettable romance. . . . Rich in texture. . . . A novel to sink your teeth into."

—*Romantic Times* (4½ stars)

"Fast-paced, heart-pounding . . . a wonderful read!"

—*Fresh Fiction*

Turn the page for more sparkling reviews!

A LADY'S LESSON IN SCANDAL

RT Book Reviews Top Pick & a Desert Isle Keeper for _All About Romance_

An American Library Association Shortlist selection

"Compelling, exciting, sensual . . . a nonstop read everyone will savor."

—*Romantic Times* (4½ stars)

"Top-notch romance."

—*Publishers Weekly*

WICKED BECOMES YOU

RT Book Reviews Top Pick

"Charming and deliciously sensual from beginning to end."

—*Romantic Times*

"Witty, often hilarious, sensuous, and breathlessly paced . . . An engaging mystery-enhanced escapade."

—*Library Journal*

"Sexy, inventive, and riveting, it's hard to put down and a joy to read."

—*All About Romance*

"Rousing . . . delightful. . . . *Wicked Becomes You* enthralls with particularly likable characters and a heartwarming romance with deeply affecting emotions."

—*Single Titles*

WRITTEN ON YOUR SKIN

RT Book Reviews Top Pick & a _Romantic Times_ Best Historical Romance Adventure award nominee

"Mesmerizing . . . a glorious, nonstop, action-packed battle-of-wills romance."

—*Romantic Times* (4½ stars)

"Wildly romantic."

—*Dear Author* (Grade: A+)

"Everything a great historical romance should be."

—*Romance Junkies*

BOUND BY YOUR TOUCH

A Best Book of 2009 in *All About Romance*'s Reviewer's Choice column

"Entertaining. . . . Historical romance fans will enjoy the adventure."

—*Publishers Weekly*

"Sophisticated, beautifully written, and utterly romantic."

—*The Book Smugglers*

"A great love story. . . . I found new layers and meaning each time I read it."

—*Dear Author*

THE DUKE OF SHADOWS

Finalist for the *Romantic Times* Best Historical Debut award

"Evocative and enticing . . . a luscious delight."

—Liz Carlyle

"Fascinating, emotionally intense."

—*Romantic Times* (4½ stars)

"Riveting. . . . emotion-packed. . . . A guaranteed page-turner."

—*The Romance Reader* (4 stars)

"Without a doubt the best historical romance I have read this year."

—*Romance Reviews Today*

ALSO BY MEREDITH DURAN

The Duke of Shadows

Bound by Your Touch

Written on Your Skin

Wicked Becomes You

A Lady's Lesson in Scandal

At Your Pleasure

That Scandalous Summer

Meredith Duran

Fool Me Twice

POCKET BOOKS
New York London Toronto Sydney New Delhi

Pocket Books
A Division of Simon & Schuster, Inc.
1230 Avenue of the Americas
New York, NY 10020

This book is a work of fiction. Any references to historical events, real people, or real places are used fictitiously. Other names, characters, places, and events are products of the author's imagination, and any resemblance to actual events or places or persons, living or dead, is entirely coincidental.

First Pocket Books paperback edition April 2014

For information about special discounts for bulk purchases, please contact Simon & Schuster Special Sales at 1-866-506-1949 or business@simonandschuster.com.

The Simon & Schuster Speakers Bureau can bring authors to your live event. For more information or to book an event contact the Simon & Schuster Speakers Bureau at 1-866-248-3049 or visit our website at www.simonspeakers.com.

Manufactured in the United States of America

10 9 8 7 6 5 4 3 2 1

ISBN 978-1-4767-4135-2
ISBN 978-1-4767-4138-3 (ebook)

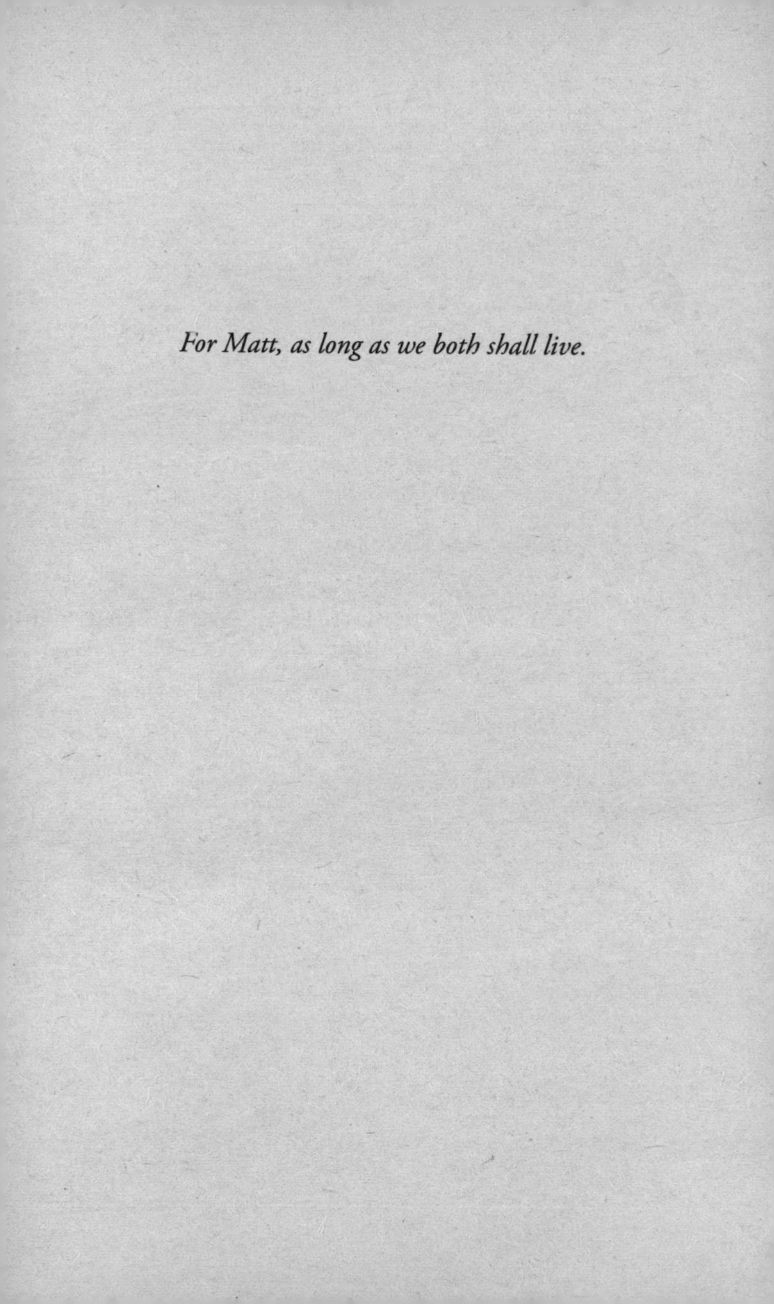

For Matt, as long as we both shall live.

ACKNOWLEDGMENTS

I am infinitely indebted to Janine Ballard and S. J. Kincaid for enthusiasm, encouragement, and understanding at all times of the day and night. Thanks also to the ladies and gentlemen at Pocket Books, especially Lauren McKenna, editor/muse; Elana Cohen, who writes the most charming emails the Internet has ever hosted; Faren Bachelis, eagle-eyed copy editor; and the marvelously talented art department. Finally, my immense gratitude to Caroline Guindon for her expert guidance in French (any mistakes are *definitely* my own), and to Ronroe, Katherine, my wonderful parents, Rob and Betsey, and the Birnholz-Farrell clan for always understanding when I say, "I can't go/come/stay—I have to write."

Fool Me Twice

CHAPTER ONE

London, 1885

Olivia drew up before the scene of her next crime. Was it her imagination, or did the townhouse *loom*? All the other mansions on this street looked polite and elegant, neatly confining themselves within rows of trimmed hedges. This house, on the other hand, sprawled. She spied a gargoyle lurking above one cornice, glowering at her. Of course the Duke of Marwick would have a gargoyle carved into his house!

She crossed her arms and glowered back. She was a thief now, wasn't she? No matter that, for all her twenty-five years, she had prayed before bedtime and gasped at curses. Now she was a criminal. Criminals should not fear anything—not even the Duke of Marwick, tyrant extraordinaire.

Brave thoughts. But her stomach was jumping like she'd eaten spoiled food.

She pivoted away, pacing to the hedges that marked the next lot. *God in heaven.* Was this the kind of woman she wanted to be? She'd told herself she had no choice, but that was a lie. One always had a choice. She could run again, flee to France, or even farther . . .

The autumn breeze carried a child's laugh to her ears. In the park at the center of the square, a little boy was playing chase with a puppy. He ran in circles, shrieking with delight as the spaniel nipped his heels. Was he all alone?

Her concern faded when she spotted the couple watching from the shade of the elm trees. They were not a nanny and footman, as one typically saw supervising the young heirs of Mayfair, but a married couple, the husband fair and slim, with an elegant gold watch pinned to his lapel. The wife, plump and pink cheeked, hugged his arm as she smiled at her son.

A knot rose in Olivia's throat. If she walked away now, it would never be safe to make a home. She would always be alone. Always running.

Strictly speaking, theft and fraud were immoral. But her cause was just, and her prospective victim, a bully. Marwick deserved a taste of his own medicine. She would not feel guilty!

She nudged her spectacles up her nose and marched back to the duke's townhouse. The brass knocker felt slippery in her hand. The advertisement was a week old; the maid's position might have been filled already. All her agonizing would be for nothing.

The door opened. A young brunette set her shoulder against the doorjamb and looked up at Olivia. "Oo-oo. Tall as a man, ain't you? Come about the position, I expect."

It had taken several days for Olivia to persuade Amanda to write the reference. But in a second, she saw that she might as well have forged it herself. Nobody was going to check its authenticity, not when they had *this* creature answering the door. "Yes," she said. "The maid's—"

"Welcome to the madhouse, then. Me name's Polly." The girl waved Olivia into the chill of the lobby, a cavernous space tiled in checkerboard marble. "It's Jones you'll want to see. He's in the butler's pantry. Don't ask what he does there; nobody can say."

Olivia followed the girl past what looked to be the scene of a fight, remnants of a shattered vase strewn along the wall. Or perhaps only neglect was to blame, for the Grecian urn by the stairs held masses of withered roses, and the air smelled sour, as though somebody had laid down vinegar for cleaning and forgotten to mop it up again.

A madhouse, indeed. It was the master who had gone mad first, Olivia guessed. Her former employer, Elizabeth Chudderley (from whom she had *stolen*), had called the Duke of Marwick a bully and a tyrant, for his ruthless opposition of Elizabeth's marriage to his brother. But this house suggested he was less exacting of his servants than of his family. How bizarre!

A bully, she reminded herself. Marwick was a boor, a monster. Cheating him would be criminal, but not unforgivable—unlike her theft from Elizabeth.

"So you'll have heard about our duke," Polly said as they stepped into the servants' passage.

For a stupid moment, Olivia thought the girl had read her mind. And then she gathered her wits. "Of course. The Duke of Marwick has done so many wonderful—"

Polly's snort spared Olivia the distasteful task of

praising him. "You don't know the half of it." And as they descended the stairs, she commenced a chattering monologue, full of sordid details that supplied the larger picture.

The housekeeper had quit nine days ago, after an episode in which the duke had thrown a shoe at her. Since then, half the maids had fled. Oh, the pay was still good, but you couldn't expect a lunatic to live long, could you? To be sure, he was only thirty-five. But the duke had not left the house in ten months. If that wasn't lunacy, what was?

"It's been grand fun," Polly concluded as they emerged into the servants' gallery. "Like being paid to see a stage show!"

"Indeed." Olivia felt slightly sick. Thanks to the letters she had stolen from Elizabeth, she knew far more of the situation than she should. She even knew why Marwick was deranged.

Several months ago, Elizabeth had come into possession of letters written by the duke's late wife. These letters revealed the duchess to have been unfaithful and treacherous. The duke, upon learning it, had turned from a grieving widower into a half-mad hermit—and perhaps a drunkard, too, for what else could have driven him to throw shoes at the housekeeper?

Polly banged on the door to the butler's pantry. "You've a new one," she called.

The door opened a crack. A hand shot out, pudgy fingers snapping up Olivia's reference. The door slammed shut again.

Polly crossed her arms and tapped her foot. "Now, now," she said loudly. "This one looks promising. I swear to you, it wasn't Bradley who summoned her." She cut Olivia a grin. "One of the footmen. Thought it'd make a fine joke to summon a painted lady for an interview. Poor Jones, he wasn't amused."

Olivia grew conscious of her own increasingly stiff posture. Did the butler have no spine? Why did he not sack Bradley?

That isn't your business, she reminded herself. The disarray of this household would work to her advantage. Her aim was to rifle the duke's belongings, for his late wife's letters suggested that he kept files on his political colleagues, dossiers that evidenced their crimes. If this was true, then Olivia needed to find the files. There was a certain man she very much needed to blackmail.

She had anticipated a great many watchful eyes ready to catch her in the act of prying. But this lot? They wouldn't notice if she stole the silver! Assuming any silver remained to be stolen, of course.

"You're lucky," Polly said, jarring Olivia from her reverie. "Old Jones is so desperate, he'll probably not care that you wear spectacles. But in the normal course, ain't much call for a maid who can't see."

"Oh." Blinking, Olivia nudged her glasses back up to their proper place. She had never considered that detail.

"And you'll have to stop coloring your hair," Polly added with a *tsk.* "Fine shade of red, but a bit too loud for service."

"I don't color my hair." She had considered it for the sake of disguise, but the lighter shades did not stick, and the darkest would have looked unnatural.

Polly gave her a skeptical look. "Right-o. Mother Nature just got frisky, I suppose."

"I tell you, this *is* my natural color." And if she *had* dyed her hair, she certainly would not have chosen the shade.

The door opened. Jones proved to be a distinguished gentleman in black tails, with bulldog jowls and hair as silver as a groat. He clutched Olivia's reference like a drowning man to driftwood. "This looks *quite* satisfactory, Miss Johnson."

Polly gave Olivia a questioning look. "*Miss* Johnson, is it?"

Mere parlor maids did not deserve such a formal address. Olivia had a sinking feeling that Amanda had not obeyed her instructions: omit from the reference any mention of Olivia's education, and emphasize instead her experience in cleaning and caring for a grand home. Not that she had any, in truth. . . .

"Come, come," said Jones, pushing himself through the doorway and all but scrambling for the stairs. "Follow me, if you please."

"Our finest drawing room," Jones announced. He waved her out of the salon, setting a brisk pace down the corridor. "You worked two years in Lady Ripton's household?"

Olivia rushed to keep up. Roman statues lined the hallway, their stiff, marbled faces gazing with disapproval on this unlikely scene: the butler, who was meant to stand at the top of the servants' hierarchy, giving a tour to his prospective underling. "Yes, sir. I served two years as an upstairs maid."

This was a lie, of course. Olivia was a secretary by training. But it was her good fortune that Amanda, her former classmate at the typing school, had recently married Viscount Ripton. This made Amanda's recommendations very powerful things to own. If the Viscountess Ripton said that Olivia had been a housemaid par excellence, then this poor, beleaguered butler would not doubt it.

"I do wonder . . ." Jones was scratching his chin. He seemed very interested in one spot in particular, a patch of whiskers beneath his ear that he had obviously missed during his morning ablutions. The silver hair there sprouted a full inch longer than the rest of his beard.

Beneath her fascinated gaze, he recalled his manners, flushing as he tucked his hand back into his waistcoat. "Are you, by any chance, lettered?"

She could have answered him in French, Italian, or German. But it seemed rather showy—and improbable, for a housemaid. "Yes, sir. I can read and write."

"I don't suppose you can do figures as well?"

That was also not among the housemaid's usual skills. But the pleading look Jones fixed on her was impossible to resist. How desperate he appeared. "Yes," she said. "I'm quite good at figures."

Relief flashed over Jones's face, followed, puzzlingly, by what looked like pure trepidation. He came to a stop by another door. "The library," he said—but before he could show it to her, raucous laughter exploded around the corner, causing him to wince. "Today is rather unsettled," he said hastily. "But I assure you, I do not tolerate such disarray on a typical basis."

His embarrassment was contagious. As the giggles came again, Olivia felt herself turning red to match him. "Of course not, sir."

Two maids spilled around the corner, one of them holding open a magazine, the other craning to gawk at it. Jones stiffened. "Muriel!"

The girls startled—and then, to Olivia's astonishment, they turned on their heels and scampered back the way they had come.

Jones scowled after them. But his spirit was sadly broken, Olivia saw; rather than summoning them for a well-deserved scolding, he sighed and shook his head. "Have you any questions for me, Miss Johnson?"

She consulted herself. "Well—wages, of course."

"Twenty-five pounds per annum, increasing to thirty after five years' service. Anything else?"

She wracked her brain for typical concerns. "When His Grace closes the house, will we travel with him? Or will we be kept on here?"

Instantly she regretted the question, for Jones darted her an agonized look. "I do not think . . ." He cleared his throat. "His Grace will not close the house this year."

Nobody stayed in London during the winter. She tried to mask her shock. "I see."

"You may have heard . . ." The butler hesitated. "I wish to assure you that His Grace is everything one could wish for in an employer."

Poor Jones. He sounded so disheartened by his lie. Olivia restrained the urge to touch his elbow in comfort. "I have no doubt, sir."

And *that* was not the kind of lie *she* had expected to

tell today. Indeed, she'd anticipated having to prostrate herself. This was, after all, the household of the most feared figure in British politics: Alastair de Grey, fifth Duke of Marwick, friend to princes, patron of prime ministers, and puppet master of countless MPs. His upper staff, she'd assumed, would be overproud and haughty, like all servants in grand houses.

But if Marwick had once governed the nation, he now failed to govern even his own home. His servants were running wild. It made no sense to Olivia. Elizabeth had spoken of him as an all-powerful bully . . . but a bully never would have tolerated this chaos.

And once she stole from him, this beleaguered butler—the only one here who showed a lick of sense—would bear the blame for having hired her.

She couldn't do it. To take advantage of this miserable fellow was too sordid. "Mr. Jones," she began, just as he spoke.

"Miss Johnson, I have a terribly unorthodox proposition." He took a deep breath, like a diver preparing himself for the plunge. "We are lacking a housekeeper. As you—as I am sure the maids already told you."

"Indeed, they did not," she lied. How far gone he was! Mr. Jones should not *depend* on the staff's gossiping. His task was to prevent it.

"Well, yes. She gave notice . . . rather abruptly. And I do wonder . . ." Jones mopped his forehead with a handkerchief. "That is, it occurs to me . . . Lady Ripton spoke *most* highly of you; why, she even said she felt you were lowering yourself to this position, having served, in her time of need, as an amanuensis, a companion and secretary—"

She had told Amanda not to embroider the point.

"Lady Ripton is too kind. It's true, once in a great rare while, I did assist her—"

"Well, here's the rub." The words tumbled over each other; it was evident that Jones was aghast at his own proposal, and wished to get through it as quickly as possible. "Until we find a replacement, I require someone to fill Mrs. Wright's shoes. You are educated; you are familiar with the ways of the better classes. I wonder if you might not step into her post—until, of course, I can find her replacement. Only until then."

Olivia caught her breath. This was a stroke of luck beyond all imagining. She needed a weapon very badly indeed. The Duke of Marwick was likely in possession of this weapon. And a housekeeper would have license to look *everywhere* for it.

But—her spirits sank—it would still be fraud. And it would still cost Jones his job, in the end. "I couldn't," she said miserably. "I have no experience—"

"I would instruct you." Jones caught her hand. "I do entreat you, Miss Johnson"—his grip tightened as his voice dropped—"to think on the *great* advantage it would do your future. To be able to say you had once served as housekeeper to His Grace. Why, no domestic of your age could *dream* of such a boon!"

Gently she pulled her hand free. He was right, of course. Had she truly been Olivia Johnson, parlor maid—and not Olivia Holladay, former secretary, now operating under her *second* alias, with a falsified letter of reference—she never would have refused the opportunity.

And so, lest she rouse his suspicions, she said, "It is a fine honor, indeed. But you must give me a day or two to think on it. To consult with myself, and see if I am worthy of it."

Olivia's humility pleased him. Smiling, he agreed to her terms.

"Oh, it's you." Mrs. Primm stepped aside, allowing Olivia to step into the shabby little hall.

Mrs. Primm behaved as though she were doing her lodgers a great favor by letting them rent rooms the size of mouse holes. Meanwhile, she hoarded the coal, so they fell asleep shivering each night. But oh, could she cook like a dream! Olivia breathed deeply; the smell of beef stew filled the air, rich and savory. "Is supper laid?"

"Laid and finished. You know I don't wait for nobody."

Swallowing her disappointment, Olivia mounted the stairs. Her stomach was growling, but hunger wouldn't kill her.

Once in her room, she knelt to make sure the lockbox still sat beneath her bed. She lived in fear that somebody might steal it.

On the omnibus, she had been tallying sums in her head, calculating her options. It was time to consider what she'd most wanted to avoid: fleeing to the Continent, someplace far enough away that Bertram would never think to look for her there.

She glanced up at the drawings she'd tacked on the wall. They were benign prints clipped from magazines: an ivy-covered cottage with a lamp burning in the window. A village sleeping beneath the snow. Treacle dreams, but she could not scorn them—or let go of them, no matter how hard she tried.

Abroad, she would always be a stranger. Forced to avoid her fellow expatriates in order to hide, she would be even more alone than she was now.

Bah! She shook off the self-pity. Such a bittersweet, sticky feeling. Wallow in it too long, and one found oneself trapped.

She unlocked the box and took the comfort of weighing her pound notes, a solid brick of savings. Elizabeth Chudderley had paid her a generous salary, and together with her mother's savings, she had enough to stay comfortably lodged for several months if she did not find work as a fräulein, signorina, or mademoiselle.

She laid down the money, and then, because she had not allowed herself to look at it in months, she lifted out her mother's diary. The leather cover needed oiling; it had begun to crack. But her mother's handwriting still looked crisp and fresh.

Mama had never feared Bertram. Had he always been a villain, it would have been easier to understand him now. Olivia skimmed past observations on flowers, descriptions of the changing seasons, of dresses newly arrived from London, and of course, of Olivia herself (*My precious angel has become a young woman; I can't tell how it happened*). The last entry was what drew her in, every time. It was the only one she didn't understand.

The truth is hidden at home.

What truth? The mystery would remain unsolved, for Olivia dared not go to Allen's End.

The stairs groaned. She shoved away the lockbox just as a key rattled in the lock.

"Am I to have no privacy?" she demanded as the door opened.

Mrs. Primm ignored this. "There's one thing," she said sourly. "I forgot to mention it before."

Olivia rose. She would not be extorted again! "I have already agreed to the new rate, ma'am. You said that was the final price. And I keep this room very neat—"

"A man came looking for you today."

Dread seized her. "What?" *Be calm.* She cleared her throat. "How curious. I can't imagine who it might have been."

Mrs. Primm had a round, rosy-cheeked face. It lent her an air of benevolence that sat oddly with her cynical tones. "I expect you'd prefer it that way. Came by foot, he did. Well dressed, but not well spoken."

"Did he leave a name?" How she managed to sound so indifferent, she didn't know. Her skin was breaking out in gooseflesh; she had to clench her teeth lest they chatter.

"Munn, was it? No—Moore." Mrs. Primm nodded to herself, missing, thank God, the small sound that Olivia could not swallow away before it escaped her. "He left an address as well, mind you, and asked that I let him know when you returned."

"And did you?" She realized she was cupping her throat, squeezing it as Moore had once done. She tucked her hand into her pocket, made a secret fist. Thomas Moore was Bertram's man, perhaps even Bertram's . . . assassin.

Mrs. Primm shrugged. "Well, he wasn't police, and I don't fancy myself a matchmaker. I told him you'd moved on."

"Oh." Olivia blinked hard and tried to master herself, for she was seized by the most inappropriate impulse to give Mrs. Primm a hug. "Thank you! Oh, thank you, ma'am." How she had misjudged the cantankerous old woman!

The woman rejected this gratitude with a sharp pull of her mouth. "I don't want trouble. You'll need to leave now."

"Do you think—that is, could I perhaps leave through the back gate?"

Mrs. Primm gave a grim nod. "I expected you might. Should you find yourself in need of a place, you'll not come back here. You follow?"

"I won't. I promise you." It was the easiest promise she'd ever made.

The door closed. Olivia quickly gathered up her belongings. Every time she fled, she abandoned more than she took. Her possessions now fit into a single valise, the weight of which felt like evidence of her own failure. How on earth had Bertram tracked her here? She'd taken such care with her movements.

Outside, in the safety of the narrow passageway behind the house, night had fallen. This footpath was the sole reason she had chosen Mrs. Primm's establishment for her lodging. But she'd prayed she would never need to use it.

She stole quickly down the rutted trail. Where would she go? Amanda had departed with her husband for Italy. Lilah, lodged by her employer, could not take Olivia in. Nor could a woman simply prowl the city at night, begging for a room. The steamers bound for the Continent all left with the morning tide. She might go to Waterloo, take the first departing train—but what would she do once she arrived, in the dead of night, God knew where?

The traffic of the nearby high street grew louder with each step, the rattle of tack, the rumble of wheels, promising her the safety of a crowd. *You are safe,* she told her racing heart. But she wasn't. Bertram's man knew that she was in London . . .

His Lordship don't want no trouble. That first night in London seven years ago, Moore had met her at the station. He had sat across from her in Bertram's brougham, the swinging side lamp painting his face then casting it back into shadow, visible and then invisible, in rhythm to the thumping of the wheels. *And you're trouble, I expect.*

Moore had lured her into the coach with the promise of taking her to a decent hotel. He'd said that Bertram wanted him to see her safely settled. After how hotly Bertram had opposed Olivia's plan to come to London, this kindness had surprised her. She'd supposed it was meant as an apology; Bertram probably felt guilty for having missed Mama's funeral.

But his manservant did not take her to a hotel. Instead, the vehicle had turned into a road that grew progressively darker, traveling into the wild darkness of the heath. And when Moore began to speak of trouble, she grew amazed, then afraid. *I won't be any trouble,* she'd said. *I told Bertram. I don't need anything from him. I have my own plans now.*

But Moore had not seemed to hear her. *He don't want no trouble,* he'd repeated. *So I take the trouble for him.*

And then he had shown her what he meant by that.

She could still feel his hands around her throat. She remembered it so vividly. One's mind did odd things when starved for air. It saw colors, lights, visions of better times, when one had felt loved.

She had fought him. But he was so much stronger.

She had woken in a ditch by the side of the road, as dawn broke overhead. Even as her eyes had opened, she'd realized she was meant to be dead. Moore never would have thrown her out of the coach if he'd imagined she would live.

When she had appeared at the typing school and asked the headmistress to register her by a different name—not Olivia Holladay, but Olivia Mather—the woman had taken one look at the bruises on her throat and kindly agreed.

Now Thomas Moore had found her again. He was looking for her even now. And she had nowhere to go.

She pulled up where the path opened onto the high street, putting her hand over her chest, willing her gasping breath to slow. She had air. She had enough air.

And it wasn't true that she had nowhere to go. She watched a hackney pass, and then another, wrestling with herself. One house stood open to her tonight. It was also a place Bertram would never think to look: the house of a man he'd betrayed.

Could she do it? Had she given up on her soul? She had stolen the letters from Elizabeth rashly, on a moment's wild whim. But this undertaking would be different. She had planned it as thoroughly as a hardened criminal.

But forced to choose between her soul and her safety, her soul and her dignity, her soul and freedom—her soul be damned! Thomas Moore could take part of the blame, for he had forced her into it. Bertram would take the rest, for setting Moore on her trail.

She hailed the next cab. "Mayfair," she said to the driver. "Green Street."

Inside the musty cab, as the wheels thumped steadily against the pavement and St. Giles receded, her panic began to ebb, her mind clearing.

She would play the housekeeper. She would find Marwick's information on Bertram. And she would use it.

This was the last time that any man of Bertram's would ever make her flee.

CHAPTER TWO

Two hands and a throat: that is all that murder requires.

Alastair sits on the floor. The wall presses like a hand against his back, trying to shove him away, but he will not go. He will stay here. In the darkness he looks into his hands, spreads and flexes them. They itch for something to break.

Simple. Murder is so simple that boys must be warned against it. The throat is a delicate instrument; the hyoid bone, once crushed, blocks the airway completely. On playing fields, boys are taught the rules by which they must abide as gentlemen: *Never squeeze the throat. Poor sportsmanship.*

But in the end, the *laws of honor* have nothing to do with games, or with honor, either. They are simply lies invented to dissuade boys from knowing their own power, and from using it to kill each other.

Why? Why not kill? There are worse deaths than murder. Alastair's wife, for instance, died alone in a rented suite at Claridge's, an opium pipe beside her. *But no,* he'd told the inspector, *no, no, it can't be that. You're wrong. There has been some mistake. She knew her limits. She knew how to use the stuff safely.*

You knew, *Your Grace? You knew she smoked the pipe?*

The sudden change in the inspector's tone had startled him. Before that night, nobody had spoken to him so. Yet this paid lackey of Alastair's own government had dared to challenge him.

Yes, he'd replied icily. *I knew.*

What arrogance, that he hadn't thought to lie. He'd been stunned, of course; grief-stricken, baffled, any number of florid adjectives that only a fool would willingly use to describe himself. Still, what arrogance! And what naïveté, that he'd ever imagined there was a safe way for Margaret to dabble in such drugs. What idiocy that he had believed her (*I take it for my headaches; it is harmless, it works better than laudanum*). Any sensible, intelligent man, upon discovering her habit, might have made the next leap: if she had kept this secret from him for so long, she might be keeping any number of other secrets, too.

But self-doubt had never come easily to him. For he did everything right, did he not? He lived well; he performed his duties with panache; he defied all the sordid legacies of his father. He had married well, and his marriage was nothing like his parents'. Margaret was the perfect wife. The opium was only a fluke.

And then suddenly she was dead of it, and Scotland Yard did not know what to do. A duchess found dead at one of London's finest hotels? Dead in a plush suite that had cost fifty pounds a night, between floors of Americans planning their tours of the Tower and the zoo? How to contain such a story? How to bury it quickest?

No one at Scotland Yard knew of the letters Margaret had written, or of the lovers she had kept, or of the countless betrayals she had made in the dark, pressing her body to her lovers' bodies, speaking into their ears of her husband's plans, the schemes with which he sought to defeat them in Parliament. On that night, Alastair had not known yet, either. He had still been telling himself a story, believing it: their lives had been perfect until now. But if Scotland Yard had known those details, they might have suspected Alastair of murdering her. And had *he* known those details, perhaps they would have been right.

He flexes his hands. *So easy.* The wall gives another shove. He digs in his heels and resists.

The death of Margaret de Grey, Duchess of Marwick, was ruled an act of nature. Her body was removed from the hotel under cover of nightfall, while all the curious Americans were sleeping. *Influenza,* the official report read. Alastair's friends consoled him. *The injustice of it. God's ways are mysterious indeed.*

But there had been no mystery, no injustice, in her death: her own stupid vice had caused it. Likewise, it would be no injustice if her lovers died. No mystery, either. It would be murder. It would be murder if Alastair left this house.

So he does not leave this house. He does not even leave this room.

He looks into his palms. His eyes have grown accustomed to the dark he has made for himself, behind these curtains that never open. He sees clearly his lifelines, supposed harbingers of fortune: another lie, as much a lie as honor or ideals. He curls his lip. *Fuck these lies.*

His language is filthy. Foul thoughts swarm through his rotted, useless brain like flies across shit. He thought once that he saw every possibility. That he would make his own destiny. That he and Margaret, together, would be everything the world required. He thought he had control, and that everything he did, was done perfectly. *I have done everything right*—or so he'd thought.

He makes fists. His knuckles crack. He feels no pain.

"Your Grace."

That is the third time someone has addressed him. He becomes aware of that, all at once. The soft voice comes from the doorway. It is female. He does not look up.

Glass clinks: the woman is collecting empty bottles from the carpet. He has not drunk in some days, though. Even alcohol has ceased to affect him. With it or without it, he feels equally numb.

"Your Grace," she says, "will you come out? Take the air, while I tidy your rooms?"

They always leave after a minute; the trick is to ignore them. But the more frequently this question is put to him, the more foolish and dangerous it seems. All of them are ignorant: the servants, his brother, the world. They fail to understand that their best interests lie in leaving him here. It is safer if he stays—not for himself, but for them.

For he knows that he could kill very easily. These hands, his own, could kill. He is no longer Parliament's brightest star, celebrated husband to a society beauty, someday to be prime minister. He is not the country's best hope, nor the corrective to his parents' foul legacy. He is not the new chapter of anything.

If he decided to take the air now—to step out, to return to the world—people would die, because he would kill them. He would kill them for what they had done.

"Your Grace." The girl is pale, tall, with hair as red as

a warning. She is too bright; she hurts his eyes. "If you will just—"

Idiots must be saved from themselves. He gropes for a bottle and hurls it.

Olivia slammed the door, then leaned against it, heart pounding. She had not started her day intending to meet the duke. But in the library, when she had remarked on the empty spots on some of the shelves, one of the maids had replied, *Oh, the duke has them upstairs. It's like a jumble sale, his rooms! Loads of books and papers and whatnot. He won't even let us in anymore.*

Papers.

Olivia had been here five days. She had not yet searched an inch of the place. Contrary to her expectations, the disorder of the household worked against her. The maids, the footmen, even the cook's assistant forever seemed to be popping up where they shouldn't. She caught them in odd places, doing everything in the world (loitering, dozing, playing cards) save their work.

How was a woman supposed to pry when potential witnesses roamed wherever they pleased?

She was attempting to impose a schedule, discipline. Jones, when he was not hiding in his pantry, approved: she had the makings, he told her, of an excellent housekeeper. *Natural talent,* he pronounced, clearly pleased with his own instinct in hiring her.

But she couldn't care less about the household, save that the errantry of its staff offended her sensibilities and was foiling her plans. What she needed was *predictability:* to know where everyone would be, at what time.

Until she managed that, she contented herself by surveying the terrain and designing a plan of search. She knew she must go through the study, top to bottom. The library also had cabinets requiring investigation. But the duke's rooms? She had never dreamed he might keep files there. She had ventured upstairs to make her introductions to him (baffled as to why Jones hadn't yet arranged it) and to take a look around.

Instead, she'd uncovered a shocking scene, at the end of which he had thrown a *bottle* at her.

Her palm itched with the urge to turn the key and lock him inside. But no, she didn't dare. That was not the act of a housekeeper, but of a jailer.

The housekeeper in a madhouse might do it, she thought.

She took a long, ragged breath. He had not been aiming *at* her. That was some kind of comfort, surely.

Or perhaps he *had* been aiming and had simply missed. It had been so dark that from the doorway, very little was visible. She'd made out shapes along the floor—books? Or piles of paper?—and the mass of the canopied bed. To the right, where a dim glow penetrated through the drawn curtains, she'd spotted *him:* the shape of him, at least, a silhouette sitting perfectly still, head bowed as though in prayer.

But he was not praying. He was mad. His insanity had a feel to it, jagged and sharp, so the very air in his bedroom seemed filled with edges.

When the bottle had shattered, she'd dropped the ones she'd been collecting. He was armed, then, with at least three more potential weapons to throw. She would not go back into his rooms until she found a suit of armor.

She smiled a little. The one standing guard outside the library might fit her.

"She just went in there." The voice came from ahead.

"No! She wouldn't dare!"

"I tell you, she did. I was listening for a bit, didn't hear no screams."

"Just wait for the bruised eye, then. You know he ain't—"

Olivia stepped around the corner. The maids fell silent, but the glance they exchanged spoke volumes, lending their silence a mocking air. It made her wonder what they saw in her face—if she looked shaken.

The thought irked her. She was *not* frightened. Only Bertram's man frightened her, and she refused to expand the list. She pulled herself straight. "Polly," she said to the brunette, "I told you to see to the morning room."

Polly wiped her hands down her apron. "I already did, Miss Johnson."

"Mrs. Johnson," Olivia corrected. That was the proper address for a housekeeper.

The other maid, Muriel, giggled. The footmen seemed to admire that giggle, for they were constantly trying to elicit it. Olivia had never witnessed so much flirtation as she had the past several days. She'd found this atmosphere mildly annoying, but now, all at once, it struck her as obscene.

The duke was drinking himself to death in the darkness while his servants flirted and giggled. *It's been grand fun,* Polly had told her. *Like being paid to see a stage show.* "What," she said coldly, "do you find so amusing, Muriel?"

Muriel dimpled as she shrugged. A petite, pretty blonde, she seemed to think her charms were universally applicable. Life would surprise her someday. "Nothing, ma'am. Only, somebody said you came to apply for the housemaid's position—"

That somebody could be none other than Polly, who returned Olivia's sharp look with a shrug.

"—and truth be told, you're the youngest housekeeper *I* ever saw."

That, no doubt, *was* the truth—and the reason the staff mocked and japed at her. Jones, who spent most of his time hiding in the pantry, was not proving the confederate she'd hoped.

But until she got the servants in hand, she dared not search the house. "How surprising to hear that," she said. "The *youngest* housekeeper, are you certain? But I suppose I must take your word for it, your experience being so very broad. You having served in so many great houses, and traveled the world, *vous avez même soupé à Versailles, n'est-ce pas?*"

Muriel's smile slipped. "I . . . I don't speak that language, ma'am."

"No? What a pity. Do you speak the language of rug brushing and curtain beating?"

Muriel cast a worried frown toward Polly, who had gaped at Olivia's French, and had yet to close her jaw. "I don't suppose I know that language, either," Muriel said.

Polly collected herself. "Dolt. It's not a language. She's saying, do you know how to brush a rug?"

"Think carefully," Olivia said. "It is the main requirement of your continued employment."

Judging by the startled alarm that flashed across their faces, the maids had not realized that she had the power to sack them. Indeed, Olivia did not feel so certain of it herself. She was, after all, "temporary"—and the household had lost too much staff already.

Regardless, her threat had the desired effect. Both

girls went hurrying to collect their maids' boxes, which they had abandoned at the top of the stairs. Polly muttered something to Muriel. Only two words popped out: *duke* and *drunkard.*

No wonder that the staff was wild. Marwick set them no good example. On the other hand, why did they humor his debauchery? Had they no self-respect? The task of a well-trained staff, particularly in a grand home such as this, was not merely to *obey* the master, but also to exert a civilizing influence. In *some* households, the staff even took pride in that role. And why not? Left unchecked, the excesses of the aristocracy would have outraged England into a revolution by now.

But *this* staff cowered as though their duty and their dignity were mutually exclusive.

"One more thing," she called. Both girls turned to look at her. "You will take no more liquor to His Grace's rooms." Let him learn a lesson. For that matter, let him be deprived of new weaponry, in case she needed to enter his rooms again. "That is an order that applies to all the servants, footmen included."

They goggled at her. Muriel recovered first. "But if he rings, ma'am—"

"You will come to me. I will handle it." *Somehow.* She would deal with that problem when it arose.

"The footmen don't take orders from you," Polly said.

"No, they take orders from Mr. Jones, who is in agreement with me." Or so he would be, after Olivia spoke with him. Marwick's brutishness should carry repercussions. Besides, if he drank himself to death, his butler would be out of a job.

* * *

"Don't move." Olivia sat at the head of the table in the servants' gallery, Jones to her right, Cook to her left, and Marwick's valet, Vickers, at the foot. Together, the four of them sat watching the bells affixed to the wall, one of which had begun to ring again, for the third time that hour.

"But we must answer him!" Vickers was round-faced, tonsured like a monk, and given to rubbing his bald spot when nervous. He was scrubbing it now vigorously.

"He's had his dinner," Olivia said. "You were just upstairs. The only possible thing he could require from us is alcohol—or hot milk." She grew thoughtful. Hot milk was said to be comforting. "Would you take him some? It might help."

Vickers clutched his pate. "You want me dead, do you?"

"I agree with Mrs. Johnson," Jones said. "Whisky will not aid him. But what of port? It *is* a gentleman's right to enjoy his—"

"Any intoxicant will do him ill. And he does not deserve our indulgence." *Really,* Olivia thought. Must she persuade them all over again? "He threw a bottle at my head, sirs. That is *not* a gentleman's right." But her motive was not wholly spiteful. She clung to the virtue in it. "Besides, if it's true what you say—if he was never violent before—why, then the liquor must account for it. You do him a service by denying it."

"Are you certain he was drunk?" Jones squinted into space. "I keep good track of the cellars, and I've not noticed—"

"You can't imagine how many bottles I found up there."

"And *you* can't imagine what he's been like," Vickers said. "The liquor soothes him, I tell you!"

"Soothes him!" Olivia sat back, gawking. "Do you call a bottle, *hurled* at the wall—"

"At least he's eating." Cook looked bleary-eyed from exhaustion, her face as gray as her hair. Every time the bell rang, she shrank more deeply into herself, so that over the course of the last hour, she had gone from sporting two chins to three. "I can't say the liquor accounts for it, but he'd barely touch his tray, this summer. He's better now."

Better! Olivia thought again of the darkness, of his sudden savage assault today. Cook called that *better*? She gripped her hands very tightly in her lap. "But surely you see that this is for his own good. Even if he *is* on the mend"—*ha!*—"liquor will not benefit—"

Jones's chair scraped as he stood. "You are new to this household, ma'am." He lifted his voice to be heard over the clamoring of the bell. "I cannot fault your intentions. But you overstep yourself to imagine that you have any understanding—"

Olivia lifted her hands in surrender. "Fine! Take it to him." What did it matter to her anyway? For all she knew, the duke kept his dossiers somewhere logical, like the study. She would never need to go into his rooms.

But the problem of the disobedient staff remained. "But how," she continued, "shall I win the respect of the staff? Pray tell, Mr. Jones. For the servant follows his master's example, does he not? And you see what this household resembles, when its master is playing the lunatic."

The bell fell still. In the silence, she found herself the object of three appalled stares.

And then Cook gave a breathy sob and looked down

at the tabletop, and Jones fell back into his chair like a sack of flour, and Vickers set his head into his hands.

Olivia felt a brief wave of triumph. Finally, they saw her point.

With the next breath, she felt sorry for them. Their employment here was no game, no masquerade; it was their livelihood.

But should the duke perish, his heir might bring a new staff to replace them. She was doing them a favor.

Cook was muffling sobs with her handkerchief. "I've known him since he was a boy. I never thought to see him brought so low. He was everything kind, you can't imagine . . ."

No, she certainly couldn't. With a sigh, she said, "Perhaps what we need is a doctor."

Vickers scoffed. "His own brother is the finest doctor in England. Much good he did!"

"Lord Michael tried his best," Jones said with dignity.

Olivia believed it. She had come to know Lord Michael during his courtship of Elizabeth Chudderley. He had not struck her as a man to do anything by halves.

She had depended on Marwick's estrangement from his brother to safeguard her masquerade here. But now, for the briefest moment, she wondered if he shouldn't be summoned. "Do you think he might . . ."

Alas, she was too self-minded to finish her sentence, for if he came, Lord Michael would recognize her in an instant. But Cook caught on, and shook her head. "He's been driven away, Mrs. Johnson. He'll not set foot in this house again."

Olivia eyed her. "You say you've known the duke since boyhood." And Cook's tearstained face was very poignant, the picture of a grieving grandmother, almost.

It would require a heart of stone to look upon her and remain indifferent. "Perhaps if *you* were to speak to him . . ."

"Oh, no. It's not my place. And I'll not go up there, I won't." Cook crossed her beefy arms and sat back, less grandmotherly now than mulish. "It's here I stay, in the kitchens. I take good care of them; I know my place."

"Convenient for you," Vickers muttered.

Olivia bit back an agreement. Cook's pride in her kitchens evidently did not extend to cleanliness: Olivia had discovered a pile of dirt sitting on the counter just this morning. "Let's trick him down here, then. When he realizes Vickers is not at hand, he'll certainly go looking . . ." She trailed off, for all three looked startled. "What is it?"

Jones said guardedly, "He will not leave his room."

She frowned. "Even if we all seem to have abandoned our posts?"

"He has not left in . . . some time."

She paused. "You mean to say he won't leave his bedroom? *Ever?*"

"I suppose he might venture into the sitting room occasionally." Jones cast a hopeful look at Vickers, who shrugged.

"Vickers ain't in the rooms often enough to know," Cook said. "I have to chase him off my girl thrice a day!"

"Hey now," said Vickers. "I can't help it if she hangs about!"

"He won't leave his *room*?" Olivia wished to be very clear on this point. She had never heard of such a bizarre condition. "But *why*?"

"Nobody can say," said Jones.

"He doesn't receive anybody, either." Vickers sounded

gloomy. "Doesn't write letters. Takes no calls. It's dashed dull around here, of late."

Olivia groped for words. "Then how on earth does he conduct his business?" For this was not merely a private gentleman. This was a peer of the realm, one of the greatest landowners in England. His concerns necessarily encompassed the welfare and livelihood of a vast number of people.

"He don't manage," Cook said. She gave a pull of her mouth, considering. "Perhaps you're right." She glanced toward Jones. "Liquor can't be helping him."

Jones thumbed his patch of overlong whiskers. "Perhaps," he allowed.

As though in reply, the bell rang again. Was it Olivia's imagination, or was it somehow ringing *harder* now?

"Somebody needs to answer it." This, naturally, came from Cook, who would not go upstairs. "Even if to tell him we won't fetch him his drink."

Suddenly everyone was looking at *Olivia*. "Oh, no," she said. "As Mr. Jones has pointed out, I am too new to take a hand in these matters."

"But it's your plan," Vickers said. "*You're* the reason we haven't answered him."

She scowled. They cared for the duke; she did not. Indeed, that thought felt like an anchor, holding her steady against their imploring looks, which, like a strong current, threatened to bear her straight into stormy waters. "He and I have not even been introduced. Surely, Mr. Vickers, it is you who—"

Jones stood. "Come, then. Let us go together, so I may introduce you properly."

Vickers mimed a tip of an invisible hat. "It was a pleasure to know you both."

* * *

As Jones opened the door to the duke's sitting room, the hinges squeaked. Olivia stood close enough behind him to sense how he flinched. His nerves proved contagious; she found herself holding her breath as she crept across the carpet in his wake.

She never should have interfered. What did *she* care if the staff failed to defend their own dignity? If they were at peace with their master's savagery, so be it; let them indulge him. And as for having to go into his rooms again—she could have encouraged the footmen to take him more bottles than any man could drink. An unconscious, stupefied drunkard would have posed her no harm.

Oh, this was a terrible flaw in her, this need to interfere and manage and *fix* things.

Jones knocked softly on the bedroom door. "Your Grace?" His voice shook. Olivia wanted to pat the poor man's arm to lend him courage, but she wasn't sure she had enough to spare. She had vowed, after all, not to return until she'd acquired a suit of armor to protect herself. So much for that.

Jones must have heard a reply, for he opened the door. "May we enter?"

A soft hiss filled the air. Along the walls, gas lamps sputtered to life. The rising light illuminated a man standing at the far corner of the room, very tall. It gilded the strong column of his throat, the sharp angle of his jaw—

Olivia felt as though she'd been kicked in the head. He was disheveled (but with a valet like Vickers, she would not have expected otherwise). His beard wanted trimming, and his shaggy hair begged for scissors. He looked, as well, underfed—his shirt hung loosely about his shoulders, and his trousers depended too visibly on the clasps of his suspenders. Together with his gauntness, the effect should have been ugly.

It was the opposite. His leanness only accented the perfect bones of his face: broad, sharp cheekbones; a straight, high-bridged nose; a hard, square jaw that framed full, long lips. She stared, feeling stupefied. Marwick had been a subject of public scrutiny ever since he had stepped into political office. But for all the things that had been spoken of him, nobody had ever called him handsome. Why not? *How* not? Broad-shouldered, whittled lean, he put her in mind of some warrior ascetic from the icy, Viking north. Only his mouth ruined the image: his full lips belonged on a hedonist.

He stepped toward them—rangy, tall, very, very blond. His single step caused Jones to bobble back against her. "I have been ringing," the duke said coldly, "for an hour."

His voice was dark and rich, like the cream on a pint of stout. She understood nothing, suddenly. He did not sound like a madman, and he did not hold himself like someone afraid to leave his rooms. He loomed, rather. He . . . *presided.*

And the chamber over which he presided, she saw, was *filled* with papers. Piles of them lay strewn across the carpet. There were also piles of books stacked about, but those papers . . . oh, so many of them!

"Forgive us, Your Grace." Jones stammered the words. "There was an emergency in the kitchens."

She had a sinking feeling. She would search the study, of course. The library, too. But all these papers . . .

here . . . in the room he never left. God must have a very dry sense of humor.

When she raised her gaze, she found Marwick's attention fastened on *her*. His eyes were a brilliant, piercing blue. Their intensity made something flutter inside her. She recognized the intelligence in them. Her gut told her to take it as a warning.

Jones spoke in a rush. "This is Mrs. Johnson, Your Grace. She is—ah, a temporary replacement for Mrs. Wright, who you may recall gave notice two weeks ago. We were left in the lurch, I fear—I know it is somewhat extraordinary, to hire someone without consulting you. But—if you recall, you gave me full authority—"

"I recall." His piercing blue eyes had not yet released her. She began to feel the weight of them as a deliberate challenge. The lion in his natural element expected submission, but she would not bow her head. She did not even blink. Had she been a cat, she might have bristled at the provocation of his look.

Instead, she was a secretary—by training, at least; and a housekeeper, by strange luck. Neither position required her to abase herself to him.

Thank God for it. For she realized in this moment how badly she would have played the maid. Humbleness came hard to her. She could not value it; too many unkind people had tried to force it on her in her youth. They had expected her to be ashamed, and so she had vowed never to be so.

Nevertheless, a curtsy did no harm. "I am honored, Your Grace," she said as she rose.

He stared at her a moment longer. Then, with a soft noise of contempt, he swung his attention to Jones. "I have told you," he said, "that you may manage the staff as you like. However." His voice hardened. "If I am forced to wait, the next time I ring that bell—"

"That was my doing," Olivia said quickly—for Jones had whimpered, and she could not let him face the consequences that rightly belonged to her.

Marwick said to Jones, "You will tell the girl not to interrupt me."

The girl! She stiffened. She was his *housekeeper*, a position well worthy of his respect. Not that she imagined a man who threw *bottles* would recognize that.

"Yes, indeed." Jones shot her a panicked look. "Mrs. Johnson, if you will wait in the hall?"

She would, gladly. She was already turning away. But—no, in fact, she had something to say. She pivoted back. "I am no girl," she told Marwick. Bully. Brute! He had tried to wreck his brother's marriage to a good woman, for no reason. He terrified his servants. His estates were probably falling to pieces thanks to his inattention. And *he* called her a *girl*? What was he, but a sulking, spoiled boy? "Admittedly, I am young—and a good thing, for an elderly woman might not have survived the shock of having a bottle thrown at her."

Marwick looked at her a moment. And then, suddenly, he was crossing the room in long strides—and Jones, the coward, was dashing into the safety of the sitting room.

She shrank back. But her feet would not let her retreat, clinging stubbornly to pride even as Marwick towered over her. Her heart, on the other hand, was a coward; it slammed against her breastbone in search of an escape.

"I beg," he said softly, "your *pardon*, girl. And now, I advise you to go downstairs and pack your things. You are sacked."

As simply as that? *No.* She did not dare glance over her shoulder to find out if Jones had heard the news. "That would be foolish, Your Grace." The sound of her voice, so fierce, gave her fresh courage. "Your staff is running wild. They need a strong hand to put them to rights."

"Get. Out."

A wild idea came to her, borne of desperation. Lowering her voice, she said, "I should hate to be forced to tell the newspapers that I was attacked by my employer, and then thrown out on my ear for complaining of it."

He stepped back as though to see her better. But as he studied her, his perfect face held an absolute lack of expression. "Was that a threat?" he asked. He did not sound particularly interested.

His monotone was somehow more terrifying than a bellow. She felt a bolt of primal alarm, the same that saved her from runaway carriages, uncovered drains, and lunatics on the street. *Run,* it said. *For your life.*

She took a breath. She knew enough of him from Elizabeth Chudderley—particularly about his reaction to his wife's letters—to know that he feared public notoriety. Elizabeth had said that he dreaded above all things that the letters would be made public. It stood to reason, then, that he would not like the incident with the bottle to be made public, either, for it certainly would make him notorious.

"It is not *precisely* a threat, Your Grace"—for she would never carry through on it; such attention would not suit her, either—"only a suggestion that you might prefer to deal fairly with me. Your household requires direction."

He stepped toward her again, and this time her feet

responded sensibly, carrying her backward until she hit the wall.

"How curious," he said. He propped an elbow against the wall above her, leaning into it, *looming* over her, while with his other hand he grabbed her jaw, lifting it the way one might an animal's. Every muscle in her stiffened as he looked into her face.

His hand was hot. Impossibly large. She spoke through her teeth. "Release me."

"Your Grace," he said very softly. "You will address me properly."

Properly? He wanted respect from her while he behaved like a common thug? She glared at him.

He pulled her chin higher. A muscle in her neck protested. Where was Jones? Why was he not interfering? "Your Grace," he said again, still just as soft. "Do say it, Mrs. Johnson. I am waiting."

She would spit in his eye first. "Do dukes behave so?" Her voice came out very hoarsely. "*Gentlemen* do not."

His eyes roved her face, his own still coldly impassive. "Oh, yes," he said, "you *are* very young. Very young and very stupid. I think *girl* is the only word for you, Mrs. Johnson. Tell me, was there ever a mister?"

She slammed her lips together to halt their trembling. Until he released her, she would say no more. She did not know which remark might incite him further.

He lifted a brow, which gave her a weird shock; it was the first animation she had seen on his frigid countenance. "Silence? But a moment ago, you had so very much to say." He placed his thumb on her lower lip, then made a firm, hard stroke. She tasted the salt on his skin.

This was not happening. She seemed to move outside her body, viewing from above this unbelievable moment: the Duke of Marwick, *molesting her.*

He withdrew his thumb. Lifted it to his own mouth. Tasting *her.* Their eyes met, his impossibly blue, not a speck of hazel or gold to break their electric intensity. A curious prickle spread through her.

He made a contemptuous noise and dropped his hand. "Disobedience," he said. "The taste of it does not suit me." He took another step back, looking at her with sudden cruel amusement. "However. The correction of impertinent domestics has always been one of my skills."

Here was why nobody commented on the beauty of his bone structure, the shape of his mouth, or the brilliance of his eyes. Perfection was not always beautiful: sometimes, it was terrifying.

"Your Grace—" she began in a whisper, but he cut her off.

"There is no Mr. Johnson, I think. You blush like a virgin. *Ma'am.*"

She turned her face away. Staring at the wall, she said rapidly, "The staff assures me that you have never been the kind of cowardly man who abuses his servants—"

His fist slammed into the wall.

She opened her mouth. Nothing came out. His fist had missed her ear by an inch, no more.

"I am precisely that kind of man," he said bitterly. "Or did you imagine you were dreaming this episode?"

She darted a horrified glance at him. Something dark and contemptuous had come into his face. He reached for the gas dial, and the lowering light masked him from view.

She wanted to bolt, but she was not certain her knees would support her. Her breathing would not settle into an easy rhythm; it jerked in her throat. What kind of man was this? What kind of monster? And she could see nothing, which would make her escape treacherous, for the floor was littered with all manner of—

Papers.

She willed her voice not to shake. "It would be easier to keep me on. Otherwise you might have to trouble yourself with terrorizing a new woman."

"You must be very desperate, Mrs. Johnson, to want this position."

Again, she caught the note of contempt. But it was not for her, she realized. He meant that it would take a desperate woman to wish to work for *him.* His contempt was all for himself.

This attitude was so at odds with what she had expected from him (arrogance, vanity, condescension) that she felt at sea. She groped for a reply. "I do not blame you." *What a lie!* "Liquor can make us strangers to ourselves—"

His laugh seemed edged with glass. "But I am sober, ma'am. I have been sober all day."

She swallowed a gasp. If he had been sober when he threw the bottle—if he was sober even now—then liquor had no role in his wickedness: the evil was native to him.

She would not let him hear her shock; she sensed it would gratify him too much. "Then what were you ringing for, if not alcohol?"

His slight pause suggested surprise. And then, with a note of mockery, came his reply: "Bullets."

Her courage shattered. She groped desperately along the wall for the door. She fled through the sitting room into the hallway, where Jones—a true coward—stood waiting. "Well?" he asked anxiously.

She shook her head and walked past him, hugging herself. Whether, with his last remark, Marwick had been trying to frighten her or only telling the truth, she could not say. But if it was the latter . . .

Jones fell into step at her heels. "Shall we send up a bottle?"

"Several." *And put hemlock in them.*

The thought was too black, too horrifying; she felt appalled at having entertained it. But had she spoken it, Jones probably would not have been shocked. By his lack of surprise, it was clear he'd given up on his master sometime ago. He had only humored her tonight as a matter of form.

Yet as she reached the ground floor, she found herself remembering the look on the duke's face. His disgust after he had punched the wall. It had been an ugly look, at odds with the treacherous beauty of his features.

She realized she was touching her lip. She scrubbed it with her knuckles. He was a bully, a lunatic. She should not spare a thought to what haunted him. There was no possible earthly excuse for his behavior.

But she did know the reason for it. She had read the duchess's letters. And as much as they had shocked and revolted her, she could only imagine what effect they'd had on Marwick.

How she wished she hadn't read them! For this sudden, fleeting sympathy was undeserved by him, and *ridiculous* of her, and . . . the very opposite of armor.

CHAPTER THREE

When Olivia woke the next morning, it was to a creeping feeling of doom. She could not even trace it back to Bertram, for it descended from above, from the room where the Duke of Marwick stewed in his villainous lair.

She breakfasted in the privacy of the sitting room attached to her sleeping quarters. Through the walls came the muffled conversation of the staff taking their meal at the long table in the gallery. To her ears, the gabble seemed muted, bereft of its typical boisterousness. Perhaps somebody—probably Vickers—had spread word about last night.

When she stepped out to give the maids their duties, her suspicion was confirmed. Polly, Muriel, and Doris greeted her very meekly, and as they filed out, Muriel whispered, "You're very brave," before dashing off.

Brave? Vickers must have gotten a garbled tale from Jones. Olivia did not feel brave at all. She felt, all at once, *oppressed.* The duke was not her concern. He could live or die as he wished.

Indeed, as long as he lived until she had a chance to search his house, she would be content.

That is awful, she thought, scowling. She did not really mean it. She was not wicked. She *did* wish the best for him—even if he did not deserve it.

Snapping out of her reverie, she found herself paused on the stairs. The tumult within her had drawn her to a stop—*exactly* the kind of inaction she could not afford.

Today, she resolved, she would begin her search. For tomorrow, no doubt, the maids would rediscover their contempt for her, and begin to flirt with the footmen again, luring them into dark rooms where Olivia had rather not be discovered, nose-deep in the duke's belongings.

All summer, the garden had hummed. From the darkness of his bedroom overlooking the flowers, Alastair had listened to the cacophony. Bees knocking into the window. The rattle of squirrels playing along the ledge. In the early morning, the birdsong leaking through the panes had woken him in a fury, his head pounding.

He'd wanted nothing of summer. This house would be his grave. Drunk, enraged, he'd cursed the life in the garden.

Now, on a late October morning, he woke to silence. The garden was dead. He could *feel* its sterility. Its silence pressed against the curtained windows like a fist ready to explode through the glass.

The silence, so loud, bore a message for him: he had missed something crucial, let it pass by. Now it would never return for him.

He rose. (Why? What point?) The long mirror atop

his dressing table showed a lean face and sunken eyes, the face of a starving wolf. "Damn you," he said to the mirror. His eyes burned; his lip curled, exposing teeth.

Once, he wielded this sneer in Parliament, a handy tool to silence his opponents. Now it functioned only to silence himself.

He resisted it. "Will you not go outside?" he snapped.

Outside: a crush of eyes to watch him. Countless mouths poised to spread news of him. *Look at what he has become. England's hope, they once called him.* Thoughts of that world, the eyes, the mouths, swarmed over him, nested in his chest, and grew heavy like stone. It crushed the breath from his lungs to think of the world outside.

In the world's memory, he was a statesman. Not a fool or a cuckold, not a man whose hubris had blinded him to his own idiocy.

Let the world remember that other man, then—even if, in retrospect, he had always been a lie, after all.

Kneeling, Alastair commenced his calisthenics. Twelve years ago, drunk at a pub in Oxford, his friends had paid an old soldier to show them his mettle. He had led them through his army routine, and none of them—save the soldier—had gotten through it without puking.

That might have been owed to the alcohol. But the routine was punishing. As Alastair pushed himself off the ground, there seemed to be nothing but bile in him. He welcomed the sensation. He had followed this routine for four weeks now, needing the exhaustion that followed. Exhaustion was the only cure for this acid in his veins, the restlessness that built like ground glass, the *rage*.

Once finished, his labored breath searing his throat, he laid his forehead atop his drawn-up knees and let the sweat cool on his skin. Here, now, only now, once a day, was the game he would allow himself to play, having earned it with physical exertion:

This silence might be any silence. This time, any time.

It is four years ago, or five. The beginning of it all. His wife is dressing in the adjoining apartment. If her mood is happy, then she sings to herself as she tries on jewels. She is dressing for a party. Every night brings parties: a politician requires friends, resources to use and abuse.

Perhaps the party is here. Margaret is an excellent hostess, as celebrated for it as her husband is for his good deeds, his noble causes, his leadership. *You chose very wisely,* someone has told him. *She will make a fine wife for a prime minister one day.* How the compliment gratifies him. How well Margaret looks on his arm, and how cleverly she converses.

But it cannot be *four* years ago. It must be five. Four years ago, Fellowes returned to town. And there it began. Fellowes, Nelson, Barclay, Bertram . . .

Alastair lifted his head. He was done with this mantra, these names of the men with whom she betrayed him. He had read her letters so many times now that he might have recited them like soliloquies, speeches from some lewd and puerile script.

My husband is a fool; he has no inkling of who I am, what I do.

He believes the bill will pass, I tell you. But he worried last night that Dawkins would waver, if only somebody knew to push him. So go find Dawkins, and promise him a few coins, and the bill will die on the floor.

I lie next to my husband at night and burn for you . . . I imagine his hands are yours, and then I open my eyes and want to wretch . . .

He stared at the broken shards of glass along the baseboard. Why were they there? After a moment, it came to him: these were the remnants of the bottle he'd thrown . . . when?

He had thrown it at the girl who had said, *I am no girl.* When had that been? In his memory, her voice seemed strangely clear, cutting through the murky sewage of his rotted brain. He recalled the vividness of her red hair, and her unusual height; but her face, in his memory, was blank, a pale and featureless oval. What he recalled instead was his own reflection in her spectacles. The reflection of a beast.

Looking at himself, he had wondered how she did not recoil. How she dared to face him so boldly.

He ran his thumbs now over his scraped knuckles. He had hit a low point, no doubt. Bullying women; that was what he did now, it seemed.

But she had not yielded her ground even then. She had challenged him again. She must be deranged. Not as deranged as he, though.

He remembered touching her, meaning to teach her a lesson in obedience. But now all he remembered was the feel of her lip. Soft. For a moment only, sensation had sparked along his skin, and it had not felt like pain.

But how predictable. His father had molested the servants. Any number of maids. Four years ago, five, Alastair had known he would never be like his father—that leering, raging, lecherous bull. Even a year ago, he had known it.

Known it. Ha. A fool *knew* many things, very few of them true.

But when had the girl come in here? Yesterday? Two days ago? Twenty?

Time passes without him now. He is trapped in this moment, which never changes. And he dares not leave it, for if he does, everything will change. The world will cease to remember how it once saw him. Instead, it will see his new face: violent, broken, shattered, *murderous.*

These shards on the floor, he sees, are his ambitions, his ideals, his foolish presumptions: *I will be nothing like my father when I am a man. I will not repeat his mistakes.*

The silence from the garden reverberates.

Olivia started her search in the library, but the very promising cabinets turned out to be filled with maps—so many, and some so ancient, that it appeared some duke had nursed an obsession for them.

She went next to the study, which she had instructed the maids to clean first today. As she turned on the lights, she saw proof of their shoddy job in the dust lining the edge of the carpet.

She gritted her teeth. This was not her concern. She was not *really* a housekeeper.

She turned the dead bolt behind her. Most studies were humbly furnished, the better to receive tradesmen. But this chamber, with its thick Turkish carpet and oak wainscoting, spoke of loftier pastimes: the business and politicking of great men. To think that Marwick had once been known as a master statesman! A Cato for modern times, incorruptible, the champion of the poor. *Ha!*

Yet amid this silent grandeur, the vacant desk and its bare blotter disturbed her. They seemed proof of tragedy, something gone horribly wrong.

She forced herself to shrug away the thought. Yes,

something had gone wrong: Marwick had married a wicked woman. What of it? He'd probably given the duchess ample reason to despise him. Perhaps, for instance, he'd *thrown* things at her.

She tugged at the top drawer of the desk. Finding it locked, she plucked a hairpin from her chignon. It took a single prod to coax the latch to yield. This talent was courtesy of the typing school, where she'd sat to the left of a future viscountess, and to the right of a former pickpocket, Lilah, who had firmly believed no girl should ever be baffled by a lock. Secretaries were a very interesting bunch.

The drawer contained several ledgers. She removed her spectacles, which did tend to blur things, and discovered that these were records of income from the duke's estates. The notes grew illegible in August 1884; by September of that year, they ceased.

As the significance dawned on her, she recoiled. In August, Marwick's wife had died. And shortly thereafter, he had discovered how she'd betrayed him.

She brought the ledger closer. Like the photographs of crime scenes printed in the newspaper, Marwick's handwriting exerted a morbid fascination. *Here,* grief had made his hand shake. And *here*, his grief had darkened and twisted, becoming something so awful that it had finally silenced his pen completely.

Bah. So he was human. What of it? He was a *terrible* human. She would not pity him.

She moved on to the next drawer, which yielded a set of twine-bound folders. Within, she found drafts of speeches, records of parliamentary proceedings, notes on debates in the Commons and Lords.

As she looked through them for Bertram's name,

she felt increasingly, unwillingly curious. Was *this* how politics got conducted? Documented here was a history of frustrated negotiations, of visions dashed by corruption and the recalcitrance of supposed allies. These papers did not tell of a puppet master, but of a man who struggled for compromises, and who employed elegant, impassioned rhetoric (here was a draft of one of Marwick's most famous speeches, on the importance of primary education) to persuade others of the justness of his cause.

These records belonged to an idealist.

She shoved them away as if they burned.

The final drawer yielded a slim stack of personal correspondence—very promising. Her heart leapt when she saw Bertram's signature, but the next moment, she cast it down in disgust—it was only a note of thanks for a dinner party. The next sheet was a draft, much scribbled upon, concerning . . .

A gasp escaped her. This was a love letter!

I have wracked my brain for a way to heal this breach between us. I promise you, Margaret, that you are wrong to think I don't care for you. When I envision my life, you are at the center of it. Without you, I see only an Eden after the fall: empty, imperfect, broken . . .

Her own curiosity suddenly revolted her. She cast down the letter. It had nothing to do with Bertram. She was not the kind of low woman who pried into other people's business for pleasure.

Or was she? Sometimes, lately, it seemed she was losing pieces of herself, all her most cherished convictions: *I am innocent; I am wronged; I did not deserve any of this.*

Instead, she was discovering new things about herself, terrible things. Just look what she had done to Elizabeth.

Elizabeth Chudderley led a fast life, treated her staff too familiarly, and offered no Christian example of temperance and virtue. But despite her life as a flibbertigibbet, she was also generous, thoughtful, and kind. She could have used the duchess's letters to blackmail Marwick into endorsing her marriage to his brother. Instead, she had decided to do the honorable thing and hand them over to him.

And so Olivia had stolen some and fled.

But what *choice* had she had? For so long, Olivia's only ambition had been to hide—first at the typing school, and then as a secretary to an elderly widow in Brighton, and finally, most happily, in Elizabeth's employ.

But at Elizabeth's house party this summer, a guest had pulled Olivia aside to mention her resemblance to a portrait he had glimpsed in the private study of his friend Lord Bertram. Olivia had realized then that it was time to run again. For the first time, the thought had made her *angry*.

She made herself retrieve the papers. But now she scanned them mechanically, her mind elsewhere.

As a rash eighteen-year-old, she had assumed Bertram, being in his forties and somewhat wrinkled, would die soon enough. Seven years later, she knew differently. He might live for four more decades. And his mania was not fading. Her very existence was evidently an intolerable offense to him.

Must she spend the next forty years in flight? Would she never be allowed to truly *live*? For the first time, this summer, she had wondered if she might not try to *fight* instead of flee.

Her opponent was far above her. Bertram was an aristocrat, with the resources to match his barony. But he had made a mistake. He had connived with the Duchess of Marwick, and she had passed his letters onward. Olivia had stolen several of them—and one of particular interest, in which he had written to the duchess:

Concerning these "dossiers," as you call them, I can do nothing but express my disgusted astonishment. The notion that Marwick would compile secret information on those who consider him a friend—well, it fills me with such profound distaste that I cannot express the half of it.

I cannot imagine what information he might think to hold over me. But for the sake of opposing his espionage, I will gladly support your efforts to undo him.

Olivia did not believe for an instant that the dossier would substantiate Bertram's virtues. He was a man too viciously devoted to his own authority. Why, when an eighteen-year-old girl had chosen to make her own way rather than live under his thumb, he had sent an assassin to crush her. Would such a man prove more virtuous in his other dealings? Whatever this dossier contained, it was likely the key to disarming him for good. She must find it.

But it was not in this pile. As she put her glasses back on, her stomach felt twisted into knots. Thomas Moore would be combing the city for her. Meanwhile, servants talked, and she knew how they would describe their new housekeeper. A redhead who stood as tall as a man? The moment Moore caught wind of that gossip . . .

The bookcase to her right held nothing but folders.

She stared at them, debating with herself. It would take hours to comb through so many files.

But her time, even now, was running out.

She rose and took two folders, all she could safely conceal in her skirts. And then, steeling herself, she started for the door. Yes, she was a thief. Yes, it was wretched. But if Moore caught her, she would be dead.

CHAPTER FOUR

"That isn't the way we do it here!" Polly snapped.

Olivia bit her tongue lest she retort in kind. Her day had begun in exhaustion, which was nothing new: for the past two weeks, she'd spent half of every night reading documents she daily secreted into her rooms. None of them, so far, had proved relevant to her cause. But she was becoming peculiarly, uneasily fascinated with Marwick's personal records.

Marwick wrote—or had written—prodigiously. He kept notes on every book he read, and chronicled his thoughts on all manner of subjects: diplomatic crises, agrarian issues, the nature of good and evil, the qualities of great men. He wrote like an angel, with an erudition that stirred her envy. She had studied Latin only for a year, and ancient Greek, never; she ended up in the library some nights, struggling to decipher his quotes with the aid of dictionaries, simply to prove to herself that she could.

What she would not have given for a chance to study at Oxbridge! But she knew that even those institutions could not guarantee such insight as his writing suggested. How to square such elegant, astonishing work with the monster upstairs? She felt as though she were reading the memoirs of a ghost, someone whom she would have very much liked to meet while he still lived.

This growing fascination was perverse and unseemly. But she had to search his study, didn't she? She had to look at every document, lest she miss the single one she needed. And so, every night, she stayed up until half past two, at which point she forced herself to bed; and every morning, before dawn, she crept up to the study to purloin new material.

Only two folders remained to be read. Cook, this morning, had very nearly caught her in the act of shoving them under her mattress. She had delivered to Olivia a list of mysteries from the kitchen: five pounds of truffles had gone missing. Where had they gone? And why was the crockery in need of repair? It had just been mended last month.

Jones, whom Olivia consulted over breakfast, could not explain any of it. The truffles had particularly concerned him; he'd set about interviewing the kitchen staff. In the meantime, Olivia went to check on the maids and discovered this scene of butchery in the morning room: Polly, brushing a rose-and-cream carpet with tea leaves. The carpet already bore several telltale streaks. "Henceforth," Olivia told her, "you will use salt."

"Salt!"

Olivia was no domestic, and even *she* knew this. "For pale carpets, one uses salt."

With a sullen shrug, Polly retrieved her brush and started to sweep again.

"Stop! You mustn't brush the leaves in. Don't you see? They're leaving stains."

Polly hurled down the broom. "Then may I go?"

With leaves strewn everywhere? "Certainly not. You will pick up the leaves, then apply the salt and finish brushing the carpet."

"Pick them up by *hand*?"

"Yes, by hand. Otherwise the stain will spread."

Polly folded her arms and glared. Too late, Olivia realized she had done the same. They locked eyes, Olivia battling a creeping awareness of how absurd this scene would look to any passerby: a maid and housekeeper so close in age that the only way they might be told apart was by the key ring at Olivia's waist.

Polly's fine upper lip twitched into a sneer. She was a pretty girl, with large brown eyes and burnished hair—and why was she not wearing her cap properly? Those curls should have been covered.

"Are you Irish?" Polly asked.

That was meant to be an insult, of course. It never failed to amaze Olivia how narrowly the world was designed: if you had no legitimate origins, you were scorned. If you had legitimate origins in the wrong place, you were scorned as well.

Luckily for her, she put no stock in conventional virtues; their main supporters, in her experience, were hypocrites. She lifted her chin, knowing if she gave so much as inch, she would never regain it. "Salt," she said tersely, "catches the dust just as well. And it does not stain the carpet."

Polly rolled her eyes.

I am going to have to sack her. The knowledge formed like a ball of ice in Olivia's gut. It seemed very wrong to destroy the livelihood of somebody—no matter how mean their behavior—to safeguard a position Olivia did not mean to keep.

A thud came from above. Polly looked up, and Olivia sent a prayer of thanks for this timely interruption.

The thud sounded again—and intensified. The crystal beading on a nearby lamp began to shiver.

Had a herd of elephants invaded the house?

Olivia turned on her heel and marched into the hallway, where she discovered the other maids, along with the valet and the cook's assistant—what was *she* doing up here?—gaping at the ceiling. "What *is* that?" she asked.

A strangled laugh came from behind her. Polly had followed. "It's His Grace!"

A fine joke. Olivia's remonstrance was cut off by one of the other maids. "That's his rooms right above," said Doris. She was a lanky, rabbit-faced girl who had endeared herself to Olivia by inclining more to daydreaming than to mutiny.

Muriel crossed herself. "Perhaps it's the final stages."

"Final stages of what?" Olivia asked.

"Muriel's convinced he has the pox," Polly said.

"Polly!"

"Well, 'tisn't me who said it!" Polly put her hands on her hips. "Though if there's a more likely explanation for such behavior, I'd like to hear it. First he was grievin' his heart out, and goin' up and down the town to make arrangements for the grandest funeral you seen since the pope. Next you know, he breaks all the mirrors, rips down the crepe, and refuses t'set foot outside. Goes the summer, and now he won't stir from his rooms—not even should the house catch fire,

I expect. And if *that's* not the pox-brain, you tell me what is!"

Olivia took a long breath. It now sounded as if Marwick was banging things against the walls. Not his head, she hoped? Or perhaps she did. No, she couldn't wish harm to his brain. It might yet heal, and it had once been very fine.

More of his servants, another footman and the porter, drifted into the corridor to gawp. What a fine fix this was. Nobody was going to brave the stairs to check on him—not even his valet, who was canoodling with the cook's assistant in the corner.

Olivia squinted up the staircase. None of the papers in the study had touched on confidential dealings. What chance was there that the last two folders would prove different? Unless he'd stashed his most private documents under a cushion somewhere, his apartment was the only place remaining to look.

God help her. She was going to have to pry the madman from his rooms.

On a deep breath, she gathered her skirts in her fists and started for the stairs.

"Oh, don't go!" Muriel spoke in a high, panicked voice. "Last time a bottle, this time a blade, ma'am!"

How did Muriel know about that? Olivia wheeled back. "Vickers, you are a *terrible* gossip."

Vickers gave a sheepish shrug.

"Be a man," Polly snapped at him. "Go up there with her!"

This unexpected support quite gratified Olivia. But it only led Vickers to duck behind the cook's assistant. "I am—otherwise occupied," he said.

"Coward," Olivia hissed at him. The other servants' answering snickers, she did not welcome. She directed a scowl down over the gathering.

The resulting silence was most satisfying.

Nevertheless, as she squared her shoulders, she felt compelled to add: "If I have not returned in a quarter hour . . ."

Summon the police, another woman might have said. But not she. The police would not suit her in the least.

As Olivia opened the door to the duke's sitting room, the noise stopped. She hovered on the threshold, debating with herself. With the hubbub over, was there really any call to check on him?

But what if he was lying injured?

Even if he was, was that really *her* responsibility to determine?

Perhaps not. But if she meant to dislodge him from his quarters long enough to search them, she would have to begin the campaign sometime—the sooner, the wiser. *Right-o.* She marched up to the inner door.

Her knock sounded rather timid for her liking. *Timidity is fatal to leadership. Men desire an excuse to believe in something greater than themselves; an incompetent braggart will win them far faster than a great man who does not advertise.* Marwick had written that in his meditations on Wellington.

She bit her lip and rapped more firmly. After a long pause, Marwick said, "Come."

He'd answered! Stupefied, she hesitated. Then she smoothed down her skirts and entered, ready to duck.

The room lay in its usual gloomy darkness, the curtains shuttered. It took a moment for her eyes to adjust. To her bafflement, everything looked in order: all the furniture intact, no shattered bottles lying about—save the remnants of the one he had thrown at her, which still glimmered in a nearby corner.

The stacks of paper had been gathered up and moved. One sat on the chest at the foot of the bed. Another lay on the writing desk by the window. Where were the rest? Pray God he hadn't burned them.

Heart quickening, she turned her attention toward the duke. He reclined on his bed, lost amid the shadows cast by his canopy. Only his eyes glittered out from the murk. "Ah," he drawled. "My newest housekeeper."

How could a man who wrote so beautifully have gone so rotten? She could not think of him as the same person who had written those essays. And she *had* to get him out of this room. What on earth had he been doing in here? He was not slurring his words, and the air held no reek of alcohol—or smoke, either, thank goodness. All she smelled was . . . sweat. Not unpleasant. But sweat all the same.

"Your Grace," she said, remembering to curtsy. "I heard a disturbance. I wished to make certain you were well."

"I suppose that's a matter for debate. *Miss* Johnson."

She resented the heat that came to her face. Had he no shame? Why would he wish to remind her of his abominable behavior at their last meeting? She was tempted to quote him to himself: *We too often mistake as a privilege of rank that breed of low behavior which, among the poor, we readily recognize as vice.*

Instead, she said sharply, "Very true, Your Grace. Bedlam is quieter. I imagined you must be disassembling your furniture."

He shifted a little, bringing his upper half into clarity. He was undressed from the waist up.

She startled back into the door frame. His leanness brought into prominence the sort of muscles generally stored beneath a healthy layer of fat—and *clothing*. "If I have interrupted—"

"What of it? It seems to be a habit of yours." He reached for his shirt, drawing it on. His abdomen flexed with every movement. Rather a fascinating effect.

She yanked her attention back to her cause. He seemed more voluble today. That wasn't saying much, but she would press the opportunity while she found it. "These rooms should be cleaned, Your Grace."

"No."

"I am informed that you've forbidden the maids entry for a month or more. And to be frank . . ." She made herself look directly at him, willing herself not to redden. "It smells in here."

Momentarily he looked astonished. It was the most animated expression she had ever seen him wear, though it consisted merely of the widening of his eyes, and the briefest lift of his brows.

And then, miracle of miracles, he *laughed*. Not for long, not with much energy, but it was definitely, distinctly, a laugh. "And what do they smell like, ma'am? Pray tell me, how do I stink?"

"Like perspiration, I'm sorry to say."

He gave her a mocking smile. "How shocking," he said. "God alone knows what I've been doing up here."

If she staged a fire, he'd flee this room quick enough.

But how did one *stage* a fire without *setting* one? Arson was a step too far for her. "It would not take above an hour," she said. "A very quick cleaning—"

"Must I sack you again?" He stood, emerging from the shadow of the canopy. His disordered, shaggy blond hair lent him a piratical quality, amplified by his wolfish smile. "The newspapers will enjoy that detail: being fired twice."

She inched toward the door. She saw no bottles at hand, but for all she knew, he might throw a chair. "Indeed not. However, I think your mood would profit from cleaner surroundings. And perhaps you might open the curtains"—*in for a penny, in for a pound*—"for if one wallows in the dark, one cannot complain if one's mood follows suit, you know."

All expression slipped from his face as he regarded her. She had the uncanny sense that she was losing him; that although the curtains could not block out *all* the daylight, he was falling into darkness again, all the same.

"The room stinks," she repeated, to goad him.

His face tightened again. "Are you aware," he said, "that you are speaking to your *master*?"

"My employer. Yes, Your Grace."

A line appeared between his brows. "Precisely what I said."

If there was one thing she could not abide, it was the sloppy use of language. She would have expected better from him, but clearly he had lost his faculties. "Not so, Your Grace. You employ me, but you hardly master me."

His brows rose. He looked her up and down. "Have you struck your head recently, Mrs. Johnson?"

She laughed.

His expression did not change. Apparently that had not been a joke. He'd lost his wit, too.

"No," she said, "but I thank you for the concern."

"It was not concern." Now he spoke through his teeth. "It was simple logic, for I can think of no other reason for your bizarre and impertinent behavior. *Again.*"

No, of course he couldn't. It would take a great leap for him to guess that she lay awake at night stricken by fear that Bertram's man would somehow locate her here; that every hour that passed led him closer, while she squandered her chance to escape to safety, somewhere far from London, and all on a desperate gamble that among Marwick's papers might lie the only chance at freedom she would ever receive—

"Forgive me," she said. "But I think of your well-being." And that was true. Her motive was not *entirely* selfish. It did . . . *concern* her . . . to see a man in his prime lounging about like an invalid. So his wife had betrayed him. So he had made himself into a strange, maniacal, bullying hermit. What of it? *He* had the freedom to make a new start. If he wished, he could redeem himself, patch up matters with his brother, acquire a new wife who would help him forget that sordid business with the last one. Recover the man he'd once been.

But all of this would be difficult to accomplish from his bedroom.

Why, she was *irritated* with him. If she could resist the impulse to pity herself, he certainly should be able to do the same.

She turned around and yanked open the curtains.

The sudden flood of light revealed an atrocious

amount of dust. Dust danced crazily in the air; dust coated the writing table; dust lined the edge of the carpet. "Goodness," she said. "It's a wonder you can breathe at all."

"Mrs. Johnson." His voice was rife with disbelief. *"Get the hell out."*

She turned, prepared to defend herself, and the words fell apart in her mouth.

To have seen him in the gloom was one thing. But in the light, his beauty was radiant. His hair blazed. His thickly lashed eyes looked as blue as jewels. His skin was tawny by design, fine-grained, and shadows girded the dramatic blades of his cheekbones. Her gaze dropped to discover that he had shoved up his sleeves, revealing blond hair that glimmered on his muscled forearms.

Light was his natural element. In it, he became blinding, a golden creature who might easily write sonnets to outdo Shakespeare's—or inspire them . . .

She turned away, disconcerted, nervous in some strange new way. Her gaze fell on the hearth. She frowned at it, then stepped forward and ran a finger across the mantel. It came away a sooty gray.

Turning back, she held up this finger for his edification, and made a *tsking* noise. "No wonder you feel unwell."

He was staring at her as though *she* were the lunatic. He looked as disconcerted as she felt. How . . . diverting. She was suddenly beginning to enjoy herself.

Oh, dear. No, no, no. This determination rising within her was unwise and unwanted. She had promised herself she would do only the bare minimum. Marwick and his disorderly house were not her problems to solve.

But the bully needed bullying. It was so obvious, suddenly. Whether or not he realized it, Marwick was badly in need of her direction. And she meant to direct him *out of this room.*

He bent down in one graceful move and retrieved something from beneath the bed. When he rose, he held a bottle. "This seems to be a language you understand."

As their eyes locked, a sense of déjà vu overcame her. In the space of a heartbeat, she placed the feeling: this was not so different from the recent scene with Polly.

He was trying to intimidate her. But if he wanted to throw the bottle, surely he already would have.

And if she was wrong?

She squared her jaw. She could survive a blackened eye from a bottle—but Thomas Moore, she was not so hopeful of. "Do you *want* to live in squalor? And all these books"—she nudged a pile with her toe and sent it toppling—"would do better on a shelf. Why . . ." Her voice failed. The collapse of the pile had knocked open one of the volumes. Surely that painted illustration wasn't . . .

She fell to her knees. "This is an *illuminated manuscript!*" She snatched it up, studying the gilded halo of Saint Bernard. "This Romanesque style—it dates from the thirteenth century at the latest!"

He said something she didn't catch, for now her eyes were darting from pile to pile, the possibilities multiplying, wondrous and fearsome at once. "What else have you got lying about on the floor?" On the *floor.* "What are you doing to these books?"

A hand caught her arm. He was pulling her to her

feet. Dragging her toward the door. But her eye had caught on something. Good heavens, it couldn't be.

She ripped free and lunged across the room, lifting away a copy of *Leviathan* and *Don Quixote* in the Spanish, to uncover . . .

She held it up, balancing it on the flat of her palms, suspended between awe and rage. "This," she whispered, unable to remove her eyes, "is Newton's *Principia*. An *original edition*."

Silence.

She looked up and her heart tripped. He was towering over her, his face thunderous. He had not finished buttoning his shirt. His collar sagged apart to expose a generous triangle of skin, and—*heavens above,* his left nipple lay exposed to her sight.

She clasped the book to her chest and goggled. She had seen a variety of male torsos in her life, most of them belonging to adolescent country boys who cast off decorum at the sight of a fishing pond. None of them had looked like *this*. He had *hair* on his chest. Who could have guessed it?

"Have you a death wish?" he snarled. "Or have you, perhaps, lost the ability to understand English?"

She backed away from him, angling toward the door. He matched her step for step, prowling like a lion on the scent of a lamb—not a comfortable analogy. But these innocent *books*. She was stumbling over them, gilt-edged, calfskin-bound, *priceless*. She must save them from him.

She had one foot out the door when she caught sight again of the illustrated manuscript. She could not abandon it here. The poor darling! She lunged forward and snatched it up.

"Put that down!" he roared.

"You may keep them *all*," she cried. "Move the entire library up here, but you *will not keep them on the floor*!"

She hopped backward and pulled the door shut in his face.

CHAPTER FIVE

"I need two bookcases from the library." Olivia took a seat opposite Jones's desk. "At once. I don't . . ."

She leaned forward to take a better look at the newspaper beneath Jones's elbow. No, she was not imagining the headline: BERTRAM'S BID PROVES VICTORIOUS.

"This cursed matter of the truffles!" Jones rubbed a hand over his eyes. "I have reviewed an entire month's worth of meals. We certainly did *not* use them. None of the dishes required them. And I've spoken with every member of the kitchen staff. Nobody claims to know—"

She cleared her throat. "*I* will find out. Only give me two strong footmen to move the bookcases first."

He frowned. "What? Where do you wish them moved?"

She knew very well how he would respond to her truthful reply. "Just give me the shelves, and I will solve the case of the truffles"—she snapped her fingers—"quicker than Scotland Yard."

"I don't think Scotland Yard cares much for missing truffles." Jones sounded mournful. "Besides, I have already spoken to everyone who might have accessed them."

Her eyes strayed again to the newspaper. In *what* had Bertram proved victorious? A glorious death, dared she hope? "Give me the bookcases," she said absently.

He sighed and shut the ledger. "Very well. Have Bradley and Fenton move them."

"Thank you." She rose. *Just walk away. Don't torment yourself.* "Are you done with that paper?"

He glanced toward it. "Oh—yes, indeed. Do you follow the news?" He smoothed a fond hand across the newsprint. "Time was, I ironed four newspapers a day. His Grace had a *prodigious* appetite for them. But now he refuses to read a one. Were it not for me, nobody in this house would have a use for them." He grimaced. "But the *fashion* magazines, Mrs. Johnson—and the racing sheets, and cheap novels—you should see the rubbish that goes into the bins each week."

She made a sympathetic noise. "I'm a great reader, myself."

Jones handed the paper to her. "Of course, I must admit that the news does not always make for *pleasant* reading." A click of the tongue conveyed his disgust. "You will see that Salisbury has filled His Grace's post. It was only a matter of time, of course, but it does pain one, to see it."

She scanned the first paragraph. Why, Bertram had been appointed to the prime minister's cabinet. And had shown a '*laudable degree of Christian humility*' in his acceptance of the post. That hypocritical snake. No wonder he wanted her dead: her very existence put the lie to his entire façade.

She stuck the newspaper beneath her arm. "At the very least, Mr. Jones, the news makes *wonderful* kindling."

Under Olivia's supervision, Bradley and Fenton carried the bookcases one by one to the top of the stairs. But as soon as they realized their next destination was the duke's chambers, they stopped dead and began to bray like quarrelsome mules.

Olivia was tempted to swat them on their hindquarters with the newspaper. "Have you no pride? Bawling like children in the dark. What do you imagine he'll do to you?"

She regretted the question as soon as it left her mouth. "Don't answer that," she said hastily, and left them squawking in the hall while she proceeded onward.

A very small part of her was nervous about this plan. The rest of her was furiously, even *self-righteously* resolved. There was nobody but her to look out for the sacred treasures lying abandoned, defenseless, on Marwick's floor. Forget his punches and bottle throwing; of all unforgivable debaucheries, she could think of none more depraved than tossing *Newton* onto the carpet.

The door to the duke's bedroom stood shut. She tried the handle and found he had locked it. Coward.

She put her face to the crack. "Listen," she said. "I do not like to use threats, but for the sake of those books, I shall."

Silence.

She took a deep breath. He left her no choice. "If you refuse to let me place your books on proper shelves, I shall slip laudanum into your food so you have no *choice* but to let me do it." She paused, expectant. It was a very foul proposal; surely it merited another sacking at least.

But he did not reply.

"Very well," she said. "A man can go without food. But can you go without water? I will drug that as well. You are hoarding a good portion of mankind's priceless heritage, and I shall not let you destroy it."

The dead bolt scraped. She skipped backward, positioning herself by the exit to the hallway, poised to flee.

He stepped into the doorway, staring at her. His hair stood up every which way, but at least he had buttoned his shirt. "You are insane," he said flatly.

"Coming from you, Your Grace, the diagnosis is very persuasive."

His eyes narrowed. He seemed curiously unfazed by her roundabout accusation that *he* was the household authority on lunacy. "Didn't I sack you? Why are you still here?"

She had been wondering that, too. "Likely because you haven't told your butler of it yet."

"I will remedy that." The door started to close. "Go pack your bags."

She crept forward. "And who will answer you when you ring? Everyone else is too terrified to come to your door."

The door paused. But he stood somewhere behind it, so she continued. "Indeed, you're lucky there's a dumbwaiter, or you would have starved by now. Say, you could send your notes down with your dinner tray."

The door opened again. He looked bored. "Eager to be sacked, aren't you?"

"No. But for those books, I will gladly take the risk."

"Ridiculous," he said mildly. "Are you sure you weren't an actress in your past, Miss Johnson? A very poor one, I might add—no doubt you were sacked from there as well. But you were well suited for farces, I don't doubt."

"*Principia* is not a joke! That book—"

"Is mine," he said. "To do with as I please."

She resented his reasoning, chiefly because she could not think of a convincing way to refute it.

Instead, she put her hands on her hips and took another step toward him. "Perhaps Jones has not *sacked* me because, thanks to me, your house no longer resembles a zoo. It's cleaner now than it has been in months, not that you would know it. But I assure you, your rooms could be cleaner, too—and far less *pungent*."

The door slammed shut.

"But I will settle for the books!" she called at the door. "Only let me bring in shelves for them!"

In the ensuing silence, she listened intently, not daring to breathe. The dead bolt did not turn. That was surely as good as an agreement.

She rushed into the hallway. The footmen were halfway down the stairs. "Come back at once," she yelled down at them, "or I will say *you* were the ones who stole the truffles!"

Bradley looked up and sighed. "We'll take it as far as the sitting room," he said. "But no farther, ma'am. I'm sorry to say we like our heads in one piece."

"But he has never actually thrown a bottle *at* anyone," Olivia said. She had gathered the upper staff into her small sitting room after supper. Jones was nursing a cup of tea that Cook had brewed to "settle his nerves," which, so he said, were suffering greatly, now that he knew what Olivia had done with the bookcases.

"You just wait," Vickers said gloomily. Whenever Jones and Cook looked away, he was sneaking slugs from a leather flask. "You only got them into the sitting room. They won't ever go farther."

"They might have, if only I could move them myself. You didn't see him—he didn't mind them so very much . . ." Olivia hesitated. "Well, all right, I'm not certain he knows they're there; he didn't come out into the sitting room to see them. But he didn't argue with me, either."

Vickers sputtered on his mouthful. "He's a bloody *duke*. P'raps you've never seen him with all his sails flying, but trust me, it ain't his way to argue with the likes of *us*. You say the wrong word, and he'll simply . . ." He drew a finger across his throat.

"That's true," Jones said—making his first contribution since he'd lapsed into a choking fit a quarter hour ago, in the wake of Olivia's confession about the new location of the bookcases.

Nevertheless, his remark was enough to win him a pat on the arm from Cook. "Quite right," she agreed. "You must watch yourself, Mrs. Johnson. Being turned out without a reference . . ." She shook her head. "You won't like it, dearie. Happened to me once, and it took years to recover from it."

"Did it now?" Vickers sat up, looking interested. "Scandalous past, eh?"

"Oh, my. Well, if you must know, I exploded the range."

Vickers's eyes bugged. "What? Did anyone die?"

Cook gave him a comfortable smile. "Not so very many. But I must say, it did give me a turn, when I saw the range here is the very same kind."

Vickers sagged back, looking regretful that he'd asked.

Olivia decided to confess something else. "He's already sacked me. Twice, in fact."

Jones began to choke again. Vickers loosed a whistling breath. "Well, that's bollocks," he said, then turned red at Cook's hiss. "Begging your pardon, ma'am. But you must admit, it's very bold of our Mrs. Johnson to stay on, after."

"It—isn't—bold," Jones wheezed. Cook pounded his back, lending his next words a very forceful rhythm: "It—is—*criminal*! Mrs. Johnson, you must"—he coughed again, violently—"pack your things at *once*!"

"How now!" Cook recoiled from him. "I wouldn't go so far as *that,* Mr. Jones. Seems to me that she's been doing a world of good, don't you say? A bookcase in his sitting room, no less. That's a very fine thing."

"It will be," Olivia said, brightening. "Once there are books on it."

Jones pulled himself into a straight-spined huff. "Mrs. Bailey, I am shocked by you! If His Grace has spoken, then it is our *duty*—"

"Bunkum," Cook said. "Lately I'll tell you what our duties have been: to duck a bottle or a shoe, or cringe away and hide downstairs, and ignore the awful noises he makes. Don't pretend at bravery you haven't got, for I've not seen *you* venturing upstairs to check on him. It was Mrs. Johnson who did that today, so I heard."

Jones looked at her. Olivia shrugged. "He was making a dreadful ruckus, and I feared . . ."

All at once, Jones crumpled in his seat. "I have failed him."

"Oh, no! Here now," Cook chided, and began to pound his back again. "Nobody meant to say *that.* My point was only that Mrs. Johnson might be the fresh blood we need. Now, now, you dear man, don't *cry* now, there's a good 'un . . ."

Jones batted away Cook's proffered handkerchief, then fumbled for his own and scrubbed his eyes. This done, he took tight hold of the bridge of his nose, drawing rough, loud, unsteady breaths that caused the rest of them to exchange looks of concern.

After a very uncomfortable minute, he finally dropped his hand. "Very well," he said. "For the sake of His Grace, my dear master, I will do a very difficult thing: I will ignore his wishes on the subject of Mrs. Johnson. Ma'am, you may remain here for the time being."

"Thank you." Naturally, Olivia would not have confessed the news of her firing had Jones not seemed to be one of those lovely sorts who could be talked into, or out of, anything. But it was good to know that the next time Marwick sacked her, she'd not need to conceal it.

She retired to bed feeling very satisfied. It was only as the fire began to die down, and she cast a look about for the newspaper she'd vowed to use for kindling, that she realized she had lost it somewhere.

In the last moment of wakefulness, she had a vision of it, abandoned on a bookcase outside Marwick's bedroom.

"How curious." Baffled, Olivia halted in the doorway to the duke's sitting room. Overnight, one of the bookcases had disappeared. The other lay toppled on its side. She tilted her head for a different view, but it brought no clarity. "Could he have moved the other one himself?"

"No chance," said Bradley, who was hanging back by several feet—which made him at least five feet braver than Fenton, who stood all the way out in the hall. "It's a heavy beast. Took both of us to budge it."

"Well, we must ask him—"

"Ma'am." Bradley fixed her with a plaintive, hangdog look. "Don't make us go in there."

"Do you take note of the *state* of the bookcase?" Fenton called from the corridor. "The shelves are *broken,* ma'am."

She looked back at it, startled. Fenton was right. But those shelves were solid oak, two inches thick. "You can't mean . . ." How on earth would Marwick have split them? Was he hiding an axe in his room?

She pondered the scene. Something was nagging at her—a feeling that she was missing something important. "Well, I suppose—" She looked over her shoulder and found that the footmen had fled once again. Sighing, she stepped into the hall. They had taken some cunning escape route, for the staircase, too, was empty.

It grew very tiring, rounding up cowards. She would deal with them later. Squaring her shoulders, she marched back into the duke's apartments and rapped smartly on his bedroom door—which yielded beneath her knuckles, creaking open.

He hadn't locked it.

He hadn't even *latched* it.

A chill crawled down her spine. He hadn't drawn the curtains, either. Through the inch-wide crack, she could see daylight pooling on a patch of carpet.

But surely this was *good* news. Taking a deep breath, she stepped through the doorway. "Your Grace . . ."

The scene imprinted itself in an instant, complete and terrifying:

He sat against the wall beneath the window, his forehead laid atop his bent knees. The sunlight gilded his hair as gold as a coin; it illuminated the dust motes floating about him. And beside his bare foot lay a newspaper—the same one she had forgotten on the bookcase last night. She could see the headline from here, the fat black print: BERTRAM'S BI—

The rest of the headline was obscured beneath a pistol.

She stared at the gun for a long, stupid moment. It was real. She was not imagining it. And it lay all too near to his hand.

She took a step backward. The duke sat as still as a statue. He did not even appear to be breathing.

He's dead. He shot himself. But she saw no blood. And surely a corpse would have toppled over already.

But if he wasn't dead . . . then he was alive, and *armed.*

She retreated another step, dreading the moment when the groan of the floorboards would betray her. She dared not remove her eyes from him. With one hand cast behind her she made a desperate, groping fumble for the doorknob.

How was it that he did not move? Perhaps he *was* dead?

The doorknob came into her hand.

His head lifted.

She froze.

He stared at her without comprehension. The angle of the light played some trick on his eyes, so they looked lit from behind, impossibly blue. The light glinted off the stubble on his cheeks; it made him blaze. He looked like a creature made of light and fire and the blue, blue electricity that crackled in his eyes.

She turned to flee—and glimpsed what she had not, before: the missing bookcase. It held tidy rows of books, neatly shelved.

A choked sound slipped from her—panicked denial, anger at herself, and at *him* for having put the books away, for having done the one thing that would now prevent her from doing the wisest thing, the *only* wise thing, given the circumstances: flying through the doorway, turning the key, and locking him inside with that pistol.

The bookcase forbade it. The bookcase sent a message, unintended yet clear: a man who shelved his books on his housekeeper's insistence was not a man who meant to kill his staff.

He meant to kill only himself.

She forced herself to face him. He still stared fixedly into space, but his hand was playing over the pistol, stroking it. What an awful, meditative rhythm his fingers struck up. "You mustn't do this," she whispered.

He did not seem to hear her.

She could not bring herself to approach him. All she could do was speak. "Please, Your Grace. Whatever it is that troubles you"—such a lie; she knew exactly his cause for grief, and it was *her* fault, she realized, *her* fault for having abandoned the newspaper where he would find it, where his eyes would fall on that headline, that last dash of salt into an already mortal wound—"it isn't worth your life."

She might have been talking to a stone for the notice he took of her. But the quality of his gaze seemed to change. To focus on something invisible to her eyes, somewhere in the air in front of him. His face tightened, seemed to harden. For a moment she wondered if he would speak—if he would rave now to the ether, and complete his lunatic resemblance.

But he said nothing. And she began to wish he *would* speak, for the silence was dreadful, deep and unnatural and dire, like the hush after a sudden fatal accident. The very house seemed to hold its breath.

She saw deep shadows beneath his eyes, almost like bruises. He looked like a man in the grip of a fever, burning up from within.

"Your Grace," she said again.

This standoff could continue forever. Either she would surrender to cowardice and go, or take hold of her courage and . . . approach.

She did not know which she would do until her feet were carrying her forward.

Shaking, she knelt down before him. She put her face in front of his, but he did not focus on her. He was in a trance of some kind. Only his fingers kept moving, stroking the pistol.

Every instinct in her, every shred of self-interest, fixated on the gun's presence so close to her—and on his hand, which might so easily trip the trigger.

"Your Grace," she said. "He is not worth your life." The words triggered a flood of anger, scalding, directed outward, across the city. Bertram was worth nothing, not even a spare look from a street urchin. A cabinet appointment? Salisbury would have been wiser to appoint a slug. "He is beneath your contempt."

Did his fingers briefly pause? She could not say.

Her anger grew. It made her reckless. "If you don't like it, get up then! You think this gun is your answer? *You* have let him do this. You have *given* Bertram your office."

No reply.

Very well. If he meant to ignore her, then she would speak to her heart's content. "You don't even answer letters," she said. "How odd, how bizarre, how *childish* is that? Why, how could Salisbury *not* replace you? You might as well have put his hand into Bertram's. And now that Bertram has your office, will he make half the use of it that you did? Will he bother to support the laborers, or to think of children in the slums? Will he fight for their schooling? Ha! He won't care if they never learn their letters. It will make them better peons if they can't read to save their lives. He cares nothing for the poor—nobody does. *You* were the only one who did."

She fell into a breathless pause, appalled by herself—by how sharply, how boldly, how *fluently* the speech had spilled from her.

But then, strangest thought, it came to her that his hair was the color of beaten gold.

And that made her angry all over again. He did not deserve to look like a fallen angel, or a warrior, either. "*You've* done this. You've given him the post he'll use to enrich himself and his friends at the Bank of London. Because he never would have had the office had it not been for *you* deciding to retire from the field!"

His lashes fell. He stared now at the gun he stroked, as though her speech, *which was the truth,* affected him not at all.

She gritted her teeth, boggled, furious. How could this be the same man who had written and delivered so many powerful, breathtaking speeches? Who had waged battle with his colleagues for the sake of the unfortunate—and whose continuous, earnest struggles were so amply documented in the files in the study downstairs?

Suddenly she was no longer afraid in the least. Let him fondle his gun. What would he do with it? The same as he did with himself: nothing.

She clambered to her feet. "I thought you lacked bullets," she said. "But I suppose it would only take one. At this rate, nobody will notice—you've driven them all away. *England* will not notice."

He flinched.

It was enough to drop her back onto her knees, to look into his face more closely. The flat line of his mouth gave her more hope. It was an expression.

"I lied," she confessed. "People would notice. *I* would notice, of course."

No reply.

Frustration bolted through her. But she remained crouched before him for one simple, stupid reason: she could not forget all those pages he had written, the gorgeous meditations on improvement, on virtue—and the profoundly messy speeches, as though he'd made drafts upon drafts, demanding ever more of himself, for the sake of people, strangers, he would never meet, who might benefit from his labor.

She looked at him now, exhausted and beautiful and locked so deeply inside himself, and some weirdly bittersweet emotion choked her. Was there no way back for him? Did he not realize he'd made the *choice* to be alone?

On a desperate stroke of daring, she reached out to touch his face—tipping up his chin, as he had once done to her far less gently. "Look at me," she said.

To her shock and triumph, his lashes rose. It gave her a jolt; as they stared at each other, her every breath felt shallower, harder to draw.

His skin felt warm, rough from his whiskers. He felt *human.* It was so easy to think of him as a monster—or as a mannequin, too angular, too perfect, to be fashioned from pedestrian flesh.

But he was only a man. Only and entirely a man. She felt the slight, irregular tremble that moved through him, and sensed the rigidity with which he held himself still. He was making a great effort to restrain himself—but from what?

"You are so much more than this," she whispered. "Why do you insist on hiding away?"

He did not answer. But he didn't look away, either. He had worlds in his eyes; they were magnetic. He was a force of gravity, and his presence, even in this blackest moment, could not be confined to the small, dark space he had made here for himself. The force of him felt like an invisible wave, overwhelming her, crushing the air from her lungs: such was the power of his gaze. He was larger than this room, larger than this house. Why had he tried to make himself so small?

"You deserve better than this," she said. "Give me the gun."

One corner of his mouth lifted. It was a dead smile; a chilling, lifeless expression. "You have no notion of who I am," he said. "Girl."

I know more than you realize, she thought. What she knew of him—his ruthlessness toward his brother; the injustice he'd done to Lord Michael and Elizabeth—had helped her justify how she meant to deceive him. But the files she had read . . .

She pulled back. Who was *she* to help him? Her motives were black, through and through.

"You were a good man, once," she said as she stood. "You could be so again. It is up to you."

"A good man?" His voice was cutting. "'A savior to the poor,' do you mean? 'A ministering angel'?"

He spat out these common praises as though they were vilest slander. "Yes," she said. His brother had loved him very dearly once. And his public works showed that he'd been worthy of that love. His wife's betrayal had deranged him, but beforehand . . . "You did great things—"

His smile silenced her. It cut through his features as sharply as a knife. "Despite all you have seen, you still believe that? You think the newspapers had it right. You are a fool, Mrs. Johnson."

She took a hitching breath. He would not intimidate her now. She crossed her arms and stared down at him. "Were you not the author of the education reform bill? Did you not take a stand for the workers who suffered in the fire at the Hallimore factory? Did you—do you not fund your brother's hospital?"

"Oh, yes," he said. "Such a résumé. Very impressive. And what you have witnessed in this house—how does that fit into this noble picture? Tell me, ma'am—by what possible contortions have you made this evidence fit with my reputation?"

She opened her mouth, but her brain could not fit it with a reply. How curious, how perverse, that he should be asking her to defend him—against himself!

She might have lied anyway. She might have made an excuse for his behavior. But even what she knew privately could not excuse all of it. "I don't know," she said flatly.

"But you do. What you have seen in this house is the truth: the man I always was. Now you know it." He shrugged. "And so do I."

This philosophical drivel suddenly annoyed her. That he would terrify her with a pistol and then spout all this nonsense . . .

She stepped back a pace. "I see you feel very sorry for yourself," she said sharply. "Forgive me, but what a *pathetic* reason to kill yourself. Even the playwright of a farce would come up with a better motive."

He laughed. "Kill myself? Mrs. Johnson, there are four bullets in this pistol. None of them are for me."

She caught her breath and prayed her comprehension did not show on her face.

"Won't you ask who they're for?" he said mildly.

"No." Four bullets would be sufficient for each of the men to whom his wife had written . . . and with whom she had betrayed him. "It's not my concern."

"When has that stopped you?" He pushed himself to his feet, rising lithely, up, up, up—he was several inches taller than she, which was a feat. She was not accustomed to having to look so far up at anyone; she could not be blamed, surely, if the act made her take another step backward. "But will you still urge me to go into the world again?" he asked lazily. "Because if I do, it will not be to save orphans."

Finally, she understood. *This* was why he refused to leave—because he knew that if he left this house, he would kill the men who had made him a cuckold.

A horrible thought gripped her: if he murdered Bertram, her own life would become so much simpler!

She caught her breath, appalled by herself—and by him, too. He looked light on his feet, easy, like a man accustomed to long, athletic days out of doors; he looked suddenly amused, in control, nothing like the mute, entranced, suffering soul she had encountered a minute ago.

And suddenly she felt outclassed. It was a startling and unpleasant and very novel experience, but somehow he had done it: he had turned the tables on her, not with brute strength but with his wits. For now, if she encouraged him to leave these rooms, she would be a party to his murderous intentions.

And he had made sure she knew it.

"I can't say I support murder," she managed. She hoped God took note of this virtue, and marked it as a counterbalance to her longer list of sins.

His head tipped as he studied her. His eyes were the shade of some deep, stormy ocean, and far too intelligent for her comfort. "And if it were not murder, but justice?"

This felt like a test designed by the devil to tempt her. "Murder is the sloppiest form of justice ever devised. It punishes the doer as much as the receiver."

"Oh, rest assured, Mrs. Johnson—I would not suffer pangs of conscience."

She stared at him. He looked steadily back, his well-shaped lips turning into a dark, easy smile.

For a twisted moment, that smile seemed beautiful to her, and infinitely seductive. Darkness became him. He was blond and beautiful as an angel, but was not the most famous angel the one who had fallen from grace?

"Have I shocked you?" he asked. "*Do* forgive me, Mrs. Johnson."

She should pretend that he had shocked her. How much more awful to admit that she envied his confidence—his refusal to be ashamed—and his indifference to God and the fate of his soul. How free it made him.

The next moment, she came to her senses. He was not free. He was the furthest thing from it. "I'm shocked by your stupidity," she said through a tight throat. "Murder might not trouble you, but once you were caught and tried and *hanged* for it, you'd be uncomfortable, indeed."

His smile faded. "No," he said. "It would not be more uncomfortable than . . ." Something raw and vulnerable flickered across his face. "This."

She knew that feeling. She *recognized* it. It was the look of a person in purgatory, unable to look with a quiet heart toward the past, and hopeless of seeing a better future.

She stepped away from it. Why should *he* feel so? He had no right. Even *she* could see his way to the future. He was a duke; what stopped him from doing whatever he liked? Only he himself did.

"There are a thousand ways to take revenge without killing someone," she said bitterly. *Give me a look at your private files and I'll take care of one man for you. Give me a tenth of your wealth, a twentieth of your power, and I will find my way very easily.* "But none of them, Your Grace, can be undertaken while cowering against a wall."

He nodded once, contemplative. "I do wonder," he said, "what it is *you* want, Mrs. Johnson."

She hesitated. "What do you mean? I want nothing."

"So it would seem. It seems you would have nothing to gain from bearding the lion in his den. Yet you attempt it, again and again. Ergo, you must have something to gain by it, after all."

She did not like this line of inquiry. But at least it was

the sort of idle speculation that a man bent on murder did not spare the time to make. "Have I bearded you? You still look rather hairy to me."

His lips twitched in an aborted smile. "Let's find out." He took a step toward her, and she jumped backward. "Yes, that's right," he said. "Keep going."

She did not want to leave without the pistol. She did not quite trust his stated intentions for it. "I don't think—" He was still coming toward her. She danced backward. In what was becoming a familiar and tiresome routine, he matched her, step for step. "It *is* very beastly"—her voice emerged rather strangled—"to *stalk* me. I wish you—"

As she stepped over the threshold, the door slammed in her face. Then the dead bolt scraped.

She stood blinking for a stupid moment. But how anticlimactic! He'd forgotten to sack her again.

She put her eye to the keyhole, which proved more effective for spying now that the opened curtains gave the room some light. He was standing some feet away, stock-still. Goodness, had he already relapsed?

He stepped out of sight. A moment later, he came into view again, holding—a book! He'd been surveying the bookcase before. The realization made her unreasonably giddy.

As he flipped the book open, he said, without looking up, "Go away, Mrs. Johnson."

How had he guessed she was spying? She felt a moment's unwilling fascination. He was not only erudite, he was *sharp*. Shrewd. Despite his derangement.

Through the keyhole, she spoke. "Those books are not properly ordered. I will come back to alphabetize them, shall I?" And to make certain he had not lapsed back into a black mood. Not when he had that pistol nearby.

He did not acknowledge her remark. Turning, he passed out of view.

"You are very welcome for the offer," she said pointedly.

His reply came in a bored drawl: "You are paid for your work here, ma'am."

For some bizarre reason, that made her smile.

CHAPTER SIX

Of course, the duke did not open his door when Olivia appeared an hour later, prepared to organize the books. But a peep through the keyhole showed him to be among the living—and reading in a wing chair, like a civilized man, pistol nowhere in sight.

Satisfied, she returned downstairs, intent on tackling the mystery of the truffles. It stood to reason that if none of the kitchen staff had taken them, somebody else must have. After asking Jones to speak with the footmen, she took upon herself the task of interrogating the maids.

The first summoned to her office was Doris, who seemed least likely to ruffle at being suspected of theft—or so Olivia had anticipated.

In fact, Doris did not seem *unruffled* as much as placidly baffled. "But why should I take the truffles, ma'am? What *are* truffles? Are they the ones what look like mud?"

Olivia hesitated. In truth, she had never encountered any. Her last employer had not inclined to French cuisine, though Elizabeth had certainly favored French wines. "What matter how they look, Doris? More to the point, they're very expensive."

"That figures, for I've certainly never tried one. So why should I want five pounds of them, when I don't even know if I like the taste?"

This naïveté seemed a bit much. "You might want them to sell."

"Oh!" Doris gave a hesitant nod. "Yes, that makes sense. But . . . I don't know *anyone* who eats truffles. Do you? Why would anybody dare it?" She looked very doubtful of their safety. "It would take a very bold person, to be sure, to eat something what looks like dirt, ma'am."

"His Grace eats them," Olivia said dryly. "They were in his kitchens, were they not?"

Doris clapped a hand over her giggle. "Oh, well, naturally, ma'am. But I certainly couldn't sell them to *him;* he'd find it a sight odd, I expect, his maid trying to sell him his own goods! And if nobody else has tried them, then who should I sell them to?"

The girl must be shamming her. "You'd sell them at the market, of course."

"Would I?" Doris looked impressed. "That's a proper good plan, ma'am! I'd never have thought of that."

It dawned on Olivia that she might not be interrogating the girl so much as providing her with an introductory guide to petty crime. "Never mind that," she said hastily. "Have any of the others acquired new items of late? Or shown themselves to be in possession of unexpected funds?"

"Why . . ." Doris looked wide-eyed. "Come to think of it, Polly dropped a penny the other day, and didn't bother to pick it up. She said it was bad luck if it landed heads down, but *I* never heard such a thing."

Olivia exhaled. *Patience.* "Truffles," she said, "would fetch far more than a penny, Doris. *These* were more than the value of all the month's meals, combined."

Doris sat back, visibly amazed. "And to think they look like mud! Is that a disguise, then, ma'am? That one puts on them, to keep them safe?"

Muriel came into her office next, and immediately proved herself to be more world wise. *Too* world wise, perhaps. "I've heard that they're an . . ." She lowered her voice and leaned in across the desk. "Afro-what's-it, ma'am. Do you follow?"

After a moment, Olivia feared she did. "An aphrodisiac, you mean?"

"Exactly. So p'raps instead of looking to us, you'd best look to Old Willy, *if* you know what I mean."

Olivia did not. "Old Willy? Who is that?" She felt certain she knew the entire staff by now. "I haven't met anyone by that name."

Muriel rolled her eyes. "*Old Willy. You* know who."

"No," Olivia said, bewildered. "I'm afraid I don't."

Muriel slammed her palms onto the desk and leaned forward. *"Who's got the oldest willy?"* she hissed.

Suddenly comprehending, Olivia shot back in her seat. "Muriel! *Decency,* please!"

Muriel gave a one-shouldered, thoroughly unrepentant shrug. "Aphrodisiac, ma'am. You look for the willy least likely to work." She crooked a pinky, nodding sadly at it. "*That's* where you'll find your truffles."

What a ribald and preposterous theory. Yet despite herself, Olivia began to mentally survey the staff. "But that would be . . ." She trailed off, appalled.

"Exactly." Crossing her arms, Muriel gave a solemn nod. "Old Jones has done it."

Polly alone took exception to the questioning. "I thought Mrs. Wright was bad enough, with all those coins tucked under the rug. You didn't pick 'em up, you hadn't swept thoroughly. You *did* pick 'em up, you're a thief. But truffles! God have mercy, I'd rather be accused of stealing coin. I'm an honest, good girl. What business have *I* to do with the French?"

"But . . ." Olivia pressed a palm to her forehead; she was developing a headache. "What have the French to do with it?"

Polly huffed. "Truffles are French, ain't they? Yes, they are. I know what's what. And I have no truck with Frenchies, thank you muchly. I'll not hear a word to the contrary!"

Later that afternoon, Olivia found herself, dazed and no better informed, in Jones's pantry. "I don't know who took the truffles. I have *absolutely* no idea."

"Nor do I," he said with a sigh. "Well, we must keep our ears to the ground, Mrs. Johnson."

"Indeed." She could barely bring herself to look at him for fear of blushing furiously. Did everybody else refer to him in private as . . . oh, she could not even bring herself to think the name.

"Rest assured," he continued solemnly, "I have dealt with such mysteries before. Sooner or later, the truth always comes out. Oh, hello, Muriel. Did you want something?"

Olivia turned in time to see the maid shake her head. Then, with a smile for Olivia, the girl flashed a curled pinky before dashing out of sight.

"Curious," Jones muttered. "Surely you did not ask them to *pinky* swear, Mrs. Johnson?"

She smothered her horrified laugh in a coughing fit, and excused herself promptly.

His Grace wanted fresh newspapers.

The gossip spread shortly after breakfast the next day, and by the rapidity with which it traveled, and the stunned amazement it left in its wake, one might have imagined that the duke had instead requested a priest for the purpose of conversion—or that he had decided to sack the entire staff.

The prevailing mood was that somber, at least, when Olivia found Vickers and two of the footmen waiting in tense silence outside Jones's office.

"I can't imagine what you said to him," Vickers muttered by way of greeting. "It's been months since he cared to read anything." He frowned. "And why do you look so happy about it?"

Pride was a great sin of hers. *Stop annoying me,* her mother had used to chide her. But Olivia had never been able to bear Mama's low moods and sulks; there was always a solution for them. Was Marwick so different? She felt certain that the duke's request for the newspaper was a very positive sign of her ongoing strategy. Aside from this whole nonsense about killing people, he'd be out of his quarters within a week.

"Never mind that," she said to Vickers. "Why are you still down here? Take the papers to him."

"We stopped taking the *Telegraph* ages ago. I had to send Bradley to market for it. And now"—Vickers tipped his head toward Jones's door—"they must be ironed."

But what if the duke changed his mind during the

wait? Didn't anyone else realize how precarious and quick his moods were? "Heaven forbid the duke gets some ink on his hands."

Bradley spoke up. "It's not the ink, ma'am. His Grace is very particular about his papers—he can't abide a wrinkle in 'em."

Was that so? Would that he were so particular about the state of his rooms.

A marvelous idea struck her. "How badly does he want these papers?"

Vickers and Bradley exchanged a dark look. "Badly enough to ring incessantly from the crack of dawn. He hasn't been up at such an hour in ages, either." He turned his glare on the door. "I wish Jones would hurry up with it. *He* won't have to face His Grace after this delay."

As though in reply, the door opened. Olivia stepped in front of Vickers and took the newspapers straight from Jones's hands. "I will deliver them," she said.

If the duke wanted these papers, he would have to earn them.

She climbed the stairs very quickly, switching the stack from arm to arm, for they still bore the heat of the iron, and burned right through her sleeves. "Your Grace," she called as she entered his sitting room. "I have the newspapers you requested."

His voice came through the door. "Bring them."

The immediacy of his reply encouraged her. She took a strategic position behind the bulwark of the chiffonier. It was not quite high enough to protect her from missiles or bullets, but it would certainly interrupt a forward charge. "No," she called, "I won't."

It took only a moment for the door to swing open. He *was* improving. He was wearing a dressing robe, as a gentleman ought while reading the morning papers.

He glared at her from the doorway, shaggy and radiantly blond. "Bring. Them. Here."

Alas, the robe, while a very fine species of embroidered maroon silk, could not outweigh the effect of his scruffiness—or the way he shifted his weight from foot to foot, as though barely channeling some violent impulse. How good to know that it was not *she* he wished to kill. She hoped he kept that in mind throughout the remainder of this encounter.

She laid the papers atop the table. "Some very interesting news today, Your Grace. I see the mayor has authorized a new lighting scheme for—"

"I will count to five," he growled.

"Shall you?" She pushed aside the topmost paper to canvass the other headlines. "How impressive—for a three-year-old, that is."

He made some strangled noise. She glanced up and found he had taken hold of the door frame. A signet ring gleamed on his pinky. Had he been wearing that ring before? She did not think so. That, too, seemed proof positive of improvement.

Less reassuring was how he choked the door frame, his grip tight enough to whiten his knuckles. She had a brief flash of her throat in such a grip; certainly the emotion on his face would very easily translate to that endeavor.

He prefers bullets, she reminded herself. "I also see"—she paused to take a deep breath, disliking the tremble in her voice—"that St. George's is planning a commemorative service for Sir Bodley. Did you ever read his memoirs? A very bold explorer—"

"How do you dare?"

The deadness in his voice was chilling. But there was no choice for her. She had to get him out of that bedroom. She forced herself to reply brightly. "Was that a rhetorical question, Your Grace? With your tone so level, it is hard to tell—"

"If I step over this threshold, you will regret it. You do understand that, *Miss* Johnson?"

That was the longest threat he'd ever issued, syllabically speaking. It also, somehow, seemed the most convincing of them. Certainly it triggered an ache in her throat, an almost physical memory of Moore's stranglehold.

She realized she was crumpling the newsprint, and forced herself to let go. So much for the ironing. Her fingertips were smudged.

"It is a short distance to this table," she said encouragingly.

His reply came very softly: "That should trouble you."

She gripped her hands very tightly at her waist. If she bent to him now, handed over the newspapers, then he would withdraw and slam the door. And she might as well book her passage to France, for she would never get a look at the papers he kept there. Not if his improvements did not lead to him *leaving his bedroom.*

"If you would . . . if you would only come fetch these papers, you might learn yourself of all the marvelous developments—"

"*Fetch* them?" He made some abortive movement and she clapped her hand over her mouth to contain her squeak. "I am not your damned dog!" he roared.

She pressed her lips until they hurt. What a mortifying sound to have made. He had reduced her to a mouse.

But what of it? *He* squirreled papers in his den like a dog with old bones. This was all *his* fault, really—wasn't it? If he only left his rooms like any normal man, she would have no need to harass him.

Yes, *there* was the dudgeon she required. It straightened her spine. She nudged up her spectacles and narrowed her eyes at him.

"No, you are not a dog. I have it on very good authority that you are a man, a peer of the realm, a duke no less. But a very curious species of man, I must say—looking so shaggy at present that one could be forgiven for mistaking you for a sheepdog." She blew out a breath. "How *can* you see through all that hair?"

He bared his teeth at her, then retreated out of sight. Panicked, she wracked her brain for some goad to lure him back. But none came to mind that she dared to speak. The point was to lure him out—not to lure him into murdering her.

He filled the doorway again, a book in his hand—something very old by the crumbling cover. "Do you know," he said pleasantly, "what distinguishes man from beast?"

A very good question. "I should think . . . a haircut."

He made a contemptuous noise. "The ability to make fire, you tart."

"Tart?" Aghast, she crossed her arms. "Termagant, *perhaps,* but tart, I think not!" And then suddenly it dawned on her what he was threatening. "You can't mean—"

"Say good-bye to this book."

"You *heathen,*" she cried. "You shaggy mongrel!"

"Mongrel I am not," he snarled. "And so help me God"—he smirked—"or shall I say, *the Devil*"—she gasped—"but if you do not bring me those goddamned newspapers this minute—"

"Woof!" she cried. "Woof woof, yap away!"

She clapped a hand over her mouth, horrified. Where had *that* come from?

He, too, seemed shocked. He gawped at her for a long, silent moment. Then he pivoted away.

"No—wait!" That poor book! She started around the chiffonier—checked when she heard him loose a roar—more leonine than canine, to be fair—and then came a great, thunderous crash.

He swung back into view. "Your books," he said with a savage grin, "have seen better days."

He had toppled the bookcase. "You boor! You—" She hauled together the newspapers and carried them in a great armful toward the sitting-room hearth. "Fuel for the fire! What use has a hermit for news anyway—"

Hands closed on her shoulders. They spun her around so violently that she lost her balance, and grabbed onto the nearest support, which turned out to be—*him.*

Her jaw dropped. Yes, those were her hands gripping his arms. *His* arms. Like iron, they were.

He was out. He was outside his bedroom.

Her fingers sprang away as though from lit coals. But her retreat was stopped cold by his grip on her elbows. He crushed them down to her ribs, and held her pinned there before him as his breath came and went as hard as a bellows.

She made herself look at him. His face was a terrible mask, the force of his rage apparent in the pulsing vein in his temple. Her gaze bounced away from his, the awful, glassy fixedness of his blue, blue eyes, and landed on the newspapers, piled on the floor.

As far as final views went, it was not so inspiring.

"You," he said very low, and then paused—a hush like the moment before the guillotine dropped.

That sentence would go nowhere good. She made her lips move, though they felt stiff as wood. "How good," she croaked, "to see you out of your room."

Bull's-eye! He recoiled from her, staggering back a pace. He looked around blindly, wildly, as though only now realizing where he stood.

Here was her chance. She would run.

And he would run, too—straight back to his bedroom.

Her joints felt rusted, congealed, so hard did they fight her as she stooped to the floor and gathered up the newspapers. "Here," she said, and held them out, praying he did not notice how they shook in her grip. "Read them on this sofa." The suggestion came out as a hysterical shrill. "The light is very fine here!"

Staring at her, he reached for the papers like a man underwater, moving slowly, slowly—but his hands, instead, closed on her wrists.

She flinched and froze, or tried to—the instinct of a cornered hare commanding her to go still. But the terrified pounding of her heart rocked her in her boots. *You're in it now,* a mocking little voice nattered in her brain.

His hands were very large; they engulfed her wrists, wrapping like hot manacles around her. His thumbs pressed directly against her pulses.

He knew precisely how hard her heart was beating.

"How do you dare?" he said softly.

She looked up into his face. His eyes had lost their glassy blankness. He was—the realization jolted through her—*looking* at her, studying her, with great intensity. And his expression was far from blank.

She stared back, surprised so completely that she had no defenses against that look. She fell into it headfirst, fascination engulfing her suddenly and completely. What did she see in his face now? What, in her own face, could possibly inspire such riveted, arrested attention?

"How do you dare?" He whispered it again, as his fingers flexed around hers. And then, without warning, his thumbs stroked over the sensitive skin of her inner wrists.

Her breath fled her. She felt a flush of heat, bizarre, weakening. "I don't know what you mean."

"Yes. You do."

His thumbs stroked again. She swallowed. The sensation bothered her. It affected her far too deeply. She felt the pull of it in her belly. She had to look away from him. In a moment, she would.

"Woof?" he said.

A blush stung her cheeks. "Well. You must admit, you *do* need a haircut."

A faint smile ghosted over his mouth. His fingers loosened; they slipped over hers as they withdrew. "Is there anyone in this house whom I could trust to wield the scissors? I have given them all cause to aim for my throat."

Was that a joke? Miracle of miracles! "Come now," she said hoarsely. "Be sensible. Dead men pay no salaries."

His smile flickered to life again, then guttered out.

He frowned and turned his face away. "Send someone to straighten the bookcase," he said gruffly.

Another miracle. "At once, Your Grace."

She picked up her skirts and dashed out the door—straight into Vickers, who caught and steadied her.

"My God," he whispered, his eyes huge. "My God, Mrs. Johnson."

She pulled free of him. She had no time for nonsense. "Didn't you hear him? You *were* eavesdropping, weren't you? I must fetch the maids. We're to clean his rooms."

Vickers dashed after her as she flew down the stairs. "I didn't hear him say that. Only that somebody was to straighten the bookcase—"

She cast an impatient glance over her shoulder. "Clearly," she said, "you don't know how to *listen*."

She returned an hour later—far longer than she would have liked, but the maids had proved ridiculously recalcitrant to accompanying her; it had taken several threats to persuade them. Threats! And *her!* She had never fancied herself a bully, but Marwick was proving an excellent tutor.

She left the girls waiting in the hallway, looking pale and anguished like martyrs on the eve of execution, while she entered to make a quick survey of the battlefield.

The reigning lunatic sat on the sofa, immersed in the pages of the *Morning Herald.*

She breathed a sigh of relief. He must have heard her, for he lifted his brows, but did not look up. "I've brought the maids—"

"No," he said, and turned the page.

She decided she had not heard him. "And the footmen will right the bookcase," she continued. "How good to see you're still out here. Well done. Of course, you must forgive me for congratulating you on such a simple trick—remaining in place; it's not as though you were a toddler, and liable to crawl off. But you must know how they talk—downstairs, I mean."

This taunt was a calculated risk. Had he any pride left? If so, it would be useful.

He blinked. And then looked up, his face darkening. *"Downstairs?"*

Yes, she knew enough of him now to guess he would not like being the subject of gossip. "Below stairs." She gave him a sympathetic smile. "Your staff, I mean."

He made some curious noise. And then he stood, knocking the sofa back a foot. "You're saying my staff is *doubting* my ability to inhabit my own bloody sitting room?"

"Oh, well"—she shrugged and gave a trailing little laugh, which sounded perhaps a *touch* more nervous than she intended—"idle hands *are* the devil's playground. And when you don't let anybody in to clean, how else are they to occupy themselves?"

He thrust his hand through his blond hair and turned full circle, as though looking for something. "Where is Vickers?" he snapped. "God damn it, how are you always getting in here?"

She stifled her own snort. But how amusing, to imagine *Vickers* trying to stop her. "Your valet is in the kitchen, loitering with the cook's assistant. When not there, you will typically find him in the hallways, flirting with the maids. I warn you that his suit on all fronts is too far advanced for comfort. I am predicting a surprise, or several, in nine months' time."

His mouth twitched. It must have been a passing spasm, not a smile, for it faded instantly. He turned on her a narrow, assessing look. "How indelicate of you, Mrs. Johnson."

Was she a *missus* now? How gratifying. "I am prone to indelicacy," she admitted. "It is a flaw."

"One of several," he bit out.

"Yes, but who's counting?"

With a snort, he sat back down. He'd unbelted his robe, and it parted now to show that his shirttails were untucked. How much weight had he lost? Those trousers barely stayed up.

What was wrong with her? Surely she had not just entertained a flicker of curiosity about what she would see if they *fell*?

His lunacy must be catching. Feeling itchy and out of sorts, she said, "May I ring for tea for you? The girls will happily clean around you, provided you promise not to menace them."

"No." But he said it very quietly.

"No tea, quite right, far too early for that. Stay right where you are. This won't take above an hour."

And then, before he could countermand her, she dashed out and grabbed Polly's wrist. "Come on, then."

Polly in turn grabbed Muriel's elbow. "I won't go!"

"Oh, Lordy," Muriel squealed, her feet sliding as Olivia dragged Polly—and, by extension, her as well—toward the door. "Doris, run for your life!"

Doris turned tail and broke for the stairs.

"Not another foot," Olivia shouted. "Back here at *once*."

Doris's shoulders slumped. Haltingly she turned back.

"I won't go," Polly shrieked. "I won't—" She fell silent in mid-squeal, her face graying.

Olivia glanced over her shoulder, and discovered the duke in the doorway, staring in plain disbelief at this scene.

"I told you, no need to get up," she said brightly. She dropped Polly's wrist. "It's perfectly all right," she said. And then, angling her body so Marwick could not see, she gave Polly a sharp shove on the shoulder.

The maids went about their business, rustling and timid as mice. He ignored them. They were irrelevant. His mad housekeeper, hair as red as a bullfinch's breast, irrelevant. All he cared for was this editorial he had uncovered, at the back of the *Morning Herald.* It had been written by a man he'd once counted a friend—a man who probably had no notion of how offensive and ludicrous this headline was: LORD SALISBURY'S JUDICIOUS CHOICE.

Beneath it, in slightly smaller print, lay the thrust of the piece: BARON BERTRAM A BOON FOR ENGLAND.

He made his jaw unlock. He took a deep, deep breath.

Archibald, Baron Bertram: a distinguished man of fifty-odd years, unctuously pleasant to his political opponents, fastidiously proper in his manners. A regular attendee of services at St. George's Hanover Square, Wednesday and Sunday both. The best, most irreproachable choice to lead the Liberals now, or so fools and naïfs believed: a godly and principled man, devoted to family and empire.

Margaret had entertained several men. But all of them had been his political enemies, save Bertram. Bertram had been his ally in the House of Lords. His co-conspirator, his main support.

Other words popped out from the article: *Meritorious. Dedicated. Humble . . .*

The illustrator had rendered a fine likeness of the smug tilt to Bertram's nose.

Alastair grew conscious of the bed in the next room. It was new, a replacement for the bed where he'd lain so many nights beside Margaret, never imagining how she made a fool of him.

Margaret would not have dared bed Bertram in this house. But for his own satisfaction, Alastair had stripped the duchess's apartment, put the furniture to auction, and disassembled that grand, canopied bed where she had slept. He had taken it apart with his bare hands and donated it to a workhouse for kindling last spring.

A small commotion broke his reverie: a thud, a gasp. He glanced up and caught the blond maid righting a vase. She froze in his sights like a fox in the crosshair.

"Go on, Muriel." His housekeeper issued this directive from the bedroom doorway, where she stood with her hands folded at her waist, supervising.

Annoyed, he laid down the paper. This woman had the peculiar ability to radiate an authority that she did not, in fact, possess. "Mrs. Johnson. Tell me something."

She turned toward him, smiling serenely. Had she looked in the mirror? Her skin was lineless, smooth and flush and freckled like a child's. Was she aware of her age? She had ample cause to fear him. God knew she had seen him in states that—he could not bring himself to think on it. She was only a domestic; what did it matter?

She had thought him on the edge of *suicide.*

He gritted his teeth. She was only a domestic. *It did not matter.* What irked him was the leisurely quality to her movements, as though she could not be surprised or intimidated by anyone—even he. Her confidence made no sense. Was she even twenty-five? What had Jones been thinking? It wasn't seemly to have a housekeeper so young. Her hair was as bright and vivid as a flag. It was bloody ridiculous, in fact. Artificial, surely.

He needed to have a word with Jones. Get to the bottom of this absurd hiring decision.

"I wonder," he said icily, "that my staff cannot pursue their duties without your supervision." She was always underfoot. "Have you no other duties to attend?"

She shrugged. "I am happy to make time for Your Grace's comforts."

Against his express wishes. Yes, he had noticed. Why he continued to tolerate her, he did not know. Boredom, no doubt. Perverse amazement at her lunacy. She had the softest skin he'd ever touched.

He shifted in his seat, disliking that last thought extremely. "I did not speak of myself," he said cuttingly. "I spoke of the staff. If they do not know their roles well enough to perform them without your guidance, then I suggest you rectify *that.*"

She nodded immediately. "A fine plan, Your Grace. In fact, I have already begun to do so. It is human nature to wish to please one's master, is it not? And I have arranged this opportunity for it." She beamed. "I fear it has been sorely lacking of late."

He sat back, astonished. How dared she rebuke him?

She offered him another beatific smile.

He scowled and averted his gaze to the newspaper. He did not like her smile. Until she smiled, she was inoffensively plain. Overly young, but with an air of intelligence—ha! A very deceptive air, no doubt owed to her spectacles and her oddly refined accent.

Her smile, however, broke the illusion that her face was a perfect square. It brought a dimple into her cheek. It drew one's attention to her mouth, which was full lipped, but only on the bottom. Her upper lip was . . .

Not his concern. And if she was, by some very gymnastic stretch of the imagination, *pretty,* then that was another flaw. Housekeepers were not pretty. Properly, they were too aged to be recognizably female.

"How old are you?" he asked, his eyes on the paper.

"Old enough, Your Grace, to appreciate the boons of cleanliness. I predict you will greatly enjoy the results of our efforts."

He glared at the headline. He should dress her down for this cheek. He should sack her. *Again.* God damn it, why was she still here?

He took a deep breath. It stopped his next words. By God. The air was taking on a clean, crisp scent that struck him as . . . agreeable.

The vixen was right. These rooms had been overdue for scrubbing.

"Mind your tongue," he bit out, and snapped the newspaper taut. Jones had done a poor job of ironing. The man should know better.

After a moment, her silence began to irk him. He had rebuked her. She should offer an apology. It set a bad example for the maids.

He looked up to say something sharp—and found

her assisting one of the girls. The maid had discovered a pile of letters sitting unopened on his sideboard. She'd begun to carry them away in bunches with her bare hands. Mrs. Johnson was whispering to her: "On a silver salver, Muriel. You know this."

"But there's so many!"

Mrs. Johnson glanced up and found him watching. "Your Grace, how shall we sort your mail? Would an alphabetical organization suit you?"

How in God's name would that help? "Just leave it there."

"To properly clean the sideboard—"

"I said, leave it!"

Her lips pressed into a mulish line. The heightening color on her face brought her freckles into livid clarity. Freckles were not fashionable; so many freckles might be counted a disfigurement. How was it that they all clustered on the roses of her cheeks?

Scowling at himself, he once again turned to the newspaper.

"Perhaps," she said, "if I were to sort them by the postmark—"

"No." The very thought of all those letters made his chest tighten. The pile grew and grew. One would imagine, with no reply, his correspondents might realize he did not wish to hear from them. But they simply kept *writing*. Christ God. Open one and he would have to open them all. Answer one and he would have to discover what the rest of them wanted. "Burn the lot."

Silence.

He glared at the newsprint. It might as well have been in Egyptian.

"Perhaps it would be easier," she said tentatively, "if

someone opened them, and sorted them by degree of urgency—"

He slammed down the paper. Four women froze as one. A strange feeling ghosted over him, ancient, barely recognizable: embarrassment.

He took a deep breath. "I do not wish to read them." His voice remained level; that was something. "I do not care what's in them. I will not answer them. Burn them, Mrs. Johnson."

Her face made a curiously transparent screen for her thoughts. He could see, in the faint twitch of her brow, how deeply she disapproved of his order. And then, in the back-and-forth tick of her jaw, the ridiculous, thoroughly out-of-line impulse surfacing in her. She was going to *argue.*

"But what if . . ." she began, and then trailed off.

As he waited, her blush deepened. She cleared her throat and looked away; glanced back at him, and then quickly away again.

He realized he was staring. There was something . . . *interesting* . . . about her face. How easily he read it. How long had it been since he had really seen anyone? How long since he had paid attention to the small details, the nuances of expression?

Why, he could remember no images from the last year. Nothing visual at all, save the garden. The garden that was dead now. But he remembered it in full bloom this summer. That was all. Nothing else. As though his revelation, how blind he had been to Margaret's nature, had blinded him to almost everything . . .

He did not even remember who had attended the funeral. He remembered nothing but the grave, which he had visited weeks afterward. *Who were you?* That had been the only thought he'd felt capable of holding. *Who lies here? Who were you, really?*

But even that had been blindness in a sense, a massive self-deceit. It was not Margaret he'd been marveling at, but his own ignorance, the immense space of all the things he had not guessed and never suspected. He, who had prided himself on foreseeing everything.

"Wait," he heard Mrs. Johnson say. One of the maids had moved to toss the letters into the fire. *That* girl was an obedient servant. "Your Grace," his housekeeper said. She moved into his line of vision; he saw, in the resolute tilt of her chin, that she had recovered her courage. Such a small observation, to reveal so much. Once, he had been very good at reading faces. Once he could have read a lie from thirty paces. "I cannot think you truly wish to burn all this mail," she was saying. "What if—"

"Yes," he said scathingly. "God forbid I should miss an invitation to a charity ball."

She frowned but made no retort. His brain supplied it for her: *There are countless important matters that might be addressed in those letters.*

"I could read them," said Mrs. Johnson.

He laid down the paper. "You," he said flatly. "*You* propose to read my private correspondence."

Even the maids were gawking at her. He noted that with vicious satisfaction. They thought her as mad as he did.

"Well . . ." Her jaw squared. "If it's fit for burning, I suppose it's fit for my eyes as well. Unless you have a secretary?"

He snorted. "No." O'Leary had been called home to Dublin several weeks—no, he realized with a shock, several months ago. "No secretary."

"Well, then—"

"I sacked him." This was not true. "He kept insisting on looking through my mail."

She laughed.

He felt his brow knit into a frown, which he directed at the breakfast tray. Had he been joking? God's blood, but his head was addled. It felt full of cotton. Bat wings and spiders and nails. How long since his brain had truly worked?

His attention drifted to the headline.

"Well?" asked the termagant. Her own word. He could not fault her self-knowledge.

What was she nattering on about? He couldn't quite recall. BERTRAM A BOON. He thought of the pistol, tucked away in his bedroom. His old life was dead. He could take it back, no doubt. But that wasn't what he wanted.

What he wanted was to wreak bloody havoc. *Let loose the hounds of war.*

"Your Grace—"

"*Yes,*" he snapped, just to shut her up.

"Thank you." He heard the swishing of her skirts as she approached. God above! Could she not leave well enough alone? "There is another thing I wished to ask you," she said as she sat across from him—sat down in his presence without so much as a by-your-leave. Now, *this* deserved a sharp word. He opened his mouth, but she beat him to it, leaning across the chiffonier to whisper, "By any chance, did you consume five pounds of truffles last week?"

What in God's name? "No."

"I thought not." She plucked off her eyeglasses, revealing eyes a startling shade of light blue. He abruptly forgot what he'd been about to say. She was polishing the lenses with her sleeve as she continued to speak. The words might as well have been gibberish.

Her eyes were the precise shade of the sky over his garden this past summer. On the cloudless days, when the sun shone brightest, *this* had been the shade of the sky. It had glowered at him like a taunt. *Not for you. None of this is for you anymore.*

She replaced the spectacles on her nose, the glare of her lenses masking the miracles behind them.

Housekeepers did not possess such eyes.

"And I will look through your letters," she finished solemnly. She rose and walked away, leaving him . . . confused. He took a testing breath. Yes, it wasn't his imagination: she left the faint scent of roses behind her.

Was that perfume? How had he not noticed it before? It was precisely as he had imagined the scent of the garden. But he had never allowed himself to open the window, for fear of being disappointed.

God damn it.

He inhaled again as the door closed behind her.

His housekeeper smelled like the summer.

CHAPTER SEVEN

"Get on your way!"

Olivia, seated at the desk in the duke's study, tilted her head to listen. That had been Polly just now, out in the hall.

"Oh, come on now, don't pretend to be cross."

And that was Vickers. With a sigh, Olivia laid down the letter—the fourteenth she had opened today that was addressed to the duke. For a fortnight she had been going through these letters, making annotated lists that Marwick received without comment and, so she suspected, never bothered to read.

In other times, other places, she might have been frustrated at her work being so summarily ignored. But the list of his correspondents read like the index in a book of modern history. Reading these letters felt as pleasurable as eavesdropping in a palace. It was not seemly for a secretary to take such private and personal interest in her work.

Then again, she wasn't a secretary, was she? She was a housekeeper, which meant the argument in the hall—

now growing progressively shriller—was her business to squash.

As she started for the door, she heard Vickers say, "I saw how you looked when Muriel came up to me before. A bit green at the gills! Jealousy, what?"

"Ha! You think I care if a trollop and a dunce—hey! Get your hands off me or I'll pop you."

Olivia opened the door. Vickers had Polly crowded up against the wall, sandwiched between the suit of armor and a hip-high Chinese vase. "Mr. Vickers," she said sharply.

The valet sprang around. "Here now!" He gave a sheepish rub to his bald spot. "I was looking for you, ma'am. Cook wants your approval on the next week's meals—"

"My foot you were looking." Polly gave him a hard shove, and he stumbled toward Olivia, who sidestepped him neatly. He spilled onto his knees.

Olivia looked down at him. His bald patch was cherry red. "Have you no work to do, Mr. Vickers?"

"What work?" Polly cried. "He thinks he's the duke himself, he does. Loiters like a pasha, and imagines us his harem girls!"

Sputtering, he clambered up. "Nonsense. Say now, Mrs. Johnson, you saw her shove me. That's not right."

Polly came violently off the wall. "You're lucky all I did was shove. I've had enough of you, you lout."

"See?" Vickers skipped backward. "She's out for me. Always hanging about; I can't take a step without finding her underfoot—"

"That's a lie," Polly shouted.

"—and for that matter, I'm not the only man she dangles after," Vickers said. "Ask about the lad that turns up every night, just begging for a glimpse of her. Ask how quickly she runs to him."

Polly turned white. "You hush up."

"Say!" Vickers grabbed Olivia's wrist. "A regular rags-and-patches production, that ruffian. I'd wager *he* could use a batch of truffles to sell."

Polly gasped. "Why, you . . . He'd *never*!"

Olivia gave a pointed look at Vickers's hand. He snatched it back. "Begging your pardon, ma'am."

She turned her look on Polly, who was shaking like a fence post in a gale. "Polly," she said evenly, "you—"

"Of course you'd believe *him*," Polly cried. "You've disliked me since the day you set foot here. But how was *I* to know you'd not come for the maid's position? I couldn't guess—"

"Polly!" Olivia set her fists on her hips. "You will go back to your duties."

Polly gaped like a beached fish. And then, with a poisonous look divided between Olivia and Vickers, she snatched up her skirts and raced off.

Olivia rounded on Vickers: short, plump, with the coloring of a dirt patch after a drought. "I must say, Mr. Vickers, you make a very poor Romeo. If I catch you harassing the maids again, you will lose your post."

"Hey now!" He squared his shoulders, a posture that would have seemed far more impressive had Olivia not topped him by several inches. "I am His Grace's own man. My position here—"

"And what *is* that position, precisely?" She did not bother to scrub the coolness from her voice. Snitches might prove handy for housekeepers, but that did not mean she must like the breed. "For by my understanding, a valet is to tend to his master's personal needs—

and I have never once seen you in his presence." She narrowed her eyes. "Indeed, perhaps that's the problem. For it would take only a single look at His Grace to understand that he has no valet at all."

"That's unfair!" He blew out a breath, cheeks billowing. "I know he looks unkempt. But you can't imagine. The last time I ventured into his bedroom, he took the shaving kit and threw it at the wall."

"And when was that?"

He pursed his lips and made no reply.

"Not recently, I take it."

"I never got the kit back," he said sullenly. "And I can't help it if he refuses my services—"

"Yes, you can. You can *insist* upon them, Mr. Vickers." God in heaven, she had managed to get Marwick into his sitting room, hadn't she? Must she do all the rest, too? At this rate it would take a year to get Marwick out of his quarters.

"I can't overrule him. Who do you think I am? He's the bloody master of the house!"

"Watch your language," she said. "And if he will not let you shave him, then at least you might hold up a mirror."

He frowned. "For what purpose?"

"To show him his appearance. He looks like an overgrown sheepdog."

His jaw set. "There's no point. It's hopeless. I'm sorry you can't see it, but I won't be made to risk myself—"

"Then I will." She turned on her heel and marched toward the stairs. "Are you coming?" she said over her shoulder. In reply, he folded his arms. She clicked her tongue in disgust. "No, of course not." Useless, the lot of them.

* * *

The sitting room was empty, but the door to the duke's bedroom stood open. Olivia flew through it and found Marwick reading in a wing chair by the window. "Put your valet to work or sack him."

He did not look up from the book. "All right."

All right? She stood there a moment, confused. "Well? Which is it?"

He shrugged. The afternoon light fell lovingly across his face, gilding his skin and picking out the laugh lines around his mouth. When he had earned those, she could not begin to guess. He was the least laughing kind of man she'd ever met.

"Will you not answer?" she said. Despite herself, her attention began to wander the room. The maids had stacked up all the papers and placed them on the bookcase—barring a few that littered his dressing table.

He looked up, following her gaze. "Yes," he said curtly. "As you see, the maids came this morning. That fulfills the extent of your obligations here, Mrs. Johnson. If you have a complaint about Vickers, take it up with Jones."

She huffed. "Jones will not sack him without your approval."

"Well, then. There you have it." He settled deeper into his chair and held up his book with a pointed air: *I am busy*.

On a stroke of daring, she walked to the dressing table and made a show of straightening the papers. To her disappointment, these were fresh notes, observations on political items in the newspapers that he'd been reading so regularly of late.

"What are you doing there?"

She hastily dropped the papers. "If the maids came in this morning, what is all this mess?" The marble countertop held a terrible jumble of rumpled cravats and apothecary bottles.

"I am not in the mood for banter," he said coldly. "You will—"

"I'm looking for your shaving kit." She pushed aside the cravats, uncovering a hand mirror and other sundries. "Vickers said he hasn't seen it since you hurled it against a wall, and I—ah!" She picked up a tortoiseshell comb. "Behold this remarkable invention. You might wish to try it sometime."

He stared at her, a faint line between his brows. And then, mouth flattening, he turned back to his book.

His inattention suited her. Picking up the hand mirror, she drifted, oh so *very* aimlessly, toward the bookcase. The stack of documents piled on the middle shelf was a foot thick. The uppermost page was a letter, dated 1883, in Marwick's handwriting, to Lord Audley—

"The kit is not on the bookcase," he said flatly.

She held up the mirror. "Here, have a look at yourself."

Ignoring her, he turned a page.

"Oh, yes, I'm sure that book is only two or three hundred years old," she said. Sarcasm might be the lowest form of humor, but certainly it was also the most satisfying. "You were content to keep it on the floor, but now you can't spare a single *moment* before reading onward."

"Hardly so old." He held it up so she could see the spine: *The Count of Monte Cristo,* by Dumas.

"Ah, a tale of revenge. Are you seeking inspiration?"

He gave her a rather threatening smile. "So far, our hero seems spineless."

"You must be in the early section, then. I assure you, after Dantes spends years and years locked away, growing into a ragamuffin, he emerges quite deadly. Why, the first thing he does is to cut his hair."

He slammed shut the book. "You are peculiarly deaf to the cues most servants know to listen for. Was there some purpose to your visit? If not, you are dismissed."

She held up the mirror again. "Here is my purpose: you look like a wildebeest. If your valet—"

"I don't believe you know what a wildebeest looks like," he said mildly.

Hesitantly she lowered the mirror. He was right; she hadn't the faintest idea what a wildebeest looked like. "Well, you look how a wildebeest *sounds* like it should look."

"That doesn't even make sense." He opened his book again. "'Sheepdog' was the better choice."

She glared at him. "Do you *enjoy* being likened to a dog? Shall I bark at you again?"

He closed the book on his finger and leaned back to look at her. "Do you *wish* to bark, Mrs. Johnson? Yes, you seem to be feeling particularly canine today—at least, you've got your hackles up." Eyes narrowing, he considered her. "The shrillness does remind one . . . But no, a poodle is too feminine."

She sucked in a breath. "How rude. Are you implying—"

"An Irish setter? A fine match for your hair. But no," he said regretfully, "I believe the only answer is a Chihuahua: all irksome bark, and no bite."

She cast aside the mirror. "I have been reading your letters," she said through her teeth. "Do you know how many of your friends wish to see you? Imagine what they would make of you if they saw you in this state."

Mistake. His face tightened. "A fine thing that I am not receiving."

"Your valet is harassing the maids. Have you no concern for the innocent women in your employ? Only give him something to do. That's all I ask."

"In exchange for what?"

She hesitated. "What do you mean?"

He put aside the book, and she felt a quick pulse of panic as he gave her his full and undivided attention. Something mocking and untrustworthy had stolen over his expression; his smile looked distinctly unkind. "Why should I give him something to do? How would it possibly benefit me?"

She gaped at him. "The welfare of your household would benefit you. And—ha!" She pointed triumphantly at his hand, which had just risen to brush hair from his eyes. "A haircut would benefit you directly."

"And give you far too much satisfaction," he said. "You do realize, Mrs. Johnson, that you take a very unseemly enjoyment in harassing me? It isn't at all fitting for a domestic."

"You misunderstand. I don't enjoy it at all." But an uneasy feeling gripped her. Why, he might be right: she had lost track of her purpose here. Lulled into a false sense of security, she had allowed herself to be distracted by putting the household to rights—and the sheer challenge of prying this mule from his rooms.

"I don't enjoy it," she repeated fiercely. But the quicker she lured him out, the quicker she could see her mad plan through. And certainly no gentleman would ever dare set foot from his private quarters as long as he looked like a wildebeest *sounded* as though it should look, and a sheepdog certainly *did* look. "I assure you, I find my duties most distasteful."

His smile spread. It suddenly seemed to bode ill for her. "Do you? Very well, I believe you. Your manner suggests a very *put-upon* feeling. If you wish so much to see my hair cut, *you* may do it."

"What?" She took a step back. "I never—that's absurd. How would *I* know to cut a man's hair? I'd make a terrible hash of it."

He made a *tsking* noise, all mocking sympathy. "Duty can be so onerous. A very good thing I pay you for it, no?"

"Let me ring for Vickers." She turned for the bellpull. "He'll be here in a blink—"

"Absolutely not. You will wield the scissors, or no one shall."

Something serious had crept briefly into his tone. Turning back, she tried to laugh. "Surely you're not saying you don't *trust* him—"

He reached for his book again. "Enough." All levity had left him. "Leave me be."

She stood there, gripped by the conviction that she was right: for whatever reason, he did not trust Vickers enough to let him do it. "Perhaps Jones could—"

"Get out."

"Fine!" She set her fists on her hips. How difficult could it be? "I'll cut your hair."

He laughed curtly. "I was not serious."

"But you made the offer, and I accept it. What—are you frightened that I'll slice your throat?"

He looked up, narrow eyed. "Don't be a fool."

"Then tell me where the kit is."

After a long moment, he shrugged. "The wardrobe."

It took a bit of rummaging to locate the leather case. When she unbuckled it, she saw evidence of Vickers's story: all the utensils, the scissors and badger-hair brush and razor, lay in a jumble, dislodged from their compartments. The case had truly taken a beating at its master's hands. But somehow, a little stoppered vial had survived intact.

She opened and sniffed it: Castile soap, lavender, and perhaps the slightest hint of salt of tartar. Essence of soap for shaving, no doubt.

She glanced up and found his brow cocked. "You've no idea what you're doing," he said.

How insightful of him. If he wanted expertise, he could ring for Vickers. But if he was daft enough to let her do this, she certainly would not shy away from the opportunity. His hair was *atrocious.* "Take a seat at the dressing table, please."

He rose, eyeing her. But to her surprise, he folded himself without argument into the chair in front of the mirror.

She took the towel from the rail on the washstand and spread it out behind him. Then she took up the scissors. They seemed quite *small* for scissors, did they not? She sawed them experimentally.

When she glanced up, he was watching her in the mirror, the smirk on his face revealing how very *much* he was enjoying her discomfort. "I prefer the Parisian style," he said. "With a touch of the Italian on top."

What on earth did that mean? She decided to brazen through it, lest he change his mind. "I would have thought the German would suit you better."

He paused. "Hanoverian, do you mean? Or the Berliner? They're so often confused."

She stared at him for a moment, undecided, and then caught the slight twitch of his lips. He was funning her! He was making these terms up. "Whichever is shortest," she said severely, and gave a threatening snick of the blades.

"Very well," he said, and bowed his head.

A little shock bolted through her. She stared down at his head, all that luxuriantly waving blond hair, and suddenly felt unable to move. This job required her to *touch* him. To plunge her hands through his hair and . . . handle him.

For no apparent reason, she suddenly recalled the feel of his hands on her wrists. His thumbs slipping across her pulse. Her stomach somersaulted.

She pressed her lips together and took a sharp breath. How bizarre. Clearing her throat, she said, "It isn't too late to call Vickers." Why did her voice sound so high? "He'll be so glad to serve you—"

"Is your spunk only for show, Mrs. Johnson? Do I detect a whiff of cowardice?"

She rolled her eyes. "It's *your* head." On another deep breath, she plunged her fingers through his hair.

It was soft. Silken, even. A gentleman's hair was as soft as a woman's. Who would have guessed?

His shoulders jerked. She glanced up and discovered him silently laughing at her. "Your face," he said. "So shocked. Does ducal hair feel like some strange new variety?"

"Sit still," she snapped—and then frowned. "There's a pun in that somewhere, but I can't find it. Ducal hair, ducal heir . . ."

"Oh, but I'm not an heir," he murmured. "I'm the genuine article, I assure you."

Why that should make her blush, she had no idea. Something in his voice . . .

She went down on her knees to remove her face from his view. Her job here was not to amuse him. She pinched up a piece of his hair—really, it was softer than her own—and snipped it off.

There. Done.

Gaining confidence, she grabbed a larger piece, and lopped that off. *Much* better. Very quickly now she progressed the scissor across the back of his neck.

"Uncovering a talent?" he said.

She ignored him. Sitting back, she surveyed her progress.

Oh, good Lord! His hair looked like the ragged hem of some thrice-patched shift.

All right, then. It would require a bit more care. She slid her fingers through his hair to take a good, firm grasp, and felt him jolt slightly.

"Have a care with those blades," he said softly.

"Don't move, and I will."

She had trimmed hair before—her mother's, once a month, always on Sundays; and she had also done so for friends from the typing school on occasion. But cutting a man's hair—the Duke of Marwick's hair—began to feel quite . . . different.

As she gathered up his locks, her fingers brushed along the base of his neck. His shoulders were solid muscle—even here, at their tops. She could feel them flex a little beneath her fingertips, and the sensation made her redden.

She shifted her hand up, to avoid that muscled bulk. But now her knuckles skated along the nape of his neck, and his bare skin was startlingly warm, very smooth.

Three snips bared his nape—and she found herself staring, somehow startled by it: the whole strong shape of his neck, thick and muscled, corded as he bent forward to allow her better access.

His spine made a hard knob of bone at the base of his neck. In public, his collar would always hide this nexus of muscle and bone, even when his hair did not. It was a secret, intimate, vulnerable place. How many eyes had beheld it? His valet . . . and his late wife. Perhaps she had kissed it. It seemed like a spot one would enjoy kissing, were one his lover.

His skin looked smooth, unblemished. Her thumb strayed over that hard knob of bone to test her hypothesis. Yes: smooth. How solid his bones felt. She pressed with the pad of her thumb. He must be so much heavier than her. His entire frame was built on a different scale, long and lean and tightly knit, but solidly strapped with muscle. The densely packed breadth of his shoulders strained through the lawn of his shirtsleeves, even now, when he was undernourished. And she could feel—

She snatched her hand away. She had been *massaging* his shoulders.

Appalled, her face flaming, she put the scissors to work again. She prayed, *prayed* that he had not noticed. But how could he not have noticed?

She heard him loose a soft breath. She dared not look in the mirror.

The silence felt thick, charged. She wanted to wince and curl into a ball. Instead, she snipped very quickly, not taking much care. The main thing was to shorten his hair without stabbing him. If it looked awful, it only served him right; Vickers could fix it later.

At last, of necessity, she finally had to move into his

view again. She kept her gaze trained on his hair; she would not have met his eyes now for a hundred pounds. She was probably still flaming with color. Thinking of it made her flush hotter. *Drat it!*

The hair that flopped into his eyes—she would have to cut that. It had provided her the cause for goading him into this business to begin with. She braced herself, breath held, before stroking the hair away from his temple.

He was staring at her.

She could feel his attention like a hot brand against her cheek. She would not let herself look, but she could envision his eyes, so intensely blue, like subsuming oceans. His breath coasted over her arm, hot, soft. As she leaned in, her wrist brushed against his cheek, and she felt the roughness of his beard. Her mouth went dry.

No. This was not happening. She snipped as quickly as she dared. This close, she could smell the soap on his skin. A clean, fresh musk. Her heart was tripping now; she could not quite manage a steady breath.

She was not the kind of woman to feel this. No intimacy existed between them. She was not helping him because she cared for him. She had a mercenary, selfish heart and a criminal intent. She was not attracted to him. Olivia Holladay did not have her head turned by any man—*least* of all *this* one.

"There," she said finally, with great relief. But she knew that laying down the scissors would not put an end to this moment. She would have done better never to have touched him.

He tipped his head, then turned it from side to side, examining himself in the mirror. Or so she sensed—for she still could not look at him directly. "Well," he said at last. "That's quite . . . awful."

A giggle exploded from her. She slapped a hand to her mouth, appalled by the vapid sound. "Yes," she said—or gasped, rather, for she wanted to laugh again, simply from nerves. "I'm afraid it—" Another giggle slipped out, mortifying, bizarre, belonging properly to some dimwitted flirt. She made herself meet his eyes in the mirror; her own were wide, dazzled; they belonged to someone else. "I'm afraid it is." He looked like a shorn lamb.

His lips twitched. And then, wonder of wonders, he began to laugh, too. "And now the stakes rise, for if you're as bad at shaving—"

"Oh, no." She stepped backward. "I won't be lifting a razor to anyone's throat. I've never done it, and I—" She turned away.

He caught her by the wrist. Her stomach flipped; it did flip upon flip, like a child's hoop, as she slowly turned back.

"But what of Mr. Johnson?" he murmured.

She swallowed. "There is none, as you already know."

"Yes," he said after a moment. "But only now do I begin to think that a pity."

She must be misunderstanding him. Surely he did not mean that to be as suggestive as it—

His thumb made a slow stroke down her wrist. *That* again. She sucked in a breath, then yanked her hand free. "I will—I will go find Vickers, to fix it—"

"What needs fixing?" he said lazily. "I believe this has been quite a success."

She fled. Only halfway down the stairs did she finally figure out what he had done—and then she came to a stop, mortified, wishing the ground would swallow her.

The duke was not trying to seduce her. No, he was

far more nefarious. For what he'd done, at long last, was find a way to drive her from his rooms. He'd made a mildly suggestive remark, and she'd startled and fled like a rabbit.

She gritted her teeth. The low, cunning, loutish beast—

He would regret embarrassing her. Oh, yes. For she would not fall for *that* ploy again.

CHAPTER EIGHT

The envelope felt remarkably fat for a reference. Sitting at the window that overlooked the garden, Alastair squeezed it, tested its weight. It must enclose five sheets at the least.

Jones hovered in the doorway, stiff and quivering in his black tails. "It was all in order, Your Grace."

"I'm sure it was." He glanced up. Jones looked far plumper than he recalled. Perhaps that was where the five pounds of truffles had gone.

He smiled to himself. After his housekeeper had fled yesterday—if he'd not guessed her a virgin beforehand, he certainly knew her to be one now—he'd stood in front of the mirror for a minute, looking at himself.

The haircut was truly awful. But it was also undoubtedly an improvement—one that she'd fought very hard to win.

Why? He could not understand it. Nothing about her made sense. She was too young, and *far* too uppity, and . . . natively sensual, though she did not know it. For weeks now he'd felt her lingering glances. Only yesterday had he realized the cause for them. His housekeeper found him attractive.

Women had always admired his looks. What a strange thing to recall—and to be startled by, in remembering. Once he had known how to charm a woman. But *this* man, the man he was now, barely remembered his own flesh. It was a thing to ignore or to punish . . . until the moment when his housekeeper's hands had begun to wander across his shoulders.

She had cupped his arms, stroking lightly, as a blind woman might feel a shape in order to envision it. She'd appalled herself, of course.

"If you b-but read the reference," Jones stammered—he'd been quite abashed, explaining how he'd come to promote a maid to the lofty role of housekeeper—"you will understand, I hope, why I felt so bold as to hire her. Her Ladyship speaks quite highly of Mrs. Johnson's abilities."

"Yes." Alastair stared at the envelope. *Read it.* That had been the point of summoning Jones, after all. Mrs. Johnson's educated manner, her peculiar effronteries, her inexplicable determination to rehabilitate him, her touch . . . well. All of it combined had finally awakened his curiosity.

He opened the flap, conscious of a brief burst of dread.

Margaret had written so many letters. The moment he'd thought he'd collected all of them, more had trickled in. Others probably still waited in cubbyholes across town, destined one day to undo him. Letters had come to represent a great evil to him. How could they not?

But as he unfolded this reference, its neat script set him at ease. And a vision flashed though his brain, of his many piles of unopened correspondence. How absurd it suddenly seemed—that because Margaret had abused several sheaves of innocent paper, he'd become unable to look upon any others.

"Ripton," he said as he read. The viscount's wife had written this reference; she claimed to have employed Mrs. Johnson for some time. "When did he wed?" Alastair did not know the viscount; the man had taken his seat in the Lords and never returned. He was more devoted to business—no doubt by necessity; his family was full of wastrels and troublemakers, who must cost him a pretty penny.

"Recently, Your Grace. Very recently, I should think."

And yet the viscountess spoke of her housemaid with the glowing familiarity of a long acquaintance. "So with whom did Mrs. Johnson serve, before Lady Ripton's marriage? Who are the viscountess's family?"

The floor squeaked as Jones shifted his weight. "Ah . . . it slips my mind, Your Grace. I will need to consult Debrett's for that information."

While Miss Johnson certainly is knowledgeable and skilled in her application of waxes and polishes, I think her potential sorely underused by such a position . . .

This was no ordinary reference, but a hagiography. Olivia Johnson was dedicated, selfless, and possessed of any number of unlikely skills: Shorthand. Typing. Mathematics. She was a past master of etiquette, an excellent hand at planning dinner parties (with a particular talent for the design of floral centerpieces), and an irreproachable manager of complex correspondence.

He snorted. Perhaps his housekeeper was older than she looked. Or perhaps hypnotism also numbered among her talents, and the viscountess had written this letter in an obedient daze.

"Jones, tell me—" Alastair glanced up and found his butler beaming at him. "What is it?"

"Oh—" Jones straightened his face. "Nothing, Your Grace." But then the smile twitched at his lips again.

"You're smirking." Startled pleasure wisped through him. It seemed his ability to read faces had returned wholesale. "Speak your mind."

"Forgive me, Your Grace. Only . . . it's so marvelous to see you taking an interest." Jones bowed low. "Pardon me; the remark was inappropriate. I most humbly beg your forgiveness, I can't imagine what came over me—"

Alastair lifted a hand. "No need." No need to pretend, or to dance around the subject: for the last few months, he had not been . . . present.

And now Jones looked like a cat in the cream, for he imagined . . . what? That the old routine had resumed? That now he would be butler again to England's brightest hope?

Ignorance, they said, was bliss. It was what came afterward—the shattering revelations—that wounded so mortally. He would let Jones wallow in ignorance for a little while longer.

He rose. Jones made a stumbling retreat, all the way into the sitting room.

For God's sake. His housekeeper was right: his entire staff seemed shocked whenever he moved, as though they imagined him incapable of it.

"Where is Mrs. Johnson now?" This reference had cleared up nothing. She seemed to him all the more baffling in light of it.

"Downstairs, I believe." Jones was wringing his wrists.

"In the study. Sorting through your . . . correspondence? She assured me that she had your permission."

Downstairs.

He smiled blackly. Very well. He was not a child. He could send for her, yes. But let the servants see that he could not only rise from a chair, he could also—O holy miracle—descend a staircase.

He strode through the sitting room. The door opened into the hallway without argument. Indeed, it swung open so easily that for a moment he hesitated, stupidly surprised.

The butler's slightly labored breathing announced how closely he followed. Only Jones's presence behind him forced Alastair out.

The hallway smelled of wax and flowers, like a church before a funeral. He refused to draw it too deeply into his lungs.

Familiar furnishings lined the path. A lacquer vase full of roses. The bust of his great-grandfather. Oil paintings of past battles, distant victories of empire. An easy walk. A short trip. Downstairs, so simple.

The thick carpet absorbed his footsteps. Why did this seem so difficult? He had *chosen* to stay in his rooms; he had not been *trapped* there. Why was his chest constricting? He reached out to touch the bank of windows overlooking the street, and the chill of the glass startled him, yanked him to a stop.

These windows had been warm when Margaret died. For months after her passing, he had paced their length. At night, they had glared like blank eyes, blinded by the darkness outside. Anyone might have stood concealed in that darkness, watching him.

And what might that onlooker see, but a fool whose

bliss had been borne of ignorance? His achievements had been flukes, happy accidents. His defeats had been deliberate, engineered by his wife.

How cleverly she had schemed against him. *She* should have been the politician. He'd often told her so, by way of praise for her advice. Now he knew so, by way of her skill at betrayals.

After a time, he had started to avoid windows. His world had contracted to his private chambers, because there he need not worry what face he showed the world. The one he had worn before her death was a lie. The one he had discovered afterward was unbearable, grotesque, too much like his father's: fit only for hiding away.

He took a deep breath and made himself walk onward. The banister came into his hand, a solid length of mahogany, guiding him down the stairs. There must be a third face for him yet to try. He could not go back to the lie he'd once been.

He stepped into the vestibule, not looking at the double doors to the street, turning away from them for the archway into the east wing. But he felt those doors like an itch between his shoulder blades: a warning, or a temptation, or an axe beginning to fall.

He passed the formal salon where so many receptions had been held. Where he had greeted guests, and conducted negotiations in corners, and felt so damned *important.* So righteous and purposeful.

This house should be burned. What was it but a testament to falsehood? It held an entire history of how much he had cared, how cleverly he had laid his plans, how devoutly he had believed in a cause wider and nobler than himself.

How fitting that it smelled like a funeral.

The study door loomed. He grasped the doorknob like an anchor, and only once he stepped inside, closing the door in Jones's face, did he exhale.

His housekeeper did not notice his entrance. Humming to herself, she stood atop a short ladder, browsing through shelves of old estate records.

Her inattention suited him. He leaned against the door and waited for his pulse to calm.

Mrs. Johnson. The spectacles, the severe chignon, the drab wool skirt and plain white blouse belonged to a governess, a schoolmistress, a spinster aunt. But her youth, her self-possession, her flame-red hair, and her wandering hands did not.

What was she humming? Not the usual music hall ditty. Surely it was not . . . Beethoven? Since when did domestics, former maids, visit the symphony?

"L'ho trovato," she cried, and with an air of triumph, plucked a book off the shelf.

His housekeeper spoke Italian.

She tucked the book beneath her arm and lifted her skirts to clear her descent. Very trim ankles, had his Italian-speaking housekeeper. One slim boot felt for a lower rung. Her stockings, he saw, were lace.

Lady Ripton must have paid her very well for a maid.

What was she doing, prowling through his estate records?

He wrestled with a sudden suspicion. She spoke in accents too refined for her position. She did not have the demeanor of one trained for service. She wore lace stockings. She talked to herself in Italian. She was far, far too young.

What of it? Did he imagine her a *spy*? For whom? He gritted his teeth. His doctors—those he had bothered to see, before he'd turned the rest away—had cautioned that paranoia was the sign of an unwell mind.

He cleared his throat. Alerted, she gasped and twisted to gawp at him. "Your Grace! *Here!*"

So even she had imagined him incapable. Why that should gall him, he could not say. Who was she, but a servant? He felt a dangerous smile form on his lips. "Here," he said. "Yes. Does that not suit you?" Why would she need his ledgers in order to sort through his correspondence?

Her spectacles slipped down her nose. Those eyes alone might have riled a man's suspicion. He did not care how blind she was. Those eyes were weapons, and she did not strike him as a woman to waste such resources.

No. Even to his own mind, these thoughts sounded ludicrous.

"What are you doing with my records?" he asked.

"I th-thought—" She still looked wide-eyed. "Your steward from Abiston. He wrote with a question about the crop yield from a seedling in use at another estate. I thought I might make notes to guide your reply."

That was not the reasoning of a maid, nor a housekeeper, either. "I read Lady Ripton's reference," he said. "Very interesting stuff. She holds you in peculiar esteem."

Did trepidation briefly shadow her face? "Her Ladyship is too kind."

"I thought so as well."

She clutched the ladder and did not reply.

When had she ever been at a loss for words? Perhaps he could not trust his instincts. But that did not mean he needed to ignore them. "Which raises the question," he said. "Why did you decide to leave her service?"

"Oh, I . . ." She put her foot on the next rung and made an awkward hop; the ledger slipped from her arm and went tumbling onto the carpet.

She'd dropped it deliberately.

No, she hadn't. *You mustn't indulge these fancies,* Dr. Houseman had chided him. *Your mind is unbalanced by grief; it cannot be trusted.*

His brother had put it more bluntly: *You've run mad.*

But it was not a *fancy* that his housekeeper spoke Italian, hummed Beethoven, and had left a comfortable position in a bid to mop and dust his floors.

She was making a swift descent of the ladder now. *L'ho trovato,* she had said: *I've found it.* What *precisely* had she been looking for? He started toward her, determined to get his hands on the book before she could look through it.

She glanced over her shoulder, saw him coming, and lost her footing. With a cry, she stumbled off the ladder.

Let her fall. But his body disobeyed, lunging forward to catch her. A grunt burst from him; he staggered backward. Mrs. Johnson was not light.

Much to the good fortune of his pride, he caught his balance—and then a shock prickled over his skin, for he registered the feel of her. Young, yes: she had the curves of a woman in her prime. A scent enfolded him, rose water mixed with soap, and beneath that, the warm note of her skin. Glowing, soft, freckled.

She made a sound like the squeak of a mouse. He told his arms to release her. Slowly, they obeyed. He took a single step back, and now his brain and body truly parted ways, for he was devouring her with his eyes, and a certain long-dead part of his body was stirring, and he *cursed* its resurrection.

How long had it been since he had thought of, imagined, wanted a woman? Not his wife, not a nightmare, not a black bottomless sin that spread across his memory, his history, like a blot of ink, but a *woman.*

A woman's body. A woman's movements. The rapid pulse in the base of this woman's long, pale throat, the flick of her lashes as she stole a glance at him, the bend of her long waist, of her wrist, as she gathered up the fallen ledger. The curve of her breast as she clutched the dusty book against it.

The shape of her lips as she spoke, their color, the hue of pale roses, the color of her scent, her skin petal soft:

"I am mortified," said those lips. "I'm so terribly clumsy."

And her voice, soft and smooth, like the slide of silk sheets across skin—how long since such graces had been apparent to him? He had not touched a woman since his wife. He had never touched a woman before her; he would not be his father, no. But in those bachelor days, *ah,* how difficult virtue had been.

His heart was knocking in a loud, painful rhythm, his belly tight with animal need. He turned away from her, bewildered and furious with himself, lest she catch a glimpse of this adolescent disgrace, his cock as stiff as a cricket bat.

He dragged in a breath, and all he tasted was her: the scent of her, the warmth. His bloody *housekeeper.*

Who was not as she seemed.

He wheeled back on her and instantly regretted it, for she was staring at him, and had not yet recalled the need to fix her damnable spectacles. Cornflower-blue eyes met his, then shied away. A frisson seemed to pass between them, a moment of unwanted understanding: they were not only master and servant. They were also a man and a woman, alone together behind closed doors, with the feel of each other still burning on their skin.

He strode to his desk, dropping into the seat, putting a bulwark of oak between them. Blindly he groped for—a pen, yes, that would do.

His blotter was covered in paper. Tallies and figures. He blinked. A pile of opened correspondence sat next to the inkwell.

Focusing, he discovered a list, names and dates beside neatly inked notes. She was constantly delivering these lists to his rooms. But now, for the first time, he read one.

Lord Swansea, September 14, re: Illuminating Company, would be honored if you would join the board of trustees.

Mr. Patrick Fitzgerald, September 14, re: signs of blight at Abiston—seed issue? Consult other estates using same supply?

Lord Michael de Grey, September 15, re: wedding: date set for Christ Church in Piccadilly on 30th instant.

He had promised to attend. But he hadn't.

Lady Sarah Winthrop, September 16, re: Harry: no word from him in three months, request you press ambassador to mount a search.

He grimaced. For the sake of the family, he certainly hoped that Michael and Elizabeth's union proved fruitful; Harry Winthrop, the heir apparent, was good for nothing but rascality, vagabondage, and opera gossip.

"I am almost caught up." Mrs. Johnson crept up with uncharacteristic timidity. "I believe I will finish by tomorrow."

"Tomorrow," he said flatly. Ten, twelve months' worth of mail, and she would manage to read through it, summarize it, and finish it within a handful of weeks.

He flicked aside the topmost page with one nail. In tidy columns, she had transcribed the sum and total of the life he had ended, abandoned, departed: all the wheedling for favors, the solemn petitions, the ingratiating overtures.

Mr. Stephen Potmore, September 4, re: your health, concerned inquiry, kind regards.

He cleared his throat. "Yes, you're expedient, are you not? Lady Ripton, I believe, mentioned that skill—an expert manager of correspondence, she called you." He glanced up, found her hovering, her gaze downcast.

At least she had not helped herself to a seat. That was something. "Sit down," he said.

Their eyes met as she sat. He did not look away, though she did.

Ah, but there was no blush like a redhead's. He fancied he could see the very capillaries dilating beneath her skin.

He took hold of himself. Attraction between master and servant went against all codes of decency. But sometimes, inevitably, it did happen. How one handled it marked one's status as an honorable gentleman. His late father, for instance, had been the classic lecher:

forever groping this one, leering at that one, no matter the woman, no matter the witnesses—his children, his guests, his own wife.

In honesty, Alastair had not minded it so much for the betrayal it signified to his mother—for Elise de Grey had been no saint, no matter what her younger son still claimed. As a boy, Alastair had seen her emerging from other men's rooms, late at night, when no one should be roaming.

No, what had bothered him was how well his father fit the caricature of a gross, oversexed aristocrat. The late Duke of Marwick had talked a great deal of high-minded business about noblesse oblige. But in practice, he'd been a sketch from *Punch,* a dirty joke for schoolboys. His divorce, the vile details of his affairs and his wife's accusations, had occupied front-page headlines for months.

Alastair could remember the pride he'd once felt in having overcome that sordid legacy. How self-righteously satisfied he had been with his own virtues.

Yet behold this list of letters left unanswered. Questions from his stewards. Overtures from old allies. Proposals from men with whom he'd done business to great reward. All of them, neglected. And even now, reminded of his responsibilities, Alastair was not thinking of rent rolls, of tenants and crops and politics, of duties and how best to atone for his neglect of them.

For that matter, he wasn't even thinking of his late wife and the men with whom she'd betrayed him.

Put that way, how refreshing: he was thinking of his subsiding erection. And his housekeeper.

He looked at her. Really *looked* at her, in this space that echoed with memories of a life that had nothing to do with him now. The ever-present rage seemed, for a moment, to recede, making way for an interest that no servant should elicit—not from an honorable man.

But where had honor gotten him? Moreover—the strange thought riveted him—what had it denied him in the past?

It was not a gentleman's business to stare at a domestic. His precious *honor* would have blinded him to the shape of this woman's mouth, wide and more mobile than she probably liked. And he was very close now, he suddenly realized, to memorizing the arrangements of her freckles. Her left cheek bore seven beauty marks (could freckles be beauty marks? He suddenly thought so) arranged like the stars of Pleiades. Her right cheek showed the constellation of Cassiopeia, minus the southernmost star.

A *gentleman* would have castigated himself for noticing these details. England's *bright hope* would have called the freckles blemishes, for he'd believed perfection to be the image of his wife—whose skin had borne not a single mole, and whose dark, foxish beauty must (so he'd believed) set the bar for all women, just as he, with his accomplishments, set the bar for all men.

Only now did he see that freckles were not blemishes, they were *lures.* And though so many of his old pleasures were dead, he understood, suddenly, that new ones would arise—such as this one: to be fascinated by a servant, whom his old self never would have noticed.

She shifted a little in her chair. His silence unnerved her, but this minute adjustment would be her only admission of it. Another realization: a servant's self-possession could rival his own.

It could surpass it, in fact.

Give me the gun, she had said coolly, unafraid and unflinching.

"Who are you, Mrs. Johnson?" He found, suddenly, that it was not suspicion that drove him, but amazed curiosity. "What brought you here?"

She sat straight, blinking like an owl. "I . . . don't understand, Your Grace."

"Lady Ripton seems to have employed you in any number of capacities, some of them quite distinguished. Yet you left her service to apply for a position as a maid. Why?"

She hesitated. "Why . . . a chance to work for you, Your Grace. For the Duke of Marwick."

"Liar."

Her mouth tightened. "If you will abuse me—"

"You'll what? It isn't as if I haven't abused you before." He shrugged and pushed aside her neatly penned notes. "Very well, let's pretend it was my reputation that brought you here. All those glorious tales of noble doings, all the encomiums in the papers." God knew the journalists had adored him. "What kept you on? When I threw that bottle, why did you not turn heel and flee to Lady Ripton? Don't tell me she wouldn't have welcomed you back. That reference might as well have been an ode."

She fidgeted in her chair. "It was . . . not entirely my wish to leave her. But I fear one of her acquaintances took an unseemly interest in me."

He thought on that. "A gentleman?"

She grimaced. "If you must apply the term so loosely, Your Grace, I will be forced to agree with you."

He caught his smile before it could spread. Her peculiar fixation on diction was better suited to a governess than a domestic.

That notion made him wonder. "You seem remarkably accomplished for one so young."

She eyed him warily. Her spectacles were an atrocity against nature. They warped the shape of her eyes and made her look cramped and sour. "Thank you, Your Grace."

A man who had only seen her without those glasses might never have recognized her as she looked now. And if he did, he might be congratulated for restraining himself from removing them from her face. They were abominable.

He cleared his throat. "Italian, for instance, is not among the usual maidservant's qualifications, I think."

Her freckles grew livid against her white skin. "I don't . . ."

She didn't understand how he knew about the Italian. He felt a sudden, purely malicious enjoyment. How pleasant it was to have her on the run for once. "You talk to yourself. And to ledgers. Quite sloppy, signora."

"Oh." Blinking rapidly, she looked into her lap, teeth worrying her lower lip.

He supposed countless women bit their lips when nervous, but he could not recall ever having noticed it before. Most women, of course, were not blessed with such a long lower lip, the shade of a blush rose. Perhaps that was why. Her mouth demanded attention.

"Well, Mrs. Johnson?" She'd best give him a damned answer, and leave off with her lip.

When she looked up, reluctance stamped every line of her face. "I suppose . . . I was not raised to service,

Your Grace. Many of my oddities are owed to my upbringing."

Now they were getting somewhere. She might as easily have said that she'd been born in Italy, but this carried a ring of truth. "And how is that?"

"My family was . . . modestly comfortable, I should say."

"Define that for me." Hearing himself, he felt amused. Now he was encouraging her craze for precision.

She shifted in her seat. "I was educated, of course."

"At a particular school?"

She shook her head. "I had tutors."

"Ah." That sounded somewhat more than modestly comfortable. "And what else?"

She frowned a little. "Of my education, do you mean? The usual program: history, rhetoric, mathematics in the morning. Drawing and piano in the afternoon." She gave a fleeting smile. "The occasional game of chess."

"Properly educated, then."

She smiled again, wanly. "Obviously, my position is not what it once was."

He looked her over, impressed with this, the first real divulgence she'd made. He had suspected it, hadn't he? Her accent, her bearing, her mannerisms all seemed odd for a domestic.

His instincts weren't so rotten, after all.

"What happened?" he asked. "How did you end up in service?"

She shrugged. "Nothing so uncommon. I was . . ." She took a deep breath. "Orphaned. And provisions had not been made. So I was forced to make do."

He frowned. "Make do? Do you mean, support yourself?"

Her smile was faint and humorless. "As you see."

What he saw was a girl not much older than twenty, who was telling, elliptically, a story of how she had been cast from bourgeois comfort into utter want. For surely only the direst of needs could drive a pampered child, provided with tutors and pianos, to apply for positions in service.

Indeed, such stories did not generally end with the hapless orphan managing to *make do* in any regard. The only accounts he could recall were moralistic parables, in which the sheltered miss encountered some predatory young buck who turned her into a kept woman. Times were changing, of course, but the world still offered few opportunities to a gently bred girl forced to work.

He let some of his skepticism show. "What of your extended family? They had no care for you?"

"My family was never so large."

"But surely there was someone." He himself had not enjoyed the warm embrace of a large family—but even he'd had his brother, Michael.

She met his eyes and let the silence sit between them for a long moment. "No," she said at last. "There was not."

He felt somehow stung by that reply. What an absurd reaction! Yet for a moment, it felt as though he were the callow youth, and she, his superior in experience.

It unnerved him. He took a brisker tone. "How old were you, then, when you first struck out on your own?"

She answered readily enough. "Eighteen, Your Grace. Nearly."

Nearly? "Seventeen then, you mean."

She looked briefly bewildered at his tone. His anger

was showing. He did not understand, any more than she, why he should be angry. But he was. "Yes," she said slowly, "I suppose so."

Seventeen. "And yet you had no connections—no family connections—to service? How then did you find your first position?"

"There is such a thing as a servant's registry, Your Grace." There was a dry joke hidden in her voice, no doubt at his expense. "One pays a small fee to discover the households where applications are wanted."

"Yes, of course." Naturally he knew of such things. "But how did you make the decision that service was the thing for you?"

She shrugged. "Anybody, they say, can wield a rag."

She was being deliberately obtuse. Many young women would have sought alternatives to scrubbing floors. "You have an education. You might have been a companion or a governess."

Now her amusement faded, leaving only cynicism in her face. "At eighteen, Your Grace? By those who sought companions, I was more judged in need of accompaniment. And as for being a governess . . . I doubt many wives would have liked that."

No, he supposed not. The last sort of governess a housewife looked for was the dewy young lady. But he was startled by her forthrightness, and she saw it. "Forgive me," she said, and then frowned down at her own hands, looking genuinely embarrassed. "I have shocked you."

He checked his snort. "That's rather a strong word for it." And then he inwardly sighed. It seemed her quibbles with diction were catching. "Surprised, however—yes. One doesn't often find would-be maids of your background. The Italian and piano, and whatnot."

Her small, pleased smile was somehow charming. And then, quite suddenly, it . . . wasn't. Though it had not altered a fraction, he could not look on it.

He stared over her shoulder. He had forgotten that there were all manner of tragedies in the world. Hers was not the greatest—but neither was his. Was there any cliché more tired than the cuckold?

The realization might have carried a bittersweet relief—for a commonplace tragedy was also a tragedy that might pass. And yet instead he felt stung, for he saw suddenly the difference between him and this girl: confronted with unimaginable loss, she had rebounded with ambition, whereas he, a man ten years her senior, had . . . how had she put it? *Retired from the field.*

She had put it more gently than he deserved. What in God's name must she think of him?

He felt himself turning red. Odd sensation. Why the hell did it matter what a servant thought? He turned his attention to shuffling the notes she had made. Gladstone had written: he wanted Alastair's help in ousting Salisbury, retaking the government. God's blood—he'd written *thrice.* The man would not give up.

Damn right he wouldn't. Alastair had won two elections for him. Provided Margaret's letters were never made public, he would certainly be remembered for that.

But what of it? He no longer gave two bloody figs for his legacy. Naturally, some lingering vestige of his old self refused to believe this. But he had no use for it: his old life was dead. *Done,* damn it.

He laid down the papers. His housekeeper was sitting rigidly, braced for further interrogation. But he had the general outline of her secret now. She had been raised to hope for better, and she could not forget it. That explained a great deal about her.

He made himself say it: "You do yourself credit." The words burned his throat, for he knew he could not speak them to himself. "You have cause to be proud."

For some reason, she went white again. "Thank you."

"And now I will give you a piece of advice." He made himself smile. "Write to Lady Ripton. Tell her you require a place to stay while you seek a new position."

A line appeared between her brows. "Are you sacking me again?"

"No. I'm doing you a favor, in fact." He rose, and she hastily followed suit.

As he walked around the desk, he kept his eyes on her face, for there always seemed to be something new to see in it. And it gratified him to a baffling degree when he spotted the precise moment she realized he was walking toward *her.* Another man would have missed the fractional widening of her eyes. But not he. He saw what others would miss. He saw *her.*

Nobody, however, would have missed the quick hop she took away from him. "Must I always exit in this manner?" she said on an awkward, breathless laugh. "Chased out by—"

He looped his arm around her waist, and she gasped. With his free hand, he caught her chin and tipped it up.

How had he ever imagined that a petite frame was the key to feminine appeal? Miniatures might be compassed in a single glance. But such an abundance of perfection, long limbs and generous hips, nearly six feet of woman, made for an endless expanse of skin. Such a woman would demand hours to properly peruse. To taste. To penetrate.

"You should find a new position," he said, "in the house of some honorable gentleman. I am not one."

He brought his mouth down onto hers.

CHAPTER NINE

From the moment Marwick had appeared in the doorway, Olivia had felt as though the world were spinning. Shock had all but knocked her off the ladder. Before she'd even had a chance to skip forward to triumph—at last, he was out!—her worst fear had been realized: *he'd seen through her.*

But *had* he? Sitting at his desk, she'd scrambled to feel him out. His questions were probing, incisive. She felt like a tennis player parrying desperately against an unexpectedly skilled opponent. Was his suspicion based on some credible cause? Had she betrayed herself somehow? Or was Amanda's overblown reference the only cause for it?

Most unnerving of all was the growing sensation that she was not facing the same man whom she'd come to know during these past weeks. Somehow, in the journey downstairs, that wild, dark, desperate man had been replaced by a lord. He wore a well-tailored suit, his trimmed and tamed hair (Vickers must have fixed it) now framing his eyes, his face, in a manner that accented the ruthless angles of his bone structure. And his every question bore the full force and the resurrected might of a man she had glimpsed only in flashes until now: landowner, politician, the scion of an unbroken line of aristocrats well accustomed to demanding obedience. It took every ounce of her wit to evade, resist, and rebuff him.

And then, with one line, he destroyed all her efforts: *You have cause to be proud,* he'd said, with no veil of cynicism or sarcasm to flavor it.

Perhaps he was right. He was downstairs because of her. She had helped effect this. That was cause for pride.

Yet shame, like a rush of acid in her throat, had choked her reply to him: for whatever triumph she might have otherwise gleaned from a duke's resurrection, it was counterbalanced by what that resurrection made possible: a deceit and a theft that would destroy the startling, open respect she saw so plainly in his face.

This unhappiness weltered through her, dulling her wits; and so when he came around the table toward her, she did not glimpse his intentions until the very last moment—when he grabbed her waist and pulled her into a kiss.

His lips were hot. As masterful as his new manner. He opened her mouth with his and she tasted his tongue, and the shock was elemental; it started in her bones. Her startled breath filled her lungs with the scent of him, soap seasoned with bay leaves, the fresh lemon rinse with which he'd washed his hair. His skin. Salt and musk.

His grip at the small of her back, the flat of his palm, powerful, steadying, as her knees sagged.

Gasping, she turned her face aside—and then gasped

again as his lips found her ear, tonguing the rim, suckling her lobe. "Wait," she said raggedly. "I don't—this won't work." Not again. She had resolved it. His lips found a spot beneath her ear and it made her whole body shudder. She stiffened and struggled out of his grasp. "You don't need to do this! I was leaving!"

He stood facing her, his full lips parted, his breath audible, his long, elegant hands flexing at his sides. Another hot wave rippled through her at that sight, at the knowledge—God help her—that those hands were flexing around the feel of *her.* "What do you mean?" he said slowly.

What was the point of this ruse? "You don't need to run me off." Her hands shook; she knotted them into her skirts. "*You* were the one who came in. I am going." She turned on her heel.

His hand on her elbow hauled her back. "Run you off?" His smile looked disbelieving . . . and then delighted. "Is that what you think I'm trying to do?" He reached up and nudged her spectacles into place. "Look more closely," he murmured. "Or perhaps you're truly blind."

He was pulling her into him. Millimeter by millimeter, he was drawing her close. And she let him do it, because there was something in his expression . . . Who had ever looked at her that way before? As though her face were a spell, a piece of hypnotism, to which he played the willing, fascinated victim. His eyes were oceans, and she was lost in them . . .

Their lips met again. She did not move. Did not breathe. Gently his mouth molded over hers. She did not understand. If he wasn't trying to run her off, then . . .

He was kissing her simply because he wanted to.

Everything suddenly became clear and bright. Her eyes drifted closed. Her hand found the back of his head, the shorn hair, still so soft; the feel of his skull, solid and curving. His mouth opened, and so did hers. Their tongues met. He was perfectly tall; they aligned as though designed for each other. His hand stroked her waist, and it felt as though he had unlocked something; her hips loosened, became sinuous, as she pressed against him.

Like that moment when the off-key string finally came into tune and joined with the chord, and the air vibrated with purity: her lips belonged with his; her body came into tune with him. Only she hadn't guessed until this moment, as the kiss lengthened and opened a world of new sensations, that rightness could sing through her, a pure and perfect completion, and reverberate through her blood, and make it leap.

This was desire. Before it had manifested only in symptoms. But here was the full illness, and in his lips lay the cure. His mouth, his tongue, were wholesome to her, hot, exactly what her body craved . . . what it *needed* . . .

"Oh!"

The shrill exclamation brought Olivia to her senses. She leapt back, whirled, and found Polly hastily closing the door.

"Oh!" She felt the word slip through her fingers, and only then did she realize she was covering her mouth. "Oh!" She looked back at him, appalled.

He gave her a roguish half smile. "Oh."

Sanity pierced her like a needle. It drew her loose limbs back into tight, rigid alignment. She narrowed her eyes at him.

He leaned back against the desk, raffish and unashamed. "Find a new employer." He shrugged. "Or, if I am so lucky, don't."

On a strangled hiss, she fled.

Once in the hallway, the door slammed shut behind her, she sank against the wall. Her legs felt weak. She stared blindly at the suit of armor standing guard opposite. *My God!* That had actually happened! He had kissed her. And she'd reacted like a wanton.

A strange smile seized her, stupid and amazed. *She* had behaved like a *wanton*. Who would have guessed it?

She made herself scowl. This was nothing to be proud of.

But Mama had always told her that passion could make one a fool, and she had never believed it . . . until now. For there came a sound from within the study, the creak as his footsteps approached the door, and all she wanted to do was remain right here, waiting for his exit, to see what he might do next . . . and what *she* might do, what *she* might learn of herself, that she had never before suspected.

Instead, she snatched up her skirts and hurried down the hall—and then skidded to a stop by the staircase. Polly stood leaning against the banister, arms crossed, brows raised.

Mortification flooded her. Good God! After all the stern lectures she had delivered on proper behavior, to be caught *frolicking* with Marwick—

"It's your half day, ain't it?" Polly smirked. "P'raps I might go out with you."

Mutely she shook her head. She did not take half days. Why risk leaving the house to be spotted?

Polly made a little chiding click of her tongue. "I

heard Jones saying just this morning that he wanted you to fetch the fancy stuff from the market."

You shouldn't eavesdrop. She folded her lips together. After what Polly had seen, how could she make such pronouncements? Oh, heavens—Polly would tell *everyone*.

It doesn't matter, she told herself. She would be out of this house within the week. He had left his rooms now, hadn't he? *Less* than a week, then.

She wanted to sink through the floor.

"Well?" Polly's devilish grin showed how much she was enjoying this—and how little she cared to disguise it.

Olivia cleared her throat. "Yes." Her voice croaked. "That's very true." To ensure the kitchens suffered no additional thefts, Jones had proposed that *she* purchase all the expensive and rare supplies, and deliver them directly to Cook, whose knee prevented her from going to market herself. "But I didn't think—"

Polly looked pointedly over her shoulder. "Oh, here comes His Grace. Interrupting again, am I? Is that why you can't go?"

Olivia sucked in a breath. "All right, then." Perhaps she could buy Polly's silence with an ounce or two of saffron.

On a sunny afternoon, Piccadilly was a tangle of omnibuses, shouting cabmen, lady shoppers promenading beneath parasols, errand boys bearing packages, and impatient gentlemen who seemed to believe everyone should yield the road to their high-strung thoroughbreds. The entirety of the city seemed out to carouse, and the aisles of Swan & Edgar's were crushed.

It took Olivia ten minutes, and a very sharp tone of voice, to flag the attention of a young female salesclerk. The girl seemed peculiarly ungratified to be making such a significant sale, a small fortune's worth of spices: cardamom, Ceylon cinnamon, mace, saffron, and white pepper. As the goods were packaged, Olivia waited for Polly to say something—some sly remark to hint at what she required to keep quiet.

But Polly showed no interest in the proceedings. Her elbows on the counter, she faced out toward the crowds, looking with transparent curiosity at the grand dames and the harried bourgeois mothers, whose brawling broods quarreled and chased each other through a sea of skirts.

As they exited back into daylight, Olivia started for the cabstand, but Polly caught her elbow. "Why not a stroll?" she said. "We've the time for it, aye? And St. James ain't a far walk."

Olivia knew better than to trust her. They had crossed swords far too often for that. But out of doors, Polly looked different somehow—far younger, less sour. The natural light lent her olive skin a flushed, vigorous radiance that one more often saw on young children. And the light in her amber eyes did not seem greedy or calculating, only wistful.

Perhaps she saw Olivia's indecision, for she said softly, "I don't want to go back to the house just yet."

And Olivia remembered suddenly how Vickers had pinned her up against the wall. "Is the valet still bothering you? I spoke to him, but—"

"It's not that," Polly said. "Only it's so pretty out, and soon it won't be. I don't like the winter."

Lingering outdoors was a risk, but surely a minor

one. With so many crowds on the pavement, and a netted hat on her head to disguise her hair, Olivia felt that a passerby in a coach would never take note of her.

With a shrug and a nod, she turned down Regent Street for the park.

In the meadow, the milkmaids were selling milk straight from the cow at a penny a pint. Olivia purchased two mugs seasoned with nutmeg and cinnamon. Polly rented a gingham cloth to whip across the grass. After a moment's indecision, Olivia set down the packages and joined her on the ground.

She had not lolled on her bum since she'd first donned a corset. Mama, who had hailed from rural Kent, had been intent on raising Olivia to a finer standard—or what she had imagined to be finer. *London ladies don't behave so:* it had been her favorite reproof. But Mama had never actually been to London. How it would have disappointed her now. For all around them, other girls were lolling on similar blankets, enjoying their afternoon away from work—and the grass, to Olivia's surprised pleasure, was quite comfortable.

The silence, however, was not. As she sipped the milk, she felt herself on edge again, waiting for the penny to drop.

The wardrobe of passersby—some grand, some humble—at last furnished material for a halting discussion. "There's a smart gown," Polly said, pointing at a woman in bronze silk. "Bit flash for the afternoon, don't you say?"

"A bit." Olivia's mind began to wander. *Find a new position,* he'd said. Was that code for *I will ravish you if you stay*? And why did the thought make her stomach flutter? She should be horrified.

"Look at the clouds," Polly said.

Olivia glanced up. Overhead was no typical London display: the sky was clear and bright, the clouds fat puffs of blinding white.

"We could be in the tropics," she said. But only if one did not note the crispness in the air—or look around the park, so English with its severely tamed trees.

Polly reclined on one elbow. After a moment, feeling very daring, Olivia mimicked her. She was practically *lying down* in public.

The slight chill was refreshing, the sun a pleasant balm on their faces. "I'm going to freckle," Olivia muttered as she readjusted the netting on her hat.

Polly shaded her eyes to deliver a wry look. "Ma'am, that milk was spilt long ago."

Startled, Olivia laughed. "True enough."

The silence between them began to feel easier. Polly gazed up, lost in the show the heavens were putting on. Olivia shut her eyes. How long since she had allowed herself to loll about, doing nothing? She could remember such afternoons in Elizabeth's employ, but they seemed distant, part of a long-ago dream.

He had *kissed* her. She had *liked* it. How could she feel so relaxed?

"Can I ask you something?"

Tensing, she opened her eyes. "Of course."

Polly inched closer, so their shoulders brushed. "You got some special knowledge of His Grace? Before today, I mean?"

"Of course not! Why should you think so?"

Polly shrugged. "He's different since you came. I thought maybe that was the reason he listened to you."

"You're wrong," Olivia said. "I never—" She must be

red as a cherry. "He is simply on the mend," she said sharply. "And a bit—disordered in his thinking, which explains what you saw. But that has never happened before." Emphatically she added, "And it won't happen again."

Polly pulled a face. "Does he know that?"

Olivia sat up. She could not remain at such close range to that searching look. "Of course he does."

Find a new employer . . . or, if I am so lucky, don't.

She swallowed. His intentions were immaterial. Now he'd left his rooms, it was only a matter of days—perhaps even hours—until she found what she needed, and fled without notice.

Polly was watching her. "You don't fancy *him,* do you?"

She hissed out a breath. God in heaven, what an idiot it would make her if she fancied Marwick. Yes, there was a certain vain pleasure in feeling oneself instrumental to the rehabilitation of a once-great man. But that was where her interest ended. She had one task here. She could not afford to be distracted by mooncalf sentiments.

And he was the last thing from a proper suitor anyway. A duke and a lunatic—recovering, thanks to her, but no matter. And not any duke or lunatic, but the Kingmaker: a man who burned with such rage that his heart rightfully should already have turned to ash. A man who stroked pistols during his sulks.

"Fancying him would make me the greatest fool alive," she said. "And I assure you, I'm not a fool."

Polly sighed and sat up. "You know how many girls have fancied their masters? Not all of them fools. But I don't need to tell you where they are now."

Olivia frowned. "Where?"

"The street corner."

"Oh." She flushed. "Of course."

More gently, Polly said, "It never goes nowhere but ruin."

Was this girl trying to *counsel* her? Against her will, she felt rather moved. "Of course. But what you saw, Polly . . . you mustn't misunderstand. And I would appreciate it if you didn't mention it to anyone—"

"Oh, they're already talking."

Olivia gaped at her. "Are you joking?" The staff thought her a *seductress*?

Polly shrugged. "You're always going up to his rooms."

How bizarre! Olivia battled a very inappropriate urge to laugh. She had always been far too gawky, far too tall, and (she would admit it) rather too *prickly* to be mistaken as a temptress. "I am his *housekeeper*."

Polly snorted. "Mrs. Wright did her best to stay away from him."

"Then that was very wrong of her. I simply . . ." She hesitated. What possible excuse could she make for her harassment of Marwick? For obviously the truth would not serve: *I need to pry him out of his rooms so* I *might pry through them.*

But perhaps she need not lie at all. For a sudden realization dawned on her. "I simply like him." To her amazement, it was true—and idiotic enough in its own right.

She could not blame Polly for bursting into laughter. "*Like* him!"

That laugh was raucous enough to draw several passing stares. Olivia waited, crimson. "He's not *so* bad." Twisted and melancholy, yes; but he was also wonderfully erudite, with a very dry sense of humor. Before his wife's death and the revelation of her betrayals, he must have been magnificent.

Gasping, Polly knuckled at her eyes. "Oh, aye, to be sure. What bunkum. Fancy him, fine; he's not hard on the eyes. Fear him, why not? But *like* the man? He's made of ice."

Feeling stubborn, Olivia scowled. "I suppose I like an underdog."

"Underdog! The *duke*? What, does he require another coach-and-four, another house in the country, before you rank him on top?"

Olivia shook her head and made herself recline again. So, too, did Polly.

In the pause that followed, she imagined that the topic had been laid to rest, and was grateful for it. She felt a little shaky, as though she had brushed up against something that might kill her. A close escape, indeed. *Fancy* him. What a disaster *that* would be.

Her mother had fancied a man far above her status, once. Mama had loved Bertram; had given him everything. And look what it had gotten her. Oh, Olivia would not fault Mama for loving a man outside wedlock. The villagers of Allen's End had made that their main pastime. Olivia had no interest in their brand of morality, which produced only unkindness and spite. But if one was to fall in love, better to do so with a man capable of returning it in kind.

"I'm waiting," Polly remarked. "Very keen, I am, to hear how a duke should be an underdog."

Olivia felt a wisp of annoyance. Class snobbery ran along both sides of the divide. "One doesn't require poverty to be wretched. Why, my former employer—"

"The viscountess?"

"No, El—" She bit her lip, shaken by how close she had come to slipping up and speaking Elizabeth's name.

Perhaps reclining was a poor idea. She sat up again, brushing stray bits of grass from her sleeve. "Yes," she said. "Viscountess Ripton."

Polly, unmoving, watched her curiously. "Plenty of nobs got *your* sympathy, eh?"

Olivia sighed. Amanda also had been something of an underdog before her marriage, though Polly was not owed those details. "A person's wealth has little to do with their spiritual state. Anyone who feels alone in the world, and put upon, and friendless—I call that person worthy of fellow-feeling."

Polly grunted. "That's mighty kind of you. Very Christian. Only you'll note that some of these lost souls *deserve* where they're at."

"You think the duke deserves his unhappiness?"

"I ain't got any complaints against him. He's never done wrong by me. But seems he mourns awful hard for a woman who was as chilly as ice in January."

"What was she like?" Olivia asked slowly. "The duchess, I mean?"

Polly pulled a face. "No, that's a road I won't help you walk down."

Olivia felt an oncoming blush. "I don't ask for *that* reason."

Polly looked away, the full curve of her cheek showing her youth. "You've a soft heart," she muttered. "Mush, I think. Better save your concern for yourself."

Olivia realized then how foolish she must look, worrying over great folk who had never known a simple care—where to get their daily bread, or whether the rent could be paid this month.

"I'm not weeping for him," she said. "You're right, his troubles aren't matters of life and death." Not . . . technically anyway. But she remembered how he had stroked that pistol. "It's only that . . . well, he's human, isn't he? And even if his suffering isn't on the same plane, it also can't feel so different from anybody else's."

"I'll have to take your word for it that he suffers at all," Polly muttered.

Was she truly the only person in England to understand that Marwick, too, had a heart?

Good heavens. Had she survived so long, safely above the fray, only to succumb *now* to feminine foolishness? And for *Marwick,* of all people?

"I don't fancy him," she said flatly.

"I won't say otherwise." Polly hesitated. "But in return, I'd like a favor. Ma'am."

Olivia snorted. "Of course you do."

The duke's journey downstairs occasioned great excitement among the staff. Over the next two days, Marwick roamed the halls quite freely—going so far as to open new correspondence and post replies (this according to the porter, who had no notion of discretion). What next? The servant's quarters buzzed. Would he *leave the house*?

Olivia was less sanguine. From a safe distance, well out of Marwick's eyesight, she monitored his schedule. There was, alas, no predictability to it. He would shut himself in his study for ten minutes or twenty, and then return to his quarters. Or he would leave his apartment only to pace the corridor outside. Where was the opportunity to slip into his bedroom without risking exposure?

On the third day, she steeled herself and accompanied the maids to his quarters for their daily rounds. The girls' moods were very grumpy, for at breakfast Jones had cautioned them not to expect holiday celebrations this year, His Grace still being on the mend. Vickers had further soured the atmosphere with bitter muttering over Polly's gentleman visitor, whom Olivia had invited inside for tea last evening, claiming him to be a distant cousin. Such, alas, was the price of Polly's silence.

Upstairs, Marwick was nowhere in evidence, but with the maids industriously bustling about, Olivia could do no more than glance again through the papers on his bookcase, none of which were of use to her. Worse, Doris noticed her interest in them. "He won't let us put those away, ma'am."

She snatched back her hand. "Oh? Well, no bother then."

"I did try to put them away." Doris sounded both proud and amazed by her own efforts. "I carried them to his trunk, where he was putting all the others." She nodded to the chest at the foot of the bed. "But he said to leave them where they was, and never touch them."

Her pulse escalating, Olivia surveyed the chest. It bore a padlock that looked far sturdier than the one on the desk in the study. "I see," she said. "Well, we must respect his wishes."

That night she sat up until the clock chimed three. Getting into that chest would require breaking the lock—which, in turn, would require more than a few minutes' solitude in his bedroom. Afterward, she would need to leave directly, for there would be no way to hide what she had done.

On the fourth day, she woke up sick with nerves, for she was determined on her course. Marwick withdrew to his study at a quarter past ten. When the door remained closed on her third pass, she grew bold. Or desperate. Some inspired mix. She made her way quickly up the main staircase, into the upstairs hall.

In the corridor she hesitated one last moment, realizing by how hard her heart was drumming how ill suited she was to these shenanigans—and how very little she wished to betray him.

She touched her lips, picturing how he had looked at her before he'd kissed her. *You do yourself credit,* he'd said. *You have cause to be proud.*

She made a fist and forced herself to think of the little cottage. Ivy along the walls, a lamp burning in the window. A place to settle. A sense of rootedness, and a garden in the spring. *Safety.*

Even if she dealt honestly with Marwick, he would never offer her those things. At most, all he offered was the road to ruin.

She opened the door to the duke's sitting room.

"Mrs. Johnson." The duke was sitting by the window in the full flood of the afternoon light, his attention fixed on a picked-over chessboard. "Did you want something?"

She grabbed the door frame for balance. A hysterical laugh bubbled in her throat. *I want you to stay downstairs until I'm done stealing from you.* "I knocked," she said. "I heard no response, so I thought . . ." She cleared her throat and straightened. "I have come to say that I agree with you: I must look for a new position. But I will stay here until you've found my replacement." That would take a little time—which was all she needed, surely, now that she'd found the courage to do this.

He glanced from the chessboard to the newspaper

folded in his hand. "What a shame," he said absently, in a tone that suggested he could not care less.

Her vanity pricked. How idiotic of her. He had probably forgotten all about that kiss. She started to pull shut the door.

"Wait." He did not look up. "The match in Hamburg between Blackburne and Mackenzie—have you read of it? This new move, Blackburne's Gambit—I'm trying to understand it. But I'm missing something."

He was sitting here working out a chess game? Surely he could have done that in his study. "No," she said tartly. "I've not read of it. I see I'm interrupting—"

"Scampering off to hide again?"

She flushed, a very irritating sensation. "I can't imagine what you mean."

He laid down the newspaper, giving her a slight, maddening smile. Vickers must have attended to him this morning, for his jaw was smooth-shaven. His hair lay in a close, even crop across his well-formed skull, the severe cut complementing the sharp bones of his cheeks and jawline. "Of course you can't," he said. "What a pity; we are back to formalities." And then, tilting his head: "You mentioned that you've played chess. Have you any talent at it? Perhaps you can help."

First he kissed her, and then he accused her of hiding from him, and now he wanted her help with a silly game? "I was not very good," she said coldly.

He looked at her for a moment, obviously puzzled. "You're a terrible liar, Mrs. Johnson. You do know that, I hope?"

And he was a terrible judge of liars. He caught all the small deceits, and none of the large ones. "Perhaps I was rather good," she allowed.

"Then come here," he said, "and help me understand this gambit."

Wariness gripped her. "I have decided," she said again, "to look for a new position."

His smile was all innocence. "Yes, I heard you the first time. You enunciate very clearly, Mrs. Johnson. It must have been all those tutors. Now come and show me what else they taught you."

On a sudden temper, she stepped inside. "Very well." If he wished to be shown up, she would not deny him. In fact, she planned to enjoy it.

Forty-five minutes later, they were still hunched over the chessboard, having disentangled Blackburne's peculiar piece of genius and then moved on, by the duke's insistence, into a proper game of their own.

Olivia studied the board with rising surprise. Marwick's opening moves had suggested a great deal of rust on his brain. She had grown careless, certain of an easy victory—until he'd suddenly recovered the way of it. Now she had begun to play in earnest again, but it was dawning on her that he might win anyway.

That rankled. She was not accustomed to being outwitted, particularly by a louche idler. She moved her knight. "Check," she said.

It was an empty threat; he had several routes of escape. But two of those routes would lead him into a very bad position, four or five moves from now.

He chose another one entirely. She bit the inside of her cheek—and then regretted it when she realized how closely he was watching her.

Her effort to straighten her face made him smile. "You would do very poorly at cards, Mrs. Johnson. Your face tells all."

She lifted her brow. "A good thing I would never gamble, Your Grace. Money is to be saved, not wasted."

He sat back, studying her. In his dark suit and crisply knotted tie, one might have mistaken him for civilized. Only the impish quirk to his mouth gave him away. "A Puritan, are you?"

"A woman of foresight, in fact." She foresaw his defeat in five moves, if he only shifted that bishop his hand was currently overshadowing.

"A sound philosophy on gambling," he said. "I agree with you: it's terrible entertainment. I never understood it." He abandoned his bishop to castle, puzzling her greatly. "Of course, the basic principles do come in useful elsewhere. Politics, for instance: what is success in that field but knowing when to calculate the odds, how to gauge one's opponents, when to hedge one's bets, and when to cast everything on a single wager?"

Squinting, she sat back to get a better view of the board. Provided he was not declining into mediocrity again, there must be some possibility she had not yet glimpsed for him. "How very reassuring," she said absently, "to hear that national affairs are best handled like a poker game."

"At best," he said wryly. "At worst, like a shoot-out in the American West."

"I suppose one might wish you gambled, then. Or dueled."

"And why is that?"

"Because England needs you." She moved her pawn forward to menace his knight.

"Let's not go back there," he said evenly. "I've only just put away my pistol."

She glanced up at him, surprised that he could speak of that incident so lightly. He offered her a rueful smile—which slipped from his lips as he leaned toward her. "How remarkable," he said. "You realize you tip your spectacles *down* when you wish to have a look at something? Or someone."

She directed her frown down to the chessboard. Bertram had once said that one could tell a great deal about a man by the way he played chess. While she hated to ascribe him any wisdom, he had a point: Marwick played with caution, taking time to survey all his options. But once his mind was made up, he moved without hesitation. And when it was his opponent's turn . . .

"Are the spectacles not meant to *aid* your vision, Mrs. Johnson?"

When it was his opponent's turn, he tried to distract her with idle remarks.

"It is bad etiquette to taunt one's opponent," she said tightly. "This is not, as you have noted, a game of poker."

"Good etiquette rarely makes good strategy."

She cast him a severe look. "Au contraire. Good etiquette is the key to civility, and civility is always good strategy."

"Goodness," he said mildly. "Could it be that you fancy yourself mannerly?"

She narrowed her eyes. "I couldn't imagine how you would disagree."

He gave an easy shrug. "How shall I say it . . . In future

positions, I recommend that you cultivate a somewhat more *reticent* demeanor than you've shown me."

They were speaking now as if she'd already left her post. Perhaps that accounted for his casual manner. He was no longer troubled by the need to maintain a proper distance between them. Not that it had troubled him in his study.

Butterflies emerged in her stomach. She promptly willed them dead.

As she craned over the board again, she thought of the bedroom behind her, and the chest she must search before her replacement was found. It would take time to arrange interviews, of course. But sometimes, if a sterling recommendation came from a family friend, none was conducted.

"Yes, precisely," said Marwick. "This silence is very becoming of a servant. A very nice show of meekness, Mrs. Johnson."

She pulled a face at him. "Now you're having fun."

He grinned. "Indeed I am," he said—and then looked fleetingly startled. He turned his gaze out the window, his smile fading.

She could sense the downward pitch of his mood. He had recalled that his role was a recluse, to whom laughter and company were denied. And in a moment, he would cast her out, thereby avoiding his own defeat. For the perfect series of moves had finally revealed itself on the chessboard.

"To answer your question," she said, "I do fancy myself a great admirer of etiquette. But I allow it has its particular place and time. Occasionally, to do a kindness, one must bend the rules." She made a pointed pause. "Were it not for my temerity, these rooms would not smell nearly so nice. And *you* would not be reading about chess matches in the newspaper."

He looked at her narrowly, as though he was marshaling his thoughts back from a faraway place. And then he gave her a half smile. "Quite right," he said softly, and reached out very suddenly to clasp her wrist.

She froze, her fingertips hovering a fraction away from her queen, her pulse suddenly in her mouth.

He lifted her hand to his lips. "A breach of etiquette," he murmured against her knuckles. "But a kindness. You do not wish to move your queen."

Let go of me: her tongue felt like clay, unable to speak the words.

"Lovely hand," he said, and turned her hand over to press a kiss into her palm.

She pulled free. A breath shuddered out of her. Her palm seemed to burn where he had kissed it. "This—this is not—"

"Your move," he said mildly.

She fisted her hand in her lap. "Why do you *do* this?"

He gave her a meditative smile. "Better to ask, why do I seem to be the first? Were the men blind as well, where you were raised?"

The chessboard had turned into a riddle. She stared at it, her heart pounding.

"Where *were* you raised?" he asked.

"Stop." She rose. "I will—"

"Very well. Sit down; I will behave." His voice was low, calming, as though he knew what he had done to her. That gooseflesh still prickled over her skin. "And I will stop the imaginary clock, too, so you do not feel baited. Take your time with your move."

Why did she sit back down? Curiosity, she supposed. She had never before been flirted with.

But new mountaineers did not begin their careers on the Matterhorn. To indulge her curiosity was tremendously stupid. She knew it, but she sat there, breathless, looking at the board, baffled by the pieces, her hand still tingling.

"I will confess that I remain curious," he said. "You *do* look over your glasses when you require a clear view. You're doing so right now."

She shoved her glasses up her nose and glared through the lenses. "I see *you* very clearly, Your Grace." And then, because he lifted a brow as though in skepticism: "I see a man who lacks faith in his own game, and so resorts to underhanded measures to distract the superior player."

He gave a strange, edgy laugh. "Is that a challenge, Miss Johnson?"

Miss again, was she? "I think a challenge would be redundant, given we are playing against each other." Her voice sounded too high for her comfort.

But really, who *was* this man? He had taken, over the last few days, to dressing formally again: his dark jacket opened over a striped waistcoat, which clung to his flat belly. Kitchen gossip suggested that he was taking five meals a day, and he looked far better for it. The shadows had cleared beneath his eyes, and the hollows beneath his cheekbones were filling in. The stark shape of his jaw had not softened, though. That was simply the architecture of his bones, which a woman would probably call flawless, if she felt inclined to admire him.

She was not admiring him. She simply *observed* the way he lounged, his long legs extended and crossed at the ankles, in a posture that seemed almost like a dare. *Notice me,* it said.

It *was* a dare. For whatever reason, he was animally attracted to her. He wanted her attention.

A flush bloomed over her skin—*all* of her skin; even the backs of her knees felt suddenly too hot. How intoxicating, how appallingly thrilling, to find oneself in an *attraction*—even if utterly, wildly, *abominably* inappropriate.

You idiot, she told herself. *You are going to* steal *from him.*

"Now who is baiting whom?" he asked mildly.

She blinked. "I beg your pardon?"

"I can only assume your intention is to discompose me." He cocked a brow. "Certainly such a fixed stare cannot be considered *encouraging*. Or am I mistaken?"

"F-forgive me," she stammered. "I didn't . . ." She shook her head and turned back to the board. There was no hope; she could not figure out his plan for the game. Casting caution to the wind, she moved her knight forward.

Instantly, he sent out his queen to menace it.

The rapidity of his move boded ill. She moved her forward pawn to protect her knight, then scowled at the board. *What* was he planning?

"There," he said. "You've done it again, Mrs. Johnson."

She looked up. And then wanted to kick herself, for she knew exactly what he meant. Quickly, she nudged her glasses back to their proper place.

"I do wonder . . ." He tilted his head, his eyes narrowing so that crow's-feet fanned into visibility at the corners. She found herself riveted by them, these small, secret signs that he had once been a man given to more serious pastimes than lounging. "Have you worn the glasses very long?"

She struggled to maintain her calm façade. "I cannot imagine how it interests you, Your Grace."

"Oh, you'd be surprised. Curiosity is a great entertainment."

"I am sorry to hear that you're in need of entertainment. Perhaps your boredom might be cured by leaving the house."

"And thereby deprive myself of your sharp tongue?" He gave her a threatening smile. "How might we blunt it? I can think of several possibilities."

She pretended not to have heard this. "Curiosity, of course, is the most dangerous solution for tedium."

"Why, Mrs. Johnson!" He propped his chin atop his fist. "Did you just imply that you were dangerous? Lady Ripton failed to mention that, I fear."

"No need for worry," she said sweetly. "I have just given notice; you may hire someone very staid to replace me."

His laugh offered her a view of his straight white teeth, and the cleft in his chin, normally disguised. "Touché."

She felt herself on the verge of a smile, and instead folded her lips together. They should not be amusing each other. Anyone looking in at this scene, anyone who did not know them, would mistake them for pleasantly bickering lovers.

What a strange thought. She understood now how lovers might be said to quarrel without animosity. It rather took her breath away.

"Ah!" He lifted his brows. And she realized she had reached to adjust her glasses again.

"They have a smudge." She removed them to polish with a handkerchief—and he promptly reached over and plucked them from her hand.

She lunged to her feet. "Give those back!"

Too late: he had held up the lenses to squint through them. Then he looked up at her, his expression amazed.

She sat down rigidly, her heart beating very fast. To wait for his inevitable remark was agonizing. He knew now that she did not require spectacles in order to see; that the lenses, while thick, were in no way corrective.

Silently he held them out to her. Their fingers brushed, and she flinched, for the contact sent a shocking spark along her skin—as though his kiss to her palm had sensitized her, and now she had no defenses.

How humiliating. She set the glasses back onto her nose, feeling sick. He would ask now about them, and there was no explanation she could offer that would not sound ridiculous.

He cleared his throat. She braced herself. But instead of questioning her, he bent over the chessboard, making an intent study of the pieces.

He was giving her a chance to compose herself.

No. She wanted to believe she misunderstood him. But a lump was forming in her throat. Kindness was a very underrated quality. She had vowed once that she would never neglect to appreciate it. Only she had never expected to find it in him . . .

She hid her confusion in a study of her handkerchief, which she folded, end over end, into a tiny, tight square.

He moved his rook. "Check."

She tucked the handkerchief away and made herself sit forward. Her king was menaced. There was an easy way out of this trap, she felt sure of it. But she could not concentrate. What reasons must he be imagining for her disguise? He must think her daft—but what of it? He himself was no model for reasonable behavior.

She shifted her queen to block the rook—realizing, a moment too late, that she had moved that piece into reach of his knight. He would checkmate her in two moves, no help for it.

His hand moved toward the knight—hesitated there for a fractional moment—and then moved onward to his bishop.

"Don't," she burst out.

Their eyes met. Again, that hot shock—as though he had touched her. His eyes were intensely blue. Sapphire was the word. "Don't what?" he asked, but there was something hot and devouring in his gaze, which said far more than his words did. She could not look away. A woman could fall into his eyes. Drown there. She would, gladly.

The thought echoed, panicking her. What was she *doing*? "You know what I mean," she said. "I've lost the game. Don't take pity on me."

Sitting back, he offered her a rueful smile. "As you pitied me during the first half of this match?"

"That wasn't pity." Oh, she did not want to like him! Especially not if his eyes could cast spells on her, and his lips could reduce her to a gibbering ninny. What a perilous combination. "A servant cannot pity her employer." And he was still her employer, no matter that she'd told him to find a replacement for her. He was the *Duke of Marwick*. Her next victim. "It was only good strategy on my part." And avoiding him was good strategy, too. Why had she come inside?

He shrugged. "Once again, you parse diction. But I *will* call it pity, Mrs. Johnson, when a slip of a girl must yield her pawns to salve the pride of a man who once fancied himself a chess master."

Had she heard him right? A slip of a girl? Nobody had ever used that phrase to describe her. It made her sound diminutive, fragile, when she stood almost six feet in her stockings.

She dug her nails into her lap to punish herself. She should not feel flattered by the idea that Marwick viewed her as feminine. He might be kind, very well. He might have gorgeous eyes. But he was not—*could* not—be a man to her. She had no wish to make a fool of herself. Say this spark between them was mutual. It only became an invitation for him to take advantage of her. And then . . . what? She would steal from him regardless.

She made herself give a devil-may-care shrug. "Hardly a slip of a girl. Why, I'm taller than most men."

His arrested look made her realize her mistake. Her remark revealed all too clearly that she had fixated on his description of her. That she cared how he saw her.

Which she didn't.

"True enough," he said. "But since I happen to be taller, I have the luxury of failing to notice that." He smiled again, a slow, openly suggestive smile.

She cast a panicked glance toward the door. That it stood shut had not bothered her before. But now the sight left her breathless.

He followed her glance. "You may open it if you like," he said casually. "But I insist that we finish the game."

"I have duties, Your Grace."

"They can wait." He toyed with one of her captured pawns. His fingers were long but not slender, his hands large, his palms broad: the strong hands of a working-man, misplaced on an aristocrat. Only his nails suggested his privilege, neat and clean. "As you say, it is good strategy to coddle one's employer."

"I never used that word." He wore two rings now: the signet on his pinky, and a gold medallion on his middle finger. "Coddle, I mean." At this rate he'd be bejeweled as an empress by spring.

"I beg your pardon. Then it is good *strategy,* as you would say." He eyed her. The smile playing at the corners of his mouth made him look boyish, mischievous. "You really did miss your calling when you declined to become a governess."

His flirting outclassed hers by far. She stood. *Here ends the lesson.* "Regardless, I am a housekeeper. And there are several items remaining on my—"

"And there's the starch." He leaned back, linking his hands together behind his head as he surveyed her. "You carry it off very well. Once you have a few lines in your face, a bit of gray in your hair, you'll be fearsome indeed. Small children will flee, and all the housemaids will scrape and cringe."

Something trembled inside her. She knew she had a starchy aspect. Did he imagine she was glad of it? She had no desire to be a Medusa. "Don't mock me."

"Oh, I don't," he said softly. "But the glasses do give you away, Mrs. Johnson."

She hesitated, riven by twin impulses: the burning desire to know what he meant, and the fear of what he might say. That he might somehow say something true.

What a terrible thing it was to wish to be known, to be *seen,* when one's life depended on remaining unnoticed.

He could not know her. A man of his station lacked the insight—and she could never permit it anyway. Nobody could know her until she was safe. She gathered up her skirts. "I must go."

"You don't wish to hear my theory?"

A flash of anger made her turn back. When had *he* ever known the kind of vulnerability a woman must suffer, when left on her own to face the world? How could he know that a woman might seek any strategy to render herself ineligible, invisible? "I am sure it will be very *entertaining,*" she said. She was, after all, a curiosity to him, was she not? A cure for his boredom, that was all.

"I don't know about that," he said gently—yes; to her amazement, there was no other way to describe his tone. "You're a woman who has made her own way from a tender age. Unusually tall, conspicuously redheaded, very young, quite intelligent, and driven from your last position by a man who took unwanted note of you." He tipped his head. "Mrs. Johnson, I would guess there is only one reason for you to wear those glasses."

"And what is that?" she whispered.

"You wear them to hide." He gave her a wry half smile. "Alas that we don't all have the luxury of a townhome in which to closet ourselves. But you are welcome here to play chess any time you wish. You are, after all, far better at it than you wanted me to know. But to my credit . . . I'd rather suspected you would be."

She gaped at him. The force of her reaction overwhelmed her: distress, shock, embarrassment, *gratitude.* For he was right. She was so much more than she permitted others to see. Yet he had seen it anyway. And imagine what it would be like—what it would mean—if his remark was an offer of true friendship. For with a man like him to aid her . . .

Why, he was one of the few men in the world with no cause to fear Bertram. Quite the opposite: Bertram should rightfully fear *him.*

But what madness! She meant to deceive him. She already *was* deceiving him. She could not bear to think his offer was genuine—that his sympathy might be more than a passing lark. For what would that make *her*?

The outright villain of this piece. *Again,* the villain.

"I must go," she said, choked.

He nodded. "Go, then."

Only after she had shut the door did she realize, with a pang, the strangeness of their final exchange: she had not been asking his permission, but telling him what she must do. And he had not *given* permission. Instead, in a very small way, he had ceded her the authority.

CHAPTER TEN

Moonlight filtered through the crack in the curtains, bringing Alastair's half-written letter to his brother into stark clarity:

> *My behavior was abominable. I would put it down to madness, but that smacks too much of excuses. I would offer my most abject apology, but that would imply that your forgiveness is possible. Believe me, though, when I say that I wish all the happiness in the world to you and your wife. And if I could undo only one thing, it would be my*

Alastair laid down the pen. He could not write a lie. If he could undo only one thing, it would not be his behavior toward Michael. The memory shamed him deeply, but the whole episode, his insistence that Michael marry to his choosing, and Michael's enraged rebellion—all of it seemed only a piece of the larger nightmare.

If he could undo anything, it would be his marriage.

Why had he wanted Margaret? Had he really imagined ambition would bind them? He had wanted a beautiful hostess of impeccable breeding on his arm. She had wanted a salve for her wounded pride. But while they had dreamed together of the empire they might build, they had never dreamed of each other.

I never would have married you. So she had told him shortly after their first anniversary. *Had you told me the whole of it, I never would have accepted you. And you knew it.*

He had imagined that she would overcome her anger. She would come to see that he hadn't deceived her, not really. He would make a far better husband than Fellowes could have done. She would realize this in time.

And in time, she had seemed to forgive him. He'd considered the matter finished.

Obviously she had not.

He walked to the window and pulled open the curtains. What had his housekeeper once told him? If the atmosphere was gloomy, one's mood followed suit. Very true. But on this night a harvest moon, low and golden, gilded Mayfair's rooftops, lulling him.

He remembered a similar moon. A spring night at St. Paul's Cathedral, and himself drunk on a narrow victory in the Commons, a margin of fourteen votes. His father had still lived, then. He himself had been a mere MP, the entire future before him. He'd sprinted up the cramped stairs to the gallery high above, so high that the air was colder, the wind scouring. London sprawled beneath his feet, the ancient river and manicured squares, the dark maws of the parks, the distant slums lit by scattered fires.

He had never liked heights, but that night, he'd not

been dizzy. The city had seemed like a private omen, a sacred charge upon him. He would protect and serve this place. He would spend his life striving to improve it. Here was his calling.

He wanted that back. All of it. His youth, the ferocity of his convictions. A time before all the mistakes. Somewhere out there tonight his brother lay sleeping, a stranger to him. Could that be undone? In one of their last conversations, Michael had accused him of giving up, of letting Margaret win. But he'd not spoken in anger. He'd seemed only . . . astonished.

It was true, Alastair supposed, that he had never been the weak one. From his earliest memories, his role had been to protect. *You are the heir.* Again and again, this message had been driven into him. *Protect the family; do honor to your name.* Even at a young age, he had taken his duty very seriously. Too seriously, perhaps, for a child. To see others suffer had caused him the sharpest anxiety—the sense of having failed, somehow, to prevent it.

Chicks fallen from nests. Cats trapped in trees. The village idiot in Hasborotown, where his family had wintered. The local children had liked to pelt the man with stones. At eight, Alastair had taken them on, and won a blackened eye and chipped tooth before Nurse and Coachman had intervened.

At home, this protective urge had proved all the fiercer. What had he been to Michael? Never merely a brother. How much simpler that would have been. Perhaps had they only been brothers, Michael would have found it in his heart to forgive Alastair for the madness of last spring. Brothers quarreled—and then they forgave each other. That was the natural way of it.

But Michael had never viewed him with the casual regard of a sibling. How could he? Alastair's earliest memory was of Michael's head tucked into the lee of his arm, Michael's tears soaking his shirtfront. It had never been their mother to whom Michael ran for comfort—even if he spoke of her now as though she'd been a saint. She had been too busy waging combat against their father to coddle her sons.

No wonder Michael loathed him. To be failed by a brother was one thing. To be failed by one whom you counted a hero—well, that was a bitter thing indeed.

Almost as bitter as being failed by yourself.

He knew he would not be able to sleep now. The view could no longer soothe him. He left his room, walking swiftly down the stairs, past the snoring night porter, for the distractions of the library.

Inside, a single lamp was burning. Its dim light illuminated—he felt a strong premonition, a sense of inevitability—his housekeeper curled up on the sofa, a billowing white dressing gown bunched over her feet. As she pored over a book, she tickled her mouth with the ends of her long red plait.

He stood there a moment, gripped by conflicting urges. A housekeeper should not be making use of her master's library. She should not wander barefooted in her nightclothes. She should not look so young, so untouched, so solid despite her slimness, so composed despite her undress.

He had invited this temerity, of course. Hell, he had hoped for it. If he could have stolen her self-sufficiency, her fierce sense of direction, by laying his hands on her, he would have done it in a moment. He had never felt more of an ass than when viewing himself through her eyes—the eyes of a woman who had been turned out upon the world at the tender age of seventeen, and had *made do.*

Was he really less courageous than a would-be maid?

"Good evening," he said.

She flinched violently, then snapped the book shut and yanked her gown over her toes. "Goodness," she said. "I didn't think . . ."

When she rose, the light was strong enough, or the robe thin enough, or his appetites imaginative enough, to discern the contours of her body: the slimness of her waist; the curve of her hips; the fecund thickness of her thighs, which tapered neatly into square knees and rounded calves.

He did not admire her simply for her courage.

She took a step toward him—or rather, toward the door. She intended to leave. She felt the way his gaze devoured her. She knew where his interests lay.

He should let her go. But she had started this, somehow. Until she had opened the curtains and disrupted his solitude, he had been content to stay lost. Did he blame her for it? Or was this anger a product of indebtedness? He had never wanted to owe anyone anything.

"What are you doing here?" he said.

She came to a stop just out of reach. Very wise. She had called herself tall, as though it was a mere matter of height, rather than abundance. So many more inches to her, so much more skin, white, smooth. He'd learned Margaret too easily, and never learned her at all. He would not make that mistake again. The next time, he would not leave the bed until he had mastered the woman in it. He would learn that trick, no matter how much study it took.

"I couldn't sleep," she said. Her voice sounded strange, unusually rough.

He reached for the light. For months, he had lacked any clear sense of his own motives. But clarity was coming back to him, bit by bit. If he decided to keep the lights low now, it was simply to blur this scene, and what he intended to do here.

The dim, rising glow showed tears on her face.

He felt disoriented, as though the room had swum around him. Crying? Why? "Are you well?"

She dashed her wrist across her eyes, a furtive and embarrassed gesture. "Yes. Of course. Forgive me—I shouldn't have come in here." She glanced beyond him. By the way she shifted her weight, he knew that she was contemplating a dash for the door.

He should let her go. He did not like the sight of her upset. It squared with nothing he knew of her. But her distress should not concern him. He would let her go.

"Take a seat," he said instead.

She obeyed with obvious reluctance, choosing the wing chair nearest the door. He picked up the book she'd abandoned on the sofa. *The Tale of the Midnight Voyager,* he read from the spine.

She grimaced. "A piece of rubbish. It—" And then she appeared to recall whose library this was, and reddened.

"Would you like another?" He browsed the shelf. Augustine seemed too weighty, though the saint's prayer held a sudden interest for him: *Grant me chastity, O God, but not yet.* "Austen, perhaps?" Always a favorite with the ladies.

Her reply was hesitant. "Oh, I . . . didn't see her books there. Yes, please."

He pulled out two titles and offered her the choice. She took *Pride and Prejudice* and then sat staring at the cover, an air of bewilderment about her, as if she did not know what to do with it.

He carried the other volume to the sofa, opening it pointedly. "Do read, Mrs. Johnson," he said.

No one who had ever seen Catherine Morland in her infancy would have supposed her born to be an heroine. Her situation in life, the character of her father and mother, her own person and disposition, were all equally against her . . .

At last, he heard the whisper of a turned page. Leather creaked as she settled into the chair.

He eased back against his own cushions. It was a forgotten luxury to share the silence with someone. He could hear, if he listened for it, the soft rhythm of her breathing. The small noises, the whisper of cotton, as she shifted again.

"You're really going to read *Northanger Abbey*?"

He glanced up, found her gawking. "That surprises you?"

She went pink. "No, of course not." Then she shut her book and rose. The flutter of her robe provided a brief glimpse of her ankles, sufficient to burn them into his mind completely. They looked all the better without stockings: trim, pale as snow. "If I may borrow this—"

"Or you may read it here," he said. "Unless you fear an impropriety."

She bit her lip. Looked between chair and door. "Should I fear it?"

He smiled. A fair question, but her boldness never failed to surprise him. "Not tonight." Not when she'd been crying.

Hesitantly she sat again. He did not miss the way she ran a quick, furtive hand over her hem, to make sure no hint of ankle remained visible. What a pity. If one must have a young housekeeper, let her be reckless with her hemlines.

"I suppose Miss Austen is not typical masculine fare," he said. "I'll confess I probably would have chosen a different book for manlier company. Something in Latin."

She fought against her smile and lost. "How fortunate for you that I'm not manly."

"My thought precisely."

Her smile faded. She looked down to her book.

He had an inkling of his own villainy then—a flash, as from the headlamp of a passing train, briefly illuminating his motives. Her tears did not matter, after all.

Where was the regret, the revulsion, which that thought should inspire? He could not locate it. She sat not five feet away, her flush creeping steadily down her throat, soon to stain the smooth wings of her collarbones. The robe bared tantalizing inches of her throat and chest that wool normally disguised, alabaster, so pale that he could see the delicate tracery of veins that surely must slip farther down, beneath the neckline of her robe, all the way to her breast. To her nipples. God, but he would taste them.

She cleared her throat. "What do you like about her novels?" Her question sounded stiff, full of forced courtesy. She had noticed his stare, and meant to draw his attention back to more proper pursuits.

"The world she paints." He watched her thumb fret with a corner of her book, rubbing back and forth over the sharp point. He had no inkling what troubled her. It disturbed him. He had the outlines of her, and a sense of her inner mettle. But the details? Her childhood. Her origins. These large gaps in his knowledge suddenly felt wrong, strange, demanding of redress.

"What do you mean, the world?" she asked.

"The portraits of families. How well she paints them."

Her thumb fell still. "They're quite quarrelsome, on the whole."

"Yes." That was exactly what he liked about them. "Messy, sprawling, imperfect. But they love each other regardless." He felt briefly surprised by himself, by this sentimental claptrap he was spouting. But she was watching him expectantly, so he shrugged and went on. "Even the loathsome sorts, like"—he nodded toward the book in her lap—"what is her name? The insufferable one, who runs off."

"Lydia."

"Lydia," he agreed. His housekeeper's half smile put him in mind of a Greek icon—a Sybil, perhaps. He could see her dispensing wisdom from some sacred cave, her long, pale face a light in the darkness, her round, deep eyes bracing a man for solemn predictions. Her hair was the color of copper, sacred metal; men would have made amulets from it in ancient times.

Bizarre, fanciful thought. Frowning at himself, he turned back to his book.

She spoke, hushed and hesitant. "I longed for such a family as a girl."

He stared at the page. Late nights, sleepless nights, made some conversations too easy to have, and some thoughts too easy to entertain. But he did not want her friendship. He should not want her confidences.

Yet he replied. "As did I." His family's unhappy history was hardly a secret. "A larger family, perhaps. Or a warmer one." Growing up in an echoing house where his parents rarely exchanged two civil words, he had recognized nothing of Austen's domestic scenes. But even as a child, he'd felt them far superior to his own experience.

Her chair creaked. "It was siblings I wanted. I think it would have made a difference."

"I have a brother. But a larger family . . ." He hesitated. Imagine it: he not the eldest, not the heir. Someone else to rely upon. "I would have liked that."

"Perhaps you will create one. Have a dozen children of your own."

"No." The denial was hard and instinctive. Children would require marriage. Marriage would require that he trust his own judgment, which had been exposed as profoundly and irreparably corrupt. Never again. It was Michael's job now to carry on the family line. He looked at her. "I will have no children."

"Oh." She turned the book around in her hands, a nervous fiddling gesture. "Well. Nor will I, I expect."

What nonsense was this? "You're still very young, Mrs. . . ." She was no missus, of course. "What is your Christian name?" The reference must have mentioned it, but he could not recall.

She blinked at him. "Olivia."

It had a musical ring. A slight bite on the *V.* A name that encouraged one to take one's lip in one's teeth. *Olivia.* It suited her perfectly.

"Olivia," he said. "Why should you think you won't have a family?"

She met his eyes. "First I must have a home."

For a brief, clear moment, he felt the stirring of his old skill, the ability to look at an opponent and divine his secret ambitions. Here was hers: a place of her own.

Or perhaps he recognized it because it had once been his ambition, as well. Oh, he'd known he would inherit houses to spare; but what he'd wanted was a *place*, distinct from his family's legacy, wholly his own.

He did not think she meant a house, either. Otherwise, would not a girl such as this—clever, bold, enterprising—have found a husband for herself, in whatever bucolic little village had spawned her?

"Where are you from?" He had asked her that before. But now, in this strange hush, he knew he would have the answer.

It gladdened him to a strange degree that she did not hesitate before replying. "East Kent. My mother's family lives on the coast, in a village called Shepwich, near Broadstairs."

"A beautiful part of England." He could envision her walking the seashore, the salt breeze lifting strands of her hair, her skin opalescent in the cool gray light. "Is that where you dream of your home?"

Her lashes dropped, veiling her eyes. She ran a finger down the page of her book. "I don't know that I dream of a specific place."

He'd been right. "What, then?"

She shrugged. "I suppose I want somewhere to . . . belong. To feel safe," she said softly.

He considered her. It made sense that a girl forced to do for herself would long for stability, rootedness. Why had she not taken the quickest route to it? "Many women leave service for marriage."

She looked up, meeting his eyes. "And many men remarry. What of it?"

He sucked in a breath. "Well. That was bold of you." Why was he surprised?

Color came into her face. "It's half past three. I am sitting in dishabille with my employer. Etiquette does not address such situations."

"Touché. Let me be equally blunt. You were weeping before. Why?"

Her jaw assumed a granite cast. "Surely a servant must be allowed some degree of privacy."

He snorted. "I have never noticed you nursing a high regard for that concept. Indeed, given that I found you in my *private* library, our definitions of it seem to differ."

Her brows flew up. "Given that you rarely leave your rooms, I could not have foreseen that I might interrupt you here!"

He rose, powered by a welter of emotions—chief among them amazement. "I think marriage might be the best thing for you. God knows you aren't cut out for service. Had you been born a man, I would have recommended you to the bar."

She gave him a look rife with disbelief, one that required no verbal translation: *now* he would judge her? "Your Grace—"

"Did one of the staff molest you? Is something awry below?"

She came to her feet. "I am well able to manage the staff. Nor would I weep over such passing trifles as disobedience from a servant!"

"Then what—"

"I will tell you if you answer me one question," she said flatly.

It was no longer clear to him who was in control of

this conversation. How absurd. He was not bound by her terms; in return for her answer, she could demand the moon, and it would make no difference to him. "Very well, then, answer me: why were you crying?"

"Because I am not the person I hoped to be. And I dislike myself for it."

That told him nothing. "What do you mean? Who had you hoped to be?"

"Someone better. Someone who abided by her ideals."

Christ. Blackly amused, he turned away from her toward the bookshelves. "Then we both were drawn here by the same mood. But I assure you, Mrs. Johnson, you will overcome your disappointment."

"As you have?"

He ignored that. "Good night to you."

"You haven't yet answered my question."

"Welshing," he said coldly, "is the duke's special privilege."

"Very well, don't answer. But I will ask it anyway: why do you read Austen if you lack all hope for yourself? Why torment yourself with happy endings if you don't believe one is possible?"

He stared at the books. This had gone too far. Why did she think she had the right to speak to him in this manner?

Why did he constantly invite it?

"You have every advantage." Her voice was fervent. "There is no reason you can't go back into the world, have everything you feel you've been denied. I tell you—if I had your advantages, I would *remake* myself!"

The taunt in her voice speared him like a hook into his chest. Yes, she probably goddamned well *would* remake herself. She had no notions of respect, of boundaries, of her own place. She had no idea of limitations. He looked over his shoulder to sneer, to deliver her the acidic set-down she so badly needed.

But the sight of her robbed him of words. She stood with the novel hugged to her chest, a tall, long-waisted girl with coloring like the autumn, hair as red as turning leaves, and there was no taunt in her face. Her expression, rather, was pale, resolute, *hopeful.* Daring him to be as brave as she was. She was constantly daring him, as though it were not the most galling, impudent, *presumptuous* business—

"Can you imagine," he said, and did not recognize his own voice, the animal viciousness in it. "Is it possible you have lived long enough, hard enough, to guess—that I would devour you in a bite, I would use you, discard you, if it meant I could experience, for a *single* moment, that idiotic naïveté in your face? A fool's bliss: that is what it is, *Olivia.* And life will break you of it. And I would break you of it, right here, if I could have it back for myself, for only a moment, God help me. Your stupid faith in something better."

Her lips parted. He had shocked her. *Good.* She believed in happy endings. She thought fairy tales had some *connection* to reality. He wanted to do more than shock her.

He realized he'd stepped toward her when she leapt back. He made himself halt. Fisted his hands at his sides. This leaping, flaming need that wracked him so suddenly was not lust: it was far darker, a more ravaging consumption. His nails bit into his palms.

But hope was a drug, was it not? And yes, he was a fiend in withdrawal. No drug would ever feel more exotic to him, or cause him to shake harder for the want of it, than hope. What a false and desperate appetite. Else why would the poor squander their coin on lotteries, and rally to the rumors of tears appearing on the cheeks of wooden idols? How did they profit from such delusions?

But if he tasted her, he might have a moment's fix. He might.

"A good thing Jones is seeking out a replacement." His voice came out as a growl. He did not believe in fairy tales. He was not going to ravish this naïf. To *hell* with her. "You will not find a happy ending in this house, I promise you."

"Nor will you," she breathed.

"You are baiting the wrong man, little girl."

"Will you never go out again?"

He lunged at her. She remained stock-still, staring up at him, wide-eyed, unflinching. It infuriated him. "Do you fancy yourself a *do-gooder*?" The words tore from him in venomous chunks. "Have you conceived, somehow, that you might *help* me?"

"No," she whispered. "Or—I don't know; I only mean to say that you—"

"You are my *servant*. You do understand that, Mrs. Johnson? It is possible I will not give you a reference. You are insolent and unmindful of your station; in good conscience, I could not recommend you."

Her expression darkened. He wondered why he had wanted so much to put a shadow in it. Thc look did not suit her better than hope.

"That is unfair," she said flatly. "And you are not an unfair man."

"Am I not?" His laughter burned his throat. "Are you *really* such a fool?"

"No. I am not." Her shoulders squared. God damn her, she was rallying; that bloody light was entering her face again. "Even at your darkest, you did nobody evil. And at your best, the good you did the poor, the—the authority with which you guided your party, and the *nation* no less, through troubled times—and the noble example of your statecraft—you could have all that again, and I don't understand—"

He grabbed her by the shoulders. Slammed his mouth onto hers. He drank her gasp of surprise and bit her soft lower lip, though some shred of sanity kept him from drawing blood. He wanted her to squeak, and she did.

She tried to break free. His grip on her arms tightened; he was hurting her, yes. *Here is reality.* No sugarcoating it, no romanticizing it: *there is no one to protect you.* He licked into her mouth and tasted her tongue. She had recently drunk tea, sugared, and she smelled like roses, always roses—

Her fingers threaded through his hair. Her lips, her mouth, moved beneath his. She was . . . kissing him back.

Had she caught fire, he could not have been more bewildered. He did not deserve this kiss. His grip went slack.

She stepped into him. The tight, hot grasp of her hands fell from his hair to his nape, to the breadth of his shoulders. She kissed clumsily, with the same blunt, aggravating enthusiasm, the same desperate fumbling hope, that he had wanted to punish with this lesson: this lesson in disappointment.

But this did not feel like disappointment. She was warm and impossibly, miraculously tall. The angles and swells of her body matched perfectly to his, her breasts crushing into his chest, her waist—his baffled hand fell there—sweetly curved. She smelled like the garden in summer; she kissed his neck and her hair came into his nose, flowers and greenery, fresh and young.

He took her by the waist and slammed her into the bookshelves. "Fine," he snarled into her mouth. "Take it, then." He was so good? "Then take it."

"Yes," she whispered back.

Yes? He understood nothing of her. He was furious with her, at how she would let herself be used, and by what kind of man. He shoved his hand into her hair, his fingers ripping through her plait, and yanked her head back to expose the tender length of her throat. She let him do it. She was an idiot to let him do it; to let him rake his teeth down this vulnerable stretch of skin.

She shuddered against him. She moaned.

He reached down, grabbed the thin lawn of her robe, hauled it up. Her calf was hot, impossibly soft; he massaged the muscle there, sliding his palm up to the tender space behind her knee, damp, secret; and then to the curve of her inner thigh, pliant, giving, a sweet surrender. She squirmed against him. Resistance? "Too late," he growled.

Ah, God, she yielded; her thigh sagged in compliance, then hitched higher, brushing over his hip. He grabbed her ankle, set her bare foot on his thigh, and cupped her quim in his palm, pressing firmly.

She cried out. "Yes," he said through his teeth. He could feel the plumpness of her lips through her drawers, the dampness of her. The sensation made it feel difficult to breathe; he groped for the slit in the undergarment and then hissed out a breath when he found the heart of her, slippery, her lips so easily parted.

She turned her face into his throat, and he gripped her head to hold her there as he laid his finger atop the throbbing bud at the top of her vulva. He pressed, rotated, and she stiffened, throwing her head back hard against the spines of books.

He met her eyes, his thumb still pressing, teasing that place at the apex of her quim. Her hair was coming down, a wild fiery halo around her pale, pale face. Her lips parted, trembling; he leaned forward and licked them. "Am I still a good man?"

Her mouth formed a single syllable. She tried twice to speak it. "Yes," she whispered.

"No." Did she not learn? He felt for her opening, eased a single finger inside her, biting back an animal sound as she closed around him, as a sob ripped from her, breathy, nearly a moan. She was tight; she tightened further as he probed more deeply. She put the back of her hand to her mouth. "Do you feel me?" he asked.

Wide-eyed she stared at him over her palm.

"Say it." He meant to speak sharply, but his voice was slowing, growing languorous. God, the feel of her . . . "Do you know what I want with this part of you?" He made himself use the filthiest word. "Your cunt. Do you know what I wish to do with your cunt?"

She swallowed. "I . . ."

"I want to fuck you," he said. "With my cock—and all my fingers, and my tongue. Go deep inside you, every inch of you, Olivia. I want to use you up. I will make you scream, and beg me to stop, and then I will bend you over and fuck you again. This is where hope leads you: do you understand? It leads you to ruin, and

I will enjoy it. I will ruin you for pleasure, and I will make you come for me, and hate yourself in the end for doing so."

She took a ragged breath. "I—you are not—you want to be so much worse than you are!"

"Worse?" He fluttered his thumb over her clitoris, and she gasped. "Watch me," he said. He dropped to his knees, and gripped her hips as she began to slump; he pinned her in place against the bookcase as he lifted her hem, parted her folds to expose her, and laid his tongue to her. He licked her in full.

The taste of her . . .

She cried out. Dimly, he heard it. But suddenly, he was only here, in the darkness, caught in his own trap, drunk all at once on the taste of her. She tasted like . . . the ocean, everything female; fecundity, life, creation; salt and copper, he thought his cock would burst. The dam broke and his hunger roared up through him, taking possession. He forgot his aim, forgot everything but this need, only this: to taste her more deeply, to paint his tongue and his lips with the scent of her.

He sucked her clitoris until her hips bucked, but it was not enough. He was an animal, yes, too long denied; he pushed his tongue into her then, as deep as it would reach; he had promised he would do it, but now it was only for himself. *Take it,* he thought.

She twisted beneath him. "Oh—oh—oh!"

She came against his lips, throbs that he could feel, her whimpering breaths igniting parts of him, base and all-consuming desires that he had not felt before. He had not known.

It was that, in the end, that made him draw back. That which kept him from opening his fly, and finishing what he had started. For suddenly, as he held her in place, as he watched her recover her senses, he realized he did not know what he had begun, here.

This was like nothing in his experience.

She was nothing like Margaret.

Margaret had never made him feel like a ravening beast.

Margaret had never made a noise.

His thoughts doused his ardor like ice water. He slowly stepped away from her, prepared to catch her if she fell. But she straightened off the bookcase. She met his eyes. She held them, when any other woman would have looked away.

It was he who turned away from her then. He who did not know where to look.

The thought gave him an odd panic. He made himself pivot back toward her. She was leaning against the bookcase, watching him, her lips parted, her face flushed, her braid unraveling over her shoulder. He had a vivid flash of what she would look like with that braid unbound, strands of fire falling across her bare white breasts, gazing up at him from his bed with this same startled revelation in her eyes.

When she reached up to touch her lips, her hand visibly trembled.

Jesus Christ.

He wanted to yell at her. The words were like solid chunks in his throat, making it impossible to swallow. *Have you no care? No sense?*

He would have liked to punch the bookcase—he deserved the pain. But she stood against it, and that would frighten her.

How was she not frightened already? From their first

meeting, when he had thrown the bottle—how had he not managed to frighten her yet?

"You are not fit for service," he said.

She blinked as though puzzled. As though he might have said anything else: as though he could have thought of anything to say in that moment that would make sense.

Only this made sense, a cheating and low kind of sense: he was the Duke of Marwick, and she, a domestic. Whatever that made him—a swine, a cad, his father's son—so be it. He retreated into the role, away from the intolerable confusion.

"Leave service," he snarled. "Find a husband. Make a hash of your own home instead of meddling in others'."

Now, at long last, she looked away. A bright flush crawled up her cheeks. Her reply was barely audible. "That would be a happy ending, indeed."

He recoiled. And then made himself laugh, though the sound burned his throat. "And now I know you're a fool. Good night to you, Mrs. Johnson."

It was his library. But she remained behind as he shut the door on the sight of her, alone and straight-spined by the bookcase.

CHAPTER ELEVEN

The hour before dawn was always the quietest. Olivia slipped back into her small room and lay down, pretending to herself that she would be able to sleep.

Instead, she listened to the sound of her heart. That it should beat so steadily seemed impossible to her, as though nothing had changed tonight, as though *she* had not changed. As though whatever had happened might have faded, leaving no physical effect.

She knew there was nothing so rare or complimentary in what had just transpired in the library. A master seducing his servant—it was a tale so old that it had become a cliché. And so, too, was its corollary: the servant welcoming his attentions. Feeling his touch like a miracle. Hungering and praying for more.

She stared hard at the pictures on the wall, seeing them in her mind's eye though the darkness kept them shrouded. In the village tableau, a couple strolled the lane: a wife who wore her collar buttoned to her throat, and a husband, plump and florid, who would inspire no heated dreams in any woman. There was a message in the picture: what a far distance lay between decency and desire.

Decency held no moral weight for her. Her mother, after all, had taken up with a man knowing he would never marry her. That did not make Mama a bad person. She had lived gently and with grace, and Olivia had no doubt she rested now in God's arms.

But while she did not count decency a virtue, it was the safer route by far. All her plans centered on it. She was not some foolish girl who dreamed of love. What she wanted was something real, something durable: a home in a little village where people would know her name and nod to her in the street. These were the things her mother had never had. The local gentry had not acknowledged Mama. The merchants and postmaster had taken her money politely, but they had never smiled at her.

Olivia aimed for such a place, where she would be known, and welcomed, and smiled upon. But her longings . . .

She slipped her hand beneath the loose sleeve of her nightgown and ran her fingers up her arm, testing herself. The gooseflesh rose again, for in her mind it was Marwick's hand that stroked her.

He had shattered her tonight. And he'd been right to warn that she would like it. *Like* it? What a pallid word for what he'd made her feel! And how easy it was, in the darkness, to touch herself and pretend it was his touch, and feel the shivers build anew . . .

Was she tuned to him now, like a violin refashioned for one player? She could believe it. *The Duke of Marwick*: like a planet, he exerted his own field of gravity. He had shaped politics, molded the nation. Why should he not reshape her, too?

She made a fist. Replaced her hand at her side and stared up, dry-eyed. The ceiling had a single crack in it, which she could not quite see in the darkness, but she could sense. Likewise, she could sense the crack deep within her.

The longer she stayed here, the wider and deeper that crack became. He was kind and then cruel, blind and then unnervingly insightful, offensive and then, without a moment's warning, so gentle that her heart could break. He had been a great man once, and he would be so again—she did not doubt that, even if he did. His intellect was too sharp, his restlessness too strong, to submit to this self-made prison forever.

He had been wronged. She knew the full extent of it—which itself was a cause for shame. He had known too much deceit already, and he did not deserve any more of it. He would never forgive her for deceiving him. But trickery was all she had to give. He thought himself the danger to *her*? She meant to betray a man who had already been horribly deceived. And she would not be able to forgive herself for it, any more than he would.

But if she walked away empty-handed, what then? Eventually he would step back into the world, which would be waiting for him, glad to rearrange itself to orbit around him once more. And she? She was no planet. She was a speck of dust. The world would not even notice her. She would be blown onward, never able to settle in her village. For all it would take was a single visit from Bertram for the townspeople to cease nodding to her, cease smiling.

* * *

The next morning when Olivia woke, she was certain she was falling ill. Her head felt stuffed with wool, and her eyes ached. She breakfasted in her rooms, and would gladly have stayed there the rest of the day, avoiding the duke like a coward—but with only her thoughts for company, the prospect quickly grew intolerable.

She decided to check on the maids' rounds of the public rooms. In the formal drawing room, she found Muriel beating the curtains while Polly held a vase up, by one hand, to dust.

"Careful!" she cried—and then came forward to rescue the vase from Polly's awkward grip. "I'll do this. Give me the cloth—you see to the rest of it."

She pretended not to see the mystified look the girls exchanged. It felt good to be occupied, busy with something other than her thoughts. The vase was fashioned of turquoise enamel, delicate birds fluttering within compartments delineated by silver wire. No doubt it was priceless. Probably nobody had admired it in months.

She ran her cloth around the vase's mouth. She had never coveted treasures, but it came to her that there might be a peculiar reassurance in owning priceless things. If you left treasures behind, people would always notice you had gone. They would wonder where you were, simply because they wouldn't understand how you had brought yourself to abandon so much.

Somebody screamed. She turned to discover a bird fluttering over the sofa; it must have slipped through the window Muriel had opened to wash.

Polly stepped forward, thrusting her broom like a jousting lance. The bird winged upward. It collided with the ceiling and reeled drunkenly along the wall.

Muriel screamed again. "Oh, get it, get it!"

"I'm trying," Polly snapped.

"Stop it." Olivia snatched up a sheet that protected the furniture when in disuse. "Let it settle."

"It shouldn't have come in," Muriel wailed.

The bird veered abruptly toward a window—the wrong one. It smashed into the glass and dropped to the carpet.

"It's dead," said Polly. "It killed itself!"

"Hush." Olivia dropped the sheet over it, then gently felt for the small body. Its warmth startled her. She scooped it up, then brought the edges of the sheets together to make a kind of sack, in which she carried it to the door. "I'll take it to the garden."

"Its neck is broken," Polly called as she left.

She walked quickly, not understanding her sudden anger. But surely even a bird deserved a better end than to die in this house.

In the garden, she laid her burden on the grass and carefully unwrapped the sheet. The bird lay there, stunned, twitching. Maybe Polly was right, and these were the death throes.

She sensed that if the bird did die, she would feel angrier yet; that her temper might become explosive, and she would look for a way to take it out on someone who didn't deserve it. Like Polly, who thought it perfectly suitable to bash at a panicked creature with her broom.

And why shouldn't Polly think so? It was only a bird. It was not a man.

She straightened, appalled by herself. Was she so stupid, so deranged, that she now likened the Duke of Marwick to a hapless bird? He did not need her protection. If he was trapped, then the cage was of his own making.

"Go," she whispered to the bird. "You're free."

Who else could say that in this house?

A latch clicked. Marwick stood in the doorway, his face expressionless. "I would like to speak with you."

She had been anticipating, dreading, this moment all morning. Now it was on her, she found her anger had a purpose after all. It rose between them like a stone wall, rendering her indifferent to his order, to the calm authority with which he said, "Come inside."

"In a minute." She focused on the bird.

"Now, Mrs. Johnson."

Alas that he could not enforce his will by coming to get her. That would require leaving the house, which he could not do—not even to step into his own garden. How unfortunate for him that she was occupied.

She knelt by the bird. It was not pretty—a wren, plain and brown, small enough to cup in her palm. But its eyes were open now, shining black beads that darted about wildly. "Hello," she whispered. "Get up."

"Olivia," he said quietly.

The sound of her name on his lips ran through her like a hot jolt. But she refused to look up. Let him wait all day. He considered himself a very bad man, after all, and didn't bad men tend to skulk? Let him skulk in the doorway to his heart's content.

She stroked the bird's tummy, very gently, with her forefinger. The bird fell still. A mistake? Had she killed it?

"Leave it be," Marwick said. "It's frightened."

It being an unusually mild day for December, perhaps she would find other things that required her attentions outdoors. Perhaps such distractions would keep her busy for the rest of the day.

The bird's wings twitched, then flapped once, twice. It could not turn itself over to regain its footing. Holding her breath, Olivia slid her hands beneath it. Sharp little claws briefly scrabbled across her palms. Then the bird froze again.

"It's playing dead."

"Are you an ornithologist?" Her voice was tart. "If so, come lend a hand. Otherwise, be silent."

His soft laugh startled her. But she did not let herself look. "Fly," she said softly, and lifted the bird toward the clouded sky. But the bird cowered into itself.

"Or perhaps it's mortally wounded," said the duke.

"Fly," she said more sharply, and lifted her cupped palms again, with more energy.

The bird did not move.

"It's dead." He spoke with an edge now. "Put it down."

"Fly!" She threw up her hands and the bird exploded into flight, plummeting once before catching the way of it and winging rapidly over the high stone wall.

Gone. She looked for it and could find no sign. "It wasn't dead."

Silence from the doorway. She turned and found him watching her, something strange in his face, which made her chest ache. How beautiful he was. How terribly misguided. What did he see when he looked in the mirror? She saw him as a fallen angel. Did he not realize angels had the choice to rise?

"Yes," he said. "Not dead. You were right."

He stepped out the door.

She goggled. Was he really going to—

Yes. He walked toward her, and she gasped and clapped her hands together—and then wished that she hadn't, for it caused him to smile blackly, and lift his palms in a gesture that said *Behold*.

"Amazing, isn't it?" He approached, tall and lean, broad-shouldered, *outside*. "One would never guess I'd just left leading strings."

"Don't joke," she whispered. In the natural light, moving with animal grace, he looked the very last thing from a child.

"Oh, believe me, I'm not." He came to a stop, glanced around, and drew a long, audible breath. His long lashes dropped. He studied the ground beneath his feet, his full lips twisting as he scuffed the dirt with his boot. "Quite dead," he murmured.

She positioned herself between him and the doorway, determined to prevent any attempt at retreat. "The bird? Oh, the garden, do you mean?" For he was staring around at the brown grass. And he was *outside*. She barely knew how to speak for the waves of shock coming over her. He looked so much younger, suddenly, as though the house had been a weight on him, and now, at last, he could stand at his full height, liberated, strong and lean. "It's not entirely dead," she said. "There are several perennials planted hereabouts—"

He smiled faintly at her. "Don't give me any nonsense about the coming spring."

A strange sound slipped from her, something between a laugh and a sob. He sounded so well. He was not going to bowl past her for the house. "I won't."

He closed his eyes and tipped his head back, as though to show his face to the sky. His hair gleamed pale in the light, flaxen, shining. She drank in the sight of him, noting every line on his face revealed by the light: the crow's-feet around his eyes, the laugh lines at his mouth, the two faint lines above the bridge of his nose. Had she made him frown and smile often enough to have deepened those lines? Would she leave a mark on him there?

The thought made her shift uneasily. She should go. Her main aim today had been to avoid him. But though she glanced toward the door, she did not move. These steps he'd just taken were too important, too extraordinary. He needed a witness for them.

He lowered his face and smiled at her. The full shape of his lips riveted her. The strong column of his throat. He was dressed for public in a pin-striped suit; he looked now like any well-bred gentleman, only more expensive, for the gleam of his merino jacket, its elegant drape, and the effortless assurance with which he wore it, would mark him out in a crowd. He looked now like a man she could never hope to know.

But last night, he had put his mouth to her most intimate place . . .

"You were right," he said.

She was flushing; she put her hands to her cheeks to cool them. If he was going to pretend it had never happened, she would gratefully follow suit. "About the bird, you mean."

A breeze swept over them, and he turned his face into it, his eyes closing again. "Among other things."

Confusion fell over her like a hot net. She wanted to ask him what he meant. She wanted her anger back, too; it was so much better than this unsteady feeling. She wiped her hands down her skirts. "I should wash. The bird was . . ."

He turned back to her, his eyes searching, the color of sapphires, only deeper, bottomless, infinitely complex.

"I wonder," he said. "What is it you think to escape right now? Another assault? Or my apology? I am sorry for last night, you know. I never should have touched you."

She felt herself grow hotter. He had put what happened into words now. She wished he hadn't. Stupidly, irrationally, his regret upset her. She would not have called it an *assault.* It seemed to strip her of her consent, belatedly, and she *had* consented. She had not been forced into anything.

"It's fine," she said stiffly. "It was nothing."

"I envy your certainty." And then, before she could think on that, he added, "A woman is coming today to interview for your post."

Of course this was what had brought him to her. No doubt he considered himself to be doing a kindness; this was part of his apology as well. She took a steadying breath. "Do you need me to speak with her?"

"No, Jones and I will handle it." His smile seemed designed to remove any sting from his reply. "I've prepared a reference for you, and a list of suitable families you might wish to work for. My remarks last night—do forget them, please." He took her hand. His broad, hot fingers bracketed her wrist as lightly as a breath. "I confess," he said softly. "I would like to touch you again."

He meant a far more intimate touch than this. As she understood him, butterflies seemed to flutter—not in her stomach, but all along her skin, invisible wings whispering over her, leaving prickles of wonder. She opened her mouth, but nothing came out.

She wanted him to touch her.

She wanted him to say, *I am not letting you go.*

"But I won't," he went on. His grip slipped away.

"You deserve better, Mrs. Johnson. For that reason, it is best you leave."

How had this happened? She had never lost her head over any man. But now, as he rescued her from the precipice, she felt how close she had come to stepping over it. Or perhaps she already had.

And she wasn't certain she wanted to turn back.

She retreated a pace, clutching her arm, massaging it to rub away the last glimmer of desire.

He watched her, his face impassive. "I am sorry, Olivia."

She gathered herself. Straightened her spine and took a hard, deep breath. She was not his victim, nor his scorned lover. She had not been cast off; she had come here for a reason, and she might still succeed.

"I'm sorry, too," she said. Not for last night, but for what she must do today. This afternoon was her chance at last. Her only chance. His rooms would be vacant during the interview. She would search them.

Alastair thought he had acquitted himself well, honorably. He had apologized, and though she did not realize it, he had rendered tribute. She could not know the effort it had taken for him to step out into the morning light, to walk to her when she would not come to him.

Outdoors, all at once, so simply.

For a moment, stepping over the threshold, he had felt his soul part with his body and float somewhere above, while his flesh, piloted by some invisible hand, nothing to do with him, continued onward. It had been her astonishment, her gasp, that had jolted him back into himself. *Leading strings,* he had joked.

A joke! His facility had amazed him. For a strange and disorienting moment, he had remembered that old part of himself that had never been at a loss, never discomposed. *Outside,* so easily, with no weight on his chest, no panic. Walking toward her.

Of course, walking toward her. It did not even surprise him. He felt as though he had been walking toward her for months. Of course she had been in the garden.

As he'd looked at her in the fresh air, he had felt himself waking from a dream. As they had spoken, the difficulty of the first step had seemed to recede into old history, becoming half remembered, dim at the edges, like a memory twenty years old. What had kept him inside for so long? The outdoor air felt like an electric shock, sharp and wild like liquor in his nose, his throat, his chest.

This girl was beautiful. The garden was beautiful. He had kissed her once, and he could kiss her again. But he owed her better; he saw that, suddenly, for it was she who had drawn him out, her and only her whom he would have walked toward.

She left the garden first, hesitantly, looking back at him from the door to check if he would be all right. Her generosity, her kindness of spirit, came home to him all at once; she did not owe him that look, or anything else. God save her from herself.

"I'll be all right," he said, and she blushed and pretended not to know what he meant, and then walked on very quickly, soon swallowed by the dimness of the interior.

A minute later, he followed—intending to go upstairs, to finish the letter to his brother, to write, perhaps, to propose a meeting. But the house was so dark.

He wondered suddenly if the darkness might not grip him again. Where was she?

He was letting her go, for her sake. He must do this by himself.

And so, instead, he found himself in the entry hall, at the front door. The porter leapt up, goggling, but Alastair opened the door himself.

He walked down the front steps onto the pavement. How easily this world he'd abandoned now received him again. He laughed. The ground beneath him felt solid, and his feet, his calves and knees and thighs, so flexible, so ready for the challenge. He stood a minute at the bottom of his stairs, surveying the empty park, the shuttered houses across the street. His neighbors, of course, had gone away for the cold season. Scotland, Italy, Cannes. He could do that, too, if he liked.

It was too much. He would think only of this square block for now, everything within his view.

He walked across the street into the park. Here, beneath the shadow of the bare-branched elms, he sat and watched the wind play in the grass, which somehow was still green, though the leaves had all gone. The bird had not been dead. Nor was the garden, really. Other birds still inhabited the branches. Bugs crawled through the grass. A rabbit had slipped through the bushes near the wall as Mrs. Johnson had asked him if she was needed at the interview.

She deserved his respect. He would find her an excellent place, and remove her from his reach as soon as possible—today would not be too soon for her. For *her*. Not for him.

A flock of birds passed overhead, bound for warmer climes.

A superstitious man would have believed that *she* had brought the bird back to life. Ages past, she might have been called a witch.

He took a deep breath and forced his thoughts away from her. He focused on his own house rising before him, its somber, elegant face. It had looked just so since his boyhood. It had looked just so through all the havoc that had transpired within it during this last year. Here was the face shown to the world in his stead. Passersby, glancing at this house, would not have guessed the state of the man within it. He realized this with some surprise.

It had a good face, this house. Dark brick, shining windows, gargoyles in the eaves.

He felt her presence in it like a lodestone, a talisman against the dark. But she was not his to keep. She deserved a good life, a good man, an honorable arrangement, for such things still mattered to her. And if she stayed, ah, God, but he would ruin her; he would willingly, instantly, ferociously, joyously—

He rose. He thought about walking farther, but decided against it; it felt safer to keep the house in his sights. He looked up at it again, seeing it as himself, feeling its solidity as an extension of his own.

A hackney drew up. It disgorged a single passenger, a woman hunched by age, in mourning weeds. Not Mrs. Wright, alas. She had refused to resume her old position; had chosen instead to accept Marwick's offer of a pension, and live out her retirement in Shropshire. But she had recommended an old friend, who had lost her home when her nephew had died. Mrs. Denton, this woman was called.

Mrs. Denton did not notice him as she climbed his

steps. She was shaped like a barrel, exactly as a housekeeper should be. He would offer her the post as a favor to Mrs. Wright, by way of atonement for that shoe he'd hurled at her.

But most of all, he would offer her the post because he didn't want to. It was for Olivia Johnson's sake that he would offer her the position.

Olivia began the search feeling calm, numb even. She did not wish to break the chest unless she had to, and the quantity of papers had multiplied in her absence, appearing on the nightstand, taking up a new shelf on the bookcase. But as she searched, heedless of what she knocked over, or pages she ripped in her haste, her actions began to summon a different mood. She tore through the papers as though she were in the grip of some silent, unfolding hysteria.

This was a nightmare. Betraying him, stealing from him. She must get through it as quickly as possible. There was no saying how long the interview would last. He might appear at any moment. Or Vickers, or Jones.

The collection on the nightstand proved useless. She moved to the bookcase, where new papers sat haphazardly stacked, or sandwiched between volumes by Melville and Aurelius, Plato and Cervantes. As she drew out the new bunch, she recoiled, recognizing the handwriting. It belonged to the late duchess.

She flipped through the letters quickly to confirm they were all of a kind. She tried to blind herself to the words, but she could not help but see that none of them were addressed to the duke.

How must it have felt for him to read this filth? In

her letters to Bertram, the duchess had boasted of how easily she coaxed Marwick to reveal his political secrets; how her single miscarriage had so frightened him that he never protested when she demanded to sleep alone; how he nursed not a single suspicion that she looked elsewhere for pleasure. She reviled him as a gullible, impotent fool.

Yet Olivia had never seen those faults in him. Other faults, certainly: too much pride, too little faith in himself, and perhaps, once upon a time, too much faith in his wife. But cruelty? No. An easy dupe? By no means; his eyes saw far too much. And as for impotence . . . Olivia had felt evidence to the contrary.

His wife had not seen him clearly. Her reasons for it, Olivia could not begin to guess. But the duchess's most common jibe—that Marwick wholly misread her—was materially contradicted by these letters, the ink of which was blurred and smeared, the creases thinned. Each page had been handled repeatedly, folded and unfolded again and again.

She stared at the lot. *I should burn them.* Reading them would not aid his recovery.

But it was not her right to decide that for him.

She put them back, carefully replacing the book that had lain atop them—then paused, frowning, and gave the book a little shake.

It was hollow.

Holding her breath, she opened the cover—and discovered, nestled in the carved-out innards, his pistol.

A chill ghosted down her spine. *I am not that kind of thief. I have a specific purpose here.*

But the purpose was self-defense. And a pistol would aid that cause immeasurably.

Undecided, she carried the pistol over to the foot of the bed, laying it on the carpet before turning to the matter of the locked chest.

As she had feared, the lock was not simple, and refused to yield to her hairpin. But Lilah, the thief turned typist, had contended with such locks. She had said once (as Amanda had gasped with shock, throwing Olivia pointed, censuring looks, looks that condemned her for encouraging such talk) that when a lock was complex, it was easier to leave it locked; to attack whatever it was attached to, instead.

Olivia had prepared for this. She had stolen a small hatchet from the garden shed. She was crafty like a thief; perhaps she was born to it, this state of evil her natural mode. How awful. She would not think of it.

There was a fractional gap between the brass plating of the lock and the wood of the chest. She fit the edge of the axe into this gap and pried. The plate loosened just enough to permit her to crack the trunk open. But the opening was not wide enough for her hand.

On a deep breath, she slammed the blade down into the gap. The clang was so loud that her heart stopped; she hunched there, daring not to breathe, waiting to be discovered.

But nobody came. She heard nothing save the deep silence of idle afternoon: the maids had completed their morning rounds, and the staff was now gathered for a late luncheon that Olivia herself had scheduled, on the pretext that they should all be together, should the housekeeper be offered the position and wish to meet them.

Her own absence would raise brows, no doubt. But everyone would think they understood it. Sour over being replaced, surely she would not desire to meet the new housekeeper.

She laid down the axe. Now she could see the mechanism of the lock, the cylindrical shaft that pierced the body of the chest. She grasped the edges of the plate, braced her foot against the chest for ballast, and pulled. It required her to rock the lock from side to side, but she made a millimeter of progress, and then another. Her arm and shoulder began to burn; she allowed herself ten seconds' rest, to recover her breath and let her muscles ease, before resuming. Another millimeter—now a quarter inch, all at once—

The lock came out in her hand.

She looked at what she had done, and she was shocked. Fear, true fear, was a cold ringing note, like the first note that opened a symphony, a single pure tone that built and built, until it shuddered out through the air, and the orchestra joined in, and became a maelstrom.

There would be no disguising what she had done to this trunk. At his first step into the bedroom, he would see it and know.

She threw up the lid. A sob burst from her. The chest held nothing. Nothing of interest. A wreath of dry roses. A wedding dress of antique gold lace, scented heavily with lavender. She pawed it aside and found hidden in one of its flounces a photograph: Marwick standing beside a small, fox-faced brunette, a woman with a face like a heart, with eyes that were long and exquisitely formed, a smile like a cat's.

Olivia stared at the woman. Margaret de Grey, late Duchess of Marwick. She was as perfectly formed as a porcelain miniature. Dark and sultry, her cupid's-bow mouth naturally glamorous. She wore a collar of diamonds that a czarina might have envied. And she had had him, and she had discounted and abused him. Why? How could she have done it?

There was no time for this.

Olivia put down the photograph and groped under the dress—then gasped as her hands closed on smooth leather.

Gently, so as not to rip the dress (But why not? Why mustn't she rip it? It should be ripped. It should be burned; *why* did he save these things?), she pulled out the portfolio.

He keeps a dossier . . .

Margaret de Grey had no doubt lied about many things—but she hadn't lied about this. The papers inside were organized into neat, alphabetized sections, the names familiar to those who followed politics: Abernathy. Acton. Albemarle. Axelrod. Barclay. Balham.

Bertram.

She slid out the papers, replaced the portfolio beneath the dress, and turned once more to the picture.

Marwick looked so young in the photograph. There was a hint of a smile on his lips—not sarcastic, not ironic. He looked full of life, hope, energy.

He had deserved so much better than the woman beside him.

He deserved so much better than to be thieved from by his housekeeper.

She sat paralyzed, gripped by numb horror. Her valise was already packed. Once below, nobody would stop her from slipping out the back passage to the street. Why was she about to weep? Why could she not look away from his face?

It is too late. You have done it. The lock is ruined. He will know. It is done.

"Good-bye, Alastair," she whispered. "Be better. Be well."

"What," came his cool reply from behind her, "are you doing?"

CHAPTER TWELVE

Fear was a chasm that opened beneath her, stealing her balance as Marwick stalked toward her. She stumbled backward until her shoulders hit the wall. "I—I wasn't . . ."

His face was terrible, rigid with rage. He looked from her, to the trunk, and then back to her. The smile that corrupted his mouth seemed to carry fangs in it.

"You are stealing from me," he said. "Mrs. Johnson."

"No." But she was. "You don't understand . . ."

It was his expression that silenced her. The way his rage collapsed suddenly and completely into contempt. "Don't I?" He studied her now as he might some peculiar specimen of trash, distasteful, tediously in the way. "What don't I understand?"

He did not sound as though he cared.

"We have a common enemy! Lord Bertram—I needed a way to oppose him—"

On a noise of disgust, he turned away. The sight of his broad back bewildered her into silence. She had imagined, somehow, that he might want to know what she meant.

He knelt down by the trunk. In a moment he would put everything together, see what she had taken, what she still clutched beneath her arm. She must tell him. *Now.* "Lord Bertram," she said. "For years he has dogged me. You must listen. I came here specifically—"

"Did he send you, then?" He opened the trunk.

"No!" She came off the wall. But when she started to approach, he sent her a look that struck like a fist of ice. "He is abhorrent to me. Believe me. I had looked for a way to stop him, and I came here when I realized—"

"And here I thought you came to apply for a maid's position."

She stared at him. "Do you—do you not even wish to hear me out?"

His laughter sounded mechanical. He lifted out the hem of the wedding dress, the brocade glimmering. "This belonged to my wife," he said. "She taught me a great deal. She left me well equipped to hear all manner of stories. I can't imagine yours will be more surprising than hers."

Her stomach cramped. She felt physically ill. That he would compare her to his wife . . . "I'm not like her."

"Oh?" He looked up at her. "Did you know her?"

His tone was all wrong. Cordial, pleasant, as though they were standing in a corner at some party, making polite conversation. "I'm not like her," she whispered.

He fixed her in a long steady look. "You mean to say, your actions do not match your character. I am mistaking you. This is not what it seems. That's what you mean?"

"Yes!" She hesitated. Where to begin? With the letters she had uncovered from his wife? But she had not *uncovered* them, she had *stolen* them. From Elizabeth—

from his sister-in-law. How would that confession make him eager to hear, to believe, the rest of her tale? "It's complicated," she said rapidly. "But if you would let me explain—my mother, she and Bertram knew each other from her childhood—and I promise you, it will all make sense—"

He rose. She told herself she would not retreat, but when he walked toward her, she hit the wall again. "Yes," he said, "I am wholly mistaken. I have misinterpreted you entirely. You have a brilliant explanation, which will show you to be not a thief, but a victim. Even, I suppose, *noble* in your motives." His words assumed a mocking edge, drilling into her brain like gunshots: "Honorable. Righteous. Misunderstood."

He gripped her arm and dragged her around, so that she looked into the grand mirror over his dressing table. Four feet high and half as wide, it showed them both: his hard mouth, his merciless, level stare. Her face looked white and blank, the face of a foiled thief, a fraud and a liar. She stared into her wide, panicked eyes. They did not look innocent.

"And yet when you pass a mirror," he said conversationally, "for a moment, you startle. You wonder, who is that, looking back at you? This criminal face, this guilty air." His lips twisted into something like a smile. "I am sure you have some excellent reason for your crimes. Tell me, while you were ransacking my belongings, did you find my wife's letters?"

It hit her, like an anvil to her chest, that nothing she said now would convince him. For he would imagine that she had invented her story on the spot, after reading the letters from his wife.

Worse, if he discovered the letters she had stolen—

his wife's letters, which she carried in her apron, for she'd meant to return them before slipping out—he would misinterpret her possession of them. *Did he send you?* he had asked.

That she had so many letters written by and to Bertram would only make her look guilty of collusion with him.

"I didn't want to do this," she said miserably. "I took no pleasure in deceiving you."

Marwick pressed his cheek to her hair. She heard him inhale, and some deranged part of her quivered to life at his nearness, at the smell of him, the warmth of his skin. The saner part of her froze like a field mouse beneath the passing shadow of a hawk. She dared not breathe.

"Of course you took no pleasure," he murmured. His breath was hot along her skin, waking perverse echoes of last night's pleasure. "Enjoying it would force you to acknowledge your own guilt. Far easier to imagine yourself the martyr, I imagine. Far easier to sleep at night. He must have paid you very well to do his dirty work."

"He did not pay me," she whispered. "I loathe him. And I do not sleep so well."

"No," he said after a pause. "Nor do I." He pulled away from her. "So tell me, *Mrs. Johnson*. In my shoes, what would you do with yourself? Would you summon the police, or would you effect a more immediate justice?"

She could not imagine what he meant by that. She did not want to find out. "I want to destroy Bertram," she said very rapidly. "You are right, I know what your wife did, and so I *know* that you and I have a common cause—"

"Oh, you *know* of that? How delightful." He paused,

looking struck. "Of course, that explains a great deal. No wonder you showed such courage. When did you learn of her adventures, I wonder? Before I threw the bottle? Before we met in the library? Before the garden, this morning? *Well?*"

She stared at him, strangled by her own deceit, and then flinched as he put his hand to her cheek, spanning her face from temple to chin.

"I am glad you know the truth," he said quietly. "I'm sure it did much to quell your fear of me. For you realized I was not worth the fear: you realized what a pathetic object of mockery I am."

She shrank into herself. "No! I never thought such a thing!"

His hand tightened slightly. Just a fraction; just enough to make her aware of how close his thumb lay to her jugular. "Oh, but surely it did comfort you," he said. "I could not be so fearsome, after all—not if the woman I'd married could conspire so freely against me, without the least fear of discovery."

"I would"—even as she spoke, she knew the stupidity, the futility of it—"I would help you to ruin Bertram. I would help you."

"Indeed?" He seemed to consider this, then nodded. "But conspiracies require trust. Could you trust me, Mrs. Johnson?"

This sudden turn threw her. "Yes," she whispered. If only he would remove his hand from her throat.

"Is that so? If only you could see your expression. You're terrified of me. How could you trust a man who terrifies you?"

She swallowed. "I . . ."

"But I have been told," he continued in that smooth,

unruffled voice, "that my judgment is flawed. Untrustworthy. I am forced to agree. *Fool me once,* so the saying goes. But here, now, with you—I've been fooled twice. So I leave it to you to help me decide, for clearly my judgment *is* foul: am I able to trust *you*? Is this the face of an innocent before me? Or do you agree that what I see in your face is the panic and guilt of a *liar*?"

The word cracked like a whip. "I never meant to do you harm! *Think!* Did I treat you like a woman who'd chosen to hurt you?"

He tilted his head, as though to see her better. "How interesting," he said, "that you imagined you had the choice."

His hand slid down her throat, cupping, very lightly, the span of her shoulder. His forefinger traced her collarbone through her wool jacket—a jacket that felt suddenly far too thin. He watched how he touched her, his expression opaque. "What is in that portfolio you dropped?"

He would discover it anyway. "Your evidence on Bertram."

"So that's why you're here? He sent you to retrieve it?"

Suddenly she was angry. After all she had done for him, could he not even listen? "He didn't send me. I *told* you. He's my enemy as much as yours. My mother—"

"Then how did you know I had material that might destroy him?"

It was time to confess the matter of the other theft. "Your—your wife," she stammered. "She wrote him letters—"

His palm covered her mouth. "Shh. Let's not speak of her, shall we? She rather ruins the mood."

As his free hand closed on her waist, she froze, then

forced herself to meet his eyes, willing him to remember himself. To remember *her,* and what had passed between them.

But his face now was a mask of concentration. And he touched her as though she were not human, but a doll, dumb, witless, fashioned for his enjoyment. His gaze followed his roving hand, which made light little touches down her body, skimming the side of her breast, shaping her waist, molding the curve of her hip, skating—she sucked in a sharp breath—over one buttock, which he palmed and then squeezed, slowly and deliberately.

It was awful. It was the opposite of what he had done in the library—which, while more forceful, had never been brutal, for she had *willed* him to do it, then. Against all good sense, she had wanted it.

"Stop it," she whispered. "I don't want this."

"But what a sweet body you have," he murmured. "And I have unfinished business with it." When he lifted his eyes to meet hers, he gave her a slow smile. "I cannot tell you how pleased I am that you're a liar."

She had only one choice. It rose in her mind now, the vision of the gun still lying on the carpet.

Her crimes had already compounded. There was no reason not to add to them. And—to hell with him! After all she had done, that he would not even *listen*—he deserved nothing from her.

His hand slid back up her body. He leaned toward her—

Now! She twisted out of his grip and lunged across the room. He grabbed her skirt, yanking her to her knees, dragging her back toward him—but her hand closed around the pistol. She rolled onto her back, and when he saw what she held, he released her. Lifting his palms, he backed away.

She sat up, breathing raggedly, and then scrambled to her feet.

"Will you shoot me, then?"

No man should ask that question with such idle curiosity. She stared at him, struggling to regain her breath, to make her brain function. Did he not care if he lived or died? "I should shoot you," she said bitterly. "You idiot. Perhaps you were right—all the stories about you were false. For what kind of politician does not know how to *listen*?"

He snarled at her. "I would rather hear—"

"Throw me the key!" She was done listening to him, too. She took a step toward the door. "Do it!"

Sneering, he pulled the key from his pocket and tossed it onto the carpet by her feet. "This is a capital offense. Brandishing a weapon with the intent to harm."

She felt suddenly airless, as though the noose were already tightening. "I don't mean to harm you," she said, and then felt all at once furious again. She had said that enough. He was deaf, a fool. She opened the door and kicked the portfolio into the hall—then lifted the gun higher as he stepped toward her. "Stay there," she said sharply.

Slowly he held out his hand. "You don't want to harm me? Give me the gun, then. If you don't mean to harm me, hand it over."

A bizarre laugh spilled from her. "And now the tables have turned! But you never gave the gun to me—so why should I do it?" She swallowed the bitter taste of that laugh and stared at him. "I wanted none of this. All I wanted was my freedom."

His head tipped. "Yes. You must want it very much, to risk the gallows."

"And you don't want enough," she said. "Your wife was a monster. But so were the men who conspired with her. And if you had shown them half the spine you've shown me, perhaps Bertram would not have been my problem to solve. Murder? How unoriginal. You might have been cleverer. You might have made them *pay.* But instead, you decided to cower here in the dark!"

She had the satisfaction of seeing him pale before she stepped out the door. And then a thought struck her.

She reached into her apron and tossed the letters at his head. "My parting gift!" And then she turned the lock, closing him in, and picked up the portfolio.

A thud came behind her. He would try to break down the door now, of course. How predictable. She squared her shoulders and walked quickly for the main stairs.

Alastair vaulted down the staircase, straight past the astonished porter for the servants' passage to the ground floor. He had not entered it in years; this section of the house was theirs, not his. She would not be here anyway. She was long gone; it had taken him too much time to batter down the door, six inches of solid oak.

He knew he would not find her, but his feet did not consult his brain. His boots hammered heavily on the wooden steps. When he reached the ground floor, domestics scattered, gawking. Jones appeared. "Your Grace! Is something amiss? May I—"

Alastair threw open the door to the housekeeper's room.

The sitting room was small, plainly furnished. It

smelled like her, like roses, like goddamned deceit. He snorted to clear his nose of it. *I am sorry,* she'd said—the witch! Not only upstairs, either: she had said it in the garden, too. She had been plotting this for some time.

His gullibility knew no bounds.

Through a narrow doorway was the spartan cell where his newest jezebel had slept. Had he found her here, he might have strangled her with his bare hands.

She was not so stupid, though. She had fled. What had she left behind?

He ripped the drawers out of the chest. Empty. The desk: empty, too. The walls were bare save three illustrations clipped out of magazines. A man and woman, hand in hand, walked a village lane. In a parlor on Christmas morning, a mother and father presented a small, bow-tied puppy to a young child. A country cottage at dusk on a snowy evening, a lamp glowing in the window.

He felt his mouth twist. The last print, he knew. It had been famous for decades. He himself had kept a copy of it as a boy, drawn to it for no reason he could name.

If the cartoonists at *Punch* liked to draw oversexed aristocrats, the illustrators at ladies' magazines were no less predictable. Their object of fixation was all the more grotesque, for it was an out-and-out lie: connubial bliss; domestic idylls; *virtue*. The lure of a home that offered protection against the cold and dark.

He could have pitied her for believing in these things. Instead, he would despise her for it. She was a fraud. She was no more entitled to such things than he. How dared she have imagined otherwise?

He ripped the pictures off the wall. One by one he shredded them, tatters falling onto the cot. Déjà vu made the world lurch. He had ripped up the first letters from Margaret, too.

If you had shown them half the spine you've shown me, perhaps Bertram would not have been my problem to solve. But instead, you decided to cower here in the dark.

He turned on his heel and strode out into the servants' hall. His jezebel was right in one regard. He was done cowering. He knew now what tied him to this house, to this city, to life itself: revenge. He was done living for ideals. He was living for himself now.

Bertram would pay. So, too, the others: Nelson, Fellowes, Barclay. And Olivia Johnson? Safety was what she desired. It would be his great pleasure to ensure she never felt it again.

CHAPTER THIRTEEN

Olivia kept her head down as she passed through the black iron gates into St. James Park. Strollers wandered down the path, sipping mugs of fresh milk and fussing over children, full of Christmas cheer. Vendors hawked baked apples, hot chocolate, and fried oysters. The grass was littered with brown paper cones stained with grease.

As she walked, she pretended great concern with avoiding the rubbish. It excused her from having to look into people's faces, and to let them see hers. She wore a staid walking dress of unremarkable brown wool, purchased secondhand from a dolly shop along with the only hat she had seen there that looked unlikely to carry fleas. A Christmas present to herself, she thought blackly. But the hat covered only half of her head; she felt the warmth of the sun on her brow, which meant that her hair was also catching the light, making a gleaming beacon for anyone who looked for her.

Nobody was looking for her. Not yet. She had been very cautious in her approach, having gone all the way to Hampstead to rent a room, these past four nights.

She had even taken the train back to Broad Street to post the letter to Bertram.

She had not signed her name. There was no use in baiting a bear before the trap was fully laid. But in the letter, she had laid out the evidence against him: enough to hang him in public opinion, and to prosecute him, too. The building society of which he was the director, and that he had hawked to the lower classes as a fine opportunity for investment, was a sham. Of the developments his investors had funded, he had built only a quarter, and the dividends had gone directly into his own pockets. The documents evidenced his crime quite clearly.

The details of her letter ensured that he would not trust this matter to Thomas Moore, or any hired hand. He would come himself, and when he did, she and her pistol would make clear to him that he must cut her a wide berth for the rest of his natural life if he did not wish to be ruined.

The bird-keeper's cottage came into view. She scowled at the knots in her stomach. There was no cause to be nervous. She was armed in more ways than one. She was not walking to her doom now. She was walking toward her freedom. God knew she had paid dearly for it.

No. She would not allow herself to think of Alastair.

There were rooms in the club in which conversation was discouraged. The dining room was not one of them—though a stranger, stumbling inside, might have been forgiven for thinking otherwise. Tracking the avid, rapt attention of the other diners, this stranger might have imagined that some miracle was unfolding at the table by the window, when in fact all that transpired was the meeting of two brothers, nothing more.

"I thought you'd booked a private room," said Michael.

The onlooker also might have wondered that these two were brothers—for the one was pale and blond, lean after a long period of deprivation, and eating heartily, for he was trying to flesh out. The other was dark haired, as robust and tanned as a farmer—but he picked at his steak like an invalid.

"You misunderstood," said Alastair. He had not booked the private room for this luncheon. Right now, he wished his presence advertised.

"I count a dozen stares," Michael said moodily. "You could have charged admission."

He'd forgotten how easily Michael sulked. "Buck up. They aren't staring at you." But he could feel the stares like ants crawling over his nape. His back felt painfully exposed, braced for the impact of an arrow.

Let it fly. He would welcome it. These past four days, he had been gripped by a rage so pure and intense that it made him giddy, like fine whisky. His calisthenics no longer sufficed to trammel it. Bloodshed would be a better cure.

Michael produced an unhappy sigh. In reply, Alastair gave him a smile, easy, confident, meant to reassure: the old routine, picked up again as easily as a shirt. "Let them look," he said. "I expect they've missed me."

Michael laid down his fork. "You've been following the news, I hope? Don't expect to find your place reserved for you. You'll need to knock down a few pins, first. Bertram, for instance—"

"I'm aware." Alastair was aware of very little else, in

fact. In the sleeplessness of these past four nights, he'd been laying plans. *Johnson and Bertram, Nelson and Barclay, Fellowes*—the chant had run through his head so often that it was beginning to take on a melody. "Do you have the records I asked for?"

Michael retrieved them from his jacket, a padded envelope whose thickness would be evident from across the room. That these were the employee rolls from the hospital would not be evident. "As you'll see, the damage from the hospital's closure was extensive." *The closure you effected for no reason,* he did not add. "We lost several doctors. I had to raise their salaries considerably to lure them back."

Alastair nodded. The hospital was a charitable endeavor, which he funded—and which he had briefly closed, during his blackest days, to punish his brother, a doctor by trade, who had founded it. "That's fine."

"You can't blame them for demanding it." Michael shrugged. "They have no way of knowing if you'll decide to shut the place down again."

"But I won't."

"Of course not." Michael stared at his plate, grim faced. "I was . . . surprised to receive your note, I must say."

They were coming to it now. It had taken only three courses and some grumbling. "My apology was long overdue."

Michael reached for his wineglass, gave it a quarter turn on the tablecloth. "It's in the past now, I suppose." He could not have sounded more hollow.

It would be easier, of course, not to force the issue. But Alastair knew that if he wanted to repair this breach, he would have to expose his throat. "Your wife would disagree with you. And if you're honest, you'll admit that you haven't forgiven me."

Michael's mouth flattened. He said nothing.

A flash of insight struck. Alastair smiled, genuinely amused. "You fear you'll send me into another decline? Is that why you're tiptoeing around it?"

"Well. You can't blame me for worrying."

Alastair caught himself lifting his own wineglass, and made his hand return to the table. He did not deserve the comfort of tipsiness for this conversation. "I disappointed you," he said bluntly. "I behaved with reckless, irrational bile. I regret it extremely. You cannot know how much."

Michael's face darkened. "She could not understand your opposition to her."

Very well, let them pretend this quarrel centered solely on Elizabeth Chudderley's—Elizabeth *de Grey's*—hurt feelings, and had nothing to do with Michael himself. "Tell me how I may make amends to her," Alastair said. "Shall I write to her directly? I'd imagined she would not want to hear from me."

"She would read a letter, I think."

"Then I'll write to her at once."

Michael leaned forward, giving him a searching frown. "If you could only explain to me *why* you did it. That is—I know how deeply you were injured, how bitterly you took Margaret's deceit. You had cause to be furious, but never at *me*, Al." Here he looked down to his plate again, but not before Alastair caught a glimpse of his bewilderment, his pain. "You had no right to force my hand. Or to endanger the hospital—and every single patient there. Three hundred of them, transferred without notice!"

Here lay the heart of the breach. "No. I had no right." Surely it had been madness that had led him to shut down the hospital. And while he would have chosen a different bride for his brother, one less beautiful, less sociable, less worldly than Elizabeth Chudderley . . . someone less confident of her charms, who did not remind him so much of his late wife . . .

That battle was lost. And he could not account for his actions, for he no longer understood them, though he remembered them with perfect clarity. How much he had cared about the wrong things—and then, how little he had cared at all.

But now there was a new battle. "Tell me," he said, "what I must do to have your trust and love again."

Michael blinked. "My trust, or my love? Because you know you have the latter. The former will be more costly to you."

This had always been Michael's special skill: to see love and trust as separate things. In Alastair's view, neither was worth having separately. "Both," he said.

Michael nodded, then took to sawing at his steak.

In the silence, Alastair grew aware again of the stares from the room. He could feel, like an open wound, the doors behind him, through which anyone might enter, any of the four men on his list, any of these men's confidants. If he turned now, he might encounter a knowing sneer, a snicker, a furtive grin. Someone who *knew.*

And he would slice those smiles off their faces. If he could not stop the news from spreading, then he would make it the worst mistake a man could commit, to know it, and to discuss it freely.

He schooled his breath. He allowed himself a single sip of his wine. He glanced across the room, making note of who nodded at him, and who quickly looked away.

This was his club. This was his seat, by the window. This was his place. Anyone who wished to challenge him would pay for it. He was taking back what belonged to him—starting with his brother's good opinion.

He turned back to Michael. "Tell me," he said, taking care to speak gently, the better to coax the dove into hand. "How may I make amends?"

Michael cleared his throat. "For my sake, Elizabeth is willing to move forward, let bygones be bygones. And as for me . . . time, I believe. That is what it will require. And your company," he added gruffly. "God help me. But for some lunatic reason, I seem to have missed you."

"Then of course you will have my company, whenever you like."

Michael flashed him a startled smile. "My God. Not even an attempt to pawn me off on your secretary? Schedule me in? It's clear *something* has changed. I think this is the first time in my life that I've ever seen you humble!"

Alastair managed a fine laugh, perfectly balanced between amusement and abashment. For if humility was what his brother needed to see, then very well, humility it was.

But it was not, of course, humility that kept his spine straight (*if you had shown them half the spine you've shown me,* Olivia Johnson had said with contempt) as they made conversation over port and dessert, with the entirety of the room still ogling him. And afterward, in the hallway, as they paused to make plans, he recognized that while he *was* truly contrite, and entirely genuine in his intention to write a pretty note of apology to Michael's wife, these feelings were more conceptual truths than embodied sensations.

He stood there, watching Michael walk out the door, and had the uncanny sense he had performed very well in a play: he had recited the proper lines with the appropriate amount of feigned conviction, and the audience had responded positively.

The falsity troubled him. His relationship with his brother had never felt rote. He loved Michael. Even now, he knew he loved his brother. But he wanted to *feel* it again. He wanted to feel something healthy, wholesome, and good. Something, moreover, that was *true.*

In time. All in good time.

He leaned against the wall, taking advantage of this odd remove to watch passersby disguise their surprise at seeing him. Old acquaintances, who probably counted themselves as friends, stopped in astonishment and hastened to speak with him, smiling and pumping his hand, expressing their gladness at the meeting.

And here, too, he excelled, managing to intimate, with his own smiles and a certain warm tone, that they had indeed been much missed, their proposals for dinner gladly received, the old confederacy officially resumed—as though nothing had changed during the endless months in which the world had moved on and he had not.

But all the time, as he made idle talk and remembered the rusted reflexes of charm, he wondered, *Do you know what a fool I have been made? Will you be wise enough to hide it, if you do? For I will not spare you, either.*

And after almost an hour, his wait ended. Bertram stepped through the double doors into the lobby.

* * *

Revenge was not a descriptive term. It was a category, within which fell a thousand possibilities, ranging from a mild snub in the street (face turned, a social death) to a blade against the neck, a jugular severed, a hot, wet murder. Savages painted their faces in the blood of their enemies. It had its appeal. But with a slit throat, the enemy could not speak—and Alastair required answers.

Bertram, of course, mistook him for a gentleman. Bertram did not imagine he was carrying a knife; otherwise, he would not have agreed to accompany Alastair down this hallway, which grew progressively dimmer the farther they withdrew from the dining hall. Bertram had a great deal of faith in the civility of his enemy. The fool.

But once Alastair had stepped into the room after him, once the lock was turned and they faced each other, he saw Bertram catch a glimpse of another possibility.

The man went pale. He retreated a pace and reached into his jacket.

"It's your choice," Alastair said.

Bertram hesitated. Then he felt down the buttons of his waistcoat, as though that had always been his intention. "Duke," he said flatly. No pretense of old friendship here, though he had once dined nightly at Alastair's house, and familiarly called him *Marwick,* and put his head close to Margaret's as they laughed at shared jokes.

There were so many reasons for savagery. Alastair saw now how stray memories might chip away at a man, a crack here, a crack there, until the wall broke, and the rage, undammed, rushed out and destroyed all in its path.

But to have his revenge, while also keeping his place

at this club, at the table by the window—to have his revenge and his brother as well, and Elizabeth's forgiveness (for that was necessary, if he meant to keep his brother)—well, for that alone, Alastair would not reach into his own jacket pocket, where he could feel the weight of a stiletto, which he knew would do its job neatly, with a minimum of gore.

"Sit," he said.

Bertram had once taken orders with unusual eagerness. For a man fifteen years' Alastair's elder, his ingratiating manner had made him slightly pitiable, if also—what irony—reliable. Trustworthy.

But Bertram had since gotten his hands on power. "No," he said. "I will not sit. But I am glad you wished to talk. There's something you'll want to hear."

"I've already heard so much from you," Alastair said. Again, so calm. This script was excellent. "Granted, the letters were intended for my wife. But you know the saying: Adam's rib. What was hers is mine, and so on."

Bertram gave him a thin smile. "Of course. And I imagine you must be feeling very pleased with yourself, for I have received your letter, as well."

"Did you? I sent none."

Bertram took a seat. "You must hope that your henchman denies it, too. Ah—that surprises you, I see. Did you really imagine that I would go myself?" He laughed shortly. "Did you imagine those documents were *genuine*? Your own wife drafted them—it was her idea, in fact."

He deserved a knife across the throat for daring to speak of her. For mentioning so casually what should be his shame and dishonor.

But Alastair kept his hands loose at his sides, his face

neutral. He gathered that Bertram felt convinced he was sharing a great coup. "I don't understand," he said. "You'll have to elaborate."

Bertram sighed. "Must I? All those sordid secrets you collected, imagining yourself somehow superior—what did you mean to do with them anyway? Did you truly imagine that honorable men would stand for blackmail?" He shook his head. "Margaret agreed with me. It simply isn't done. And if you were vulgar enough to try it . . . why, she thought, and I agreed, how fitting it would be if your blackmail was turned against you. If the evidence you collected was, in fact, forged—and in such a way that, should you ever attempt to use it, *you* would be exposed as the villain."

Alastair held himself very still. The files on Bertram that Olivia Johnson had stolen—*these* were what Bertram meant. "They were false," he said softly.

"You fool!" Bertram's color was rising. A redhead could never hide an emotion as piquant as triumph. "Of course they were false. Did you truly imagine me so idiotic as to get myself tangled up in a land swindle? But no, you thought yourself so much cleverer. And so you've destroyed yourself, Marwick—for as you may have gathered, I did not make that meeting today. Scotland Yard paid the visit in my stead."

Alastair felt something shift inside him, minute but profound: the center of his gravity, readjusting. "I see."

To feel so right—to feel one's instincts, with savage bitterness, confirmed—and then, after all, to be so wrong, to be so *blind:* Olivia had not been lying about her intentions.

She had tried to use the documents to blackmail Bertram. *We have a common enemy,* she'd said.

Was this relief? Why? He took a great breath, for he felt suddenly drunk, though he'd not finished his wine.

Bertram interpreted this breath as a sigh of despair. "Yes, indeed, now you're seeing the way of it. And for your own sake, you must hope you paid your man well enough to resist interrogation. For when he confesses your role in it, what will the world think? That you hired a man to blackmail me with documents that you forged. Ruination, Marwick. A laughingstock extraordinaire! Yes, I hope you paid your man *very* well."

Looking at him now, Alastair saw, with fresh eyes, the significance of details he had not thought to notice before:

The man's square jaw. His unusual height. And his hair, carrot red, even in the darkness of the room.

He felt his lip curl. He knew something of how a man earned enemies. But Bertram's deeds must be blacker than he'd imagined. "Perhaps you're right," he said. "But I wonder if you guessed that my henchman would be a woman—ginger, by the name of Olivia."

Bertram gave a gasp. And then he leapt from his chair for the door.

"No." Alastair grabbed his shoulder, hauled him around. And then, with great satisfaction, he made a fist and slammed it into Bertram's nose.

Bertram dropped to the ground.

Alastair stood over him, breathing heavily. His knuckles throbbed, the sweetest sensation he'd known in a very long time—or at least, since that night in his library.

He shook his head to rid it of that thought. "Dead?" he said.

No reply.

Kneeling, Alastair felt for a pulse, and found it beating strongly. Convenient; this would give him a fine head start.

"Never fear," he said as he rose. "I'll take very good care of your daughter."

Alastair had been instrumental in drafting several measures for prison reform. As he followed the jail keeper down the moldy corridor, he wondered what he had been thinking. It was very useful to have a penal system so dependent on bribery and corruption.

The keeper took the precaution of looking through the peephole before unlocking the door. Intriguing. Olivia had obviously made quite an impression during her arrest. To believe the official account, she'd been waving Alastair's pistol and threatening to take off somebody's head.

Quite credible, that story. A wonderful system they had at work here: lies, money, mold. "Leave us," he said.

The jail keeper hemmed and hawed as though working himself up to an argument. How quaint. Alastair let his own face telegraph his opinion of the prospect.

The man snapped his mouth shut and pocketed the key. "When you're finished, sir—"

"Your Grace," Alastair said softly.

"Simply ring," the man said in a more subdued tone. He nodded to the small bell by the door. "A guard will come to lock up."

Alastair waited until the jail keeper's footsteps had faded. The bell, the iron door, the reek of filth and damp, the narrow peephole—positively medieval. When he laid his hand on the latch, he was introduced to a layer of cold, slimy moisture.

He pushed open the door. In the moment it took his eyes to adjust to the dimness, he heard her gasp. "You *came*!"

Her greeting threw him off. The gratitude in it struck at some small, tender, rotten spot inside him. She came into focus in the dimness, standing two feet away, bedraggled, straw clinging to her skirts, her right cheek swollen and purpling. "How did you know I was here?" she asked hoarsely.

"That doesn't matter." *She brandished the gun,* the jail keeper had told him. *She was hollering that she would shoot anybody who tried to lay a hand on her.*

The point of that bunkum was apparent now. Short of a proper murderess, perhaps even a cannibal, the public would scruple at police striking a woman.

He scrupled. That the police, whose sacred duty was to protect, would abuse a slip of a girl . . . Contempt burned through him.

He resisted the impulse to go to her, to tilt her chin up to the meager light from the murky window and make certain her eye was intact. She had stolen from him. Made a fool of him. Lied to him. These were her just deserts. It was not *his* job to protect her.

"I can help you," she said. "Do you believe me now?"

He felt his upper lip curl—an animal reaction to this confusion swelling inside him. *She* could help *him*? She had decided to take on Bertram singlehandedly. See how well it had turned out.

If you had shown them half the spine you've shown me, perhaps Bertram would not have been my problem to solve.

He recognized the childishness of his anger. He was sick of being shown up by her.

Her hands nervously kneaded her skirts. "Please," she

said. Her knuckles were bloodied. Had she thrown a punch? Or—the image flashed through his mind, sudden and vivid—had they dragged her? Had she grabbed onto the gravel, the walls, to save herself—

He gritted his teeth. "Very well. Tell me, Olivia, why I shouldn't leave you here to rot."

Her lips trembled. And then, quite suddenly, her strength seemed to leave her. She fell onto her knees in the straw, and the gasping breath that tore from her sounded too much like relief. He had not promised he would help her. He should warn her of that.

But instead, he knelt and took hold of her elbows. "Are you all right?" Whose words were these? Whose concern was this?

"Yes," she whispered.

His grip wanted to tighten. He understood suddenly that this was *his* concern. *She* was his concern. He was no longer going to hide in the dark, for she had pulled him out of it. He would not hide even from himself.

To hell with that! She was a thief. She had deceived him. Stolen from him.

But she had also brought him into the garden. She had shown bravery that he had no choice but to admire.

He made an angry noise and let go of her. "Don't lie to me," he said. "We're done with lies. You will speak the truth to me, or nothing at all. Now, tell me: are you all right?"

She swallowed, the noisy sound of a very dry throat. She looked past him to the door, and then around the little cell, a certain blind quality in her gaze, as though she was only now discovering where she was, and did not trust her vision. "Yes," she said unsteadily. "And I will tell you—everything. But quickly! Once Bertram realizes I am here . . ."

Her naked fear struck some chord within him, a shocked and startled note that reverberated. How had he missed her fear? In his bedroom, when he had manhandled her, he had thought her afraid of *him*. But he saw now that he'd been mistaken.

He could not make sense of it. This terror was for Bertram? He had not understood his wife's choice of lovers, Bertram least of all—and now he could not understand Olivia Johnson's fear. She had never flinched in front of him. But the mere mention of Bertram made her shake.

He grabbed her arm again. His fingers flexed on her smooth skin; he wanted to run his hands over her, to check for hidden wounds, because she was a liar, he could believe nothing she said, not even her protests that she was well.

Their eyes locked. Of course she would not look away from *him*. "Tell me why you fear that bastard," he said. "What do you think he will do to you?"

She lifted her face, showing him Bertram's chin, Bertram's hair clinging in matted curls to her temples. But her eyes were her own, an oceanic blue, the blue of prophetic heavens, cloudless summers. "He will kill me. He has already tried once."

He let go of her. Recoiled. *Preposterous.* A single punch had knocked Bertram unconscious. And she thought him a murderer? A man did not kill his own blood.

Yet he could not dispute that she believed it. Her conviction showed in her pallor, in her desperate eyes. And to see her look like that, when she had never so much as flinched from him . . .

He took a long breath. Rage, confusion, amazement . . . his emotions were pinwheeling; he could not understand any of them.

He found himself groping for another script to guide him. But there was nothing now in his brain but his instinct, his rotten instinct, which wanted to smash something. Or tie her up, swaddle her in gauze, lock her away somewhere he could study her until he understood . . . something. Something important, to which he could not yet put a name.

He made himself look at her. It was not difficult. Taking his eyes off her would be the challenge. *What are you?*

Something was missing. "Where are your spectacles?"

"They smashed them."

There was the anger, boiling up again, scalding. How stupid; she did not even need them to see.

He turned away, pinched the bridge of his nose. Found himself staring at the door. From this side, it looked even more of a relic from the dark ages. Streaks of rust resembled blood. The dents must be where—his mind's eye supplied the possibility—some past occupant had banged his head, over and over, frantic for escape.

Christ, how was she so alone? How was it that she had been *grateful* to see him here? How had her own goddamned father put her into this mess?

He turned back. She visibly gathered herself, straightening, jaw squaring. She would not beg him. Even her eyes had ceased to plead. She merely watched him, resolute, ready to hear his decision.

She had not gotten her dignity from Bertram.

He held out his hand. Her lips parted. She seized his fingers and he hauled her to her feet—too easily. She was not light, but she was not as heavy as she should be.

Her bones should be made of iron, for what else was fit to support her bravado? It would shame generals. Emperors. Professional pirates.

If anyone was going to break her will, it would be he. Not Archibald bloody Bertram.

He pulled her out the door, past the silent bell, down the hall. In the guardroom, the jail keeper and one of his thugs had begun a game of cards. When they caught sight of Alastair, the keeper stood. "How now, Your Grace! What is this? That woman is a prisoner of the Crown—"

Alastair dropped her hand—ignoring how her fingers clung, how he had to shake them off as he stepped forward. It made something in his chest twist, to feel her reaching for him. It was so unlike her. "This woman was waylaid without cause. The pistol was mine, which she was carrying to be repaired."

The man flushed. "A likely story!"

He felt a strange smile twist his lips. The jail keeper retreated a pace. "You doubt my word, sir?"

The man looked uneasily to his guard, who found a new purpose in reshuffling the deck. "I—perhaps you didn't know, Your Grace. But this woman is involved in a very bad business, a scheme to blackmail Lord Bertram—"

"Indeed? You mean to say that Bertram, a member of our prime minister's cabinet, is in the business of being bamboozled by other men's domestics?"

The keeper shifted his weight. "I . . . am not privy to all the details, but the charge sheet—"

"Yes, you'll want to keep your eye on that. The newspapers would be glad to print it. What a curious lark. Rather awkward for Salisbury, of course. Indeed, the

PM should be apprised before all of London begins to laugh at the fool he appointed. Will you inform him, or shall I?"

The jail keeper stammered a few incoherent syllables. Finally he found his retort: "This is intimidation!"

"Is it?" Alastair inspected his nails. "I had imagined that intimidation required a busted face, at the least." He looked up. "Or was my maid abused for no cause?"

"Perhaps . . . there was some mistake. She was loitering in the very spot that the criminal had promised to wait—but perhaps that was only a coincidence."

"I will leave it to you and the baron to decide. In the meantime . . ." Alastair lifted a brow. "Get out of my way."

The jail keeper swallowed and inched aside, clearing their path to the street.

CHAPTER FOURTEEN

In the guardroom, Marwick had faced the jail keeper like a predator encountering a new species of food. His smile should have exposed fang. But once outside the prison, he seemed to withdraw into himself. He handed her silently into the carriage and then settled in a brooding silence on the opposite bench.

Olivia kept her eyes on the window, for she barely knew how to look at him. For four days she had nursed her anger toward him. But the moment he had stepped into her cell, her hard work had been undone. He had *rescued* her. How could she recover her resentment? She had wondered before what it would be like to have him as a friend. Now she knew it meant *freedom*—quite literally. The Duke of Marwick could pull a prisoner out of Newgate as easily as some other man might bully a beggar into ceding the sidewalk.

She gazed at the bustle of afternoon traffic. How odd that sunlight still shone. She felt as though she'd lived through a century or more of terror since walking into St. James this morning. She touched her cheek and found it hot and tender.

"Here." He moved onto her bench, took hold of her chin, and angled it toward the window. The intimacy, the presumption, made her go still.

She could not quite forget how he had touched her in his bedroom. If he tried that again, gratitude be damned—she would punch him.

But after a moment, he released her and sat back. "Yes, quite nasty," he said calmly. "Was it a baton?"

"Only a fist." *Only*. She shuddered.

He remained on her bench, studying her. He was too broad shouldered, his legs too long, to share the space comfortably. His thigh pressed against hers; his knee came into her soiled skirts. She should mind it. For every inch she ceded him, he no doubt intended to take a mile.

But she rather liked the feel of his body against hers. It was not desire; she was too exhausted for that. But he was tall, strong, powerful; he would make a very good shield. A bodyguard . . . She caught her thoughts from wandering. He was no knight. But he'd rescued her from prison, so for the time being, she'd let him crowd her as much as he liked.

The carriage leaned into a turn. She glanced out and discovered the receding shape of Swan & Edgar's. This was not the way back to his house. "Where are we going?"

"You'll soon find out. They said you pulled my pistol on them. True?"

"Of course not." She hadn't known the police could be so vicious. She had been waiting for Bertram outside the bird-keeper's cottage in St. James Park. The older policeman had walked up to her and struck her across the face. "They didn't say a word. They didn't even ask my name. They'd been watching me, staring for a bit, and I'd felt . . ." She laughed unsteadily. "*Safer* knowing they were there. And then, all at once . . ."

"Bertram must have given them some incentive."

He believed her now? She felt a great relief come over her, weakening, like a plunge into a hot bath. "Yes, I think you're right." What sweetness to finally have someone who understood, if not the whole of it, then enough to see the blackest implications. Finally, she was not alone in glimpsing them.

But when she turned to him, his expression ended her relief. There was no sympathy in his face. No revelation, no understanding. He watched her the way a cat might watch a mouse hole: narrowly, with dark plans.

"What am I to do with you?" he said quietly.

She swallowed. "You might thank me. Were it not for me, you'd probably still be sitting in your bedroom."

His mouth flattened. "How you do go on about that. But your entire campaign was designed to facilitate your theft. Is that not so?"

"It did . . . *begin* for that reason."

He gave her a faint, mocking smile. "And then? Did my chivalry win you over?"

What could she say that he would believe—or that she would wish to admit? *Against all reason, I grew to . . . care for you.*

He would laugh his head off. Or worse, take it for another lie, and shove her from the coach.

"You stole from me," he continued, his gaze level and unblinking. "Lied to me, defrauded me, pried through my possessions, which you then used to blackmail a peer of the realm. Would you not say this puts me in a difficult position?"

A strange prickling started behind her eyes. Goodness, was she going to cry? How mortifying. She put a hand over her face, hoping he would think it was simply the pain in her cheek that troubled her. "If you hand me over to him now . . ."

He made a contemptuous noise. "If I'd wished to do that, I'd have spared my shoes the prison mold. Tell me: why did you blackmail him?"

She dropped her hand. Let him look at her. Let him see she spoke the *truth*. "I wanted him to leave me alone. He has harassed me, hunted me, for seven years now. Once he hired—he hired an entire *team* of private investigators." They had nearly caught her, too. She'd been three years into her first position, with the banker's widow in Brighton. That had been the first time she'd fled in the night.

"Why? What does he want of you?"

"I have no idea! His obsession has *never* made sense. If I knew, I promise, I would tell you."

"Then tell me this." He settled back, bracing one elbow against the back of the seat, making himself comfortable. "Who is he to you?"

She bit her lip. They were drawing near the heart of a secret she had never spoken to anyone. "You must understand, the last time his man caught up with me, he . . . tried to choke me to death."

His face darkened. "But you escaped."

"Yes. I was lucky; I knew nobody here. I'd just arrived in London." She had waited four days for Bertram to come to Kent for her mother's funeral. Finally there had been no choice but to go forward without him. All during her mother's long illness, she'd planned ahead: found the typing school, written for admission. Bertram had forbidden it, but she did not care. She was not her mother. Her life would not be shaped by his whims. The funeral concluded, she'd gone from the churchyard directly to the railway station.

On her arrival in London, Moore had been waiting on the platform. *His Lordship wishes me to see you safely settled.* And then, that ride to the hotel, which had transpired not to be a hotel at all . . .

"He tossed me out of the coach and left me for dead," she said. "Seven years ago, now. That was the beginning of it."

Marwick studied her, his vivid eyes unreadable. "And you truly have no idea why he pursues you."

"No."

"I told you not to lie."

She shrank back against the window. "I don't . . ."

"He's your father. A small detail you've omitted."

Her breath stopped. *He knew?*

"The resemblance is clear," he said. "Once I looked for it."

God help her. She pressed her forehead to the glass and closed her eyes. "I would rather resemble the devil. Perhaps they're one and the same."

"Tell me. What is your real name?"

"Holladay." She whispered it. "It was my mother's name."

"The mother from East Kent."

It surprised her that he remembered. She nodded.

"Olivia Holladay, whose mother hails from East Kent."

He sounded as though he didn't believe her. "Yes!"

"Are you certain?" His voice was cruel. "Are there any other names you'd care to share with me?"

She tried for an equally cutting tone, one that would slice through the knot in her throat. "I hadn't imagined you the kind that enjoys kicking a dog when it's down. How *easy*."

For a moment, he did not speak. And then he said, "Look at me."

On a deep breath, she opened her eyes. A single tear spilled. He reached out, grim faced, to wipe it away with his thumb. "You will be honest with me." His voice carried no inflection. "You're no dog. You're hardly beaten."

His words, in some twisted way, were almost kind. But his touch was not. He stroked her cheek again, roughly, brutally, as though that tear had been an offense against him. "We have a common enemy," he said. "You were right about that. And I do mean to destroy him." He paused, his thumb digging like iron into the top of her unbruised cheek. "But please note: I have not yet decided what to do with *you*."

He watched himself touch her. It seemed impossible that her skin was so soft when the mettle beneath it was steel. The disjuncture angered him. It seemed proof that deception was at her very core, bred into her, as much a part of her as her eyes or her hair.

Why did she weep now? It seemed baffling, infuriating, that she wept here, in his coach, though she hadn't in the prison. As though *he* were the villain.

He let go of her. The coach was slowing as they pulled into Brook Street. He kept a flat here—once used by his brother, now empty. It was well suited to his purposes.

She sat quietly beside him. If she still wept, she did it soundlessly. He would not look at her to check. She had a swollen cheek; that was all. It would heal.

"So you hate me now," she said quietly. "How convenient for you. As though everything I did for you no longer counts, because I deceived you."

He clenched his teeth. He had cause for hate. In his old life, he would never have forgiven her for her crime; his pride alone would have forbidden it.

But it was not pride that galled him now. It was her temerity. Her idiocy *staggered* him. Who was she? A lone woman. No family to protect her, to save her when she slipped. She was profoundly alone. And yet, despite the great risk to herself, the lack of any net to catch her, she had acted. What if he were another man? *Any* other man. A man whose pride had not been shattered so violently by his late wife that he no longer cared to guard it. If he were any other man, she would still be in Newgate. How much she had dared, with so very little by way of defense. *That* was what galled him.

"Fair or not," he said flatly, "your fate is in my hands now. For as you saw today, you are powerless. And I am not." Compared to her, his power was limitless. Did she not see that? How had she dared to go against him?

"That must be pleasant." Her voice was bitter.

The coach stopped. "Come." He opened the door and stepped out. She could find her own way onto the pavement.

But when she stumbled on the step, he cursed and took her by the forearms, lifting her safely to the ground.

She did not thank him, which was wise of her. The feel of her burned his palms. She should not feel so soft. She should feel like iron. He remembered the expression she had shown him in the garden, her face as he'd walked toward her . . .

He released her. "Follow me," he bit out. He didn't want to look at her.

Marwick led her through a discreet door set into a brick building not two hundred yards from Claridge's Hotel. Wasn't that where his wife had died? Olivia vaguely remembered Elizabeth mentioning it, having heard it from Lord Michael.

At the top of a narrow, creaking staircase, she stood aside so the duke could unlock a door. It opened into a simple bachelor's apartment, two rooms sparsely furnished. The front room, which was larger, held a slim bed, one chair, a desk. The dressing table was covered in a thin film of dust. Nobody had lived here in some time.

Of course, Marwick probably had keys to any number of rooms across town. He owned a good portion of the city; she had seen the rental incomes in his ledgers.

"Sit," he said.

Since he stood in front of the single chair, she took the bed. Her head pounded. Crying had not helped. Why had she cried? She wanted to kick herself. She was not weak.

His boots thumped hollowly against the floorboards as he walked to the window and latched the shutters. The room grew abruptly darker.

"Oh, look," she said tiredly. "You're returning to old form."

"Fewer jokes would serve you better." His boots thumped as he returned to sit across from her. "So tell me. In my place, how would you deal with this betrayal?"

Perhaps he meant to kill her.

No. She did not believe that. But the idea triggered an icy thought: perhaps he *was* reverting. He had been betrayed before, and it had made him deranged, for a time. Now, in his view, history was repeating itself. What cause had she to hope for mercy?

He had not saved her, after all. He had simply reserved her punishment for himself.

Bile burned her throat. She pressed her hand over her mouth, suddenly fearful that she would be sick.

"There's a chamber pot by your foot," he said. "Take care with your aim."

She lunged for it. The violence of her illness left her weak and clammy. A washbasin stood in the nearby corner; she rinsed out her mouth and then sat back on the bed, breathing hard.

He came forward, his features clarifying. When he reached for her face she jerked her head away, but he would not brook refusal. He gripped her jaw, pulling it around. They stared at each other.

"Did you strike your head somehow?" He sounded bored. "Your pupils look even enough to me."

She was glad for his hostility. It was simpler this way. If the past did not matter—if he meant to forget all of it—then she could forget, too. She needn't feel any guilt for what she'd done. "I'm fine," she said. "Let go of me."

His hand dropped. He stood staring down at her. "I am going to give you a very simple choice."

"How good to know I'll have one."

"Oh, you've already had choices. You could have chosen to stay in Newgate, for instance. Those documents were forgeries. You would have been called to trial for creating them."

She blinked. "What? *Forgeries?* You forged them?"

His smile was thin as he took his seat again. "Bertram did—in collusion with my late wife. When, if, I ever used them, I was to be made a public fool."

She pondered this for a moment. "So then I saved you from that as well."

He leaned forward onto his elbows, nostrils flaring. "You paint a very rosy picture of yourself, don't you?"

"And you paint a very black one."

His eyes narrowed. "No matter. *You* will take the blame for them. You'll be tried for fraud, forgery, and extortion. And I doubt the courts will treat you as kindly as they would have done me. That is one choice for you."

He was trying to terrify her, and doing a very good job of it. She reminded herself desperately that his threats had always outstripped his actions. "And the other choice?"

"Obedience." The word cracked like a whip. "Bertram has an interest in you. That makes you valuable to me."

She exhaled. "You know that's no choice at all."

He crossed his legs and drummed his fingers atop his thigh. "Where is your fine grasp of precision, Miss Holladay? It is a choice. It simply isn't one you like."

He was punishing her. It was, from one view, only what she deserved; from another, he was even being generous. He could have left her to rot in Newgate.

But these were both views from *his* eyes. She was done trying to see his perspective. "What do you mean by obedience?" she asked. "What will you require of me?"

His smile mocked her. "Whatever the circumstances demand."

She hesitated. "The circumstances of your revenge against Bertram, you mean."

He followed her meaning. He took a very thorough, insulting survey of her body, head to toe. "What a deviant it would make me," he said, "to demand *that* from you. Why, one might be forced to conclude that I had a particular taste for treacherous women." He gave her a half smile. "It *is* possible."

She gritted her teeth. On one thing, they would be clear. "I am nothing like your wife. I did not fool you for my pleasure. It had nothing to do with you, don't you *see* that? Or are you too pigheaded and vain?"

"So you continue to protest. Very well." He reached into his jacket and extracted a pocket watch that he laid beside him. "You have five minutes to tell your story. If I am satisfied, we will discuss the specific nature of my offer. And if I am not . . ." He made a soft click of his tongue, a preemptive chide. "The authorities don't know the half of what you've done. In addition to forgery and extortion, there is also the matter of your theft from me."

She stared at him. He had not managed to intimidate her when she'd been his servant. Why permit him to do so now? Her pride demanded better of her. "Not only that, Your Grace. You mustn't forget my theft from your brother's wife. I was her secretary—did you know that? All those letters, I stole from her. Indeed, in the interest of good relations, you should give her a chance to convict me, too. And perhaps Lady Ripton?" She would make sure he never blamed Amanda. "For I forged a reference from her. Yes, why not contact her as well?"

His pause suggested surprise. She took a ridiculous pleasure in it.

But then, with a shrug, he said, "Good. A piece of honesty; you are learning. Well, do begin your tale, Miss Holladay. The clock ticks."

And he settled back, lacing his hands over his belly, looking for all the world like a very skeptical critic prepared for a second-rate show.

Five minutes to tell him everything. The challenge focused her—and revealed to her, with miserable clarity, how neatly her entire life might fit into a cliché: the cliché of the bastard child.

"Bertram met my mother when she was very young," she began. "She was only sixteen when I was born. He installed her in a village called Allen's End—that is where he kept her. Us, I mean. He has property very near there, but the cottage was rented from a local family."

He remained silent, watching her. The light slipping through the shutters laid bars of shadow across his face, through which his eyes glittered.

He was not going to encourage her. Very well. "He and my mother were very happy when I was young." She hesitated. "I was, too, I suppose." The village lay on a tributary of the River Medway. With an apple tree to climb, a garden in which to hide, and the entire countryside to explore, Allen's End had seemed a paradise to her. It had been her mother who felt the village's scorn most keenly.

"He loved her," she said. "He did, in those early years. And he must have been kind to me, for I have . . .

dim memories, very dim, of calling him Papa. Being dandled on his knee." She felt her mouth twist out of her control.

"What changed?" He spoke softly; she barely heard him. She did not like to think of Allen's End anymore. The villagers had been kind to her as a child, but as Olivia had matured, they had begun to treat her with the same contempt they showed Mama. *Like mother, like daughter.*

How curious then to realize that her imaginary village, the place she would belong, looked so much like the place she had been desperate to leave.

She frowned into her lap. "What changed? He married, of course. That American woman."

"The heiress to the Baring fortune."

She nodded. "I remember his first visit, afterward. I knew something important had happened, for he brought me a present—not books or a new dress, nothing so ordinary, but a doll, a porcelain doll from Paris, the most splendid doll you could imagine. She had real hair, the very same shade as mine . . ."

She had always loathed the color of her hair. Some of the village children had called her *Ginger-girl*, which they had not meant as a compliment. But when she'd been little, Bertram had called her hair beautiful. *The rarest and loveliest shade.*

She shook her head. *Bah.* "The doll wore a miniature replica of a Worth gown, made by Worth himself. I can't imagine how much it cost." She shrugged. "I played with it for a few days. I adored it. And then I built up my courage and smashed it."

* * *

Her wistful expression did something strange to Alastair's chest. It contrasted so shockingly to the hardened courage she'd been attempting to embody before. "You *smashed* it?"

Her smile was thin. "I was only seven, but I knew a bribe when I saw one."

He had an unwilling vision of her, freckled, knobby-kneed, her thin face terribly serious as she laid the doll she loved into the dirt and lifted a rock. "You must have had cause, then."

"Well. By that time . . ." She sighed. He watched her closely. A concussion would make her sleepy. He waited, willing her not to yawn.

When she drew herself up again, he relaxed. Curtly she said, "She must have seen the notice of his marriage in the newspapers. From the very moment he arrived, as soon as he'd given me the doll, they began to quarrel. He left again to the train station that same night—I was so confused; he always stayed for a week at the least, and I'd been . . ." She grimaced. "Looking forward to it. But he was gone; and the next morning, Mama took me and left, too."

"Because he had married someone else."

She shook her head. "It makes no sense, I know. He stood to inherit a barony. She was a farmer's daughter. He couldn't marry *her*."

But there was something brittle and bleak in her words that he did not like. "Love has made mésalliances for greater men than he."

She hesitated, head tilting. "Did *you* love your wife, then?"

He took a long breath. "You must have a death wish. Is that it? How amusing."

Their eyes locked. In the dim light, her skin looked so flawless that the effect was uncanny. She seemed made of porcelain, not flesh; too delicate, too breakable, the smattering of freckles only for verisimilitude. She must look very much like the doll she had smashed.

The notion made him strangely uneasy. He wondered if she had seen the resemblance. If she had felt, for a moment, as if she were smashing herself.

No child should have recognized a gift for a bribe. But he knew how wise children could become—his own parents had taught him such lessons, too.

"I think you did love her," she said softly. "I think you would have answered the question very cuttingly, if you felt comfortable with your reply."

Her audacity should not be able to surprise him any longer. But he still did not understand how she did this: how she shifted the balance of power between them so suddenly that he felt compelled to reply, to prove himself, to be *accountable* to her.

He had learned how to shift it back, though. He rose, crossed to the bed. As he sat down beside her, she froze.

"Too late for caution, Miss Holladay." He reached out, slipped his hand beneath the heavy weight of her hair. It was coming down in pieces, as soft as he'd remembered; siren's hair, the color of fire. He gathered up these locks into a mass so thick that his fist barely proved sufficient. He tugged very lightly, tilting her head back just a fraction. "This is how lambs are slaughtered," he said. "Did you know that?"

Her eyes found his, wide, her lashes fluttering. He was terrifying her. Good. He needed to know he was still capable of it.

"You'd make a poor butcher," she managed.

Brave to the end. He lost the stomach, all at once, for bullying her.

He loosened his hold, allowing her to relax into a more natural posture. "Why do you care if I loved her?" he asked. "Never say, Olivia, that you have developed an *interest* in me?" He stroked his thumb down the rim of her ear, hearing with satisfaction the shudder of her breath. "Something beyond your larcenous aims? Surely your mother's example taught you not to aim so high."

She jerked away, removing herself from his reach. "You do cruelty very well. Is that why your wife loathed you?"

He marveled at her. "You truly don't know when you're beaten, do you?"

"Am I?" She shrugged. "I haven't yet finished my story."

"But your five minutes are up."

He heard her breath catch. And then she closed her eyes and bowed her head. "Fine," she said quietly. "Do what you will."

The bare patch of her nape riveted him. Such a vulnerable, tender spot. "What I will," he mused. He tracked his knuckle down her throat, then traced back up to her chin. Gently, he nudged her face toward his.

She blushed, but did not open her eyes. "I feel nothing."

"I see your face," he murmured. "I see the lie."

Her brow tightened. "You see nothing."

"I see it all." He slid his hand down her arm, feeling for the slim bones of her wrist. Her fingers curled within his, a reflex; her fingers hid from him in the cup of her palm.

He pried them out one by one, gently, for fingers

were easily broken, and hers were too elegant to abuse. How curious: he'd imagined, a thousand times, what he might have done to Margaret had he uncovered her betrayals while she was alive. But never in any of those black fantasies had he imagined wanting to touch her like this.

This woman was not Margaret. The betrayal was not the same.

The revelation broke over him as gently as a breeze.

He lifted his hand to cup her skull. So strange to be able to compass it so easily. Odd, wrong, that all her vivacity, the force and passion of her, should be contained in such a small, neatly shaped head.

How much of his anger—for he was still angry, yes, only it existed, side by side, with fascination—how much of it was for her, and how much for himself? The things he saw in her now, even now—resolve; tenacity; determination; dignity . . .

If those things were true . . . if he separated them from her betrayal . . . how could he not covet them?

"So your mother loved Bertram," he said. "And you believe I loved my wife. Does this mean you imagine us to be equal fools?"

A line appeared between her brows. "Mama wasn't foolish. She was only . . ."

"Confused," he said.

Her eyes opened. They stared at each other. Some sticky web seemed to settle around them, enclosing them in a lush, weighted silence. Here was confusion in its purest form: finding oneself magnetically attracted to one's poison.

He smoothed her hair away from her brow. Her pupils still looked even. She was his responsibility now.

Whatever happened to her, it would be his doing. "Do you still feel sick?"

She gave a small shake of her head.

"Excellent." He leaned forward. Put his lips against her mouth.

She took a sharp breath. But she did not lean back.

He kissed her lightly, and then shifted so his cheek pressed against hers. He would be the author of her fate—not random chance; not an accident; not Bertram, or any other man. Softly he spoke into her ear, as his fingers felt down her spine. "When your mother left him. Where did she take you then?"

"Shepwich," she whispered. "Where her . . . family lived." He could feel how her muscles tried to tighten beneath his touch; how, with gentle pressure here, and a small rub there, he could make them unwind, and force her to check her sigh.

"What happened in Shepwich?" He rubbed his cheek against hers like a cat. Let her feel the scratch.

"It was . . ." She sounded breathless now. "Not a happy reunion."

"Ah. They wouldn't receive you?"

"They tossed us out."

A sad tale, but hardly unusual. He took her lobe between his teeth, nibbled lightly. He licked it, and tasted the salt of her skin. "And so what did she do then?"

"We—went back—to Allen's End. *Must* you touch me like that?"

He paused, his hand now at the base of her spine, his fingertips just brushing the swell of her buttocks. "How do you want me to touch you?"

He felt her swallow. But she did not speak.

"Do you want me to touch you?" he said.

A shudder ran through her. "I wish . . ."

"I don't care what you wish," he said. "I only care what you *want*."

Her chest rose and fell on a deep breath. And then, very slowly, she lowered her face into the crook of his shoulder. "I wish I did not want," she said very softly.

A savage triumph flooded him. He tightened his grip on her lower back to channel it. "And then. What happened then? After you returned to Allen's End?"

"Nothing." Her lips brushed against his throat as she spoke, and all his senses concentrated and collected around that single point. "But things were never quite right between them again. He visited much more . . . rarely. And when he came, they would spend their evenings in cold silence. I couldn't understand . . ."

He closed his eyes, breathing her. "Why she went back to him?"

"No. She had no choice in that, really. I couldn't—I still don't—understand why *he* came back. Why he continued to visit, year after year. He was so . . . resentful. As though he had no choice in it."

Her words were growing sluggish. He caressed her spine, long, soothing strokes. "Perhaps she had some compulsion over him. If we could learn what that was, it might prove useful."

"I don't know what . . ." She hesitated. "In fact, there is one thing—something she wrote, the last entry in her diary: *The truth is hidden at home.* But I never knew what it meant."

He did not immediately reply. For as they sat here in silence, her weight against him, a strange feeling was swelling in him.

So he was not his father, after all. He battled wicked

thoughts, dark urges; he would press himself on this woman very soon. But he was not his father. His father had never wanted any woman in particular. And Alastair only wanted this one. This was possessiveness he felt.

"We must go to Allen's End," he said. "Find out what your mother meant."

But she did not answer. And when he eased away to look into her face, he realized she had fallen asleep, her head in the crook of his shoulder.

Olivia woke to darkness. Groggy, she listened for the chatter of the servants in the gallery, but heard instead the muted rumble of traffic, as though from a high street. Where was she?

The prison. She bolted upright. Marwick had rescued her! Where had he gone?

She spotted a dim line of light beneath the closed door that led to the back room. She stared at it, trying to collect her wits. She had not slept so deeply in months, it seemed.

The last thing she remembered was sitting with her face pressed into his skin. Had she fallen asleep like that? And he had not woken her . . .

A bittersweet longing flooded her. She braced herself against it with a long breath, and caught the reek of the mold in the prison.

The jug on the washbasin still held some water. She rose and silently picked her way to it. The water was not too cold. She wet a cloth and cleaned her face. But what of the grime beneath her sleeves, and under her petticoats? Bits of prison, reeking, still coated her skin.

Disgusted, she hauled up her skirts and swabbed clean her calves and knees. But it was not enough.

She glanced over her shoulder. No sound came from the next room. The light under the door did not flicker.

Quickly, she unbuttoned her bodice. During her time as an unhappy lodger in Mrs. Primm's arctic boardinghouse, she had developed a talent for washing quickly. Her stays were fashioned for a working woman, and unfastened from the front. She placed them beside the basin and mopped her chest and arms.

Her back throbbed. She remembered falling onto it after the policeman had struck her. How long ago that seemed now. Weeks, months.

A particular spot troubled her, just below her shoulder blade. She twisted but could not quite reach it. Sweating from terror: she had not known such a thing was possible until those long hours alone in her cell—

A hand closed over hers. "Let me."

She froze. Her stays sat discarded by the basin. She was naked from the waist up.

Where was the panic? Was she simply too tired for it? Or was it that this moment felt, somehow, inevitable?

He had threatened her. Yet she had fallen asleep in his arms, and he had laid her down to rest. How deeply she had slept. It was one thing to sleep alone, and another to sleep in the presence of a man whom she knew would allow nothing to happen to her—except for what he willed.

Perhaps she was the deranged one here. For she felt safer with him than she ever had on her own.

She opened her hand. He caught the cloth before it fell.

His first strokes startled her. There was nothing seductive in them. He cleaned her skin with firm, expedient movements, as though he were a nurse tending a patient, or a servant wiping a vase. When he found the sore spot beneath her shoulder blade, she made some stifled noise, and he paused.

"Hold on to the washstand," he said.

"Why?"

The next moment she had her answer: his thumb found the spot and began to dig, rotate, massage.

Her head flopped forward. She bit back a groan. Under the pressure of his hands, her muscles unraveled, growing limp, pliant. "Why are you doing this?" she whispered.

"There is a Chinese proverb," he said at length. "'Save a man's life, and you are responsible for him.'"

"So you feel responsible."

He turned his kneading knuckles into her shoulders. "No more than you do for me."

She felt a fleeting thrill. There was the admission she'd been pressing for. She'd had a role in his recovery. "I passed your test, then."

Another pause. "I'm not sure the test was for you."

His hands eased across her shoulders, skated down her arms, and closed in a warm, solid grip just above her elbows. His knuckles brushed so close to the sides of her breasts. They stood silently, breathing together, the water in the basin casting a ghostly reflection of their silhouettes. He loomed behind her, but she felt no fear. She felt . . . protected.

"Shall I let you dress?" He sounded meditative, as though thinking aloud, the question put to himself rather than her.

In the library, he had tried to prove to her that he was not a good man. She sensed his indecision now. The battle within him.

Perhaps she did not need him to be good. "Do you mean to help me with Bertram? I don't mean murder," she said. "He has children." She tried never to think of them. She had let herself look up their names once in Debrett's, and had regretted it ever after. "But do you mean to help me with him?"

In the pause before his reply, she heard the rumble of traffic on Brook Street, the jingle of tack. What time was it? She felt adrift in this strange, fraught darkness, pinned between the washbasin and his body, large and hard behind her. She did not want him to move away.

"It seems so," he said.

She turned to face him. Here, in the shadowed corner, she could not make out his features clearly. But she faced the light coming through the shutters, and by his indrawn breath, she gathered that he could see something of her: her bare breasts; her squared shoulders; enough, at least, to make him gasp.

"You're beautiful." He sounded angry.

Had he sounded ardent, she never would have believed him. But his anger, she believed. She reached out and found his cheek, stroked her thumb along the corner of his mouth. His jaw hardened. He would never admit as much, but she recognized power when she possessed it—as she did now over him.

The revelation spread like an intoxicant through her. It fizzed in her blood. He was angry because he *wanted* her. Because he could not hurt her. Because he meant to help her, after all.

Why *had* he rescued her? Why had he not arranged to hand her back to the police? He knew her story now. She gave him no special advantage over Bertram. "I think you failed your test," she whispered.

His hand came over hers, gripping her palm, pinning it against his rough cheek. "Don't be so sure. You don't know me, Olivia."

"Don't I?" Who but she could be said to know him, now? And what she had seen of him, what she knew of him—everything that nobody else did—was what he loathed. She understood him. Like Mama, he judged himself more harshly than anyone else ever would.

But she had never been able to abide dark moods—not in Mama, and not in him. She leaned forward and found his lips with hers.

A breath tore from him, hot against her mouth. He stood very still as she pressed her mouth against his. Tension radiated from his clenched muscles. His hands found her waist. Flexed there twice.

And then he dragged her into him, into a kiss so hot and deep that it felt like the resumption of something, rather than its beginning.

I agree with the radicals; I place no stock in virginity. She'd once said that to her friends at the typing school, taking private amusement in their shock. *After all, it's very easy to resist men, isn't it? But managing to pick the right one—that is truly worthy of praise.*

Nobody would judge this man the right one. He was fashioned after Byron's own model: mad, bad, and dangerous to know.

But she knew him as no one else did. He was not the man he'd once been; he was the man that only *she* knew. And when he took her face between his palms and tilted back her head and pressed his tongue deeper into her mouth, questions of wisdom became irrelevant. She kissed him back, eager, ravenous.

In the library he had taught her about pleasure: how

it was at once shared but also private, greedy, provoked by him but involving places known only to herself. She felt it again now, low in her belly, hot flutters that collected into a delicious weight, a hot pulse stirring between her legs. She put her hands over his where he gripped her face and felt the strength in them. She heard the soft sound he made, near to a sigh.

He had made that noise because of her. She smiled into his mouth.

He grabbed her wrists and bowed his head to kiss each one, like a vassal paying tribute. She watched him do so and felt, for a dizzying moment, taller than him, a presence larger and grander than her flesh could contain. By his own account, he had seen her, recognized her, as brave, intelligent, resourceful. And he wanted her, against his will. Yes, let him bow his head; let him admit to being conquered.

And then he flicked his tongue across her palm and she was pulled back into herself, abruptly a slip of a girl enfolded by his larger body, cradled against his hard chest, gripped by his muscled arms, this man who had swept her out of Newgate. And this, too, exhilarated her. She *wanted* his protection. She wanted all of him.

He walked her toward the bed. The mattress hit her thighs and she clutched his waist for balance, but he was prepared for this. Cradling her skull, he lowered her onto the mattress, then came over her, taking her in a long, hot, languorous kiss as he laid himself atop her inch by inch, the planes of his body sparking small shocks along her breasts, her belly, her thighs which he nudged apart and laid himself between. The heat of his abdomen, where his pulse beat strongly. The weight of his upper chest. He laid himself against her with leisurely, masterful care, as a master artisan might bring together the two pieces of a diptych.

He put his mouth to her brow and breathed against her for a ragged moment. "You want this," he said hoarsely.

She opened her eyes. She knew how to listen to him; she could hear the question in his words. Braced on one arm, he hung over her, his face tense, urgent. She reached up to touch his cheek.

How sober was Alastair de Grey, the Duke of Marwick! How shadowed, how complex and inscrutable—like an uncut gemstone that, in odd lights, suddenly revealed itself clear and sparkling. The light was his hidden kindness, the goodness he tried so hard now to deny. But it flashed through his face as he beheld her. His expression softened.

"Do you want this?" he asked.

Olivia knew there was not, after all, anything so virtuous in decency. Certainly it would not give her greater courage. And according to him, she already had enough.

She stroked his cheek, which prickled from stubble. Vickers was an awful valet. "Oh, yes," she said. "I do."

He loosed a breath, then leaned down to take her lobe between his teeth, flicking it with his tongue as his hand roamed her body, butterfly touches that set off small tremors at her waist, the side of her breast, her throat. The pads of his fingertips brushed up her jaw. He outlined the slope of her cheek like a blind man reading braille.

Her own hands grew curious. She slid them over the angles of his shoulder blades to the small of his back. The rise of his buttocks was tight, ungiving. She turned her nails into it.

He made a sharp sound—between a groan and a gasp. He broke free of the kiss and laid his head into her throat, so his hair brushed against her chin. His ragged breathing heated her collarbone. "There's a moment," he said. "A moment . . ."

She slid her fingers through his hair, holding him there. In the distance, some cheap clock struck the midnight hour with tinny, hollow bangs. "A moment for what?"

He raised his head. "I loathed the spectacles," he said, very low. His thumb traced her brow once. "They did hide you."

She turned her face to kiss his wrist. An hour ago, a month ago, a year ago, he had been untouchable. And now, in the space of minutes, he was suddenly hers to touch as she liked. Who said life did not hold miracles?

His hand slid under the small of her back, nudging her up. "Come."

She sat with his help, let him draw her to her feet. Robbed of support, her breasts felt heavy and loose. His lips parted as he looked at her. He ran his thumb across her right nipple, and a sound slipped from her.

He kissed her flat on the mouth. His hands slid down her body; he caught her skirts and lifted the dress off her, then untied her petticoats and lifted her out of them.

"My God." He stepped back, gazing at her. "You were hiding more than your eyes . . ."

The wondering note in his voice made her flush. She sat back on the bed, and he nudged her all the way down. When he came over her again, the angle turned him into a featureless silhouette, like a figure from a dream.

Her dream-lover had hot, wandering fingers. They

cupped her breasts, tested their weight. His thumb outlined her nipple, causing her to shudder; pleasure yawned open inside her, demanding she part her legs, push herself up toward him, so she might know once more what she had experienced in the library.

But he had other intentions. He lowered his head; his lips closed around her nipple, a shocking sensation. She heard the sound of his suckling, and it made her hotter yet. The softness of his lips, the wet heat—she gasped—of his tongue, the momentary edge of his teeth as he tested her liking for that . . .

What leapt through her was a pulsing, urgent demand; she grabbed his head, pulling it harder against her.

"I would spend a thousand years here." His voice was rough. "Would you have me?"

"Yes." Here was what she had forgotten to say, what she had needed to say all along: "Yes, yes, yes."

But it became a lie the moment he began to suckle her again, for she realized that this would not satisfy her; a wildness was running through her now, spreading her hunger across a dozen different places, all throbbing, all in need of his attention. Her mouth, which needed his tongue, and the place deep in her belly, which was heavy and full, the place between her legs that felt too empty, throbbing with need. She groped him blindly, like a mountaineer in the dark, looking for the places that would progress this journey. She massaged the muscled bulk of his upper arms, pressed roughly down his flanks—

He sat up and shrugged out of his jacket. Off came his waistcoat; his suspenders, his shirt. She had seen his bare chest before, but now she could reach out and press her palm against the rippling planes of his belly, and feel them contract as he drew a sharp breath. He caught her hand, bit her fingers lightly, sucked them deep into his mouth; his eyes found hers, and the flick of his tongue, the grip of his lips, felt like a wicked promise. He licked down her palm and bit her inner wrist. "Patience," he said, and only then did she realize that she had said *Please*.

His trousers came off next. She was so much bolder than she'd guessed; she sat up to help, and their hands stumbled over each other. He laughed, and his clear exhilaration struck her as sweet and marvelous, and she laughed, too.

He was beautiful. His legs were long and lean, his calves tightly knit, his thighs shelved with muscle. She ran a wondering hand up the length of his quadriceps, feeling the hair, so much coarser than her own. Her hands paused at his hipbones, beneath which a notched indent angled down on either side to frame that part of him that would shortly concern her most. He had given it a name, in the library.

Holding her breath, she laid her hand over his cock.

He hissed, and then—when she tried to draw away—caught her hand and held it there. He showed her how to stroke him, this length that felt impossibly hard. Yet the skin was so soft.

As she explored him, he reached between their bodies to find the spot—precision; she had read of the term—her clitoris, pressing and rubbing in a way that concentrated, suddenly and fiercely, all the vagrant pulses of desire into a single aching demand. The part of him that she gripped suddenly felt like an answer. She understood now.

He came over her then, and positioned himself, pushing into her with one finger, and then another. She arched beneath him, and then his fingers were replaced by a larger, harder pressure, for a brief moment painful, and then filling her completely.

Stunned, she lay beneath him, looking up at him in the darkness, uncertain of what to do.

He put his forehead to hers and began to move.

It was, from that first thrust, more than she had imagined. For it was not simply the smell of him, the weight of him, his grip as he held her in place, the strength of his hips, which ravished her.

It was everything intangible that had allured her before—the intensity of his looks, his uncannily sharp perceptions, his cleverness, intellect, and power. When he thrust too deeply, and she winced, he noticed it; he began to move more shallowly. When the angle of his hips struck a strange, queer spot that made her whimper, he heard it, and repeated the move, until her fingers began to scrabble across his back, and animal noises came from her throat. His intangible qualities became the talents with which he made love to her. Even his cruelty ravished her: she felt it in the demand his body made of hers, this steady, incessant, thrusting possession.

She felt herself balanced on a strange, wild, intoxicated laugh: *And you think I do not know you?* She was enveloped by him—possessed in a way only she would understand. And he knew her; she was seen and known by him. This ravishment was a joint production, she and he *together*.

She surrendered to it. He was whispering words to her, his cheek pressed to her temple, and the words were hot and vulgar, and what they were doing was hot and vulgar, and so was she. She felt wild with his assault, and voracious, desperate for it never to end. For with each sharp movement of his hips he was striking some place deep inside her that swelled and twisted and tightened. It was stronger, more frightening, more wonderful even than what had happened in the library. He was going to break something in her and the shattering would be worth how it destroyed her, for this mounting desperation had to be satisfied; it must be—

For a desperate minute she lingered on this awful, wondrous edge, hearing noises from her own mouth that she did not recognize, that he drank as though they were ambrosia and he starving; and then he began to whisper to her, an instruction she could not follow: "Come," he said. "Take it. *Come,* Olivia."

The convulsion seized her: her greediness made incarnate, inner muscles gripping him, demanding more, more—and then . . . at last . . . releasing her from the frenzy, leaving her limp, boneless, replete.

He groaned, long and low, and then gathered her to him. She kissed his shoulder, salty from sweat. He murmured something. "Sweetness," he said. He stroked her cheek as they lay together, in the darkness of the room.

The clock chimed half past twelve in tinny tones.

He wanted to say something. But the words eluded him. His voice would shake if he spoke. He would say something he later would regret.

He stroked her arm, hoping she might read into his touch whatever a woman might need to know, to hear, in such a moment, after such a . . .

Such an *event*? That was not the word for it. He could think of no word for what had just passed between them. Sexual congress was clinical; it described only the mechanisms of body parts. But what had just occurred seemed to involve his soul. He felt lighter. He felt unburdened of something.

He put his face into her nape. The smooth length of her back pressed against his chest; she adjusted her hips, the soft flesh of her buttocks easing away from him a little. He resisted the urge to pull her hips back into his. He breathed deeply, and the scent of her stirred him—a stirring that against all odds promised to build. He would be ready for her again very soon.

He angled his face so her hair brushed along his forehead. He imagined it was her hand, smoothing his brow.

A man who had been married should know his bodily capacities. But he could not compare this with that. This woman with Margaret. The two women, the two experiences, were so profoundly unalike that they did not seem even to belong in the same category. What other explanation could there be for why he should feel so awkward now, so profoundly naked, in a way that transcended by far the bareness of his body?

He was not sure he liked it. He should be done with uncertainty. God above, was there not a time, finally, when a man was done with surprises?

But this surprise was . . . sweet. It was sweeter than he had the will to name.

He looped his arm around her waist, then held his breath as her hand tentatively covered his own.

Whom did she think she grasped in the darkness? That man whom the newspapers had heralded? Or the man who had gripped a pistol and spoken of murder?

But the hand she now held belonged to another man entirely: one who felt, all at once, like a green boy.

Perhaps this confusion was renewal. He was relearning himself. And here, in this bed, his first lesson in this new life was so extraordinary and unexpected that *better* did not describe it.

She rolled to face him. He could not resist the urge to stroke her hair from her brow, for she would not do it to him, and the longing, strangely, was as well satisfied this way, with him doing it for her.

Her eyes were dark pools, her face a blur. "I had never . . . done that," she said.

"I know."

Her breath whispered out, a hot rush across his chest. "I should have asked beforehand." She spoke so softly that he could barely make out the words. "It is . . . important to me . . . not to be with child. Not like this."

He understood. From her halting words this afternoon, he knew that she had cause not to wish bastardy on another soul. "I did not spill inside you. Do you understand what that means?"

Her head jerked—a clumsy nod. "That I'm safe. Yes?"

And as simply as that, compassion twisted through his heart.

What was he doing, taking her to bed? This brave, unlikely girl who did not know when she was beaten . . .

He eased off, putting space between them—no wider than a finger's width, but too wide for his body's liking, for his greedy cock, which already had stiffened again. "You're safe," he said quietly. "On the morrow, we go to Allen's End."

She turned into his arms, then. Her head settled in

the crook of his shoulder. He held still, unnerved. Her weight on him felt like the physical manifestation of guilt. And then, as she sighed and nestled more deeply into him, it began to feel like something else entirely, much more dangerous.

She lay with trust against him. She fit perfectly beneath his arm.

This meant nothing, he wanted to warn her. *This was for my own pleasure. I have promised you nothing. I am no man to make promises, anymore.*

But he could feel from the limpness of her body that she had fallen asleep again, and these words seemed no way to wake her.

CHAPTER FIFTEEN

By train, Allen's End was only two-odd hours from London. Olivia remembered how this revelation had once amazed her. She had spent most her life watching her mother wait, pale and frustrated, for Bertram's rare appearances—and when he'd arrived, how he had grumbled, what a fuss he had made, over the pains of the journey! Olivia had imagined Bertram like the Marco Polo of her picture books, and Allen's End, the end of an English Silk Route, reached only after braving innumerable perils.

Even once she was older, she'd imagined that there must be more to the journey than the maps suggested. To a girl of fourteen or fifteen, after all, Allen's End did *feel* like the end of the world—a place that time had abandoned, with London as distant as China.

But on a dreary evening seven years ago, she had boarded the train at half-past six. And at a quarter before nine that night, the conductor had announced Charing Cross. Olivia had been nursing enough determination and grief to carry her all the way to China, so her prompt arrival had left her vaguely disappointed.

Now she was making the journey in reverse, in a first-class compartment that Marwick had booked completely—for privacy, he'd said. That announcement had amply distracted her. She'd envisioned all manner of reasons he might require privacy for the journey, most of them torrid. Could one be ravished on a train? How would the mechanics work?

She'd rather looked forward to finding out. It had been somewhat anticlimactic to wake alone in the flat this morning, with no more evidence than a smudge of blood—hardly respectable even for a nosebleed—to prove what had happened last night. And in the morning light, after a solid, dreamless rest, she'd felt so much better, so much more herself, that all the mad events of yesterday—the ambush at the park; the hours in prison; Marwick's rescue, and the strange, feverish hours that had followed; the feel of his skin against hers, and that shocking, complete possession—all of it seemed fantastical, half remembered, like a fading dream.

Only the small smudge of blood said otherwise.

When Marwick had finally appeared, she had expected . . . something, she wasn't sure what, to have changed between them. But there'd barely been time to exchange greetings. He'd entered like a storm cloud, a valise in hand, which he'd opened to reveal a dress that she'd been forced, last week, to abandon, it having been in the possession of his laundress at the time of her flight.

"Change," he'd said. "We have tickets for half past nine." And any chance for revelations (to say nothing of shyness, or another go at debauchery) had been lost in the haste with which he'd hustled her into the coach, out through Charing Cross station, and onto the train.

Now Marwick sat across from her, making a silent perusal of the stack of newspapers he'd purchased on the platform, which somehow had kept him thoroughly absorbed for the last two hours, though she knew that in the normal course, it did not take him half that time to read every paper that London had to offer. He was deliberately ignoring her. Why? In her confusion, she could not quite find her bearings.

She stared at his hands.

Those same hands, long-fingered, rings gleaming (three of them now; they were, as she'd predicted, accumulating), were the same hands that had touched her last night. Those full lips (now pressed in a grim line, though a moment ago they had looked quite relaxed) had wandered over her body and spoken hushed, fervent words against her skin. *I would spend a thousand years here,* he'd said.

The memory made her breasts feel odd and tight, too full for her stays to contain. She took a deep breath.

He looked up. *"What?"*

She gave him a guileless smile. "What do you mean, *what*?"

He looked pointedly back to his newspaper.

With a sigh, she looked out the window. The morning was gray and wet, and the constant drizzle made it look as though the marshy bogs were boiling. She felt his eyes on her. But when she glanced back, he was absorbed in the news.

She shifted in her seat, making the springs creak.

His eyes still on his reading, he slid a newspaper across the table toward her.

She had already tried to read one, but she had not been able to focus. Now, dutifully, she scanned the headlines again, wondering at how little interest they stirred. It was not her way to look on tidings of national crises, of unrest in Afghanistan, of Russian threats and famine in Egypt, with the indifference of some vapid miss.

She frowned. Had he *done* something to her last night? She did not believe that a woman's virtue lay in her physical integrity. But had he corrupted her somehow at the *mental* level? For all she could concentrate on was *him*.

He was slumped in his seat, the newspaper hitched at an angle that obscured his face. Frowning, she studied what she could see of him. His jacket fell open to show his flat belly beneath a pin-striped waistcoat. His trousers clung to his lean hips and the length of his muscled thighs, which had felt hard to the touch, and flexed so powerfully . . .

His thumb was stroking over the newsprint. This slow, idle stroke riveted her. He had been *inside* her.

And now he would not even look at her! Suddenly, she could not bear his aloofness. "Was I such a disappointment to you, then?"

His thumb stilled. "What?"

"Last night? Was I such a disappointment?"

The newspaper lowered, revealing his widened eyes. *"What?"*

Perhaps *his* mind had been corrupted, too. "Your vocabulary seems much diminished this morning."

He folded down the newspaper to reveal his whole face. He must have shaved while at his house this morning. His jaw looked clean and sharp against his tightly knotted tie. Her fingers itched to feel the temporary smoothness of his skin. "You're making no sense," he said levelly.

"*You're* behaving oddly all around. I believe I'm the one who should properly feel shy. I am the woman, after all."

His jaw squared. He laid down the newspaper. "Don't be ludicrous."

That retort seemed somewhat more forceful than merited. She felt a glimmer of mischief. "You're not feeling shy, are you?"

To her amazement—and, yes, her delight—the color rose in his face. "*Shy,* by God—"

"You're avoiding my eyes," she said. "You could not have hustled me out of that flat more quickly this morning. And now you're refusing to have a conversation. Are you afraid that you disappointed *me*? For I assure you, it wouldn't have been possible. I wasn't expecting much—"

He made a choking sound.

"Oh, dear." She reached for her discarded cup of tea, brought an hour ago by the obsequious conductor. "Would you like some of this? And don't misunderstand me; it was quite nice. Last night, I mean."

He pushed the cup away. "I don't want any damned—" Teeth snapping together, he stared at her. "Are you needling me deliberately?"

"No." *Perhaps.* "Only I'm simply wondering—"

He raked a hand through his hair, knocking off his top hat. "You are the most brazen, shameless . . ."

She stiffened. *Shameless,* was she? "Forgive me; am I meant to pretend it didn't happen? Or simply that I didn't like it?"

He froze, hand planted in his hair. Something else came into his face then, narrowing his eyes and lending him a predatory air; his nostrils flared, and a slight smile worked its way onto his mouth.

"No," he said. "No need to pretend. I could feel how much you liked it."

She felt overwarm, suddenly. "Well, then . . ."

"But it has not changed anything else." He straightened and took up the newspaper again, staring at it—though not, she would wager, seeing a single word. "We will work together to undo Bertram. But that is all you may expect from me. You understand that, of course."

It should not have stung. But some stupid, girlish, hopeless part of her *was* stung by his coldness—a very large part of her, in fact. Almost all of her.

Which in turn made her feel numb with horror.

What had she expected? That he would bemoan his own dishonor, and propose marriage? He never meant to marry again. And, even if he did mean to marry, what could he offer her? A dukedom, very well. She made a sour face at herself. But what she wanted was safety. A place to *belong.* Not a husband who would wake up one morning desiring to reclaim his old life, only to discover that he'd married a bastard who fit nowhere in the world to which he wished to return.

She wanted nothing from him. "I wouldn't dare expect more," she said coolly. "A man of your lofty position? Of your *marvelous* accomplishments? Why, I should count myself fortunate to have enjoyed your attentions for an hour."

He looked up at her, frowning. "That is not what I meant."

"Oh? Pray tell, what did you mean?"

He sat back, eyeing her. "I am not . . ." The quick pull of his mouth suggested frustration. "I am not in the market for a mistress."

She made fists beneath the table. "How convenient, as I am *far* too accomplished for that position. Anyway, mistresses are made through repeated provisions of their services. And last night was a fluke."

"Was it," he said flatly.

"Indeed. It was a very difficult day. I was hardly myself. Having recovered my senses, I have lost interest in such business."

His eyes narrowed. "Then perhaps I will arouse your interest again."

A thrill pierced her. She resented it extremely. "But now the novelty is gone."

Bracing his weight on one elbow, he leaned across the table. "We haven't even begun, Olivia."

There was a dark promise in his voice. It seemed to melt straight through her. She leaned in, scowling, until their noses nearly brushed. "Indeed? Then I must take lessons some other time, then. From someone *else*."

"The hell you will." His hand closed over her upper arm; he hauled her forward into a kiss—openmouthed, tongues tangling. Her eyes fluttered closed. All right, perhaps *once* more—

The bang of a door made her spring backward. "Station approaching," the conductor said sourly, and the disapproval in his voice—he must have seen them kissing—was, Olivia thought, the perfect welcome home.

This morning, asleep in the dawn light, Olivia Holladay had looked no older than sixteen, and Alastair had risen from the bed on a revolted realization. He had ruined her. This girl who had managed to make her way in the world without falling prey to the thousand dangers that beset a woman . . . he had ruined this girl, and he had no intention of saving her.

So what? he had asked himself on his walk to the townhouse. This was, after all, part of being a villain. Villainy was not simply the red raging glory of inflicting well-deserved pain; it was also the curdling knowledge of having inflicted injustice. A villain simply did not *care.* Only the victims did.

But this victim did not appear to know she'd been sinned against. Indeed, she seemed made of some new substance, impossibly and unnaturally resilient, cooked up in a chemist's basement against all laws of nature. On his return to the flat, she had greeted him far too cheerfully for a ruined woman. She had met his eyes without a blush, and now she'd harassed him for failing to do the same. Nothing he had done to her last night had eroded that uncanny self-possession that she had no right to possess. A bastard, a servant, a girl who changed names as easily as a hat.

He could not come to terms with her. Even now, as the train groaned to a stop, she sat glaring a challenge at him. How did she do it? He understood the source of his own assurance: his power was his armor. When he'd first walked back into his club, he'd felt its deadly potential as distinctly as the stiletto he'd carried in his jacket. But she, who had nothing, walked through the world with her chin held as high as his, and nothing seemed to shame her. How was it possible?

He knew why he wanted her. Just as an engineer coveted strange new devices, he wanted to strip her, disassemble her, study her parts, and make her secrets his own.

But hadn't he done that last night? Yet he felt no closer to understanding her. All he seemed to have gained was a deeper awareness of his own damnable fascination.

That fascination unnerved him. It exerted a compulsion toward her that felt far too much like all the things he'd done away with: obligation, duty, ideals . . .

She was a bastard and a liar. He owed her *nothing.*

And so, yes, he sat in silence, making no effort to put her at ease. But she didn't require it anyway. What *did* she need from him? His coin, perhaps. Not much else.

He put that coin to use when they disembarked at the station. A fly would have sufficed for the half-hour's trip into the village, but the only vehicle on rent was an ancient brougham, the interior of which smelled musty, reminiscent of Newgate. As they turned onto the road, he discovered that the springs, too, needed replacement; the coach rattled and bounced like a seesaw.

He forbade himself to watch her. But of course he did. As the coach passed over the first bridge, an ancient stone arch that seemed comically overstated for the trickle it traversed, he was watching closely enough to see her composure briefly falter. Her lips tightened. She went pale.

What was she looking at? He saw only a windmill on the distant grassy rise, and closer to hand, as they reached the other side of the bridge, a crumbling stone church, pockmarked by centuries of salted winds. The wheels found a rumbling purchase on cobblestone, and the whole coach began to vibrate.

"It's not far now," she said, lifting her voice. "Just around the second turn, past the apothecary."

The village was predictably, tediously picturesque, a medley of Tudor-era shops and whitewashed cottages tucked behind picket fences where, in spring, roses would bloom. Nobody seemed to be out.

She was doing a good job now of staring impassively at the sights. It was the very blankness of her expression that gave her away. When was her face so deadpan, unless by dint of effort? "Is it as you remember?" he asked.

"Of course." She spoke without inflection. "A place like this never changes."

"You don't like returning here."

She shrugged.

He felt a strange lick of anger. She was forever needling him, provoking him, asking him what she had no right to know. *Did you love your wife? Will you not return to public life?* But she never offered him her own secrets. She required him to pry them out, to make guesses, stabs in the dark. "You grew up here," he said. "Did you leave no friends behind?"

That earned him a strange look. "The daughter of the fallen woman?" She offered him a slight smile. "This corner of the world takes virtue very seriously. Stop here," she added, sitting forward. "This is the house."

The atmosphere in the little, holly-decked parlor felt strongly familiar to Alastair. As introductions were made and tea served, he tried to identify it.

Their hostess, Mrs. Hotchkiss, was the widow of the man who had leased this house to Olivia's mother. She was slim, nervous, elegantly graying; she kept forgetting how to address Alastair, cycling rapidly between "Your Grace" and "Your Lordship."

Her friend Mrs. Dale, whose visit they had interrupted, made no attempt to contribute. Her attention was all for a button on her cuff, which she picked at skeptically, as though testing the skill of a seamstress she was hoping to find reason to sack. She marked each of Mrs. Hotchkiss's blundering addresses with a loud, pointed sniff.

Mrs. Hotchkiss was reeling off the fates and fortunes of various villagers whom Olivia presumably must have known. Country folk in these parts were apparently prone to early deaths, financial misfortunes, and accidents involving ladders, horses, and wells. Just as Alastair's patience began to wear thin, Mrs. Hotchkiss said, "But gracious me! How I ramble—I haven't asked about you, Miss Holladay."

"Yes," Mrs. Dale said in a voice as dry as month-old porridge. "It is a matter of curiosity, no doubt."

"It's clear you've done very well for yourself in London," Mrs. Hotchkiss went on brightly. "Such company you keep now!" Here she turned on Alastair a marveling look.

"*Quite* interesting," Mrs. Dale said.

Olivia faced her in a sudden, forceful manner. "Is it, Mrs. Dale? Pray tell, what precisely interests you so?"

Mrs. Dale's mouth crimped. "I couldn't say. I'm certain I lack the knowledge required to speculate. One does wonder, of course, what happened to your *face*. But perhaps that is common in your circles."

Olivia touched her bruised cheek. For his part, Alastair finally located the cause of his déjà vu. The profusion of doilies, the women's narrow, outmoded skirts, the framed prints of the Queen, the ticking of multiple clocks, and the pretty fragrance of wilting Christmas wreaths had all briefly disguised it. But the last time he'd found himself in an atmosphere so charged with tension, he'd been on the floor of the Commons, faced with a last-minute betrayal before a very tight vote.

"I fell," Olivia said calmly. "I was distracted by an evil sight—not in London." She then shifted in her seat, turning her back on the woman. "Yes," she said to Mrs. Hotchkiss, "London has treated me very well, ma'am. Thank you for asking."

"And what is it you *do* there?" Mrs. Hotchkiss asked.

Olivia's expression remained studiously neutral. "I trained as a typist. Since then—"

"And was that what led you into His Grace's company?" Mrs. Dale glanced toward him. Her eyes were dark, shining, without depth. "Or was it, perhaps, some *family* connection?"

Mrs. Hotchkiss made some abrupt gesture—distress, quickly controlled. *Ah.* Alastair understood now: Mrs. Dale thought he was unaware of Olivia's bastardy. Accordingly, she was angling the conversation toward that subject.

He broadcast mild puzzlement. "No, indeed. Miss Holladay served as secretary to my aunt, in fact."

"And now you play her escort." Mrs. Dale gave him a thin, skeptical smile. "How *unusually* decent."

She clearly imagined their relationship to be the opposite of decent. In the middle ages, she would have been the first to light a faggot when it came time to burn the witch. *Charming.*

Alastair shrugged. "It was my aunt's last request that I see Miss Holladay settled."

Mrs. Dale lifted one thin, dark brow. "I am surprised she required help. She was always so very *clever* at her business. It must have slipped Mrs. Hotchkiss's mind," she added to Olivia directly, "to mention that I am a grandmother. It was a very happy day when my son wed Miss Crocker. She is everything one could wish for in a daughter."

Ah. He gathered that at one point, Mrs. Dale's son had glanced Olivia's way instead.

"A grandmother!" Olivia said warmly. "But I should have thought you a great-grandmother at the least!"

Mrs. Dale's mouth tightened.

"Well, but then you must have some purpose in coming here," said Mrs. Hotchkiss hastily. "That is—if His Grace is helping you to settle matters, Miss Holladay."

This was his cue. He rose. "Perhaps, Mrs. Dale, you might walk with me. I should like to hear about the history of Allen's End."

Mrs. Dale did not rise. "For Mrs. Hotchkiss's sake, I must remain while she speaks with Miss Holladay."

That statement held a dozen possible inferences, all of them profoundly insulting to Olivia—and by extension, to any man who had seen fit to give her the care of his fictional aunt.

Very evenly, holding her reptilian eyes, he said, "You will walk with me, Mrs. Dale."

The lizard had another moment's mutiny in her. Then, folding her lips, she rose. "Very well. Miss Holladay . . ." She looked down her nose at Olivia. "I assure you, His Grace will find Allen's End much changed, much *elevated,* since your departure."

She stalked out in a crunch of old-fashioned taffeta. He lingered a moment, not caring to offer her his arm as she made her way to the road.

"I am sorry for that," Mrs. Hotchkiss said softly—not to him, but to Olivia, who shrugged.

"It's all right," she said. "I expected no better."

* * *

Outside, the temperature had plummeted, and gray clouds were gathering, pressing low toward the earth. Alastair spotted Mrs. Dale hurrying off down the lane, her skirts twitching briskly. How remarkable. In his experience, there was never a shortage of country matrons who wished to boast that they had strolled with a duke.

He stood by the gate, rubbing his hands together against the chill. Nearby, the horses stirred, causing the coachman to murmur some soothing remark. To the right lay a panoramic view of curving fields and grazing sheep. To the left, down the winding road they had traveled, stood a stretch of shops and cottages. It was a scene from some painting of a pastoral idyll, but he was gathering it had been far from paradise for Olivia.

He heard the door open. Only a single set of footsteps tapped down the stones. Olivia looked composed but pale. "Nothing," she said. She crossed her arms against a sharp breeze. "She's been living here for two years. There's not a nook, she says, that she hasn't looked into."

Her dispirited tone disturbed him. In the gray light, her skin looked bloodless, her bruise livid. How had he not thought to ask after her cheek this morning? "Are you in pain?" he asked.

She touched her face. "It's only a bruise," she said, and then laughed. "Or a brand of infamy, depending on whom you ask. I should have bought a pair of horns to wear, too!" She glanced around suddenly. "Where did she go?"

"Hustled off before we could even have our walk."

"You sound very sorry about it." A cynical smile came

onto her lips. "She's gone to spread the news, no doubt. Shall we walk? Let them have a look at the jezebel?"

He hesitated, frowning. Why on earth would she want to linger in this cesspool? "If there's nothing of use here—"

"But I've had an idea." She started down the road toward the shops. He snapped to the coachman, signaling him to follow, and fell into step beside her. As they passed the next house, he saw a curtain twitch in the front window, as though someone indeed had been alerted to watch for them.

"'*The truth is hidden at home,*'" Olivia said. "But this was never her home, was it?" Her profile looked serene; she did not seem to notice they were being spied upon—not only from the house to their left, but from the house on the other side of the lane, where, in the front window, Alastair could make out a shadowy form blending into the darker drapery. "She never meant Allen's End. She meant Shepwich!"

"It's possible." But he said it absently, for uneasiness was prickling over him. The overcast sky, paired with the empty road scoured by brackish wind, lent this place a forsaken quality. How it had produced a woman like Olivia, he could not begin to guess.

Up ahead on the wooden boardwalk, a small group of matrons emerged from a shop to huddle together in conversation. He picked out the paisley shawl of Mrs. Dale.

Olivia's steps seemed to quicken. She took a firm grip on his arm, hugging it to her—an embrace far more comprehensive than propriety allowed. He looked down into her pale face, not deceived by her pleasant smile. "These fools aren't worth your time," he said.

The wind pulled loose a strand of her brick-red hair, fluttering it gently against her cheek. "True," she said. "But I am taller than them now. And I have a duke on my arm. Let them see it."

Another truth struck him, distasteful, bitter. "I'm worse than a bruise," he said. "You know what they will assume."

"And they'll be right, won't they?" She said it lightly. "But I'll wager I can outstare them, and that will satisfy me greatly."

Mrs. Dale broke away from the group, hurrying off down the road, while the other women turned as one to watch their approach.

Anger was building in him. "Stop this," he bit out. "Why would you willingly make yourself a spectacle?"

"You yourself said it, didn't you? I'm brazen. Shameless."

He sucked in a breath. "I never meant—"

"Didn't you?" Their boots thudded hollowly on the wooden steps that led up onto the promenade. "Be at ease, though. *You* have nothing to fear. I'm certain they will bow and scrape very nicely to you. Even if you weren't a duke, the *man* is never blamed for it."

He groped for words. But the only reply was very simple. "I'm sorry," he said quietly. "I spoke recklessly, earlier. Without thinking."

"Of course." She jerked her chin toward a bakery, where someone was drawing down the shades. "The baker, Mr. Porter, was very kind to Mama—but not his wife. She turned away from my mother in the street."

"Fools," he said.

"Virtuous churchgoers, in fact. It was Mrs. Porter, along with Mrs. Dale, who conspired to have Mama expelled from the congregation. She had no proof of her christening—that was how they got her."

Christ. That was unspeakably petty and cruel—and also the quickest, most effective way to isolate someone in a community as small as this. He turned his hand in hers, tightening his grip.

But she snorted and pulled free. "I was glad of it. The vicar gave the most tedious sermons!"

He forced Olivia to a stop twenty paces from the cluster of staring women. He remembered his own words to her in the coach: *Did you leave no friends behind?*

Once upon a time, he had never been so carelessly cruel.

"I was lonely, too," he said. "As a boy. My parents were judged, mocked, ostracized. That should not have been my burden to bear. And this is not yours."

Something naked and vulnerable came into her face then, which he never wanted to see again. It was in his power, surely, to make certain she never looked so. Otherwise, what was the use of power?

"Not everyone was so awful," she said softly. "The vicar told her it didn't matter. But she never went back to church. In fact, she rarely went out at all after that."

Something clicked inside him. He took a sharp breath. "She wouldn't leave the house."

Gently she said, "You thought you were the first to discover that solution?"

He felt stunned, as though he'd been slammed into a wall. "But you never hid." Was that bitterness in his voice? Or mere, raw wonder?

"They were never worth hiding from." She looked over his shoulder. "And there is the milliner," she said. "Bertram had to bring hats from London. Mr. Ardell would not sell to her. His wife forbade it."

"I'll buy you every damned hat in the place."

She wrinkled her nose and locked eyes, over his shoulder, with the women at the end of the boardwalk. "I shouldn't want any," she said, loud and distinct. "They're all quite dreadful."

He turned to join her in staring. Two of the women were near to Mrs. Hotchkiss's age, but the third was young enough to be Olivia's peer, though her expression looked so sour that it aged her. "It is unfortunate," he said, "how these little towns tend to collect all the rubbish."

The elder two women whirled away and thudded down the stairs to the road. After a moment, the sour-faced girl snatched up her skirts and followed.

"Oh," Olivia whispered. "That *did* feel pleasant."

The coach had drawn up beside them, the horses stamping. "You've run the gauntlet, then," he said. "Let's leave this pit."

Olivia allowed him to help her into the coach. But when the door closed, she said immediately, "It was no gauntlet. A gauntlet hurts those who run it. But I never cared for their good opinion."

"Of course not."

"Really. I didn't." She gave him a strange little smile. "Don't imagine I wanted them to apologize for the past. I only wanted to walk in my mother's footsteps for a minute—now that I'm fully qualified to do so. But as it turns out, I can't. For she always did care what they thought. And when I was young, I decided that nobody would ever be able to ruin me but myself. Only today I know that I've kept that vow. Their stares made no difference to me."

He gauged her in silence. She meant it. This was not a show, a brave face.

"But I do wish," she added, "you would not call me shameless. For I do value *your* opinion." She wrinkled her nose. "Though perhaps I shouldn't."

"It was not an insult." God help him if he ever used it as an insult again. "I invite you to be as shameless as you like."

She tilted her head, giving him a look of smiling puzzlement. "Indeed? But I did seem to scandalize you on the train. And I should not like to trample your tender sensibilities—"

He took her by the waist and pulled her across the carriage onto his lap.

She was soft, startled, laughing, a wriggling hot bundle in his arms. "Oh, dear," she said, and whooped as she lost her balance; he steadied her by the waist, and she looped her arms around his neck with a broad smile. "You seem to *prefer* me brazen," she said.

He put his face in her hair, dragging her into his lungs, hard, deep breaths full of her. Let her settle in his lungs. Let her penetrate every pore. She smelled like roses, but he knew now that it could not be a trick of perfume; the soap at the flat had been castor and lye. This scent was not the essence of flower water, but the essence of *her,* some alchemical design of her strange nature. Her miraculous nature. Rose-scented mettle, indifferent to convention.

She spoke again, less steadily: "I think I prefer me brazen, too."

He had no reply. He was lost in the feel of her hair. He rubbed against it like a cat, letting it brush over his eyelids, his cheeks. He did not simply admire her. He *coveted* her, and his rapacity was not merely lustful. He had wanted once to steal her hope, but if he could have walked an hour in her skin, he would have done so, just to feel how such mettle might be worn so elegantly, encased in such soft, fragrant flesh.

He took her ear between his teeth and licked the rim, making her gasp. One could say this was only lust, of course. He meant to take her here, to push himself into her body and make her moan. But lust was only an itch, mechanically satisfied. Lust was like hunger, and a man's appetite was as easily sated by plain bread as by foie gras.

This was not simply lust. It was not only his body that needed her. It was not only her body that he needed.

He tilted her in his arms, leaning her back, her head supported in his hand, to drag his mouth down her jaw. He tasted her throat, salt, cream, and felt her shiver. Her body moved at his bidding; he lifted her, turned her again so she sat against the seat. He cupped her breast, stroked it, and made her shudder again. Feeling her body answer to his seemed to unhinge something inside him, a floodgate, some crucial safeguard that kept him in check. A tide of need, raw and pulsing, blotted out his brain.

He let her feel his teeth—the scrape of them against her neck, and then the flick of his tongue. She whimpered. He would seduce her body, snare it, if he could not capture her mind, lure her to confess all its parts to him, to reveal her secrets willingly. He slid off the bench and coaxed her to lie down across it; she let him lower her, her body pliant, her wide eyes the shade of wild skies on the moors. Wildness could be tamed.

He sank to his knees on the rattling, cold floor and came over her, lowering his mouth to hers, sealing her mouth with his lips. *Speak only to me.* He felt cunning and calculating and ambitious and—suddenly—fiercely jealous of moments when she had spoken to others, all the words she had given away, the wit she had squandered on those who did not properly appreciate it, even the courage she had shown those village harpies, who were blind and would misrecognize it as depravity.

Her closed mouth suddenly seemed to deprive him of his right. He opened it with his lips. He kissed her tongue, her teeth, her inner cheeks; every inch of her mouth would be his now. He slid his palm down to the neckline of her gown, finding beneath it the smooth rise of her breast, the pebbling peak of her nipple, which he rasped lightly with his nail until she moaned.

"In a . . . carriage . . ." She sounded dreamily amazed. He was not sure, in truth, how it could be done. But a half hour remained before they reached the station. He would invent a way. Like a scientist, he would devise a way to take her apart. He would own her by the end. No one else would get the chance.

He inched down the bodice of her dress bit by bit, taking great care, because he would not allow her to be disgraced in public by a rip or tear; no one would look at her again as those women had (though she had never been touched by their scorn; it existed in a different universe from the one she assembled, by the force of her unyielding will). He coaxed her breasts from the obnoxious pressure of her stays, which, because God was kind, were leather, and spared him the challenges of lacing and whalebone. And then he took her nipple in his mouth while he watched her face.

Her mouth fell open. She tried to cover her eyes with the back of her hand. He pulled her hand away and held it down, in a firm grip, beside her: she would not deny him the sight of her reaction to him.

Her groan was animal. Animal, yes, vivid and vigorous and free. She had the coloring of a fox, her hair a wild pelt, red and copper and russet and orange, sunlight and fire trapped and refracted. He suckled her as he lifted her skirts, and felt up her long, smooth limbs. When she tried to sit up, to assist him, he forced her back down with another, deeper kiss. He did not require assistance. *Be still,* he did not say, because he did not want her cooperation; it was her submission he craved, and it was his challenge to earn it. *Give yourself to me.*

Her knees, once bared to the light, proved to be plump and curving, dimpled, an invitation to his mouth. He had not lingered over them that night in the library, a sin for which he had been suitably punished by her later betrayal—her deceit, in the heated retrospect of this moment, seemed almost too mild for the guilt of his omission, in ignoring her knees. When he nibbled at the inside of her thigh, she squeaked; and then, as the coach slowed, she clamped her legs shut. "Wait!" she gasped.

But the changing rhythm of the wheels showed that they had slowed only so the driver could transition onto the smoother course of the highway. Alastair licked the seam of her joined thighs, and then, when they proved stubborn, he ran his hand up to her quim, his thumb pressing firmly through the thin lawn, and said, "Give me this."

Her legs fell apart.

He felt for the split in her drawers, and then probed softly, delicately, through her tender, damp folds, the gentleness of his touch a deceit of its own, masking the savage feeling growing in him, feeding like a ravening beast on the noises she made. He lifted her skirts and found her with his mouth again, God above, it seemed he had waited centuries to relive this possession—and he licked and sucked until she whispered, "Please," and then licked into her until she said it again.

God, what he would not do to hear her beg! He made her say it once more; he made her choke it out, and felt her nails turn into his back, and still it was not enough. How to prolong it? He eased off when he felt her hips buck; he breathed lightly on her until her body retreated from climax, and then he laid his mouth on her and devoured her again. She was gasping, but was it enough? Villains tied women to train tracks; had she proved mute, had she resisted, he would have tied her to the train tracks until she cried for mercy, and then he would have fucked her on the rails, against a tree, on the grass, until she knew how to cry out for him, until she had learned her lesson fully. There was no goodness in him. But in the smell of her, in her groan, he saw a good use for his evil. He saw a way to accept it, to use it, if it would make her moan.

He sat up and lifted her on top of him; she bobbled, clutching his shoulders, breathless, flushed, her lips damp, open; he had a glimpse of her tongue and leaned forward to suck it into his mouth as he unfastened his trousers.

Her hand closed around him. He gasped. It was the first sound, perhaps, he had made. She guided him, her hips moving awkwardly; he grasped her waist and re-adjusted her, and then—ah, her quim opened for him, inch by inch as he pushed inside her. He felt her grow wetter yet, and hotter, as she closed around him. Her forehead fell to his shoulder; he cupped her skull, *stay there,* she was safe there, pinned, and with his other hand he directed her hips, showing her the way of it, until she moved against him as he moved into her.

Always. The word beat into his brain. He would stay in her always, her weight a grounding burden, what kept him in place as he kept her in place, his arm around her. He would take her body again and again, and God help anyone who tried to come between them, for their bodies belonged together, his in hers, she pinioned, penetrated, *his*. This alone he knew. Her hot wet depths posed a challenge that only his body would answer; he would teach her how to be greedy, he would use her and let the world go to hell. She would have no room to think of anything else; he would fill her so completely that thoughts would find no room to penetrate.

He reached between them, rubbing her, stroking, and she lifted her head and cried out. He gripped her, held her still, and forced her to take the pleasure, to follow it. She contracted around him, pulsing spasms gripping his cock, and he felt his own climax rush over him, the hot seed that would plant him inside her, make her truly his own, himself a part of her forever—

No.

He thrust her away from him, onto the bench. He would not betray her so. He put his head into the wall, and worked himself—two strokes was all it took. He spilled onto the ground.

When he turned back, breath ragged, he found her disheveled, skirts around her thighs, hair mussed, pins strewn across her lap. They stared at each other. He felt unable to hide what must be in his face. He did not know what to do. She deserved more; she deserved better. He could not offer her any of what she deserved.

He did not move, though the urge to gather her to him, to kiss her face and throat, was fiercely powerful: to deliver a final imprint, to warn her that she must not forget what he had just shown her. Her body was his. But what could he offer in return?

He did not move. For ownership was a lifetime's proposition. No other measure of time made sense to him. And that was absurd. And he had nothing to offer. He did not trust himself enough to offer what he might.

"Well," she said shakily, and licked her lips.

The sight stabbed through him, a sweet, hot pain. He could think of nothing to say. Words did not make sense with her. All the words that might frame her—bastard; liar; housekeeper; thief—were wrong. But there were no words to replace them. And no words that made sense, when linked to him. Not *wife*. Not *mistress*. And not *stranger*. Never again.

CHAPTER SIXTEEN

Olivia remembered very little of her only visit to Shepwich, which had not lasted above an hour or two. She remembered a house, infinitely large and empty. An old woman who had tried to pull Olivia onto her lap—but Mama had snatched her back. And she remembered an argument, very angry, as Mama wept.

These were not details that provided much help in locating her mother's childhood home. But Shepwich itself was smaller even than Allen's End, no more than a dozen houses sparsely arranged around the bend in the sandy road, and the proprietor of the general store, who greeted her with curiosity, answered at once: "The Holladays? Aye, you'll want the white house half a mile down the lane with the old stone barn in back. Can't miss it. A relation, are you? You've the look of a Holladay, about your eyes and . . ." He gestured toward his nose.

"Yes," Olivia said, "a relative," and beat a hasty retreat to the coach, where Marwick was waiting—his presence, she'd felt, being somewhat too grand to induce easy admissions from a shopkeeper.

She gave instructions to the coachman, an easygoing young man who'd proved remarkably tolerant at devoting his day to haring about the countryside. Inside, Marwick was slouched against the wall, looking sullen. The effect of sexual congress obviously varied widely: it rather enlivened her, but *he* always behaved afterward as though he'd been hit hard on the head. "What do you think of my nose?" she asked him.

He pushed himself up from his slouch, and frowned at the item in question. "I never have, particularly."

"Exactly," she said with satisfaction. Her nose was straight enough, if a touch too large for true beauty. But she deemed it in no way remarkable. "Yet the man in that store said it marked me as a Holladay."

She did not intend the remark to pose some revelation, but Marwick looked arrested. He leaned forward, considering her so narrowly that she felt, after a moment, somewhat flustered, and held her hand up to block her nose from his view. "It's a very normal nose," she said. "Don't tell me otherwise."

The corner of his mouth twitched. "I wouldn't dare," he said. "It's a lovely nose, in fact."

She dropped her hand and ogled him. "A compliment! I change my mind: my nose must be the eighth wonder of the world!"

Expression darkening, he settled back against his bench. "I've complimented you before."

"Have you?" She shrugged. "Very well."

"I have."

She saw no point in arguing. She looked out the window, aware suddenly of a certain nervous flutter in her stomach. This stretch of Kent, the last ribbon of fertile soil before the ground turned to salt and sand, was the land of her ancestors. Flat green fields stretched endlessly beneath the gray sky. If these people, the Holladays, tried to slam the door in her face, she would *not* weep. Had it not been for the . . . interlude . . . on this very bench, she would have been primed to rage at them. Instead, she decided she would task Marwick to coldly intimidate them.

"I've told you you're beautiful," he said.

She glanced at him, startled. "Oh, yes, of course. But that was during . . ." She felt herself blush. Peculiar how one could do things without shame, but not be able to speak of them.

His smile now was deliberately suggestive. "It counts," he said. "But I'll say it again, lest you feel skeptical: you are beautiful, Olivia."

She frowned at him, puzzled by why he might say so. "I'm not, particularly."

He frowned back at her. "Yes," he said. "You are."

What nonsense was this? "You and I both know what beauty looks like." A waspish tone had crept into her voice. She did not like to be patronized. "Your late wife was beautiful. The very picture of beauty."

It was a calculated decision, mentioning her. Olivia expected it to end the conversation. But he merely shrugged. "She was lovely to look at," he said. "But not beautiful."

She smiled despite herself. "That's ridiculous. Do you mean to say that beauty lies in a lantern jaw?" She touched her chin. "A perfect square?"

His eyes followed her hand. "Determination," he said. "Resolve. Yes, those things are beautiful."

"I'm talking about my *jaw*."

"That is what your jaw looks like to me."

She felt a fluster of confusion. Was he serious with this mad babble? But he appeared quite serious. He was gazing at her with perfect sobriety.

She suddenly could not hold his eyes. She looked out the window again. If he was mocking her . . . "Obviously you find me attractive," she said. "And I'm handsome, no doubt. I have all my teeth. But that's a different thing from beauty. That's all I mean."

"Self-possession," he said. "Dignity. Gorgeous qualities. I see them in your straight spine. In the way you hold yourself, your carriage."

Did she hold herself so distinctively? She had never realized it. She felt a flush of gratification, quite unfamiliar, stemming as it did from her neglected vanity. "Don't be silly."

"I'm the fifth Duke of Marwick," he said. "Also the Earl of Beckden and the Baron Wellsley. I am many things, but I am not *silly*."

She rolled her eyes at the clouds.

"Resilience," he said. "In the tilt to your chin." Dryly he added, "It verges on stubbornness, of course, but all the virtues extend into flaws when carried too far."

She cast him a quick, mocking glance. "In the manner of compliments that edge on criticisms?"

He smiled at her. She looked away again, but now she was holding her breath, hoping (ridiculous of her!) that he might go on.

And he did. "Passion in the vibrant colors of your hair," he murmured. "I see new shades every time I look at it. I've counted at least nine."

He'd been cataloging the shades of her hair?

"Intelligence in your brow. Thoughtfulness in the way it has furrowed, as you try to figure out whether

I'm speaking truthfully. Which I am. And you would be wise to believe me. I've been making a study of you for quite some time now. Yours was the first face I'd seen in months, after all. The face I saw through the darkness. And it seems that I know it even better than you do, if you doubt your own beauty."

She'd been holding her breath, and now she could not catch it. She looked back at him wonderingly, and the expression on his face . . . It was sober and tender and intent. She had wondered, in his garden, if any man would look this way at her again. She'd never dreamed that he might be the one to do it.

But that had been her secret hope.

"You're mad," she whispered. She felt shaken. "Perhaps *you* need the spectacles."

He gave her a gentle smile. "Humor and wit, in the quirk of your lips. And in your eyes . . ." His smile faded. "Hope."

She swallowed. He had commented on that before, in the library.

Would you always look at me so? She bit her lip to stop the words, and put her hand over her chest, which twisted painfully. For she knew the answer to that question better than he did. He thought he would never recover his old life. But one day he would. The world would not be content to move forward always without him. And he, eventually, would not be able to endure the sidelines.

He would stop looking at her like this once he remembered who he was.

The coach began to slow. She made herself look out. She did not recognize the house. It was only a single story, weatherboarded in white, barely larger than the cottage in which she'd grown up. A stone barn stood a short way beyond it, through a field of waving grass.

"Of course," he said as the vehicle rocked to a halt, "the final element, which shows nowhere in particular, and everywhere at once, is your courage."

She took a deep breath.

"I know you're ready to face these people—your family, Olivia. But there is no need for you to do it. You can stay here while I speak with them. And then, if they wish to meet you, they can make the approach themselves. I think you deserve that—to be the one who is approached."

Her throat closed. He had not mentioned kindness. That was *his* quality, which she lacked. But it suffused every part of him, though he fought so hard to hide it. Perhaps she was the only person in the world who managed to see it so clearly in him. Even he himself seemed blind to it. "Thank you," she said. "But today . . . I seem to want to do it all." He thought her very brave, but without him, she would never have dared approach those women on the promenade. By his side, she discovered new parts of herself fashioned from steel and armor, parts that she liked very much. She would take advantage of them now. "I want to get through it all in one fell swoop."

He moved onto her bench. "For luck then," he said, and lifted her hand for a single kiss that she felt all the way through her bones.

Mrs. Holladay, white haired and petite, had the rosy cheeks and bright eyes of a figure in a fairy tale: the white witch who saved children from wolves. But she wore the weeds of a widow, and when she received them at the door, her courteous greeting was sluggish, dulled by obvious fatigue.

Her mourning black, and the lock of hair she wore at her wrinkled throat, silenced Olivia. Marwick spoke for them both, but he only shared his own name, and conveyed that they had come on a matter of delicate but urgent import. "You should sit," he said, "before we speak."

Mrs. Holladay ushered them into her parlor, where tea was laid. After handing them each a cup, she said, with a polite but bewildered smile, "How may I help you, then?"

Olivia took a breath. "You won't recognize me. But my mother was Jean Holladay, your daughter."

Mrs. Holladay dropped her cup. Tea splashed across the carpet, but she did not seem to notice. She stared, lips trembling. "Oh. Oh. Oh, you've come home!" She lifted a hand to her mouth. "If only Roger had lived to see it . . ."

Roger, it transpired, was Mrs. Holladay's late husband, only two months' deceased. She rushed to find a photograph of him, then changed course and flew outside. Olivia heard her tasking the coachman to take a note to the neighboring farmstead—the denizens of which must have worked to spread the news very rapidly, for within a quarter hour, the parlor had filled with strangers, all of them claiming to be Olivia's relations.

Cousins, uncles, nieces and nephews, dear old friends of her mother's, swarmed to introduce themselves. Amid this strange and ardent welcome, Olivia found herself quite unable to cut to the point of her visit. She felt numb, overwhelmed, a cold point of sobriety amid tears and laughter. Marwick, now seated on the sofa watching her with an inscrutable look, now cloistered in the corner in conference with a farmer (whose trousers were still coated with stray bits of hay), proved no help at all. But when she finally extricated herself from embraces and found a seat again, he somehow managed to appear beside her, asking in a low voice if she was all right.

Of course she was. She reached for her resolve. "Mrs. Holladay," she said (making clear with a pointed look that she did not mean any of the four other Mrs. Holladays, two of whom had babes in arm). "I must speak with you privately."

"Of course, dear!" Mrs. Holladay proposed a supper, and this seemed a signal for everybody to disperse, with promises of a quick return, and a dish or two each to contribute.

Once the three of them were alone again, Mrs. Holladay (*Grandmother, you should call me*) took a seat opposite, taking up her knitting, beaming as her needles clacked.

Olivia took Marwick's hand. Mrs. Holladay's rheumy gaze flicked down to take note of it, and somehow, that faint whisper of propriety finally jarred Olivia into speaking the question that, once voiced, sparked a burn of anger: "Why are you being so kind to me? You turned my mother away from your doorstep when she most needed you. Why?"

Mrs. Holladay dropped her needles. "Gracious, child! Turn her away? Did *she* say that? We never did any such thing!"

Curiously, Olivia felt Marwick's surprise more than her own. It registered very clearly in the sharp squeeze of his fingers around hers. "But you did," she said. "I remember it. You quarreled with her, and then we went away in the dark, and she said we couldn't stay."

"But that's because she refused to listen to us." Mrs. Holladay sat forward, looking white as paper. "We told her she needn't put up with him. We told her she should sue him in court. And she refused. She wouldn't do that to him, she said. As though she owed him anything! And yes, by heaven, we quarreled with her for that—your grandfather would have no part in letting that rascal abuse her. He wanted justice. He would have sold every inch of this land to fund a lawsuit, if she'd only allowed it."

The woman might as well have been speaking in tongues. But a strange, prickling foreboding came over Olivia. "A lawsuit?"

"Yes, a lawsuit! How else were we to go about it?"

Marwick spoke then. "A lawsuit on what grounds?"

Mrs. Holladay made a disgusted noise. "On the grounds of bigamy, of course! How could he marry that American girl, how *dare* he do it, when he was already married to my daughter?"

Olivia sat on a fallen log, by the edge of a pond choked with lily pads. The dark water glimmered in the late afternoon light. As if winter had forgotten about this stretch of Kent, many of the branches still bore leaves, and the air was temperate, scented by mulch and sap.

She heard Marwick coming long before she saw him. Branches cracked underfoot, and then a stone flew past her, skipping across the pond's surface.

"Well done," she said.

"I can do better." He came to sit beside her on the log. After a brief study of the ground, he plucked up another stone and proved his claim.

She rather thought she knew how that stone felt when it made the final plunge. Surprised to be so suddenly out of its depths.

She had listened as long as she'd been able. But when the family had begun crowding into the parlor again, carrying dishes and bottles, full of merriment, her numbness had cracked. She had excused herself to the washroom, then ducked out the door and followed the path through the scraggly wood to this pond.

"They must be wondering where I am," she said now.

He shrugged. "They're aghast that your mother didn't tell you the truth."

She bit down hard on her cheek. Yes, all right, it was anger she was feeling. Anger and . . . deep, deep injury. "She must have had her reasons."

He said nothing.

"She loved him." A jagged laugh spilled from her. "This, above all, is the ultimate proof of it." To have protected him against his own evildoing, even at the cost of her own happiness.

"She might have loved you better," he said quietly. "To have put you through such a childhood—"

"Don't." She snatched up a rock and hurled it. It did not skip once, but it made a mighty splash as it sank. "She loved me very well. What could *you* know about it? And who knows? If she hadn't taken his bigamy quietly, perhaps he'd have sent a man to throttle *her*."

"Perhaps," he said after a pause. "I suppose it does

solve the mystery of why he hounds you. If he feared you had the proof of his marriage to your mother . . ."

Tears pricked her eyes. Why now? She had been staring dry-eyed for half an hour. "What a joke. I don't."

He turned to her. "Olivia. You do."

She dashed a hand over her eyes. "Do I?"

He brushed his thumb over her cheek, his handsome face grave. "That's what your mother meant by that line in her diary. The 'hidden truth'—that's the parish register. Your grandmother explained the whole of it. The night your mother brought you here, the family conferred with the rector who had married your parents. He decided to hide the register—a very wise decision, for the church was later burgled. A few pieces of silver went missing, along with the registers—save the one which the rector had locked away."

"Oh." The syllable seemed to flop out of her mouth. She stared at the ground where it would have landed.

"So it can be proved," he said.

She nodded once.

His hand found hers. "Is that all you have to say?"

She glanced at him and felt a strange flutter of anxiety at his frown, which she identified after a moment: concern that she had disappointed him. She pulled her hand free and stared at the lily pads again.

She had never felt obligated to anybody but her mother—and perhaps Elizabeth Chudderley, for whom she'd felt such deep gratitude for employing her without a proper reference. But what was this uneasiness now, but proof that she felt beholden to *him*? Beholden not only in simple matters, like their shared aims in regard to Bertram. She also worried over his moods. She wanted him to be . . . happy.

But she knew that his happiness lay in his return to a world she could not join. Lovely. She'd fashioned a perfect pit for herself.

She cleared her throat. "It has certainly been . . . odd," she said. "The afternoon."

"Odd in the best of ways." She heard in his voice that he was attempting to cheer her. "Had we a copy of Debrett's, we could edit it."

She did not want to think on that right now. It would be a rageful undertaking to reflect on the consequences of exposing Bertram—and she had spent long enough in this dark mood. She was not a woman to sulk. Better to focus on the simpler, happier facts: she had a family. She had a place. She had everything she'd once longed for.

Yet where was her triumph? Why did she not feel compelled to return to the house, to meet everyone, to bask in their welcomes, their affection so easily offered?

They didn't know her. They had no idea who she was, only that a woman they loved had birthed her. But the man sitting next to her knew her. And he was all she needed. All she wanted.

God help me.

She watched him toss another stone, then let herself take his hand. Only that. "I never could do that," she said, after the fifth skip finished the stone's run.

"It just takes practice. And a pond, of course."

"Then that's what I lacked. The only pond in Allen's End was the cow pond—and I promise you, the smell kept me away."

"Little girls are so picky."

She laughed despite herself. "I can't imagine the young heir to the dukedom got his practice in a stinking cesspit!"

"More of a small lake, really." He grinned, and ran his thumb across her knuckles. "Far more manicured. There was a gardener's assistant whose only task was to keep it cleared of weeds."

She tried to match his smile. This was one of the happiest days of her life, wasn't it? And he was sharing it with her. He was here with her—for now.

"I wonder," he said, but did not continue.

If her happiness depended on keeping him, she was sunk. "I wonder, too." She felt very cold, suddenly.

He glanced over at her. "Go on."

She shook her head. "You first."

He gave her a half smile. "I wonder what we, both us, would have been like, growing up in a place like this."

We. Some bittersweet feeling constricted her chest. She tried to pull her hand away, but his grip tightened, and after a moment, she surrendered to it. "I think we would have been spoiled rotten," she said.

He gave a low, rusty laugh. "No doubt you're right."

They sat hand in hand, unspeaking, as the light changed around them. The pond reflected the late afternoon sun, bits of pollen and fuzz drifting in the sunbeams that fell through the trees. Bubbles rose on the water, popped, and disappeared. A fish surfaced, mouth gaping. Somewhere in the distance a bird called out.

"You would have thrived here," he said. "The brightest girl in the district. Petted and admired by everyone. That's what you deserved."

Her throat felt tight. "But I would not have learned to speak Italian, I fear."

"Oh, you would have found a way."

She shrugged. Perhaps she would have. But it would have required the desire to learn Italian—and bereft of others' contempt, of the hostility and suspicion of Allen's End, what would have planted her so firmly before her books? She might have spent her afternoons playing chase and hunting treasure instead. Shouting and quarreling and jumping rope . . . learning to make friends, instead of learning how to hide herself.

She cleared her throat. "If *you* had grown up here, I should have *had* to learn chess. Otherwise who would have explained Blackburne's Gambit to you? You're hopeless on your own." She looked at him from the corner of her eye, and saw that he was smiling. Encouraged, she said, "But you still would have gone into politics. You'd have made a fine MP, in time—a true hero of the common people. We would have called you . . ." The notion amused her. "The salt of the earth."

He laughed. "There's a wild idea. But I'm not so certain. It's a hard road from the paddock to Parliament."

"You would have found your way." She dared to tread on dangerous ground. "You did not get your ideals from your father. You discovered them on your own. You would have found them here, too."

He glanced at her, visibly struck. "Yes," he said slowly. "All my ideals. You see how they've guided me, this last year."

The words were cynical. But his tone was speculative, testing. She pressed his hand in encouragement. "Those ideals are part of you still. You only took a rest, Marwick. You needed a rest. But soon you'll take up the gauntlet again—very soon, I think." And there would be no place for her then.

He gazed at her. "Perhaps. If I remember how to care about such things."

"You still care."

"I've learned to care about different things now." Very gently, he reached out to brush her cheek. "You should call me Alastair," he murmured.

She swallowed. Suddenly it seemed important to say something. "We would have been true friends, had we both grown up here." She made herself say it: "Alastair."

"I think you're right. Olivia." He stroked her face. "And we might have come here, to this very place, to sit and talk, as friends do."

"Very often. And perhaps . . ." She smiled. "Not only to talk. This is where you would have kissed me, I think. The first time. When we were both . . . sixteen?"

"Fifteen," he said. "Fourteen."

"Precocious young things!"

"Yes," he said. "Brash. Barely out of childhood. And the first time I kissed you . . ." He leaned toward her, and she inclined to meet him. "It would have been like this," he said against her mouth.

His lips were warm, indescribably sweet. It felt as though he sought something from her, something precious that must be coaxed rather than taken. And she gave it to him, gladly.

After a long minute, he turned his face to kiss her temple. "You would have been shocked," he whispered. "But no more than I, at my own temerity."

She put her face into his shoulder to hide her smile. "Is that so?"

"Well. A rude country boy. No large experience. I should think he'd be shocked."

"But as a farm girl, perhaps I wouldn't be. Farm girls are saucy, I think. When you pulled away in shock, I would have dragged you back for another kiss."

"Would you?"

She liked the startled pleasure in his voice. She lifted her head to show him her smile. "Oh, yes," she said. "Like this."

His kiss had been slow and wooing. But country girls had little patience for that. She licked his lower lip, made him groan; then she slid her hand through his hair and pulled his mouth hard into hers.

In a flash, hunger leapt between them: electrical, overwhelming. His palm pressed flat against her lower back and held her in place as he angled his head, kissing her more deeply yet.

But then, like a motion in a symphony, there came a moment when they both paused by tacit accord. "I wonder," she said against his lips, "how saucy I would be? I would know you so well, after all. But until this moment, you would have only been a friend."

He loosed a soft breath. "But there was never really an 'only' about it. We would always have known, somehow, that it would be more."

"Yes." She caught his hand, kissed his palm and then pressed it to her cheek. "I think I would be very bold. I wouldn't feel any fear. You would be so safe . . . and not safe, all at once. I would trust you completely, somehow."

"And I would never fear disappointing you." He put his face into her hair, so his voice came out muffled. "Because I would require your trust like I required air. And if you were bold with me, then it wouldn't feel like boldness. It would feel like wisdom."

"Would it?" she whispered.

"Yes. Because we would both know that you need never plan on kissing anyone else."

She felt dizzy, breathless. "And how would I know that?"

"You would know that I meant to marry you."

She could barely speak. "Would I?"

"Yes. Before the next harvest," he said roughly, and pulled away from her. His expression now looked black as he gazed out at the pond.

She loosed an unsteady breath. It was only a fantasy. But didn't he see how painful such games must be? Did he imagine she would have slept with any man who rescued her from prison? Did he not know what it meant that he could say *I know you*?

She had wanted a place. Now she had one. But now she realized that not *any* place would do.

She frowned at herself and reached for good sense. "I would refuse to marry you, of course."

He cast her a fleeting, one-sided smile. "That would be a mistake. You deserve love. And a family. All those children you once told me you won't have."

She recoiled. "Don't tell me that." Why did he taunt her like this? Why did he dare her to dream of love, while he sat across from her? "*You,* of all people!"

"I, of all people." He repeated it softly, then turned to her. "Indeed. Let me tell you, then, the truth you once asked of me. I wanted to love my wife, Olivia. I believed I did. I certainly thought her everything worthy of love, when we married."

Oh, God. She sucked in a breath. She had not wanted to know it. Not really. But he was holding her eyes and she could not look away, even though she knew the blood was draining from her face, and she lacked the skill to mask how he wounded her.

"I loved the idea of her," he said evenly. "The perfect wife for a man of my station. Well bred. Elegant. Not a woman who would be led astray by passions or tempers, as my mother was." He paused. "But she had her heart set on another man. Roger Fellowes was his name."

She covered her mouth. Fellowes had been one of the duchess's lovers!

"Yes, you'll recognize the name from the letters, of course. He was her first revenge on me—the first man she took to her bed. But they met years beforehand, during her first season. He was not moneyed enough to win her father's approval, but they were set on each other. I knew it. Everyone knew it. But I wanted her, regardless."

She felt suddenly afraid. "Why are you telling me this?" Now, of all times; and so calmly, his voice only darkening when he spoke of his own role in it.

"Because you need to know." He watched her, his face impassive. "Had you asked me three days ago, I might have told you that I could trust nobody else. But now I think the problem is that I cannot trust myself—what I feel, what I believe. And you should know why."

She had a terrible, sinking feeling. This confession was not a sign that he longed to unveil himself, to grow closer to her. It was, instead, a warning of why he would never do so.

"I knew she did not want me," he said. "But I thought I could win her anyway." He picked up another rock, turning it over in his hand. "She was too good for Fellowes. And I was the heir to a dukedom, after all. President of the Union Society at Cambridge. A double first behind me, predictions of fame abounding. I'd already made a splash in the Commons. I would be prime minister one day; everyone said it." He gave a pull of his mouth, mocking himself. "In short, I was precisely the kind of man she deserved. And she, ideally designed for me: educated, well connected, mannerly. How could she rebuff me?"

His smile was a grim slash across his features. He paused for a long moment, seeming to look inward.

"Her father came to me," he said at last. "He had noticed my interest in her. I knew if I confirmed his suspicions, he would take some measure to remove Fellowes from the picture. But I told him the truth. I wished to marry her."

She guessed where the story was heading now. Finally, she began to understand his wife.

He blew out a breath. "I can only imagine what picture you drew from those letters. That she was deranged? But she wasn't. She had cause to loathe me. Her father offered Fellowes a handsome bribe to decamp to the Continent. He told me so the same day that Fellowes booked passage abroad. I could have stopped Fellowes. But I didn't. He let his love be purchased away, after all. Why should I reason with such a man? And when Margaret collapsed into heartbreak, I stood ready to help her, to offer an antidote for her wounded pride. She had no notion of why Fellowes had abandoned her, and I never breathed a word of it. But a year after we wed, he came back from Italy. And he told her his own version of the truth. That he was forced away, instead of bribed."

"She blamed you," she whispered.

He shrugged. "Of course. Wouldn't you?"

She recoiled. "Never put me in her shoes!"

He looked at her then, a long, clear look that seemed to see to the heart of her. "No," he said quietly. "I don't."

She exhaled. And he was silent for a time, long enough for a chorus of birds to begin chirping around them.

"She accused me of colluding with her father," he said finally. "Cheating her out of her only chance at happiness, and I was not . . ." He sighed. "*Patient* with her. Fellowes had abandoned her. And she and I had been happy—had we not? This was love . . . was it not? Mannerly, polite. Never an argument between us."

That did not sound like love to Olivia. It sounded like courtesy. But she said nothing.

"I couldn't understand," he said, "how she might prefer such a man to me. And she seemed, finally, to agree . . ." He trailed off, his mouth twisting. "I thought we had reconciled. Only, as it turns out, we had not."

"You blame yourself," she said. No wonder he had no compassion for himself. No wonder his anger had taken so long to turn outward, toward Bertram and the others. "You blame yourself for what she did to you."

"I blame myself for a good many things—delusion being first and foremost. I thought we had made the perfect marriage. That love was bound to come, to develop naturally. That I had become a man utterly unlike my father, and made a marriage that would answer for all the sins and mistakes my parents had made." He shrugged. "In retrospect, my blindness is extraordinary. I was arrogant, ignorant—"

"No." All at once, she understood him completely. He was still blind, entirely. "The problem was not *you.*" A choked laugh escaped her. "Bertram was not worthy of my mother's love, either. But she loved him all the same. Don't you see? Love is not *earned.* And it's not born of perfection. It—"

"You call that love?" he said sharply. "The cause of all her difficulties—and yours. That isn't love; it's *idiocy.* Selfish, thoughtless—"

She rose. "How *dare* you judge her?"

His jaw hardened. "Very easily," he said as he stood. "You deserved better, Olivia. And she might have fought for you. Instead, she placed the interests of a scoundrel over her own child."

She opened her mouth, quivering with rage—and what came out instead was a sob.

She clapped a hand over her lips, appalled. But oh, God, he had lanced her as expertly as an assassin. For within the space of a minute, he had shown why he would never trust his own feelings for her, and why she should not have trusted her mother's.

She heard him curse. And then his arms were around her, and he was forcing her face into his shoulder, though she resisted him. His murmured apologies washed over her. She did not want them. She willed herself to be as hard as iron in his embrace, indifferent to him.

"You deserve to be put first," he said into her hair.

He meant it as a comfort, no doubt. But it was the cruelest thing he'd ever said. "And who will do that?" she choked. "You?"

His arms tightened. But he did not reply. Of course he didn't. For all his sins, she could never say he had lied.

She pulled away from him, roughly wiping her eyes. "I want to go to London. Now, at once."

He stared at her, face haunted. "Olivia . . ."

"I want you to arrange a meeting with a lawyer, a very nasty one."

"Let me handle it." He reached out to touch her, but she stepped backward. His hand fell, curled into a fist. "Stay here," he said. "This is your family. You ask who will put you first? They will. They are so eager to know you—"

"They are strangers!" She hugged herself, hating him, though she could not say why. "No. I am going to London." She took a ragged breath and lifted her chin. "I am putting *myself* first. And I want to look into his eyes when he finds out he's ruined."

CHAPTER SEVENTEEN

"Beat you to it!"

Olivia stepped behind the shelter of a broad oak, her heart in her throat. Across the street, the door to a townhouse had just opened, discharging three footmen with luggage, and then a nanny and two boys, neither of them older than nine. The boys raced each other down the stairs into the waiting coach, jostling each other, their faces alight.

She had not allowed herself to think on them before. But in the law office, when the barrister had pulled down a volume of Debrett's to contemplate the affected parties, she had stared at those three names printed so small beneath Bertram's entry and felt something break inside her. In the wake of its shattering, her cold rage had deserted her. She had barely been able to speak.

She had not known how to explain what ailed her. She had asked Alastair to return her to the bachelor's flat on Brook Street so she might rest. But instead, she had lain awake through the long slide of the morning, this first morning of the new year, thinking of the names: Peter, James, Charlotte.

On the doorstep now appeared a nanny, who made her way sedately down the steps. Trailing her was a little girl of four or five, whose hair was as red as Olivia's. The girl managed the first step, then wobbled around to face the doorway. "Mummy, *up*," she cried.

Olivia dug her fingers into the bark. That little girl was her blood. Her half sister.

An elegant brunette stepped into the clouded afternoon. She was adjusting her hat, a confection of feathers and lace that perched atop her chestnut curls at a rakish tilt. She wore eighteen years of marriage very lightly. At the right angle, she would look no older than thirty.

Her hat settled to her satisfaction, she bent down, putting her face on a level with her daughter's. Some private conference passed between them. The girl nodded, then hooked her arms around her mother's neck and laughed as she was lifted.

Lady Bertram carried her daughter down the steps to the coach.

Olivia loosed a breath. Anger, frustration made a sick, toxic churn in her gut. She should have listened to Alastair; should not have set foot outside the flat without him. Had she listened, they would have paid a call together, this very afternoon, to this handsome brick house. No children would have greeted them. For the luggage being strapped to the roof of the coach suggested a long journey. Olivia would never have seen the faces of the half siblings who must pay now for their father's crime.

The footmen, having strapped down the bags, sprang

off the coach to the ground, causing the vehicle to rock gently on its springs. She heard a muffled whoop from the interior, the glee of an excited boy ready for adventure.

Lady Bertram emerged from the coach, following the footmen back into the house.

Olivia made herself look away. The path she had walked through the trees curved out before her. It was only ten minutes' walk back to the flat. She could return there, wait for Marwick. Never speak of this outing.

But how would she forget the little girl? That girl looked so much like her, they might have shared a mother as well as a father. And the boys, their eager innocence . . .

A frustrated syllable lodged in her throat, sharp and solid, choking. *No!* But she could neither voice it nor swallow it. She waited, staring again at the darkened doorway, as though an answer might appear there, one that would crush these doubts swarming through her.

She knew that little girl's future. It was taking shape right now as the barristers drew up a suit, as they laid plans to expose an old injustice. In an office in Chancery Lane, a little redheaded girl was being turned into a bastard. And nobody knew better than Olivia how Charlotte's future would look from now on. The sly remarks, the veiled leers, the snickered gossip of the self-righteous—how much worse would these be for a girl whose father was a cabinet member, the PM's right-hand man? His disgrace would draw the attention of the nation. This little girl would not be able to escape infamy simply by boarding a train. It would follow her everywhere, documented in newspapers from Cornwall to Scotland.

That would be Bertram's fault. Not Olivia's! Her rage insisted that she place the blame where it belonged.

Yet she *would* be the instrument of this scandal. She

would be the actor who ensured that for the rest of their lives, these children would always see a dim flicker of recognition after introducing themselves to strangers. *She* would be the cause for the moment that followed, that sinking in their stomachs as they waited to learn whether they would be scorned, or pitied, or generously spared.

She had borne the indelible mark of bastardy without pain. But would they? Would that little girl know how to lift her chin, square her shoulders, and dismiss the weight of the world?

By keeping silent, she would care for them better than her father had ever cared for her. But then there would be no justice—and moreover, no *safety*.

She put her fist to her mouth, biting hard on her knuckle. How completely she'd forgotten her original aim! Alastair had distracted her. He had, quite unwittingly, filled her head with empty dreams. He offered her nothing permanent, only the brief, fleeting distractions of pleasure. But somehow she had built castles on air. She was still not safe. He would not be with her forever.

But it wasn't necessary, she thought suddenly, to make a public matter of this secret. All she needed to safeguard herself was to ensure that Bertram knew he could never hurt her—not if he wished his marriage to her mother to remain unknown. The truth could remain locked in a lawyer's vault. The moment something happened to her, it would be exposed—but only then. That was all Bertram needed to know.

The baroness emerged from the house, wearing the slightly harried air of a woman beset by last-minute errands. She was a woman who loved her children: that much was evident. She would certainly want to know if their happiness depended on her husband's good behavior. Her confident carriage, the arrogant tilt of her hat, made Olivia feel certain that she had the kind of poise and savvy required to *ensure* Bertram's good behavior. As long as it protected her children, she would certainly keep him in line.

Olivia could put an end to all of this right now, safely, with the aid of the baroness.

She took a deep breath and started across the grass. "My lady," she called as the baroness reached the coach. "I must speak with you."

The woman startled, and then stared at her as one might a loathsome insect. "Must you?"

She thought Olivia a beggar, perhaps, for Olivia's dress was much soiled from recent travel. "You don't know who I am, but I assure you, I—"

"Oh, I know who you are." The baroness rapped smartly on the door to the coach, which swung open. Into the interior, she directed her next words: "Mr. Moore," she said. "Come handle this, please."

Alastair threw open the door. "Where is she?"

Bertram, ensconced in an armchair before the fire, looked up in goggling astonishment. "What in the devil!"

Footsteps came thudding up. A footman grabbed Alastair's elbow. "Your Lordship, he busted through—"

Bertram leapt to his feet. "Are you deranged? Coming in here like this!"

Deranged? Alastair choked down a black laugh. For two hours he'd waited in that empty flat, time crawling past, the door standing shut, listening for her footsteps.

And perhaps, yes, in that slow crawl of time, he'd begun to lose pieces of himself, for sanity had supplied no solid reasons for her continued absence. She would not have run off; he'd given her no cause.

Or had he?

Since their conversation by the pond in Shepwich, she'd not seemed herself. Why had he not demanded, pressed her, for an explanation? Cowardice: he did not want to know what bothered her. He did not want to be forced to deny her the words she so clearly needed to hear. He could not love her. He could not keep her. In his old life, she would have had no place. In his new life . . . he had no faith in himself with which to make promises.

But in this new life, he waited with his heart inching up his throat, with anxiety edging into anger as the minutes dragged onward. What strange hell was this, in which a man could not keep a woman, but found her absence so profoundly terrifying that his overriding instinct was to kill someone to ensure her safety?

He withdrew his pistol from his jacket. "Deranged," he said. "That's a fine accusation from a man who would murder his daughter."

"What in God's—" Bertram sucked in a breath and stepped sideways. "Not in front of my children!"

Only then did Alastair notice the two young boys sitting cross-legged in the window seat, wide-eyed, a game of checkers forgotten between them.

Their pale, stricken faces checked his rage for a single moment. And then it flamed hotter yet. "Would that your concern encompassed *all* of your children. What have you done with her?"

Bertram looked over Alastair's shoulder. "Take the boys away," he said urgently to the footman.

For a single dark moment Alastair contemplated forbidding it. Using the safety of these children as a barter for Olivia's. "Perhaps it would edify them to learn what you truly are."

Bertram took a shaking breath. "Please." He brought his hands together at his chest, clasping them into a prayerlike posture. "I have done nothing to her. Please, let them leave."

One of the boys whimpered.

Alastair stepped aside to clear a path to the door. "Get them out."

The older one sprang to his feet and flew out. But the younger remained, his jaw squaring, a stubborn look that reminded Alastair, with a painful stab, of Olivia: what she must have looked like, as a child. "I won't leave you!" the boy said to his father, who did not deserve such loyalty.

Bertram knew that much, too. He made an angry sound. "Go now, I say!" He grabbed the boy, dragged him off the seat, and shoved him across the carpet toward the door.

"This is about that woman, isn't it!" The boy craned to look back at Alastair, a brown cowlick flopping across his eye. "She ruined our trip!"

"What woman?" Alastair snapped.

Bertram shot him a warning look. "Do not involve him in this."

He spoke grimly. "Ask him what he means."

Bertram paused in the doorway, every line of his body suggesting furious reluctance. Finally, he put his body between Alastair's and his son's, and knelt to say, "What woman? When did you see her?"

The boy darted a glance between them. "Mummy

said it was her fault we couldn't go to Houghton today. But Mr. Moore said he would take care of her." In a whisper, he added, "Mummy said not to tell you."

Bertram touched his son's hair very gently. "It's all right." But when he closed the door, he laid his head against it a moment before turning. "I had no idea," he began, but Alastair cut him off.

"I am longing to kill you. I thought I knew the urge when we met at the club. Then I learned you had sent an assassin to throttle her."

Bertram came off the door. "In God's name, man, you are raving! I have never lifted a hand against her! I have never once—"

"No, you sent your man to do it—and today as well, it seems." Alastair sighted the pistol, his vision seeming to telescope, so all he saw were Bertram's lying, bloodshot eyes. "Such a pity that I will not shoot," he said softly. "Provided you tell me, right now, where she is."

"Moore! Moore is not my man!" Bertram plowed his hands through his hair. "He has never been in my employ! He is my wife's . . ." His hands dropped. He cast a blind, panicked look around the room. "My wife," he repeated. He focused on Alastair. "I know where she is. Come—come with me at once!"

Olivia opened her eyes. The room danced crazily, chairs hopping from side to side, the carpet falling toward the ceiling. She closed her eyes. Her head throbbed. She could feel her heart jumping in her chest like a frightened rabbit.

But somehow she was still not afraid.

She opened her eyes again. Took a long breath of air

that felt like liquid flame. Moore liked best to choke her. She felt surprised every time she regained consciousness, but he apparently had a talent, or a flaw: he had throttled her into fainting four times now, but had not yet managed to kill her.

Then again, she hadn't yet given him the answer he wanted.

"Where is the register?" he asked.

She squinted through the dimness of the room. She hoped it was dim; she did not remember him hurting her eyes. But her head pounded. She didn't know why. Her memories felt jumbled. How long had she been sitting in this chair, her wrists tied behind her? She flexed her hands. Blood prickled painfully through her fingers.

"Where *is* it?" A chair scraped, banged against the floor. He came toward her. Perhaps he'd never had a choice in being a thug. He looked born to the part: short, squat, thickly muscled, with grizzled hair shorn close around his square head. His eyes were an almost colorless gray.

She was not stupid. She stared at him and did not answer.

He knelt down before her, taking her jaw in a painful grip, as though muzzling a disobedient dog. She did not like to see him from so close. His skin was smooth, almost lineless, a strange contrast to his graying hair. She closed her eyes.

His grip tightened. Pain formed a whimper in her throat. She did not loose it. She felt numb. It was strange, so strange, that she wasn't yet afraid.

"Don't be stupid, girl."

She heard the puzzlement in his voice. He was a beast; he knew the smell of fear, and he recognized its absence, too. He understood her no better than she did.

"Do you want to die?"

She said nothing. A bell started ringing in the street outside, the kind used to alert passersby to animals being driven to market. They could not be in Mayfair. Livestock did not walk those streets.

He let go of her. "Like your father." He made a disgusted scoff. "Stupid, stupid as the day is long."

That idea pierced her strange remove. She could not let it stand. "Nothing like him," she rasped.

"Stupid!" He spat the word. "Bloody dog. She never should have married him."

Almost, she smiled. "On that, we agree."

He slapped her.

She saw a star flash as her chair rocked backward. His hands bit into her arms, yanking her upright before the chair hit the ground.

They stared at each other. She thought of the pistol she'd once possessed. She would have killed him, had she held it now. What had Alastair once said? It would not have troubled her conscience to have this man's blood on her hands.

"You needn't be such a fool," he said slowly. "You tell me where you keep the register, you give it to me, you can go."

He truly did think her an idiot.

"She'll not care what you do with yourself afterward," he said.

She swallowed. All her spit had dried up. Her mouth was as dry as dust.

He pulled a face, then rose and walked across the room to pour himself a glass of water. His body was compact, his strides neat and athletic. He was ageless; he was the devil incarnate, perhaps.

He turned back to study her, wiping water from his mouth with the back of his hand. His swallow was loud, satisfied. Taunting her. She rubbed her tongue along her front teeth and breathed deeply. It hurt.

"My mistress has no ill will against you," he said. "You understand? If you tell me where the register is, you need never see me again."

His *mistress*? "You . . ." She understood suddenly. He was not Bertram's man, after all. He was *Lady* Bertram's man. He worked for the woman she had approached this afternoon, thinking herself so cautious, so clever, in avoiding the main threat.

A laugh sawed through her, hoarse, croaking. A mistake. His face tightened. He tossed aside the tin cup. It clattered against the wall. His neat strides ate up the floorboards; he approached, fist rising. "The next sound you make," he said, "will be your confession, or your death rattle."

She closed her eyes. It must be death. There was no other way to explain her serenity.

A splintering sound rent the air. Moore wheeled around. The door burst open.

She realized then why she had not been afraid. She had known somehow that Alastair would come.

He lunged for Moore, and his face was the face of the man who had closeted himself in a dark room to prevent murder, but now was in the light. His fury was quick, bare knuckled, graceless. He slammed his fist into Moore's face, knocked him to the ground, and then stomped the man's throat with his heel. Moore looked up, his expression one of mild surprise, like a man who expects rain and finds sunshine instead. Alastair knelt down and pummeled him again. Blood spattered.

Moore's heels scrambled on the floorboards. Wet, sick sounds rose. A crack like the snap of bone. Moore's boots fell still. Alastair punched him again. And again. And again.

"Alastair," she said softly.

He went still. So suddenly. The silence was shocking.

He turned to her, droplets of blood sprayed across one high cheekbone. His blue eyes were wild. But they fixed on her.

"Untie me," she said.

He rose stiffly. Walked around her. His hot fingers closed on her wrists. A groan came from Moore, and she sensed Alastair jerk.

"He's not getting up," she said. Moore's eyes had not opened. He lay insensate, his nose a pulp.

The rope loosened. She pulled her hands into her lap, massaging them. They were beginning to shake. They felt very cold. She was cold all over.

Alastair was in front of her. His hands on her shoulders. He was looking at her throat. Probably it was bruised. "Olivia," he said. His gaze lifted. She looked into it and felt a strange jolt. *She* was shaking.

He pulled her into his arms. He was so much warmer than she. Suddenly she was crying. Here was where she felt safe. She had not been afraid because she had known this would be the conclusion of it: she had known he would come. Here was safety, he was safety. She was safe.

"You won't keep me," she whispered. She wasn't his. His world had no place for her. How would she ever feel at home? Never, never again.

She felt his hand brush up her back, along her cheek, feeling lightly, as though he feared to break her. "What?" he asked. "What did you say?"

A deafening explosion. Alastair shoved her behind him. Pivoted.

Moore's chest was smoking.

"He moved," came a voice she knew too well. Disbelieving, she leaned around Alastair and saw Bertram in the doorway, still aiming his gun at Moore's body.

"He did not move," she whispered.

Bertram cast her a bleak look. "Perhaps not. But he would have, eventually."

"Yes," Alastair said. "He would have."

CHAPTER EIGHTEEN

The hotel suite at the top of the Savoy was the finest room Olivia had ever been in. She lay among piles of pillows, feeling dazed and slightly ridiculous, as the hotel doctor examined her, clucking and muttering. "A very bad business," he said. "Footpads, in this area of town! I urge you, Your Grace, to report this to the police."

Alastair stood by the doorway. He'd been prowling the room as though in expectation of new threats popping out from the woodwork. "My cousin requires rest," he said, clipped, "not some fruitless interrogation from a two-bit inspector. I trust I can depend on your discretion."

The doctor snapped upright, stripping off his stethoscope. He vented his offense by slamming his bag shut. "Naturally," he said. "Mrs. Lewis's name shall never cross my lips."

Once the door had closed, Olivia smiled. "Another alias," she said. "How many more shall I collect, do you think?"

Alastair sat on the very edge of the bed and looked at her. "No more, if I can help it."

She looked back at him, battling the warm flush of pleasure that wanted to creep through her. This sense of well-being was a trick of the tincture the doctor had given her for the pain in her throat. It made her sleepy, loose limbed, careless with details. She might mistake Alastair's concern now, which was circumstantial, for lasting affection. Eternal affection. She might imagine, in this moment, that he meant to ensure she required no additional aliases by caring for her this way forever.

"Why did you bring me here?" she asked. By agreement with Bertram, they had left him behind in Moore's flat, so he might report to the police that his wife's manservant had attempted to extort and then attack him.

"You needed a doctor," he said flatly. "And rest. That wretched little flat on Brook Street would not do."

"You might have taken me back to your house, though." It was becoming, in her mind, some sort of mythical place where she had once belonged, and by virtue of belonging to it, had belonged with him, too. She knew the realization should alarm her. But she felt too fuzzy, light and floating, to grasp the cause for concern.

"I could have," he said hesitantly. "But of course the staff would have . . . leapt to conclusions."

Yes, of course. They all thought her a thief. Had Alastair brought her back there, installed her in a bedroom, they would have assumed he was taking revenge in a very sordid way.

She found she did not care. "What difference does it make?"

"It makes a difference to me," he said. "I will not have you looked at so."

She hesitated, puzzled, a little dumb. Her thoughts felt so mushy. "Looked at how?"

"The way those shrews looked at you in the village." His jaw made a hard square. "No one will ever look at you that way again."

A laugh tumbled from her. She touched her lips, surprised at the airy sound. "Oh, Alastair. That isn't in your power."

"Isn't it?" He gave her an inscrutable look. "I think it might be."

She caught her breath, wishing suddenly that she were sober. That her wits were sharp enough to untangle his meaning without her having to ask . . . "How?"

A knock came at the door. He gave an irritated pull of his mouth and rose. "That will be Bertram."

She watched him walk through the door into the sitting room. Listened to the muffled exchange of masculine conversation. And then, after a minute, came the distinct sound of Alastair's voice. "No," he said. "You will not speak to her."

She pushed herself up. "Let him."

Alastair appeared in the doorway, face thunderous. "In your condition? Absolutely—"

"I'm all right." This was the best, the only condition in which to speak to Bertram. Everything seemed hazy, blurred around the edges. She did not want to remember this moment too clearly—the moment in which she saved Bertram from his just deserts. "Let him in," she said again. "Really, Alastair . . . I do know what I'm doing."

His mouth made a flat line. He pivoted. "Five minutes," he said.

Such an autocrat! She might have smiled, only the sight of her father killed the urge. He looked exhausted, shadows beneath his eyes, like a man tortured by a secret he knew must emerge.

He looked exactly as he should. She stared coldly as he approached.

"I don't . . ." He turned his hat in his hands. "I don't know precisely what to say to you."

"What a surprise."

He grimaced. "I deserve that. But I—"

"And more." The doctor's potion had not muted her emotions entirely. She felt anger, bright and burning. Perhaps it would never burn itself out. "You deserve far more than that. You owed my mother everything. She could have destroyed you. How she loved you enough not to do so, I will never understand."

His hat crumpled, the brim breaking. "I was twenty-two when I wed her. I understood nothing. Do you hear me? I was young and stupid, and wild—"

"And so was she. But her love never wavered. You have more proof of that than any man alive."

He hung his head. She heard his unsteady breath. "Yes," he said. "She was far better than I deserved." He looked up again, and she saw pain in his face. It made her angrier. What right had *he* to feel pain? "I want you to know," he said, "that I had no hand in Moore's actions. He was my wife's man—her bodyguard, from the time she was very young. And I think he must have been mad. I cannot believe my wife had any hand in what he did—"

Alastair made a sharp, scornful noise. "That won't fly."

Bertram rounded on him. "You don't know her. She's not a murderess."

"I don't intend to know her," Alastair said coldly. "You will make arrangements to ensure that I never do. Send her to an asylum. Or back to America—it makes no difference. But she will not remain in England."

"She's the mother of my children!"

"Three of them, at least," Olivia said bitterly.

That drew him back around, desperate now, pleading. "Olivia, I promise you—"

She scoffed and glanced to Alastair, who shook his head in clear amazement. "I am not so desperate as to accept promises from *you*," she said.

"Besides," Alastair added, "I doubt very much she will wish to stay, once her children are made bastards, and her marriage exposed as a bigamous sham."

And therein Olivia saw a solution.

"My God." Bertram took a step back, clutching the hat to his chest now like a shield. "You speak of destroying three innocent children—"

"I will never say a word," Olivia cut in—causing him to halt, jaw agape.

"Olivia." This from Alastair, disbelieving. She lifted a hand to signal him to wait.

"Your wife goes to America," she said to Bertram. "And you go with her—after resigning your office." That would be justice for Alastair, too. "And nobody will ever know that you were married to my mother."

Bertram's mouth worked around an objection. "I . . . I cannot simply leave! And *resign*? I am a member of the cabinet—"

"I saw her face this afternoon," Olivia said. "I believe she knew what her man meant to do. And if I did not believe she loved her children—if I did not believe she had grown criminal only to protect them—I would have stayed at Moore's flat to tell the police everything. But as it stands, I will say nothing—if you go abroad. And whether or not she loves your children, I think a woman inclined to dispatch assassins is no woman whom you wish to raise your children unsupervised—so you should gladly go. It is your chance to be the kind of father you never were to me."

He stared at her for a long moment. "You have much of your mother in you," he said faintly. "You imagine she was the victim—but I promise you, she never let me go unscathed."

"Am I meant to feel sorry for you?" She wanted to throw a pillow at him. No, something much heavier. A bottle. She looked hopefully to Alastair.

His face was thunderous. He would be angry with her for this, no doubt. But his focus now was on Bertram."You've heard her offer," he said darkly. "It's far more generous than what I'd planned for you. But it will do. Now get out, and let the next thing I hear be the news of your resignation from Salisbury's cabinet."

Bertram shook his head, then returned his hat to his head, where it sat crumpled. "I cannot accept this," he said grimly. "This is not over." He turned and walked out.

Silence filled the room. Alastair stood looking at her. She took a long breath. "So much for nobility," she said. "I did not wish to punish his children. Or to rob you of your revenge. But it seems you'll have it anyway. What a fool he is!"

"Indeed. We knew that." He sounded strangely distracted. "Olivia, you would have given up your chance at legitimacy."

She blinked. "What of it?"

"He has money. Not much. Most of it is his wife's. But you stand to inherit what remains. You do realize you would have lost that?"

Amazement was not enough to prevent her yawn.

"Do you really imagine it matters?" She covered her mouth, jaw cracking. "Even now, Alastair. I don't care for the money so much. I know how to make do. I'm a . . . very fine secretary."

His smile was fleeting; when it faded, he looked very serious, indeed. He came to the bed and sat beside her, brushing her hair from her eyes. "I should have someone run to a proper shop. Fetch you something better to wear than a hotel robe."

His touch was soothing. Her eyes fluttered closed. "You're spoiled," she murmured. "This robe is far too grand for secretaries . . . or housekeepers."

His hand stilled, cupping her cheek. "And for a duchess?"

She opened her eyes. He was looking at her gravely, with an expression almost of trepidation. This was not the look of a man who had just said the remark her ears had heard. She'd slipped into a dream, maybe. "I'm falling asleep," she said. "Will you go home? Or will you stay here?"

He took a long, audible breath. "Olivia, you deserve better."

She blinked and sat up a little. Surely she hadn't heard him right, before. But what could he mean? From fatigue to painful alertness in one moment; her heart was suddenly drumming in her mouth. How sick with heartbreak she would be in a moment. "I don't understand," she said carefully. "Better than what?"

His hand flexed on her cheek. And then it slipped down to tangle with her own hand, his grip firming. "Better than to be someone's lackey," he said. "Someone's secretary. Someone's servant."

She frowned. "You're a terrible snob."

"Better than to be looked at the way men look at servants," he said. "Better than to be looked through. Better than to be looked down upon."

Disappointment began to leach through her. This was no romantic speech he was making. "It isn't so bad," she said. And then she shook herself and lifted her chin as best she could, propped up on all these pillows. "My skills are more than respectable. I am very good at what I do. Not everyone can do it! You recall, I am not a housekeeper by training. I can speak four languages; I know shorthand—"

He stopped her mouth with his. Confused, she let him kiss her; and then, after a moment, his kiss distracted her from confusion, so all she could think of were his lips, light, thorough, gentle, the beginning strains of something more . . .

He pulled back. "Olivia," he said, "I am making an argument for you to marry me. It's very awkward, but I do not require a wife who speaks foreign languages or knows shorthand. I do intend to hire a secretary separately."

She gaped up at him.

"I see I asked badly." A rueful smile quirked his mouth. "Perhaps I do require a wife with secretarial skills. And Italian, and . . . what other languages do you speak anyway?"

"French," she whispered. "German."

"French, then. And German. I cannot have a wife who doesn't speak German," he said solemnly. "Does that strengthen my case?"

"No." For suddenly her heart had sunk. She pushed him off her and sat up as he began to frown. "You're repeating your mistakes." She ran a hand up her aching face, pressing her eyes until she saw stars. *Just say yes, you fool.*

But she couldn't. Now he had asked the question, she could admit it, with fear: she loved him. She loved him enough to say yes.

But because she loved him—and because she liked him, too; liked him more than was wise, and more than he deserved—she could not say yes.

"Alastair," she said, "you loved the idea of marrying Margaret. But you never loved her. You're doing it again—you love the idea of . . . of what? Of saving me from sly looks? Of playing the hero? But you don't love— "

He laid a finger over her lips. "Don't," he said quietly.

They sat together for a moment, frozen, staring at each other.

She took another ragged breath. It felt ice cold. *She* was ice cold, suddenly. "I want a place," she said softly. "And though you think you offer one to me now, it isn't the kind of place I want. Don't you see? You're a great man. You were before, and you will be again. And once you resume that life—"

"I will *never*." His jaw squared. "Can it be that you still don't understand?" He let out a wild laugh and rose off the bed, dragging his fingers through his hair. He pivoted back to her. "I am done with it!"

"So you think." She was so tired. She fought her eyes, which wanted to close; but even the panic of missing this moment, this crucial moment, could not stall her cracking yawn. "I'm not . . ." She pinched her arm hard to rouse herself. "I'm not a fool," she said. "There is no place for me in the PM's life."

He shook his head very slowly. "You have no idea what you're saying."

Her eyes closed over her tears. "But I do," she whispered. "I . . ."

She woke very gradually, her consciousness seeming to filter up through layers of light. As the world brightened behind her lids, she became increasingly aware of the aches and twinges in her body. Lady Bertram. Thomas Moore, dead. Bertram refusing her offer.

Alastair, proposing marriage . . .

Her eyes flew open. She stared at the strapwork ceiling, rigid with horror. She had *refused* him. Oh, God, she had refused him!

She sat up—and froze. He was sitting at a chair drawn up to the foot of the bed. Beyond him lay a breakfast tray, a scrap of eggs remaining on the plate.

"Good afternoon," he said evenly.

She clutched the covers to her throat—and then winced and regretted it. Gingerly she felt her neck.

"It looks even worse than it feels, I'll wager." He sounded strangely cheerful, but his eyes never once moved from her face. "But you must feel rested. You slept sixteen hours."

"Sixteen . . ." She looked to the broad windows that overlooked the Strand. The curtains were thrown back, showing a cloudless blue sky over the tall buildings across the lane. "Goodness." She cleared her throat and cautiously glanced back toward him. Had she dreamed the proposal? Or better yet, had the proposal happened, but she had only dreamed the rejection?

For now, alert, refreshed, she was feeling far less virtuous. She remembered all the objections she had lodged last night. She knew them still to be true. But she no longer cared. Let him regret the marriage one day. But until then, let him be hers. "Alastair," she began nervously, "I . . ."

He tossed a newspaper onto the bed. "Look at the headlines."

Hesitantly she picked it up. The headlines showed nothing of particular interest. A minor train accident in York. A new steam engine that promised a quicker trip to Egypt. "What of them?"

"Enjoy them," he said. "Tedious, mundane, and utterly benign. They will not look so within a week."

The newspaper crumpled in her grasp. "What have you done?"

He rose. In the bright light, he glowed like burnished gold, his handsome face gilded, his eyes a deep, piercing blue. "I have circulated the letters," he said.

She stared at him. "You . . . what?"

"I had them copied. Michael is carrying them about. The club was his first stop, so the news"—he glanced toward the grandfather clock in the corner—"should be halfway to Scotland by now, I would think."

She groped for words. "But . . . *why*?"

He shrugged. "If you think on it, it's a very neat revenge. None of Margaret's lovers will escape unscathed. Public opinion will ruin them. Nelson is bankrupt; he's been angling to marry an heiress, with the promise that he's soon to be ennobled. That engagement will be broken, I imagine, within a day. Fellowes also loses his chance at marrying well. Barclay will find his political power much diminished, for it would behoove nobody's career to ally with a man who made his political successes through underhanded conniving with someone else's wife. And as for Bertram . . ." He smiled slightly. "I believe he will prove far more willing to take your offer, should you still feel willing to extend it. He'll certainly be tossed out of the cabinet. I would not be surprised if he's bound for America within the fortnight."

She gaped at him. His cool delivery suggested that he had rehearsed this speech beforehand. But she could see no sign in his face of what it must have cost him to take this measure. "But you, Alastair . . ."

"It had to be done." He shrugged. "One could never be sure there weren't more letters out there, waiting to emerge. Better to release the others now, when I was prepared for it. The scandal will die down eventually."

She wished suddenly he would come toward her. That he would touch her. But last night's conversation sat between them like a solid presence, obscuring her understanding of his expression, his manner. And—why, these two matters could not be unconnected, could they?

She slipped to her feet. If he would not come to her, then she would take the risk and go to him. She padded barefoot across the carpet, wobbling slightly but steadying herself as she advanced. He watched her approach, making no move to meet her. But when she reached him, he let her take his hand, draw it to her chest. How dear his touch was. She breathed deeply. Their eyes met, clung. "Why did you do this now?" she whispered.

"You said you did not believe my intentions." He spoke very low. "But I have demonstrated them. I do not intend to go back to that old life, Olivia."

She swallowed hard. This was not what she'd hoped to hear. "But your talents . . ."

"I may go back into politics one day." He paused. "With Bertram gone, there will be an absence."

She hesitated. "Then I don't understand . . ."

"I will never be the man I once was." Very gently he smoothed her hair from her brow. "I am a new man. A better one, I think. No wiser, though. The difference is, I once thought I knew right from wrong. That I saw with perfect clarity. Only now, I know I don't. I know I must depend on someone else for that clarity. And you, Miss Holladay, are clear-eyed." He smiled ruefully. "And the opposite of shameless: you are too virtuous for your own good. You have offered to sacrifice your inheritance, your rightful name, to protect children who will never know you. Perhaps you might be willing to guide me. A politician requires such guidance."

Wonder prickled over her. "I . . . think you underestimate yourself. Your Grace."

He dragged in a breath. "Oh, God," he said very softly, and it sounded to her ears like a prayer. He bowed his head for a moment. And when he lifted it, his face was stark, his anxiety so plain that it shocked her. She had never seen him look so afraid. "Can you love me, then, Olivia? Not that man, but this one. The one I am, not the one I was."

If this was a dream, she prayed to never wake. "That man never knew me," she whispered. "Only you know me. Of course it is you whom I love."

He took her face between his hands and kissed her. She swayed on her feet; had it not been for the firmness of his grasp, she would have fallen. But his grasp could be depended upon. She put her own hands over his and kissed him back.

After a minute, when they parted for air, she said, "But

you have not said the same. And I might point out that we met when you threw a bottle at my head, and then punched a wall—so forgive me if I require assurance."

He laughed, a giddy sound. "I will remind you," he shot back, "that you were a housekeeper, who obeyed no order I ever gave. My frustration was somewhat justified."

She kissed his knuckles. "It's a very rocky foundation for love. You must agree."

"Au contraire," he said. "You were never afraid."

"I knew you would never hurt me."

"I was a perfect villain."

"Never, not really."

His head tilted as he studied her. "I wanted your courage," he said quietly.

"And I, your brilliance." She thought of all those speeches, half written, pearls that history would treasure. "Your insight." She hesitated. "The way you look at me, Alastair. You *see* me."

"I do," he murmured. "Olivia, I know exactly who you are. I don't love the idea of what you might be. It is you I love. That, I know."

She smiled, a foolish smile that seemed to stretch wider than her cheeks. "So may we go home now? Your staff will recover from the shock eventually, I think."

He laughed. "If they don't, you may sack the lot of them."

"Never," she said, and then thought better of it. "Only, perhaps, Vickers."

They were married a week later, in a private ceremony attended only by Lord Michael and Lady Elizabeth de

Grey. For one cowardly moment, on hearing Alastair's plan to invite them, Olivia had been tempted to oppose it. Most would account this a very curious "peace offering," as Alastair called it: to invite a woman to the wedding of her former employee, who had stolen from her, and would now be her sister. "And outrank her to boot," Alastair had added impishly.

But Elizabeth had always been very bohemian. On the morning of the wedding, she announced her arrival by bursting into Olivia's sitting room with Hanson, her lady's maid, in tow. Hanson, looking beleaguered as ever, laid a glimmering gown across the sofa, which Elizabeth gestured to dramatically. "Your wedding gown, you cheeky sneak. You must dress properly, you know, for with any luck, you'll only be married once."

Olivia rose, hoping her own discomposure was not as apparent as Polly's and Muriel's. Their jaws hung nearly to the floor, and no wonder. Elizabeth was a renowned beauty, dark and voluptuous, but she made an even more magnificent sight than usual, for the pose she struck put on display her belly, which looked far too round for a woman only three months married. "Am I to congratulate you . . . ?"

"Indeed," said Elizabeth, patting her much-expanded waist with a smile. "Now send out your maids. You know Hanson's a hand with hair. And you have a *great* deal of explaining to do."

Stunned, Olivia retook her seat. Hanson set about heating the curling iron while Elizabeth prowled like a cat on the hunt. "Start at the beginning," she ordered Olivia.

Olivia took a deep breath. "That would be an apology. I—"

"No!" Elizabeth waved this away. "Skip that bit; begin with the most interesting parts. How on earth did you end up in Marwick's house?" She looked around, wide-eyed. "A very fine house, no doubt—but *Marwick's*? Now, I've had some of it from Michael, of course, but secondhand news grows so patchy. Tell me everything, and mind you, honesty is part of your atonement."

And so, as Hanson dressed her, then pinned and trussed her hair, Olivia recounted the whole tale—or most of it. But she avoided all reference to bottles and books and pistols and libraries, and by the end, Elizabeth had fixed a very skeptical eye on her in the mirror.

"Give me that," Elizabeth said to her maid, and shooed the woman out so she might fix the wreath of orange blossoms atop Olivia's head herself. Once it was firmly settled and pinned—only a couple of stray stabs to mar her makeshift performance as a maid—she lowered herself to a nearby stool. "Now I suppose you can give me the *real* story? Starting with why you stole the letters from me? Michael had the news of Bertram's bigamy from Alastair—but why on *earth* did you run away without saying a word?"

Olivia slowly turned—not only because she had dreaded this moment, but because this gown, a cream silk brocade, was far heavier than any she was accustomed to wearing. "I'm so sorry," she said, hushed. "I . . ." She felt herself turning scarlet. "I was mad with panic, and I don't expect you to forgive me, but—"

Elizabeth gently touched her wrist. "Mather. Or—pardon me, Holladay." She laughed. "Olivia, I should call you—for we're to be sisters now." Her brows arched, a silent statement of amazement, to which her smile lent a wondering quality. "I never doubted for a moment that you had a sound reason to take those letters. But you know me well enough, I hope, to believe that I would have helped you. Or don't you?"

Olivia found herself blinking back tears. "I do. I should have. But Bertram . . ." She took a ragged breath. "I did not want to draw trouble on you, ma'am."

Elizabeth grimaced. "No, no, sisters do not call each other *ma'am*." A mischievous expression crimped her mouth. "I do hope you will feel free to draw trouble onto Marwick, at least? I cannot say I would find him the easiest man to marry." She gave a mock shudder. "But he's certainly able to handle a few villains. Say . . . are you *certain* you don't wish to change your mind? We could steal away to Waterloo, you know—it's never too late to flee!"

Olivia smiled. "He is quite fearsome, isn't he? At first glance, at any rate. But I do believe that's part of his allure."

"Hmm." Elizabeth eyed her. "Very well, we will stay. But I must ask—you have seen the morning's papers, haven't you?"

She nodded. News of Bertram's resignation occupied the top headline, along with the information that he had been spotted boarding a steamer bound for New York. "Yes. It's no surprise."

Elizabeth hesitated. "It will keep the journalists busy for a week at least. But you must know . . . it's only a matter of time before the rest of it makes the papers, too. The editors are beating their brains to find a way to print those letters without coming up against the obscenity laws."

Olivia sat down. "We're ready for that," she said quietly.

"But aren't you afraid," Elizabeth said gently, "of the repercussions for you? The two of you, I mean."

Olivia shrugged. Alastair had made a point of visiting his club yesterday. Nobody, he'd said, had dared *not* meet his eyes. "A man who would willingly distribute letters that paint him as a cuckold is a man who might do anything. That is not a man to cross."

Elizabeth nodded, frowning. "Yes, I'm certain Marwick will find his way back into politics without difficulty. But the social consequences, my dear . . . You'll be the center of a million stares! At least for a time. I'll do everything I can to smooth your path, of course, but it will not be the easiest time to announce a marriage . . ."

Olivia laughed. "You mean, people will talk. They will gawk and whisper. But they would have done it anyway. In the eyes of the world, I'm a bastard, a woman who was in service. Our marriage will be a mésalliance. People would have stared regardless."

"And will you be able to bear it?" Elizabeth hesitated. "I have endured that kind of attention. It's a heavy weight to bear the way others stare. . . ."

Smiling, she repeated what Alastair had said to her recently: "All that matters is how we look at each other. How I look at him." She blushed and looked down at her hands, at the pearl bracelet he'd given her. He was right, she realized wonderingly: it did match her skin.

"Well." Elizabeth sat back; she looked impressed. "I never would have guessed you had a taste for scandal, darling." She grinned. "But I did remember how well you look, when turned out properly." She waved Olivia up and turned her by the shoulders to face the mirror. Together they gazed at her reflection.

She barely recognized the look of herself—glowing, alight. The gleaming cream brocade made her pale skin look rosy, and set off her scarlet hair.

But she did recognize the way it *felt* to look beautiful. It matched the way she felt when Alastair looked at her. She finally matched in the mirror what she saw reflected in his eyes. "Shall we go?" she asked softly. Suddenly she could not wait any longer.

Arm in arm, she and Elizabeth made their way down the scrolling staircase. The servants had lined up to watch, and she almost did not let herself look into their faces, for fear that some sneer would ruin this moment. It had been very unsettling and confusing for them to receive her again, not as a member of the staff but as their future mistress.

But she steeled herself, because Elizabeth was right: the days ahead, until the scandal died, would take courage. And she did not lack it. The Kingmaker had assured her so. So here was an opportunity for practice.

But what she saw, when she looked up, were smiles and nods—and a single scowl from Vickers, who ducked his head when she met his eyes. She glanced past him and found Cook beaming at her, clutching a basket, tilting it now to display—

Startled, she came to a stop. Why was Cook showing her a load of dirt?

Cook arched a brow. "Truffles," she said pointedly. "For your wedding breakfast, ma'am."

Olivia remembered suddenly a certain bucket of dirt

she had once discovered in the kitchen and had tossed away, thinking it part of the filth that abounded in the unkempt household.

"What is it?" Elizabeth whispered. "Second thoughts? Shall it be Waterloo, after all?"

She felt a wisp of annoyance—very fitting for a sister-in-law. And then she laughed. "I am not jilting His Grace," she said.

"Drat. Very well, I'll behave."

And they recommenced their passage without further interruption, into the formal drawing room, where Alastair stood with Michael at his side.

There was a time when he never stood in the light. But sunlight poured in through the windows now, painting him in gold. She followed the pull of his sapphire eyes across the carpet; his hands closed over hers, firm and steady, hands that would be hers to hold until the end of her days.

The chaplain began to speak. She barely heard him. It was only the two of them here in the light. And when it came time to kiss, she turned her face aside and whispered into his ear, "There's one thing that troubles me."

He pulled back, frowning. "What is that?"

"I found out who stole the truffles."

His frown deepened. "What? How?"

"Rather ask who. It was *me.* I threw them out, thinking them rubbish."

He laughed and took her face in his hand. "I suppose I'll have to sack you as my housekeeper, then. How fortunate you found another position."

And then, as Elizabeth and Lord Michael applauded, and the servants began to cheer, he kissed her. And she kissed him back, though her mind did wander again to the truffles, for Doris was right: who would eat a food that looked like that?

"Pay attention," he murmured. And then he kissed her again very persuasively, and all thoughts of Doris and truffles and dirt faded away, leaving only him.